THE TEMPTATIONS OF LOVE . . .

It was a long time before she could fall asleep. She kept reliving that surprising kiss and the delicious feeling it had spread through her. She knew beyond doubt that this was what Harriet felt when Jeremy kissed her. No wonder her cousin sometimes looked as if she were in another world! If ever Eban had kissed her like that, she'd be counting the days till he got back.

Swiftly she pushed the thought of Eban away from her and let her mind fill with romantic fantasies featuring Tom Fulton and herself in the starring roles. Two hours later she fell asleep, murmuring his name . . .

The Dark Side of Passion

BARBARA BONHAM

SPHERE BOOKS LIMITED
30-32 Gray's Inn Road, London WC1X 8JL

First published in Great Britain by Sphere Books Ltd 1981
Copyright © Barbara Bonham 1980

TRADE
MARK

Printed and bound in Great Britain by
©ollins, Glasgow

1

It was a robin that awakened her. The sweet, cheerful
notes brought a smile to her young lips as she turned
over onto her back and opened her eyes. The upstairs
bedroom with the steeply pitched ceiling conforming
to the lines of the roof was gorged with sunshine.
Through the slightly opened window near the head
of her bed came the familiar odors of salt and sea, but
mingling with them this morning was another smell,
that of green things coming to life under the warm rays
of the sun. It was the heady fragrance of spring, bearing
the promise of unknown yet exciting events. It was that
stimulant that brought Vianna Chadwick, two months
away from her seventeenth birthday, bounding out of
bed and over to the window. Maybe this would be the
day when it happened!

With large eyes several shades darker than the sky
that showed behind some streamers of white clouds,
she surveyed the harbor. Samuel Chadwick, captain of
a whaler, had built his house on Front Street between
the cooperage and the apothecary. Not for him a home
on a back street, where his view of the sea would be
cut off by trees and other houses. He would feel
smothered, he declared. By leaning out of her window,
Vianna could see down the street past the other shops,
beyond the sail loft and rope walk, to the Govans Harbor lighthouse that stood at the tip of the spit of land
that curved into Cape Cod Bay. Up the street to her
right she could see past other shops and houses as far
as the shipyard. Early as it was, the waterfront was

busy. Half a dozen ships were tied up at the wharves and were being either loaded or unloaded, the men's voices rising to Vianna in the clear air along with the constant creaking of straining ropes and timbers.

Her gaze fastened on Eban's ship, the *Andover*, its bare masts and spars drawing straight black lines against the sky, the blue gown of the buxom female figurehead on the bow glowing brilliantly across the hundred or so yards that separated Vianna from her fiancé's vessel. Eban was nowhere in sight; in fact, there was little activity about the ship. That would change in a few days, when they began loading her for her voyage to the West Indies.

The thought of Eban on that bright May morning in 1848 brought with it the gritting frustration that had plagued Vianna ever since their engagement, two weeks ago. When was the romance going to begin? How much longer must she wait for the look, the kiss, or the caress that would send her blood singing through her veins and loose the tumult of emotions that lovers were supposed to feel?

From the cooperage next door came the pungent smell of oak barrel staves being steamed and softened for shaping. Jeremy Walters was probably already at work, perhaps helping his father make the very casks that would carry the provisions for Eban's ship. Now if Eban were more like Jeremy . . . Vianna experienced a surge of envy for her cousin, Harriet Sawtell, who was to marry Jeremy in just three weeks. That romance was everything she and Harriet had dreamed about these last few years as they had read novels forbidden by their parents but secretly borrowed from one of their girl friends and as they had speculated about the most important event in any girl's life, which each of them was awaiting with fluttery anticipation—falling in love. They discussed their ideal men, and they wondered what it would be like to be really kissed—not the type of kisses stolen down by the rope walk ever since they were ten years old by the boys they went to school with, but passionate kisses given by a man who desired you. Their dreams and speculations grew vague beyond this point. The forbidden novels and girls' gossip had provided only the faintest notion of what followed the passionate kisses.

Harriet was the first to find romance. Suddenly she was in love with Jeremy, a boy both she and Vianna had known all their lives. And he was in love with her. Vianna wasn't sure how it had happened or precisely when, but one day Harriet's conversation was filled with phrases like "Jeremy says" and "Jeremy thinks" and Jeremy this and that, and her freckled face was suffused with a light Vianna had never seen there before. What was even more disconcerting was a strange timbre in her voice and an expression deep in her eyes that Vianna couldn't read. Until that moment there had been nothing about her cousin that was unknown to her. Harriet was only five months older than Vianna, and they had grown up as close as sisters. As the romance developed further, Vianna watched in dismay while her cousin turned into someone that at times she scarcely knew.

Jeremy Walters was unarguably the most handsome man in Govans Harbor. His lithe, narrow-hipped body and thickly lashed blue eyes had for a number of years attracted admiring glances from every girl in town above the age of thirteen, including Vianna, and he had spread his charm impartially among them all until suddenly they realized he had singled out Harriet Sawtell for his attentions. Although Vianna would scarcely admit it to herself, she was surprised. Her cousin was not especially pretty, not at all a match for the handsome Jeremy. Her sandy lashes gave to her round face the lashless look seen in old paintings. Nor did her thin, narrow-shouldered body offer the plump, feminine curves that brought a glitter to the eyes of the young men around town, of whom Jeremy once was the most bold with his looks and remarks. That Harriet was lovable Vianna knew beyond doubt, but she hadn't expected the gay and charming Jeremy Walters to look any deeper than a girl's outward appearance. The knowledge that he appreciated Harriet's subtler charms made Vianna think more highly of him, for despite the undeniable fact that she found him physically attractive, she had decided he was a bit too conceited and pleased with himself for her taste. Had it not been for that, she might have been jealous of Harriet and resented the fact that he had chosen Harriet instead of herself.

What jealousy she felt was caused by the feeling that Harriet had always held a part of herself back, a part she was now sharing only with Jeremy. Had her cousin held this part of herself back deliberately? Vianna didn't think so. Love had unlocked the door. Fascinated, envious, Vianna yearned to enjoy the same mysterious emotional experience.

She could have had almost any young man she set her heart upon, but Govans Harbor was a small seaport, and she couldn't picture herself settling down for life with any of the group of boys she had grown up with. For years she had been telling herself she had plenty of time, that one day someone would come along who would capture her heart, someone who, because he was a stranger, would be exciting and romantic. When Harriet fell in love with Jeremy, Vianna realized suddenly that she was without any prospect for a husband except Eban Stanbro, who had paid her a lot of attention while he was at home a year ago. She began to weigh his assets. He was nine years older than she and therefore practically a stranger, especially since he had been going to sea since he was twelve years old and was seen about Govans Harbor for only brief periods between voyages. A new whaling ship was being built in the Govans Harbor shipyard for the firm of Bell and Townley, and Eban would be given command of it when it was finished. Vianna appreciated the fact that as Eban's wife she would enjoy the same social position she now had as a captain's daughter. In addition to all of these favorable factors, both of her parents liked and respected Eban. In fact, Eban had sailed as second mate under Vianna's father for one voyage early in his career, and Samuel Chadwick had returned full of praise for Eban's seamanship and his ability to handle a crew.

Yes, Eban would be a prize, Vianna decided. And besides, she was running out of time. She couldn't wait any longer for the handsome stranger to arrive and sweep her away on a tide of passion. If Harriet was in love, Vianna wanted to be, too; if Harriet was getting married, Vianna too would choose a husband and start a home and family.

Always the proper gentleman, Eban had written of his intentions to Vianna's father months ago without a word to Vianna or her mother, sending the letter with the captain of a whaling ship bound for the Pacific, where Samuel Chadwick had been for twenty-two months, accumulating a cargo of whale oil. Vianna's father was pleased by the prospect of seeing his daughter so well married and had sent his blessings by way of the first ship he encountered that was returning to Massachusetts. The letter reached Govans Harbor one week after Eban's ship docked there, whereupon Eban began an earnest courtship that resulted in a proposal offered and accepted. Now, two weeks later, Vianna was still waiting for the mysterious change she had observed in Harriet to happen to her.

The age-old power of spring to stir the senses gripped Vianna on this bright morning, and as she breathed in the soft air as she stood at the window, a strange longing sent an ache through her firm, young body. She couldn't put a name on it; she had never felt this particular sensation before. Its initial effect was to make her feel weak, but then a restlessness overwhelmed her, and she felt as if she wanted to cry out and go running down the street toward she knew not what.

She squeezed her eyes shut, then opened them quickly. A picnic, that's what the day called for! A lunch eaten on the beach, the hot sun, and a couple of lovers like Harriet and Jeremy to fire the blood! Surely Eban would succumb to such enticements, drop his cool reserve, and reveal the desire that he must feel for her. So far she had seen no sign of it, and she had gradually realized that her feeling for him was not going to achieve the passionate flowering that Harriet's had for Jeremy unless it received some stimulation from Eban. Time was growing short. Soon he would be leaving for the West Indies, and she had the scary suspicion that if their relationship did not burst into flame before then, it never would.

Today, then, was an opportunity that must not be missed.

Vianna swiftly threw off her nightdress, washed, and slipped into a pink checked dress that, despite the demureness of the white collar, provocatively displayed her well-rounded bosom and slim waist. Standing before the maple bureau that matched her bed, she brushed her blond hair. Then, pulling it back softly to leave a wave over each ear, she secured it with two ivory combs at the back of her head, allowing it to fall into a cluster of loose curls about her shoulders.

The combs, like the brooch she pinned where the ends of her collar came together, were scrimshaw, made from whalebone and decorated by her father during the long days or weeks of waiting for the next whale to be sighted. He had shown her once how scrimshaw was made, how the tooth or piece of baleen, or bone, was sanded until nice and white before the picture was etched upon it with a sharp tool or sail needle, the lines then filled with India ink.

As she pinned the brooch, with its finely etched rose, at her neck, a longing to see her father arose in her. She adored him, yet in her almost seventeen years of life, they had spent only a total of ten months together, generally two months at a time between voyages. Those brief periods, plus an occasional letter from him and daily reminders of him in her mother's conversation, kept her close to him in spirit despite the thousands of miles that separated them. Her loneliness at this moment was especially acute. She needed him here to tell her she had not made a mistake in agreeing to marry Eban.

The robin's exuberant song rang out clearly in the morning air. Vianna's mood brightened once more, and giving the brooch a pat, she turned and hurried down the stairs.

Mary Chadwick was already in the kitchen, fixing breakfast. A crisp blue apron covered her gray dress, and her whitening blond hair was secured at the back of her head with a pair of combs almost identical to those of her daughter. Her face was surprisingly smooth for her age, soft and white with a faint blush of color in the plump cheeks. It glowed with affection as Vianna entered and greeted her. "I'm warming the fish cakes left over from supper last night. They'll be ready in just a few minutes. Do you want some applesauce?"

Vianna shook her head, far too excited to be interested in breakfast. "It's such a pretty day that I want to do something special. Like have a picnic on the beach."

"What a lovely idea! We can take our lunch and spend the whole afternoon there."

Vianna's hand went to her brooch, rubbing it nervously. "Well, I . . . that is, I thought Harriet and I——" Her voice trailed off.

For an instant Mary Chadwick's pleasant face fell, then she recovered quickly. "You and Harriet, of course. You girls don't have much time left to do things together. Once she's married, things will be different." She tried not to show her disappointment.

Vianna was the living center of her mother's life. Mary Chadwick had learned to live without her husband. In fact, she had never known what it was to live with him, because he was already a whaling captain when she married him. He had taken her with him on his first voyage after their marriage, but she had proved such a poor sailor, experiencing unrelenting seasickness, that he had had to put her on the first ship they met that was returning to New England. It was not until his return three years later that she conceived Vianna. Although Mary Chadwick's sister, Mercy Sawtell, lived in Govans Harbor, Mary's life had been unbearably lonely until her daughter was born, and when there were no more pregnancies, all the great store of love in Mary Chadwick's generous heart was showered on Vianna.

Without realizing what she was doing or why she was doing it, she strove to keep her daughter a child, waiting on her, making no demands of her, forging ties of dependence that would hold Vianna to her as long as either of them lived. She dared not face the possibility that someday Vianna might get married, and she believed that threat lay far in the future until Eban Stanbro began paying court to Vianna. After a brief period of panic, she realized that if Vianna married Eban, it would change both her and her daughter's lives very little. Eban would be gone most of the time. Vianna would still be hers; the only thing that would change would be that they would no longer live under the same roof, but perhaps even that problem could be managed. During Eban's long voyages Vianna might choose to return to her childhood home.

Vianna had seen her mother's face fall when the older woman realized she was not the picnic companion her daughter was thinking of. Experiencing a rush of sadness at knowing her mother had been hurt, Vianna added swiftly, "If it's this nice tomorrow, Mother, we'll have our own private picnic, just you and I. Today, though, I thought it would be fun for Harriet, Jeremy, Eban and me to spend the day together."

Mary Chadwick busied herself at the stove, turning the fish cakes in their skillet. The fire in the cookstove put too much heat into the small kitchen. She pushed up both of the low, many-paned windows behind the table. "Surely the men will have to work today."

Vianna sat down and poured herself a glass of milk from the blue and white pitcher. "I'll bet we can coax Jeremy away from work. I'm not so sure about Eban, but I know he's not really busy right now. Can we have what's left of the spice cake? And can I buy some lemons for lemonade?"

Her daughter's childlike enthusiasm for a beach picnic drove away the momentary pang of rejection Mary Chadwick had felt. Smiling as she placed two fish cakes on Vianna's plate, she said, "Of course you can have the cake, and when you go after the lemons, buy a pound of bacon for sandwiches."

"And cheese!"

Mary Chadwick laughed as she slid the other fish cakes onto her own plate. "You'd better talk to Harriet and her mother before you buy cheese. Mercy is going to insist on furnishing part of the lunch, I know."

As Vianna had suspected, persuading Eban to take the afternoon off was the only problem her plan faced, but he agreed at last. The four of them walked to the south edge of town and took the path that bordered a stretch of marshland that would lead them to a small cove. The day had grown increasingly warm, but the sea breeze was strong and cool. Harriet and Jeremy held hands as they headed toward the beach, so Vianna made an excuse to fall behind, hoping the sight of the two lovers up ahead would get Eban in the right mood to make the most of this effervescent day.

He did seem to be in a lighter mood than usual, Vianna was encouraged to note. Not that his gaiety came anywhere near matching that of the rest of them. Eban at twenty-six possessed the gravity of a man twice his age, due largely, Vianna's mother assured her, to the fact that he lost his mother when he was only five and had been going to sea since he was twelve.

The gravity showed plainly in his gaunt face and was accented by the earnestness of the deep-set gray eyes. That he wasn't more handsome was a secret regret of Vianna's, but she always reminded herself that it was a strong, masculine face, full of character, and that he would be the kind of husband a woman would be proud of. He was big and strong of build, too, if rather ungainly. There was nothing of Jeremy's lithe, slim-hipped grace about him. Was the fact that he was not particularly attractive one of the reasons her love for him had not yet sprung to full life? Vianna thought about this as she watched Harriet and Jeremy cavorting playfully on the path ahead of them. Perhaps, but she was more inclined to think the reason was Eban's stiff reserve, and that's what she intended to break down this afternoon.

When he made no move to follow the example set by the lovers up ahead, Vianna grasped his arm as if overcome by exuberance, and exclaimed, "Oh, Eban, isn't this the most beautiful day you've ever seen? Aren't we going to have fun?" Then she let her hand slide down until it reached his, and squeezed it.

He smiled down at her. "It's a fine day, my dear, but I can't help feeling guilty because I'm not at the ship."

"But there isn't much work to be done there now!"

"True, but . . . I'm sure I'll enjoy the picnic. I haven't been on one for longer than I can remember."

She sent him a coquettish glance. "I'll make you forget your nagging conscience and turn you into a carefree boy again."

"Impossible," he said, chuckling.

Giving his hand another squeeze, she warned, "Don't be too sure!"

The cove they had chosen was formed by an outcropping of huge rocks. Here they would be protected from the stiff ocean breeze. No sooner had they spread the two beach robes on the sand than Jeremy wanted to eat.

"We just got here!" Harriet protested. "And it was a long walk. Can't we rest a few minutes?" She pulled off her bonnet and shook out her copper-colored hair.

It was an orange bonnet and clashed dreadfully with her hair and her green dress, but that was Harriet. Mismatched colors, crooked stitches, missing buttons, boiled potatoes still hard at the center—such details were cheerfully overlooked by the entire Sawtell family. Yet in his sailmaking Harriet's father, Isaac, was so exacting that there was never any complaint about his work among the ships' captains whose lives depended on the quality of those sails.

"Rest?" Jeremy exclaimed, sitting down on the robe and crossing his legs under him. "Since when was eating hard work? Let me have one of those sandwiches."

Sitting straight-backed, her legs thrust out in front of her, Harriet sent him a lazy look and drawled, "Are you going to order me around like this after we're married?"

"Of course." He gave her a grin that would have melted the resistance of a girl far more independent than Harriet. Rolling her eyes in mock dismay, she reached for the basket Eban had placed in the middle of the robes and began to set out the food. Vianna helped, wondering if she and Eban would ever lose the formality that still clung to their relationship and achieve the teasing familiarity Harriet and Jeremy enjoyed.

Full stomachs and the warm sun made them drowsy. Conversation died. Jeremy lay with his head in Harriet's lap. Now and then they murmured together as her hands played with his hair.

Vianna moved closer to Eban, who was leaning back on his arms, his crossed legs stretching so far in front of him that his boots rested in the sand beyond the edge of the robe. He was gazing off to his left toward a spot a quarter of a mile up the beach, where a man and a boy were forking seaweed into a farm wagon. Placing a hand over his, Vianna asked softly, "What are you thinking about at this moment, Eban?"

"I was thinking about how I used to help my father

gather seaweed to spread on our fields. He preferred kelp to rockweed. He reckoned it to be richer in minerals."

Eban's older sister, Susannah, had taken charge of the household when her mother died. She hadn't been in her teens yet, but she'd made a home for her father and brother on their small farm until John Stanbro's death. When a year later she'd married Kermit Baker, who worked in the clock shop, she sold the farm and took Eban with her to her new home. He was eleven years old, and although he and Kermit got along well together, he decided to sign on as cabin boy on a ship going to China to see if the life of a sailor suited him. It had, and Vianna knew that as his wife she would have to endure a lifetime of long separations from him. The thought had not troubled her thus far, because the emotional bonds between them were still tenuous.

"We were a day out of Liverpool," Eban was saying, "when we spied a great field of kelp. We saw that there was something caught in it. It looked like a sea chest, so we drew alongside, and sure enough, that's what it was. We brought it aboard and knew from the barnacles on it that it had been in the water a long time. The lock was so encrusted that we had to saw it off. What do you suppose we found in it?" He turned toward Jeremy and Harriet with a look of amusement.

The other couple had been lost in their own private world and had not been listening to Eban, who, insensible to the intimate withdrawal of the lovers these past few minutes, was puzzled by the blank looks they now gave him.

"What was that?" Jeremy said apologetically.

As first mate Eban was not accustomed to inattention when he was speaking. There was the faint snap of reprimand in his voice as he repeated, "The sea chest. What do you suppose we found in it?"

"A bottle of rum."

Eban stared, incredulous. "How'd you happen to guess that?"

A grin swept the sensuousness from Jeremy's handsome face. "Some of your crew were telling the story at the tavern a couple of weeks ago. Sorry to spoil your story, Eban."

"Oh, well——" Vianna saw her fiancé master his annoyance and take command of the story again. "It was quite a moment, though. We were prepared to find anything in it from Spanish gold and jewels to love letters. Nothing so commonplace as a bottle of rum, though it was still sealed and enough to give the whole crew a swallow around."

Jeremy yawned. "That makes me dry. Is there any lemonade left? And cake?"

Harriet tweaked his nose gently. "We just finished eating." There was a huskiness in her voice, an unfamiliar depth of tone that brought Vianna's glance swiftly to her cousin's face. It was flushed, almost swollen by sensations Vianna could only guess at.

"Sometimes I'm tempted to give the sea a try," Jeremy declared. "Making barrels day after day gets plenty tiresome. I think about you sailors out on the ocean—moving, always moving, visiting foreign lands, seeing strange sights and peoples—and I think I'd like to experience some of that excitement. Then I get to thinking about those months and years you're away from home, and I lose my desire for it. I'm a man who has to warm his feet at his own fireside each night." When he gave Harriet a look that said it was more than his feet he wanted warmed each night, her hand trembled as she poured his glass of lemonade.

"It's a calling," Eban explained—a bit smugly, Vianna thought. "If you have it, you can never be content living ashore."

Not even with a young, eager wife, apparently, Vianna told herself, realizing with a sinking heart that Eban would never need her in the way Jeremy needed

Harriet. Yet maybe precisely because of their long separations each return from a voyage would be like a second honeymoon.

Jeremy drank thirstily, then stretched his arms above his head. "It's for sure I don't have the calling. For me, dreams of the sea will always be better than the reality would be." As he lay down with his head in Harriet's lap once more, he murmured something to her that brought her finger swiftly to his lips as if in reproof or warning, and they withdrew again into their private world.

Vianna felt their withdrawal sharply, especially since Eban seemed disinclined to talk any more. He lay back, his head on the robe, his eyes closed. Vianna sensed that he was as far away from her in spirit as Jeremy and Harriet were. Disgruntled, she sat watching the green waves rise until they curled over on themselves whitely and collapsed with a crash. Was nothing about this day going to warm Eban's blood? Was he immune to all the sensual stimulants of the spring weather, the two lovers, and even to her own feminine attractions, which she was certain she possessed?

She sat in lonely isolation for a long time, finally sighing and turning toward her cousin and Jeremy, hoping they would allow her to share their company. Instead she saw their eyes locked in a look that set her own body aflame and cause her fingers to dig convulsively into the robe. They were getting married none too soon, she decided.

A sudden restlessness seized her, jerking her to her feet and sending her forward to the several pools the waves had worn in the tawny rocks that erupted from the sand at this point on the beach.

Through the perfectly clear water of the nearest pool she observed three sea perch swimming about. She knelt, and gradually the fish and the sandy bottom faded from her vision and she saw her own face against the background of blue sky reflected there. A wave of blond hair fell softly over each ear; the soft mouth appeared supremely kissable; the large blue eyes carried hints of the passion she knew was slumbering within her, just waiting to be awakened. When were she and Eban going to become lovers? When were their emotions going to reach the pitch that those of Harriet and Jeremy had obviously reached?

Behind her she heard the thud of boots on sand and felt something cut off the hot rays of the sun falling on her body. An instant later, Eban's face appeared above hers in the pool. The jutting brow ridges shadowed the gray eyes so darkly it was impossible to read their expression, but there seemed to be a smile beneath the dark mustache, which was all that was left of the full beard he had come into port with six weeks ago.

"If we had a net, we could catch them," he said.

"I would rather just watch them swim. They move so effortlessly. Watching them makes me feel heavy and graceless."

"It's the medium they live in that allows them to move with so little effort. One thrust of any object in the water will set it into flowing movement. Moving through air as we do, we display a different kind of grace."

She gazed back at his reflection in the clear pool, anticipating that he meant to turn his observations on the gracefulness of the human body into more personal channels. When no compliment was forthcoming, she stood up, glancing past Eban's tall form toward the other couple, who we still oblivious to everything but themselves. Above the roar and crash of the waves it was impossible for Vianna to hear what they were saying, but the bemused expression on Harriet's freckled face and the caressing way Jeremy's fingers were moving up and down her bare arm set Vianna's imagination soaring.

Eban had never touched her like that. In fact, he had kissed her on the mouth only once, the evening she had said she would marry him. The kiss had been more of a seal to a bargain than an ardent expression of love. She hadn't enjoyed it, either. His lips had been hard and dry, his mustache prickly. There had been no evidence within herself or Eban of the rapture she had always imagined a kiss by one's beloved would evoke.

"Why don't we go for a walk?" she suggested, tearing her eyes away from the other couple. "They'd obviously prefer to be alone."

"What? Oh, yes, I see." Eban shot them a second look, as if just noticing their absorption in each other. "Embarrassing, isn't it? One couldn't expect any restraint from Jeremy. He's always been one for the girls. But I am surprised at Harriet, permitting such liberties."

"She's in love, Eban!" Vianna's tone was snappish. Had he no understanding at all?

"All the more reason they should behave circumspectly."

Irked, Vianna started up the beach. Eban strode along beside her—silently, to her relief. If she had to listen to any more of his stuffy remarks, she'd scream. Recalling the smoldering glance that she had caught passing between Jeremy and Harriet a few moments ago, she experienced a flash of such acute frustration that she picked up a small stone and hurled it petulantly at a mackerel gull wading in the foam at the water's edge. The bird squealed a protest and flew off, continuing to register its outrage as it wheeled above them.

I'm being cheated, Vianna thought. When I accepted Eban's proposal, I expected to change the way Harriet has changed, but I haven't, and it's all Eban's fault. He's about as romantic as that stupid gull!

Her eyes fell on a cave worn in one of the taller rocks. It had been a favorite place to play when she and Harriet were children. An idea came to her. She and Eban had never really been alone. Their courting had taken place in her mother's parlor, at church, and at other social affairs. Today there had been Jeremy and Harriet, who, instead of inspiring him with their amorous behavior, might have inhibited him. The cave was small and rather dark and just the place to attempt an assault upon Eban's coolly restrained emotions. She wasn't certain what she would do once she got him up there, but she would think of something.

She called Eban's attention to the cave. "Harriet and I played in it many times when we were children. We used shells for cups and dishes. Rockweed did for everything from cake to codfish."

Eban halted, gazing up at the cave thoughtfully. "I'm surprised your parents permitted you to play in it. If you had forgotten the time, you'd been caught there by high tide."

She chuckled. "Our parents never knew, of course. They always cautioned us not to play in it for that very reason."

"But you disobeyed them?" There was reproof in his voice. "Naughty girl."

"Oh, Eban, for heaven's sake," she chided, shaking his arm none too lightly, "didn't you ever do something you weren't supposed to do?" *And won't you do it now?* she pleaded silently, as a sudden wildness seized her. *Sweep me into your arms, carry me up there, and make fiery love to me. Show me you desire me, and under the stimulation of your kisses and caresses I'll finally experience the mystery of love.*

"I never intentionally did anything I wasn't supposed to do," Eban was saying, "and from the time I was twelve years old, I was given orders and expected to carry them out like a man."

At this reminder of his harsh childhood, pity pulled Vianna's attention away from her own needs to Eban's, and pressing his arm close to her side, she said, "You've missed out on a lot of fun, and I intend to help you catch up. I want to make you very happy, Eban."

"You already have, my dear. He drew her hand through his arm and patted it. "It will be a source of great satisfaction to me during my voyages to think of you back here, maintaining my home, raising my children."

Maintaining *my* home, raising *my* children! Was that all he wanted of her, to serve as a symbol for him while he was away, representing his success? She studied his weather-cured face. How much of his undemonstrativeness was caused by his sense of propriety, and how much by an innate coldness? Perhaps there was no passion in Eban; perhaps not even after a minister had placed the seal of approval of both church and society on their union would Eban turn into the lover she yearned for.

Suddenly she had had enough of this day. All of its loveliness and promise had been wasted. Romance had quivered in the air, only to fall forlornly to the ground to be crushed underfoot like a fragile scallop shell. "The breeze is turning cold," she said dully. "We should be starting home."

"But it's still early. You should have brought a shawl, my dear."

Gritting her teeth, Vianna agreed with his sensible advice, adding, "However, I didn't, and I'm chilly." She had withdrawn her hand from the crook of his elbow some moments before, and now she started back down the beach toward the spot where they had left Harriet and Jeremy. Vianna noted that the other couple viewed their return as something of a nuisance, and they amiably declined to return home with them.

"I'm not at all cold," Harriet hastened to say, "and there's too much of the day left. I don't want to go yet." Her face was suffused with a strange softness.

"Go ahead," Jeremy urged. "We won't look upon it as desertion. Just leave us the rest of the cake and lemonade."

They couldn't wait to be left alone again. Vianna

was made even more aware than before of the aridity of the relationship between Eban and herself. "I'll see you tomorrow, Harriet." She headed through the deep, dry sand, and with the crunching sound of Eban's boots behind her—smashing romance to bits—picked up the path that led back into town.

2

The next morning Vianna confided her doubt about her fiancé to her cousin as they made their way toward Mrs. Prentiss's Millinery Shop to buy more thread for the wedding dress Harriet and her mother were making. It was going to be another beautiful day, which only added to Vianna's wretchedness. The fragrant air, the golden splashes of daffodil beds, the serene white clouds that hung in the sky all created an ache inside her breast that she was afraid would never be relieved. A block to their right, behind the row of houses and shops that faced the wharf, she heard the creak of timber and rope from the ships docked there. Eban was probably aboard his ship this minute, making up for playing truant yesterday.

"Do you think Eban really loves me?" she asked, interrupting Harriet's account of the problems she and her mother were having with her wedding dress.

"What? Oh——" Her cousin avoided looking at her, choosing instead to glance toward the schoolhouse they were passing. From inside came the sing-song murmur of a group recitation. Not too many years ago they had sat in a couple of those desks, learning, memorizing, but knowing that those particular lessons would have little application in the lives they would lead someday, each of them dreaming of the faceless yet handsome man around whom their lives would revolve. "Of course he loves you."

"Not the way Jeremy loves you. Do you know he's kissed me on the mouth only once?"

Harriet's sandy-lashed eyes swung swiftly to her now, incredulous.

"It's true," declared Vianna. "And I've been kissed better behind the rope walk."

Harriet's step had slowed. "Eban is older, not only in years but because he's lived in a harsh, man's world since he was a boy."

"Shouldn't that make him more of a man rather than less?"

"Eban is man enough, I'm sure. He's of a very serious cast of mind, though. Kissing, just for the sake of kissing, may seem a waste of time to him."

Vianna studied her cousin's profile, the round cheek dotted with freckles the same color as her hair, the very short chin, the nose that turned up ever so slightly. "You don't think he could be . . . well . . . cold, do you? Uninterested in the love part of marriage, I mean." Funny, she was thinking, that I should feel this embarrassment with Harriet, from whom I've never had any secrets, nor she from me—until Jeremy, that is.

Harriet laughed. "From what I've seen, and from what Jeremy has told me, *all* men are interested in that."

"Maybe, but he made a remark yesterday that made me wonder." The open back door of the ship's chandlery sent forth the smell of tar and turpentine into the morning air as Vianna told her cousin what Eban had said about maintaining *his* home and raising *his* children as if she were to be not a source of love awaiting him on his return from his voyages but a possession that would be a constant reminder to the town of his importance and success.

"It does seem an odd thing for a newly engaged man to say," Harriet admitted. It was several moments before she added, "And he does seem rather cold, but," she hastened to add, "I'm sure that will change after you're married."

"What if he doesn't?" Vianna almost wailed.

The two young cousins stared at each other in mutual

anguish. Neither of them knew the answer to that mournful question.

As the day of Eban's sailing drew nearer, Vianna's desperation grew. He would be gone two months. Would she have no memories to sustain her during that time? None that would set her heart clamoring for his return, make her arms hungry to hold him close once again?

It seemed not. Eban's behavior toward her changed in no degree during the next ten days. On the eve of his departure, Vianna decided that bold action was required. She devised a plan. If it shocked him, she did not care. Even if it did, and he responded in spite of himself, the risk would have been well taken, and she would have the passionate memories she needed to excite her while planning for the wedding that would take place upon his return.

That last night, at Vianna's instigation, Mary Chadwick invited Eban to have supper with them.

"Perhaps we should let his sister have the pleasure of cooking for him on his last night home, dear. I'm sure he will come by here later and spend the rest of the evening with you."

"I'm the woman he's going to marry," Vianna reminded her mother. "Surely I'm more important to him now than his sister. He'll want to come here to supper, I know. Please, Mother?"

Knowing how precious those remaining hours before sailing were to a seaman and the woman he loved, Mary Chadwick capitulated and extended the invitation, which was accepted at once.

When Eban arrived that evening, he was carrying a bulky package, which he presented to Vianna as she invited him in. "I will not be here on your birthday, so I will give it to you now."

"Oh, Eban, how nice!" She flashed him the brightest smile in her repertoire of smiles, swiftly thinking that here was a good excuse to initiate her plan of the evening. She pulled him into the parlor for maximum privacy. Her mother was in the kitchen and would not be able to hear or see them.

She laid the package on a carved mahogany table that stood behind the sofa. The table, brought from Africa by her father, gave off the tangy fragrance of furniture wax as the rays of the late afternoon sun fell on it. The room was filled to crowding with Chinese porcelain, laquered Japanese boxes, and other exotic mementos of Samuel Chadwick's travels. The mahogany table and a round lamp table that stood between two chairs were draped with brilliant shawls of Indian silk.

Vianna untied the twine from her package, and as the foreign looking paper fell away, she withdrew a cream-colored shawl. "Oh, it's lovely!"

Eban looked pleased. "It is knit from Shetland wool."

Vianna unfolded it and handed it to Eban. "Help me put it on."

He appeared slightly puzzled at being asked to do something she could do in an instant with no more effort than a flick of her wrists, but he obliged, draping the closely knit woolen garment across her shoulders.

Catching his hands before he withdrew them, Vianna leaned her head back, tilting it so that she could gaze up into his eyes. Trying to put a huskiness into her voice, she murmured his name and waited, her lips inviting his kiss. When it didn't come, she stretched her neck, but before she could get her lips to his, he stepped back, saying, "There is more. There. In the bottom of the package."

Thwarted only momentarily, Vianna unfolded the soft paper covering the smaller gift to disclose six Irish linen handkerchiefs. She shook one out gently and fingered the lace border lovingly. "They are exquisite. Almost too fine to use."

He laughed. "But you will use them."

"Indeed I will." Vianna stood on tiptoe to kiss Eban. He turned his cheek. She put her hand on his chin and turned his face so that she could place her lips squarely on his. She had no idea what a passionate kiss should be like, but assuming it included a lot of pressure, she kissed him so hard her teeth hurt her own lips. What it was doing to him she never found out, for at that moment her mother entered the parlor. Eban jerked away so violently that Vianna staggered, momentarily off balance. Red-faced, he said with as much dignity as he could manage, "Good evening, Mrs. Chadwick. I've brought Vianna's birthday presents, and as you can see, she was reacting impulsively, as always."

Startled by what she had walked in on, Mary Chadwick nevertheless spoke in a light tone. "My daughter is still a child, I fear, but," she continued, beaming affectionately at Vianna, "that is a large part of her charm."

Child! Vianna ground her teeth. Her mother was as bad as Eban. Would neither of them recognize that she was a woman, with adult dreams and desires?

"A new shawl!" Mary Chadwick exclaimed, coming forward to touch the soft wool that draped Vianna's shoulders. Against the fading light, her gray-blond hair shone white. The plum-colored silk from which her dress was made had been one of the gifts Samuel Chadwick had brought home from his last voyage. "It's Shetland, isn't it? There's no other wool like it anywhere in the world. And Irish linen handkerchiefs! Eban, you certainly know how to please a woman."

Vianna nearly laughed out loud, and not wholly from amusement. Yet perhaps tonight she would discover that her mother's remark was true after all.

She suffered impatiently through dinner while Eban and her mother carried on a conversation that scarcely included her. Mary Chadwick was clearly enjoying having a masculine presence at her table again, and Eban talked freely of his most recent voyage and the one to come. Annoyed at being ignored, Vianna finally broke in and said, "We had letters from Father today. Captain Hobart of the *Century* brought them from Lahaina.

He wrote that hunting had been good this season. He's taken more than a thousand barrels of oil."

"Well, he has had a successful hunt, then," Eban remarked.

"Eight hundred of those barrels were taken off Cape Thaddeus in June. It was a grand cut." Mary Chadwick's fair, plump face glowed with the excitement of such an unusual event. "Only a few ships were there, since it was early in the season for that area. That's why Samuel took so much oil in such a short time."

Eban's black brows rose sharply as he laid down his knife and fork. "What a stroke of luck!"

"Or perhaps God in His mercy was being kind. It took Samuel thirty-eight months last time to get a full load, and he was away from home for forty months. If he continues to have good hunting, this may prove to be a much shorter voyage. He's been gone only nineteen months." Some of her elation faded as she added, "Of course, this still won't put him home in time for your wedding."

Eban set his coffee cup down and smiled into her saddened face. "Such is the life of a sailor and a sailor's wife and family. But we are a tough breed. We can bear what others cannot."

Vianna broke in again. "It's such a nice evening, Mother. Can you manage the dishes alone so that Eban and I can go for a walk?"

"Why of course, dear, go——"

Eban interrupted with a protest. "Vianna, for shame, leaving your mother to clear up alone. You help her with the dishes, and I'll take you for a walk afterward."

Take her for a walk! As if she were a child or a dog! Livid, Vianna was on the verge of retorting that if her mother didn't mind, why should he? But making him angry might spoil her scheme, so she clamped her lips together and set about clearing off the table.

By the time the dishes were washed and put away, her annoyance had cooled and been replaced by butterflies in her stomach. As she hung up the dish towel, she giggled to herself. She couldn't have been more nervous if she had planned to seduce Eban, and of course she had no intention of going that far. All she wanted to do was melt the frost that perpetually coated his emotions and lay naked the hunger that according to Harriet *every* man carried inside him.

Dusk was falling when she and Eban left the house. She wore her new shawl against the coolness that arrived quickly as soon as the sun had set. There was no hint of winter left in either the feel or the smell of the evening air, however. The perfume of lilacs followed them wherever they walked, and a mockingbird sang its medley of songs despite the waning light.

Vianna unobtrusively guided their steps toward the point where the lighthouse stood. The bank and the ship carver's shop were dark, but light streamed from the windows of the tavern and from the open door through which came the sounds of laughter and raillery. "Do you ever miss the comforts and amusements of a town when you are at sea?" Vianna asked. Eban had tucked her hand sedately into the crook of his elbow and was walking with measured tread down the bricked sidewalk that fronted the shops.

"Not at all. In fact, after two weeks ashore I grow bored. I enjoy the routine aboard ship, and I like to stand on deck and see nothing but ocean no matter where I turn my eyes. That is home to me and always will be. I'm sure you are prepared to accept that, because your father is, of course, the same breed of man that I am. We can love our wives and children deeply, but our souls find contentment only when we have a ship moving under us."

"I understand, and I don't mind as long as I know you love me." They had reached the firehouse, the last building along Front Street. Up ahead, across an empty expanse of brick paving and sand, was her Uncle Isaac's sail loft, beyond that the rope walk, and finally the lighthouse. There was still light enough to see

Eban's expression as she peered up at him and asked solemnly, "You do love me, Eban, don't you?"

The question embarrassed him. He had never used the word *love* in his proposal or in any of their private moments together. He didn't use it now, saying merely, "Of course I do, my dear. Why else would I have asked you to be my wife?"

Not a satisfactory reply at all, she reflected, sighing. Yet if she couldn't make him say it, maybe she could make him reveal his love for her physically. When he suggested they turn and go back along the next street, she pleaded to go on down to the lighthouse. "It's still early, and it is our last night together."

He patted her hand. "If you like."

Behind the sail loft the rope walk stretched for a thousand feet toward the lighthouse. Here the tons of rope required by Govans Harbor ships were twisted and braided. The mingled odors of tar and hemp that hung about the long building never failed to evoke a sense of wickedness in Vianna, not that she had ever done anything naughtier than let a boy kiss her here, but she had heard rumors of other forbidden things taking place in this spot.

As they walked beside the long building toward the point, Vianna drew closer to Eban. There wasn't another soul in sight. The lantern in the white wooden lighthouse pulsed above their heads, and across the water the running lights of a fishing boat returning with its day's catch bobbed and dipped. Slowing her step, Vianna pressed her breast against Eban's arm. He seemed not to notice. She did it again, harder this time, feeling his solid muscles against her soft flesh. Still no response. Was his jacket sleeve so thick he could feel nothing?

She pulled her hand from the crook of his elbow and caught his, squeezing it warmly and exclaiming, "Isn't it a beautiful night? Truly a night to remember all those nights you're away." Making it appear an accident, she managed to bring Eban's hand in contact with her thigh. Instantly he stiffened his arm, drawing it close to his side and hers with it. It was a moment before she dared sneak a glance at him, but unfortunately it was now too dark to read his expression.

"This is the best season to begin a voyage," he said. "The weather is good, and I'm filled with the need to be doing something productive."

"Maybe once we're married you won't feel bored and restless when you're ashore. I'll do my best to make you content, Eban." She tried for as seductive a tone as possible, and when he made no reply, she abandoned all subtlety. Crying, "Oh, Eban, I shall miss you so!" she threw her arms around his neck and kissed him. This time she used more than pressure. She ground her mouth against his, forcing his lips open along with her own.

Like iron hooks his hands gripped her arms, tearing them loose from his neck and forcing her body away from his until they stood at arm's length from each other. "Vianna, stop that! Whatever in the world has got into you tonight?"

"Nothing, except that I love you and I'm going to miss you," she replied innocently.

"You are much too impulsive. It is not proper to kiss me like that."

"Why not? Are we not betrothed?"

"Yes, but not married."

The flashing lantern in the lighthouse was too high to offer any illumination at their level, so she could not tell from his face whether her kiss had stirred him in the slightest. There was certainly no evidence of it in his voice, which was as stern as any he had ever used with her. "Are you sure you'll be wanting me to kiss you like that even after we are married?" she asked earnestly.

"No lady would kiss any man like that, not even her husband," he replied stiffly.

"No matter how much she loved him?"

"Ladies don't express their love in that way."

The doubt about the wisdom of accepting Eban's proposal, which had started as small as a mustard seed more than two weeks ago, blossomed with Eban's last remarks. Desperately she asked, "And you? Will you ever kiss me like that? Do I stir you at all? You never even look at me that way Jeremy looks at Harriet."

"He fails to show proper manly restraint. Jeremy is a wild one, and it is good that he is finally settling down."

"I think Harriet is very lucky to be getting a man who loves her so much and is not ashamed to show it."

She had spoken tartly; Eban spoke placatingly. "There are many ways to show love, my dear."

She would not deny that, but she had the depressing suspicion that there was one method of expressing it that Eban would not employ with any passion or enthusiasm. She no longer had any confidence that marriage would uncover any ardor in this man. Maybe Jeremy did like girls too much, but Vianna wished fervently that Eban were more like that.

"Come, my dear, we must have no disagreements on my last night home." He leaned forward to peck her on the forehead, then turned her firmly around and led her back in the direction of town.

Vianna went unresistingly, defeated. The intimate shadows and evocative odors of the rope walk accentuated her despair. She was never going to experience the passion and mystery of love the way Harriet had. Her marriage to Eban would be one of chaste kisses, "proper" behavior, and unremitting boredom. Her throat swelled achingly, and it was only by summoning up all the self-control she possessed that she kept from weeping.

3

Mary Chadwick attributed her daughter's disconsolate silence the next day to the fact that Eban's ship was sailing. Those days when Samuel sailed away were the saddest of her life, and believing Vianna was suffering the same bereavement, she offered sympathy and support but no words of comfort. She knew well there were no words to ease the pain of these hours. She accompanied her daughter down to the wharf after an early breakfast, and there they found Susannah Baker, standing near the *Andover* among a sizable group of people who had gathered to watch the ship sail.

Eban's sister was a tall, large-boned woman with dark hair. In the shape of her face and nose she resembled her younger brother, but there was none of his sternness in her expression. Her gray eyes surveyed the world serenely; her smile came easily and with great warmth. After several miscarriages early in her marriage, she had failed to conceive again, but childlessness had cast no blight over her cheerful nature. She called a greeting to the Chadwicks and beckoned to them. "They're just taking on the last of their fresh water. There's Eban up there near the hatch, see?"

Vianna's eyes had already picked him out, not that she was making a special effort to find him. After last night she felt as if her heart had grown as cold as Eban's. His departure elicited absolutely no regret. What would there be to miss once he was gone—a paternal kiss on the brow, a pat on the hand? She could get those anytime she wanted them from Uncle Isaac.

"Yes, there he is, Vianna," Mary Chadwick said, scanning the ship with a practiced eye.

With barely concealed irritation, Vianna said, "I see him." Clad in duck pants and checkered shirt, he was directing the men who were laboring to lower the heavy water barrels into the hold. Up on the bridge the captain stood talking with the two ship's owners, calling an order down to Eban occasionally. To anyone unfamiliar with the last-minute tasks to be done on board a ship preparing to get under way, the activity on deck would seem disorganized and random, but the citizens of Govans Harbor who had collected to watch the *Andover* depart could have told a landlubber precisely what each sailor was doing and why. It was this bustle that Vianna watched, not Eban, for she was always fascinated by the courage of men who, with nothing more substantial than a small amount of wood and canvas, set forth to challenge the mighty ocean. Susannah, like Vianna's mother, attributed Vianna's silence to unhappiness over the prospect of the coming separation from Eban, but not being a seaman's wife, she believed that words could comfort.

"The time will go fast, you'll see," she told Vianna. "You'll be planning the wedding, and you'll be so busy that before you know it Eban will be back and you'll be getting married."

Vianna gave her a faint smile. She was fond of Susannah. Why couldn't Eban have been the same sort of warm person his sister was? Had she made a mistake? It was a question she had asked herself many times last night before she finally fell asleep, but she always came smack up against a second question as she did now. What course was open to her, even if she had made a mistake? In Govans Harbor a broken engagement was only a mite less scandalous than a divorce. It simply wasn't done. Once you made the

commitment to marry, you did, and you stuck it out
no matter how bad the marriage might turn out to be.

She was so preoccupied with her predicament that
she scarcely heard Susannah's continued efforts to cheer
her up. Finally Eban's sister gave up and fell into quiet
conversation with Mary Chadwick, leaving Vianna to
what she believed was the anguish of seeing her loved
one sail away.

By the time the *Andover* left the harbor, Vianna
had decided she had to get some information from
Jeremy through Harriet. She knew so little about men.
Maybe she was getting upset over nothing and an explanation would show her she really had no problem
at all. When she told her mother she would go see
Harriet instead of returning home with her, Mary
Chadwick said, "Ask Mercy if she's finished with the
pan I sent those rolls over in last week. I want to bake
again tomorrow."

Dishes taken to the Sawtells or things borrowed by
them had a way of never finding their way back to their
original owners except after a long wait or a direct
reminder. No one minded, however, because the Sawtells were so generous in return.

The Sawtells' house was two hundred years old and
had a fireplace in every room, and Aunt Mercy still
did her cooking in the huge one in the kitchen. Vianna
had been surprised when Harriet hadn't come to the
wharf that morning. Now she saw why. The breakfast
fire was no more than coals now, but Aunt Mercy was
sitting close to it, hemming a new petticoat for Harriet's
trousseau, and Vianna could tell from the way she held
her left arm that her rheumatism was plaguing her
again. A few feet across the wide-boarded floor Harriet
was punching down bread dough at the big round table.
There was a dusting of flour on the worn braided rug
at her feet. Mercy Sawtell's usually flushed face was
pale, and her blond hair, normally bunned at the nape
of her neck, hung loose and unbrushed down her back.

Her smile was bright, however, when she greeted her niece. "The *Andover* has sailed?"

Vianna nodded. "I'm sorry your shoulder is bothering you again. Wouldn't you be more comfortable if you just sat and didn't try to do anything?"

"My stars, child, I can't sit with idle hands! I'd go crazy."

"I thought there must be something wrong when Harriet didn't show up for the sailing." Vianna sat down at the big scarred table where her cousin was working the bread dough on a floured area. How was she going to manage a private conversation with Harriet?

The problem was solved immediately when her cousin said, "I'll be finished with this in a minute, then I've got to go to Mr. Fickett's and get some fish for dinner."

So it was only a short time later that Vianna was spilling out her doubts to Harriet as they made their way along the cobbled street to the fish market. Now that the *Andover* had sailed, there was scarcely a person to be seen on Front Street. There was plenty of activity nearer the water, however, around the ships that remained at the wharf. When Vianna came to the point in her account of her attempts the previous evening to arouse some ardor in Eban, when he declared no lady kissed even her husband the way Vianna had kissed him, Harriet declared in surprise, "That's nonsense."

"That's what I thought. Whatever could Eban have meant?"

Harriet shook her head. "I can't imagine."

"Well, will you ask Jeremy? Tell him everything I've told you, and ask him what he thinks. Honestly, I think there might be something wrong with Eban, and I don't want there to be, because if there is, I wouldn't know what to do."

Harriet's lashless eyes were puzzled. "What do you think might be wrong with him?"

"Maybe he doesn't really love me, I don't know. But he certainly doesn't act like Jeremy."

Harriet giggled. "He certainly doesn't."

"Will you ask Jeremy?"

"Of course."

"How soon can you ask him and tell me what he says?"

Harriet slowed her steps as they approached the fish market. "I'll be too busy helping at home today to see him, but he'll come by tonight after supper, like he always does. I'll ask him then and tell you tomorrow."

"If I come over early in the morning, can you think up some excuse to talk to me in private?"

"I'll think of something," Harriet promised.

It seemed like an awfully long time to live with uncertainty, but there was no choice. Vianna skipped breakfast the next morning, despite her mother's protest, and with the excuse that she was anxious about Aunt Mercy, she hurried over to the Sawtells' house. The family was just finishing their breakfast. Isaac Sawtell was drinking his final cup of creamy, sugared coffee. Vianna thought he looked like what she had always imagined an elf would look like—small and wiry, with sharp features, a pointed chin, and curly gray hair. Harriet's two brothers were still working on stacks of flannel cakes swimming in maple syrup. Joseph, at sixteen, was small and wiry, like his father. His features were softer, however. He looked younger than he was, but every ship's captain and owner was aware that he was on the way to becoming as fine a sailmaker as his father. Nine-year-old Nathaniel was a different story. Thin, already tall, with front teeth too big as yet for his mouth, he was bored with sailmaking, bored with school, and counting the years until he would be twelve and old enough to go to sea. To his great delight, he'd been given the nickname "Cap."

"You're up early," Isaac Sawtell remarked to Vianna. "Better have a couple of the flannel cakes."

"No, thanks, Uncle. Mother and I were anxious to know how Aunt Mercy's shoulder was today."

"I walked the floor with it most of the night, but the pain eased some about sunup." Fatigue dimmed the older woman's cheerful tone a trifle.

"That's good news. Mother will be glad to hear it, too. She said to tell you she'd be baking today and would bring over a pie for your supper." Vianna caught the eye of her cousin, who sat sleepily over an empty plate.

"Come up to my room," Harriet said, pushing herself up off the chair. "I want to show you something."

Green eyes gleaming devilishly, Nathaniel cried, "She got nothing to show you. She just wants to tell you how many times Jeremy kissed her last night before Papa finally kicked him out."

Over her shoulder Harriet said, unruffled, "He didn't kick him out, and I didn't keep a count of his kisses. I couldn't. There were too many."

Harriet's room was very small, holding a single bed and a narrow chest of drawers. Pegs driven into the fading pink wallpaper held her clothes. She sank down on her unmade bed with a yawn. "Jeremy did stay late last night."

Vianna sat beside her, exclaiming, "Did you ask him?"

Harriet propped herself on the pillow, her feet still on the floor. "It's sort of embarrassing. Are you sure you want to hear it?"

"Of course I do. Come on, Harriet. I *have* to know what Jeremy thinks about Eban."

"Well," Harriet began hesitantly, "Jeremy says there are some men who believe decent women don't and shouldn't enjoy the lovemaking part of marriage. Eban might be one of these."

"That's not true, is it, about decent women, I mean?" Vianna folded and unfolded a crease in her blue striped skirt, adding in a small voice, "If it is, then I suspect I'm not a decent woman."

Harriet gave a throaty chuckle. "Neither am I, if decent means numb." Hastily, she expanded on that remark. "I don't want you to think I've done anything with Jeremy I shouldn't have before we're married, because I haven't. But I know when he starts kissing me on our wedding night I'm not going to be lying there as lifeless as a figurehead. And he won't want me to. He says there are men, though, who prefer that their wives lie there like corpses and just wait for it to be over."

Vianna asked miserably, "Do you suppose that's what Eban expects of me?"

"Even if he does," Harriet said, trying to sound hopeful, "he might change his mind once he finds out what it's like to have you love him, too. Jeremy says these men who think they want their wives to just lie there don't know what they're missing. And, Vi, you don't know for *sure* that Eban's going to be that kind of husband. He might turn out to be the most passionate lover you could imagine."

Vianna was still nervously pleating her skirt. "I hope you're right. If only there were some way of finding out before it's too late!"

In the next two weeks her problem receded a bit, pushed aside by the excitement and the many details to be worked out before Harriet's wedding. The fact that Eban was gone helped, too. Out of sight, out of mind, Vianna reflected wryly. She even felt some relief that he was no longer around. The doubt and frustration she had begun to feel since she'd accepted his proposal faded without the constant reminder of his presence. A feeling of freedom, which she hadn't realized she had lost, came back. It was particularly strong the night she ran over to the Sawtells to tell them her mother's yellow climbing rose was sure to be blooming by Friday, when the wedding was to take place, and that they could have all they wanted to decorate the house with.

She delivered the message rather self-consciously, because when she entered the Sawtell kitchen, she discovered a new face among the familiar ones of her relatives and Jeremy. Eight people crowded the kitchen, which had been heated so much by the supper fire that the door and windows were open. Isaac Sawtell sat in a wooden rocking chair at one corner of the cooling fireplace, smoking his pipe. The rest sat at the big round table, above which hung a large whale-oil lamp. Mercy Sawtell was hemming a towel, and Joseph was quietly leafing through Nathaniel's book of ships, which his younger brother had abandoned when Harriet's company had arrived. When Jeremy introduced the stranger to Vianna as Tom Fulton, she exclaimed, "Oh, yes, hello! You're to be the best man."

He and Harriet's fiancé had become close friends two years ago, when Jeremy had gone to Pennsylvania to try farming with an uncle. That experiment had lasted only one season before Jeremy decided he preferred working in his father's cooperage. They hadn't seen each other since, but the ties of friendship forged during those months had remained strong. When Jeremy wrote Tom, asking if he'd be best man at his wedding, Tom had accepted at once. And here he was, standing to acknowledge their introduction.

Vianna examined the face before her and liked what she saw. Tom Fulton wasn't as handsome as Jeremy, but he didn't miss it by far. With his reddish brown hair he could have been a Sawtell, but his skin was fair and without a sign of a freckle. There was a straight wedge of a nose above a full-lipped mouth, and smoky gray eyes that met hers boldly. "I've always been the best man," he said, grinning at her and ducking the playful blow Jeremy aimed at him.

Nathaniel cried, "Tom's the smartest one, I know that for sure." His green eyes sparkled.

"How do you figure that, Cap?" Jeremy demanded.

" 'Cause he's not marrying my sister!"

Through the laughter Harriet, ignoring her younger brother, told Tom, "My cousin became engaged recently. Her fiancé is first mate on a merchantman bound for the West Indies."

"And her dad is a whaling captain, which is what I'm going to be when I grow up," Nathaniel declared.

Harriet sighed. "Papa, can the four of us go into the parlor, where we can visit without being interrupted?"

"Go along, but leave the door open. You're not married yet."

The four of them withdrew to the square room with its horsehair sofa and stiff chairs. The formality of the furnishings put no constraint upon the men. They joked and, with apologies to Vianna and Harriet, fell constantly into reminiscences of the high jinks they'd perpetrated back in Pennsylvania.

Vianna found their tales amusing and realized she was having more fun than she'd had in a long time. She realized something else and faced it with utter honesty. She found Tom Fulton more attractive than any man she'd ever known. While Harriet and Jeremy sat on the sofa holding hands, she and Tom sat straight across from them on cedar chairs softened with patchwork cushions. A dried-up bouquet of lilacs that should have been thrown out several days ago stood in front of the cold fireplace. Finally Tom turned to Vianna. "So your father is the captain of a whaling ship. Is that pin you're wearing a piece of scrimshaw, then?"

She was wearing her pink checked dress with the brooch pinned as usual between the rounded points of the collar. When she said it was indeed scrimshaw, Tom displayed great interest, fastening his eyes on her breast so intently that she felt warmth flood her cheeks.

"We don't see any of that in Pennsylvania, but I've heard of it. I take it your father made the pin?"

"Yes, and the combs in my hair."

As he raised his eyes to her head, they met hers and held for an instant before moving on to the combs. "What kind of flowers are those he's drawn?"

"Forget-me-nots."

His eyes dropped again, ostensibly to the pin at her throat, but it was her whole bosom that burned under his gaze. Fluttering her hands, she began to babble. "I begged Father to teach me the art of scrimshaw once when I was little, but the results were so clumsy I burst into tears. He told me I'd get better as I got older, but I didn't. I'm absolutely awful at drawing. On paper, ivory—it doesn't matter. I just can't do it."

He brought his gaze slowly up to hers. "I'm sure you have other talents."

One of her flickering hands found the brooch and grasped it convulsively. She tried to speak, but no sound came out. She cleared her throat and managed a breathless "None that I'm aware of."

Later, when the three of them decided to walk her home, Tom asked her more about her father's work. Behind them Jeremy and Harriet dawdled, falling ever farther back, using the dark and the distance to create a measure of privacy for themselves. "I've heard these whalers are gone from home three, four, five years at a time."

"It's true. They hunt the whale grounds until they have a full cargo of oil."

"That's a mighty long time to be at sea."

"They aren't at sea all that time. They put into a port now and then to reprovision. Father was in Lahaina in the Sandwich Islands the last time he wrote."

"Are the common sailors paid very well for their work?"

"They get a share of the cargo. When Father returned last time, the common crewmen were paid seven hundred dollars when the shares were figured up."

"And that was for how many months at sea?"

"Forty."

Tom whistled. "You've just killed my interest in signing on a whaler. I've had enough of farming, and I intend to go out and see something of the world, but I won't do it by becoming a sailor."

"Not all ships are away as long as whalers. My fiancé will be gone only two months."

At the mention of Eban their conversation died. Behind them the silence of their companions was as intimate as words of love would have been. Neither Vianna nor Tom glanced back, nor did they look at one another. The windows of the houses they passed glowed yellow, and occasionally through one that had been thrown open to the warm night came the sound of voices. The oil streetlamps had been lighted, and each spilled a golden circle on the bricks at its base.

Vianna was sharply conscious of Tom's physical presence. Though he was not especially tall, the breadth of his shoulders made him appear larger than he was, and emanating from that lean, virile body in waves was something Vianna couldn't name. She felt it, though! Every vibrating current of it! It set each cell in her body tingling. She savored this new sensation, analyzing it to discover all its subtle characteristics. She was sorry when Tom interrupted her meditation with a question.

"When are you getting married?"

"Probably about the middle of August. Eban should be back by then."

"That's a long time." The light from a window shone in his eyes as he turned toward her.

Vianna didn't reply, because she didn't agree. If the wedding could be put off for several years, she'd feel a lot better about it.

Tom grinned. "You could change your mind in that time."

"It's too late." The words slipped out before she could stop them. Offering a hasty explanation, she added, "What I mean is, a girl weighs her choice carefully before she accepts a proposal, and once she says yes, there's no turning back." Somehow, Vianna thought distractedly, she'd ended up back where she began, and her explanation had accomplished nothing.

"In that case, there's no danger for either of us if I kiss you," Tom said, moving swiftly as he spoke to capture her in his arms and carry out his announced intention.

Caught off guard, Vianna had no chance to avoid his embrace until he had already begun to kiss her, and by then she had no wish to stop him. This was what a kiss should be like, she thought dreamily. Warm lips nibbling to taste hers, sending shivers up her spine, then settling firmly to draw out her individual flavors and textures. A peculiar sensation spread through her stomach, almost like a pain yet so pleasant she was sorry when he finally pulled his lips away from hers.

"Any man who would sail away and leave you is a fool," Tom whispered, his arms still around her.

She was too pleased with the compliment to care about the criticism of Eban. Not wanting him to know how strongly his kiss had affected her, she asked lightly, "Do you make a habit of kissing young women who are betrothed to someone else?"

"They're the safest kind, providing of course their fiancés are not around to object."

"That's wicked."

"That's what makes it so much fun," he said, and kissed her again.

Vianna knew she should make him stop and she could have, but they were between streetlamps, hidden in the shadow of a tree that stood before a darkened house, and Harriet and Jeremy were far behind, so there was no one to see them. Besides, she was enjoying herself too much, and she had only been teasing when she declared it wicked. What harm could it possibly do? Tom Fulton would be gone in a week.

They would never see one another again, but she would have a romantic memory to recall for the rest of her life.

His kiss was different this time, forcing her lips open and . . . good heavens! What was he doing? Her eyes flew open as his tongue entered her mouth, then closed again as that strange sensation grew in her stomach once more, stronger this time. The warm organ probed her mouth gently, then suddenly her own tongue came alive, urgently seeking to join with his. Tom's arms tightened around her until they hurt.

Abruptly he pulled his mouth from hers; a tremor went through his arms as they relaxed yet continued to hold her. "I was mistaken," he said huskily. "You're a very dangerous girl to kiss."

"I am?" She felt enormously pleased.

He was silent a moment, then said slowly, "You've never been kissed like that before, have you? Or kissed anyone back as you did me just now?"

"Not exactly." She wasn't going to reveal her total inexperience to him.

"I suspect then that your fiancé doesn't have any idea of the kind of woman he's getting."

Vianna bristled. "What do you mean by that?"

"Everything good," he assured her. "You've got a lot of love in you just waiting to be turned loose. When that finally happens, you are going to make a fine wife. Now I'd better get you home before I get us both into trouble."

She wasn't sure what he meant by that, but she liked the sound of it. It made her really feel like the dangerous woman he said she was. She was sorry when he said good night at the door. She'd had so much fun that she hated for the evening to end.

It was a long time before she could fall asleep. She kept reliving that surprising kiss and the delicious feeling it had spread through her. She knew beyond doubt that this was what Harriet felt when Jeremy kissed her. No wonder her cousin sometimes looked as if she were in another world! If ever Eban had kissed her like that, she'd be counting the days till he got back.

Swiftly she pushed the thought of Eban away from her and let her mind fill with romantic fantasies featuring Tom Fulton and herself in the starring roles. Two hours later she fell asleep, murmuring his name.

4

When Vianna opened her eyes to her sun-filled bedroom the next morning, the first thought that came to her sleepy mind was of Tom Fulton. She came wide awake, propping her pillows behind her so that she could sit up. When Harriet had told her months ago that Jeremy's best friend was coming for the wedding, she hadn't given it a second thought; however, now that she had met him, she felt herself drawn irresistibly to him. As a matter of fact, she began wondering how she could arrange to see him again as soon as possible. Was he, at this very moment, next door at the cooperage, visiting with Jeremy and his father while they worked? The very idea that he might be so near set her heart to fluttering crazily.

Washing and dressing took only a few minutes; then she was down the stairs, calling to her mother in the kitchen that she had seen Harriet go into the cooperage and was going to speak to her for a few minutes.

The wide doors of the cooperage were open, letting in the sun and the sea breeze. In the walk-in hearth that filled the far end of the building a fire was burning. Some new casks stood along one wall, and Jeremy was rolling another into place beside them as she entered. In the middle of the shop, Mr. Walters was setting curved staves into a wooden bottom. Tom Fulton was not there. Mr. Walters, a taciturn man with a big nose and a jutting Adam's apple, gave Vianna a quiet but friendly greeting. Jeremy was surprised to see her.

"I thought I saw Harriet come in here," she lied.

"Haven't seen her this morning." A grin curved Jeremy's sensual mouth. "She'll probably be by later, though, as usual."

As he checked the brazier, where some oak staves were steaming, Vianna, trying to convey no more than politeness, said, "I think your friend is nice."

Jeremy nodded his dark, glossy head. "Tom was a good friend to me at a time when I was sort of lonesome and homesick. He's pretty interested in the way we live, isn't he? He's got a landlubber's romantic ideas about the sea. He was going to wander around town today and look things over. Said he wanted to visit the rope walk, and Mr. Sawtell invited him to come up to the sail loft."

So he wouldn't be hard to find. "He sounded like he was interested in going to sea until I told him Father's crew drew seven hundred dollars for forty months' work."

Jeremy chuckled as he helped his father insert some staves in a machine that pulled them together so that the men could slide iron hoops over them. "Tom's one for trying new things, but I can't see him cooped up on a ship for months at a time."

Now that she'd found out what she came for, Vianna took her leave and went home to breakfast. She didn't feel in the least hungry, but her mother would have to be given some explanation if she disappeared for the rest of the morning, so she hurriedly ate and then said that Harriet hadn't been at the cooperage after all and that she was going to the Sawtells' now to see her. Instead she headed for the sail loft. Her appearance there would occasion no comment, and besides it was at the end of the street. If she walked slowly, and if Tom happened to be in one of the other shops, there was a good chance he might see her as she passed. There was no doubt in her mind that he would come out and speak to her—not after the way he'd kissed her last night and the things he had said to her.

As it turned out, he was at the sail loft. The three men—Tom, Isaac, and Joseph—appeared small in the huge, almost empty room. Space was needed for the enormous pieces of canvas that were sewn into sails. Even the stove was suspended from the ceiling on cables to hang a couple of feet above the floor, enabling Isaac to spread canvas under it. Here as at the cooperage the wide doors had been thrown open, admitting the bright morning light.

Using the same excuse that had served her well twice in the past hour, Vianna said, "I thought I'd find Harriet here. Good morning," she said casually to Tom, who was standing beside Isaac's chair, watching the older man push his three-sided needle through the canvas with a leather palm strapped to his hand. Across the room, Joseph was doing the same at his side of the sail. Vianna discovered she couldn't meet Tom's eyes, but she felt his gaze on her like a warm beam of light.

"She isn't at the house?" Isaac Sawtell asked, looking like a grizzled gnome bent over his work.

"I . . . uh . . . didn't stop there. I thought I saw her come in here."

"She's probably home sewing on that dress of hers. If she and her ma don't hurry up with it, I'm going to have to give them a hand in order to finish it in time for the wedding. Never saw two women make such a to-do about a little bit of sewing."

Turning to Tom but still avoiding a direct look, Vianna asked, "Are you finding all this interesting?"

"Lord, yes! Making these sails is a whale of a job."

Under the cover of their laughter at his pun, Vianna sneaked a close look at him. She hadn't been mistaken last night. He was as attractive as any man she'd ever seen. His reddish brown hair waved above a wide brow and was cut to reveal small, neat ears. But it was his mouth, with the curved, full lower lip that had nibbled hers with such a shivery result, that drew her eyes.

"I was about to visit the rope walk," he was saying. "Maybe I could get you to be my guide—if you're not busy, that is."

"I'd be happy to."

They took their leave, going down through the warehouse below and out onto the path that led to the rope walk, stretching its long length toward the lighthouse point.

"I hope you slept well last night." Tom's grin was teasing.

"Soundly. And you?"

"Not well at all." He didn't elaborate, letting her read what she liked into his reply while he continued to grin at her.

"Sometimes our sea air does that to people who are not used to it."

"Too stimulating, I suppose. At least that's the way I found it." He surveyed the wooden building they were approaching. "I remember Jeremy telling me stories about this place. Not what went on inside, but what went on outside. I can see its attraction, off by itself like this where no one is likely to notice what goes on. I would guess from what I learned about you last night that you don't come down here often."

They had reached the entrance, and Vianna was glad. It gave her the chance to ignore his last remark and to avert her face to hide the blush that bloomed in it. She introduced Tom to the owner, Mr. Hobson, and while Tom watched the spinner walk backward the length of the building, forming the hemp fibers wound around his waist into a yarn as a wheel twisted them, she surreptitiously studied this friend of Jeremy's, perplexed by the variety of mysterious feelings he evoked in her. What was there about him that caused this effect? He was more handsome than most men, but it was more than that. Of that much she was certain, because Jeremy was handsome, but she had never felt this way around him, even before he made it clear that he preferred Harriet to any other girl. Why would looking at those broad shoulders and lean hips make her light-headed?

She failed to find the answer to those questions as she guided him around town for the remainder of the morning, nor did any answers come to her during the rest of the week when she made further excuses to encounter him during the day. There was no need to manufacture accidental meetings in the evenings, because Harriet and Jeremy made sure she was always present to entertain Tom, thus providing themselves with more privacy. Tom invariably managed to steal one kiss, sometimes two. Vianna had decided she was obliged to protest, but she was careful not to discourage him completely. She meant to learn all she could about kisses, realizing she would never have a better teacher.

The night before the wedding, the two men went off by themselves to celebrate Jeremy's last night of bachelorhood. When Vianna learned of their plans, she felt a sharp disappointment, but Harriet, awash in last-minute details, welcomed the extra time. Vianna and her mother made several trips to the Sawtells' house, carrying armloads of yellow roses along with two enormous Chinese porcelain vases, and then stayed to help arrange the flowers and place them around the house. The parlor mantel was cleared so that it could be hung with greenery the next afternoon. The wedding was set for five o'clock and was to be followed by a supper for which Mary Chadwick, as well as Mercy Sawtell, had been roasting and baking all day. It was the first time Vianna had seen her aunt in a pother about anything. She and her mother chuckled about it on the way home.

"I shouldn't laugh," Mary Chadwick declared. "I'll be in even worse shape when my time comes to prepare your wedding. My nerves aren't anywhere near as steady as Mercy's. Have you gotten any ideas from all this about what sort of wedding you'll want?"

To answer truthfully, Vianna would have had to

admit she hadn't given her own wedding a thought. As a matter of fact, she found that the idea brought a sudden depression to her spirits, which for the last few days had been gloriously high. "Not really. I suppose I'll want one very much like Harriet's."

"I think that would be lovely."

Vianna dismissed the rest of her mother's comments about tomorrow's fete, recalling that Tom would be leaving the day after and life would revert to ordinariness. Loneliness, too, probably, because with Harriet married, things were bound to change. Her cousin wouldn't be as free as before, unable to provide the unrestricted companionship they had shared for as long as either of them could remember. Later, in bed, Vianna felt overwhelmed by all these changes taking place in her life. Until now her sixteen years had been happy and uneventful. In the last six months that had all changed, and it made Vianna so sad that, to her surprise, she began to cry. She fell asleep with her pillow damp from tears.

Something awakened her, some sound she couldn't identify as she struggled up out of a deep sleep. Surprised to find her room dark when she opened her eyes, she lay unmoving, frightened. What was it? There it was again. A soft thud against her window, like a bird flying against the glass; but what kind of bird would be abroad in the middle of the night? Still uneasy, but curious, she left her bed and padded over to the window that overlooked the cooperage. Pulling aside the thin, starched curtain, she peered out, glad that she hadn't thrown this window open tonight. Below, in the shadow of the cooperage wall, she saw movement. The moon was bright, but she was looking into it and couldn't make out what had moved. Then a form stepped out of the shadow and waved to her. It was Tom! She pushed up the window and waved back, giving a finger-to-lips warning to make no more noise and using further sign language to let him know she was coming down.

Turning back to her room, she realized she couldn't meet him in her nightgown, and it would take too long to dress. She considered her predicament for only a moment before her eagerness to join Tom drove her to abandon propriety. She pulled her heavy winter wrapper from the closet, tying it tightly around her waist as she crept out of her room, past her mother's door at the end of the hall, and down the stairs, guided by the moonlight streaming through the fan-shaped window above the front door. Easing out of the house, she gasped faintly as her bare feet touched the cold brick walk. Then, lifting the long skirt of her robe, she ran through the dewy grass between the buildings to where Tom stood waiting.

He stood in the open, his white shirt gleaming across his shoulders and cutting to a dark V at the neck. A lock of hair fell across his brow, lending him a rakish look. He watched her, grinning, as she hugged the shadow of the cooperage in her awareness that she was not dressed properly to be meeting a young man, or any man for that matter. The sight of him, so boldly handsome, set her heart fluttering. "What do you want?" she whispered.

"You." There was a vibrant note in that single syllable that made her step back suddenly from his reaching arms.

"No, Tom," she said, fending him off. "I shouldn't be down here. I'm not even decently dressed. Mother would be horrified if she found me out here talking to you like this. I can only stay a minute. What are you doing here? I thought you and Jeremy were celebrating."

"We were. I broke it up. I told Jeremy he couldn't get too drunk, because he had to be in good shape for his wedding tomorrow. But the real reason I took him home was that I wanted to see you. I haven't been able to think about anything else for the last two hours." He reached for her again and caught her this time before she could evade him, burying his face in her throat. "Sweet," he whispered, "sweet as honey," and pressed his lips against her skin as if to draw out the nectar he found there.

A melting warmth spread from Vianna's throat down and through her whole body. When he raised his head, her lips eagerly met his, tasting the rum on his tongue, growing as dizzy as if she had actually drunk some herself. One of his hands was pulling her tied wrapper open, and she pushed it away, but when he persisted and in the struggle touched her breast, she caught her breath and froze. He had never taken such a liberty before, and she knew she should not permit it now, but when he cupped her breast and ran his thumb lightly over the smooth tip that thrust against the thin fabric of her nightdress, her breath came out in a small moan and her mouth went slack beneath his. The exquisite pleasure came as a complete surprise; she had never dreamed that such a caress would send liquid fire through her body. She stood wrapped in delight while his thumb continued its gentle flicking motion. Her eyes were closed; she was aware that he dropped his head, and the next moment she gasped as his tongue burned through her filmy gown and began doing what his thumb had been doing.

Grasping for what shreds of strength his caresses had left her, she put both of her hands on his cheeks and lifted his head. "Please, no." Her words were barely audible, but Tom understood. His arms loosened reluctantly and she slipped out of them to lean weakly against the rough wooden siding of the cooperage, a trembling hand pressed to her feverish brow.

"You're as heady a brew as the rum they serve at the Life Buoy." Tom's voice was hoarse, but he was smiling. He stepped over into the shadow beside her, putting one shoulder against the building and crossing his arms over his chest. The night was so quiet that the sound of the waves lapping at the wharf could be heard. The beam from the lighthouse regularly rent the dark sky over the roofs of the Chadwicks' house and the cooperage.

Flattered, Vianna gave a soft, shaky laugh. "It is well known that the rum at the tavern is full strength, and I suspect you imbibed of it generously tonight."

"I won't deny it. After all, it is not every day a man's best friend surrenders his bachelorhood forever."

"You make it sound like a great sacrifice. Is bachelorhood such a precious state of being?" she asked coyly.

Tom considered her question for a moment, then grinned. "Perhaps not. Bachelorhood, like virginity, can be surrendered with gain rather than loss, if the circumstances are right."

She reproved him. "You are too bold!"

"I apologize. The rum has loosed my tongue."

Even though his face was shadowed, Vianna felt his burning glance roving her body. The woolen robe was far too warm for the June night even without his searing gaze; under them both, her skin grew moist and suffocatingly hot. She longed to fling open her robe and let the night air cool her.

"I shall hate to say good-bye to you, Vianna Chadwick." His voice was soft; it caressed her name.

An aching sadness wrapped itself abruptly around her heart. "When will you be leaving?"

"Day after tomorrow. Early in the morning. So you see, I don't have much time left to gaze upon your beautiful face." He laid his fingers lightly on her cheek. "Or to listen to your throaty laugh." His fingers trailed softly down her throat as he added, "You can't know what the sound of that does to me. Not much time left, either, to taste those sweet lips." Leaning forward, he kissed her lingeringly.

Vianna closed her eyes. She felt like a candle left too long in the hot sun. When she began to sway, Tom put his hands on her waist to steady her. Her thin gown might not have existed, for all the barrier it offered between his skin and hers.

"Nor do I have much time left to touch this silky

body that is a torment to me day or night." His voice had grown husky and his mouth found hers again, crushing it this time as his hands moved voluptuously over her back, sliding down to her buttocks and pressing her tightly to him. For the first time in her young life she felt the hardness of a man. Her body arched instinctively to meet it as desire licked through her body like an orange flame. Then reason returned to her bemused brain. She tore herself away from his spellbinding hands and body, slumping against the cooperage. "I must go in." Her voice was so hoarse she couldn't recognize it as her own.

"Vianna." That's all, just her name, but it was a plea that almost robbed her of what little self-control she had left. He stood there, one wide shoulder in full moonlight, the other in shadow, his muscular body leaning toward her slightly as if he were about to take her in his arms again.

"No," she sobbed and, gathering up her skirts, she ran away.

In her room once more, she leaned against the closed door, heart pounding, trembling in every limb. Slumped against the solid paneling, she moved her head from side to side in an agony of frustration, still wanting Tom's hands caressing her skin, his body pressing against hers, his lips pouring fire down her throat. Pushing away from the door, she walked unsteadily to the window and peered through the curtains. Both moonlight and shadows were empty. She exhaled a long, ragged breath, part disappointment, part relief. If he'd still been down there, she wasn't sure she could have prevented herself from running back to him.

Slowly she removed her wrapper and hung it up, then took herself back to bed, where she lay smiling and hugging to herself the knowledge that at last she knew what it was like to be kissed by a man who found you so beautiful and desirable that he was driven almost beyond the limit of his control. And, what had proved to be even more fascinating, she had discovered that she, too, could be aroused to the same torrid emotional pitch. She was a woman, there was no doubt about it, and a passionate one besides. If Eban thought he was marrying some lukewarm creature who would be satisfied with a few chaste pecks on the cheek, he was in for a surprise.

But she wouldn't think about Eban. She still had tomorrow and tomorrow night to spend with Tom.

To her dismay, her mother and her Aunt Mercy kept her so busy the next day, running between the two houses for this and that, hurrying to this shop or that for last-minute items either for the wedding or the supper afterward, that she had no time to seek Tom out. So she caught not so much as a glimpse of him until she arrived at the Sawtells' house for the umpteenth time that day, but dressed this time for the wedding that would take place shortly.

She was wearing a new gown of blue lawn that exactly matched the color of her eyes. Silver ribbons wound through the sleeves and around the neck, with a wider silver band encircling her slim waist. A filigreed silver necklace, made by the Indians in Peru and brought home by her father from his last voyage, graced the expanse of white throat above the square neck of her dress. Her mirror had told her that she looked especially attractive, and now she saw her self-assessment more than confirmed in Tom's eyes as they swept over her. He and Jeremy were standing in the front yard with Mr. Walters, Isaac Sawtell, and Harriet's two brothers. The sun was still high, and they stood in the shade of a large maple tree. Tom, like the other men, was dressed in a frock coat and high collar, looking older and breathtakingly handsome, yet so formal and strange that Vianna would have felt intimidated had it not been for the naked admiration in his glance as it caught hers. His russet hair was neatly combed back off his brow in a wave that shone like his wide satin bow tie, which was very nearly the same color.

His smile was as intimate as his glance, and she wondered if her mother had noticed, but Mary Chadwick was greeting the other men.

"How nice you look, Nathaniel."

Harriet's younger brother grimaced and yanked at his collar. "I feel silly. I don't see why I had to get dressed up like this just to watch Harriet and Jeremy get married." A haircut had tidied his curly hair, and his freckled face had been scrubbed until it looked shiny enough to crack if he smiled, which he wasn't doing.

His father, looking like a dressed-up child himself except for his grizzled hair and lined face, cautioned his son sternly, "Stop pulling at your collar before you bend it."

Mary Chadwick put a hand on her nephew's flaming head and said sympathetically, "It will be over soon. Then you can have all the cherry pie you can eat." To Jeremy she said, "You look very cool for a bridegroom."

Jeremy grinned. "Then my looks are deceiving, ma'am."

During these brief exchanges, Vianna managed another look at Tom. She suspected he had never taken his eyes off her, for they met and held hers with a boldness that brought memories of last night's caresses flooding back to her. She blushed and looked away quickly as she followed her mother into the house.

Scarcely half an hour later she was trying to picture Eban and herself standing in front of Reverend Baxter in a flower-filled room, exchanging vows that would unite them forever as man and wife. The Sawtells' parlor was heavy with summer heat and the fragrance of yellow roses. Vianna stood on Harriet's left, Tom on Jeremy's right; behind them sat the relatives in rows of chairs. Vianna heard the faint swish of women's fans as they stirred the hot air around their faces. Beside her Harriet's freckled face was incandescent with happiness, her thin body enticingly lovely within the cream satin wedding gown. The profound emotional significance of this day had worked magic upon her rather plain face and made her beautiful. Vianna marveled at the transformation. Would she glow like this on her wedding day? A troubling doubt swept her, making her miss her cue to take Harriet's bouquet as her cousin prepared to receive her ring from Jeremy. She leaned forward to watch Tom hand the gold band to the bridegroom with a broad smile. The sight of that firmly curved mouth sent a delicious shiver down her perspiring back.

A few minutes later the ceremony was over, and while the family members came forward to congratulate the newly married couple, Tom drew Vianna a bit to one side. "You look so ravishingly beautiful I am hard pressed not to take you in my arms here and now and kiss you as you deserve to be kissed."

She smiled and said coyly, "Thank you for saying I am ravishingly beautiful. About the rest I am not so sure. How do I deserve to be kissed?"

"With fire and fierceness and a hunger great enough to relish the feast your lips and body offer." He was smiling, too, but there was flame in his smoky gray eyes.

The impact of his words parted those lips he desired so much, and Vianna felt herself sinking into those burning gray depths. She made no protest as he took her arm and led her casually out of the parlor, but as they went down the hall toward the kitchen, she offered half-heartedly, "We shouldn't."

"No one saw us leave. Of that I'm sure." Tom pulled her into his arms the instant they entered the deserted kitchen, proceeding to kiss her exactly as only a moment before he had declared she deserved. Last night he had been a reckless young man, drunk on rum yet manageable. Today it wasn't only his frock coat and starched collar that had dispelled his boyishness. In his kiss and in his arms she felt a man's strength and resolve. This new assertiveness was even more exciting than his youthful boldness. His hands around her silver-belted waist arched her supple body while he moved his hips with sensual slowness against her own. All this time his mouth was feeding greedily upon her soft lips, sending the world spiraling dizzily away from Vianna, leaving only herself and Tom, wrapped in a mist of sweet desire.

The voices of her mother and aunt as they walked down the hall toward the kitchen yanked her back to reality. Tearing herself out of Tom's arms, she stumbled blindly toward the open back door, seeking some breeze to cool her flushed cheeks. Tom followed, urging in a low voice, "Meet me tonight at the rope walk."

She had no time to answer, as he went past her and out into the yard at the same moment her mother and aunt came into the kitchen.

"I wondered where you'd gone, dear," Mary Chadwick called to her. "Here, put this apron on and start cutting the pies."

During supper and the visiting that came after, Tom and Vianna had no opportunity for so much as a single private word. Good sense told her that she could not meet Tom later as he had urged. His kisses, once just pleasant and interesting, now aroused her to a point where her self-control hung by a fragile thread. And there was this new element today, this masterfulness that might snap that gossamer strand, sweeping her into the ultimate mystery that should be reserved for man and wife. She dared not risk that. Much as she longed to be with him on his last night in Govans Harbor, to enjoy more of the magic his caresses performed upon her senses, she would play it safe and say good-bye to him in the presence of her mother when the party broke up.

So for the rest of the evening she remained at his side, behaving discreetly enough that no one could fault her behavior, yet extracting as much sensual pleasure from his nearness and his secret glances as she could. How she envied Harriet! Her cousin was flushed and bright-eyed, her laughter soft and low, as if anticipating the rapture that awaited her once the party was over and she and Jeremy went off to the cottage they had rented. For his part, Jeremy couldn't keep his eyes off his bride. More than once Vianna caught him gazing at her cousin with an expression that was at once tender and lustful. At the thought of what would happen once the newlyweds were finally alone, Vianna's imagination took wild leaps into uncharted areas, leaving her taut and breathless.

About nine o'clock the guests began drifting away, showering the bride and groom with wishes for many happy years together. Tom, Vianna, and her mother were the last to leave. Mary Chadwick had remained to help her sister tidy up the house a bit. Isaac Sawtell was in his customary place beside the fireplace, smoking quietly. Joseph and Nathaniel sat at the big round table, sharing the only remaining slice of cherry pie. The festivities had proved too much for Nathaniel, and he was quiet for once, his head propped sleepily on one hand as he ate. Cool air flowed through the opened house, and the men looked less uncomfortable in their formal clothes. The vases of roses gave off their fragrance so generously that the house smelled like a garden. The newlyweds stood holding hands in front of the cold fireplace, radiant and charged with an energy that had kept them on their feet for the past two hours, but Mercy Sawtell, upon emerging from the parlor with her sister, sank immediately into a chair beside her youngest son.

"It was so nice that you could come for Jeremy's wedding," Mary Chadwick said, smiling warmly at Tom. "I've enjoyed meeting you, and I hope we'll have the pleasure of seeing you again someday."

Vianna waited through Tom's gracious reply, then said, "Good-bye, Tom. If you should ever change your mind about going to sea, I'm sure you couldn't find better ships and captains than here in Govans Harbor."

Holding her proffered hand, Tom replied, "Fascinating as I found your industry here, I'm afraid I'd make a poor sailor."

She shook her head slightly in reply to the question his eyes were flashing her. He paused for a moment and then bowed politely. "However, if ever I should decide to give the sea a try, you can be sure I'll come to Govans Harbor to find a ship." A gleam of mocking amusement came into his eyes as he added, "Thank you for giving me your time when Jeremy was busy. You have helped make my visit one I'll never forget."

Vianna dropped her glance hastily. Retrieving her hand, she hurried to Harriet, flinging her arms around her. "What can I say that I haven't said before?" Her throat tightened, and she blinked back tears. "I wish you all the happiness in the world."

Her cousin's face still wore a glow as creamy as her satin gown. With a tight hug, she murmured, "Thanks, Vi. This won't change anything. I want you to come to see me every day, just like always."

"I will." Swallowing the growing lump in her throat, Vianna turned to Jeremy and kissed his cheek. "Welcome to our family."

"Thanks, and I want to echo Harriet's invitation. Come and see us anytime you like." There was no doubting his sincerity, but it was obvious to Vianna that he was giving these farewells only a fragment of his attention. His restless movements betrayed his impatience to be left alone at last with his bride. Harriet was holding his arm with both hands, the rapid rise and fall of her breasts revealing her own anticipation of the event she most surely had been dreaming of for months.

As Vianna stepped back, she bumped into Tom, who had been waiting to offer his congratulations and farewells, too. He put his hands on her arms quickly to steady her, and for a moment they were close enough that Vianna caught the male smell of him, a combination of tobacco, bay rum, and an indefinable scent unique to men. In the instant their eyes met, he possessed her so intimately that it stopped her breath. He stepped back, murmuring an apology, leaving her feeling dizzy and shaken. Mary Chadwick noted her daughter's confusion but attributed it to the emotional embrace the two girls had exchanged. Taking Vianna's arm, she gently led her out of the house.

They were down the walk and out in the street before Mary Chadwick offered soothingly, "Things won't be all that different between you and Harriet. She still wants to see you every day, and in a little while you'll be married and with a home of your own, too, and you'll have everything in common again."

"I suppose you're right." But she didn't really believe it. As Eban's wife she couldn't imagine that she would have much in common with Harriet. Their marriages would be so different. The passionate love her cousin and Jeremy shared would be missing in her own life. At the thought of what she would never experience, of the glorious moments that lay ahead of her cousin in the next hours, a sob escaped Vianna. Gathering her child close, Mary Chadwick said, "There, there, dear. Things will look better in the morning, you'll see. It's been an emotional day. I suspect you are not the only one who has shed a few tears."

Vianna went straight to bed after they got home, but she was far too keyed up to sleep. Her body seemed made up of nerve endings, tingling, prickling, causing her to toss and turn, and finally driving her out of bed to kneel before the open window, letting the breeze off the water cool her feverish body. An unidentifiable longing filled her until she felt as if she'd burst. Rubbing her forehead against her arms as they rested on the windowsill, she sighed, wishing now she hadn't indicated to Tom that she wouldn't meet him. She felt smothered, in need of open spaces and more air than the narrow stream that came in the window.

Deciding a long, brisk walk would relax her, Vianna

pulled her nightgown over her head, donned a short-sleeved gingham dress, and started down the stairs.

"Vianna, is that you?" her mother called from her bedroom at the head of the stairs.

"I'm going for a walk. I can't sleep."

"Can I heat you some milk?" There were stirring sounds, as if Mary Chadwick had sat up in bed.

"Thanks, Mother, but I think a walk is what I need."

"All right, dear. If you decide you want something to eat or drink when you get back, call me."

Vianna let herself out of the house and set out at a fast pace down the street. It felt good to be moving. The only place of business open at this hour of the night was the tavern. Otherwise Front Street was dark, lit only by the widely spaced streetlamps. She met no one as she strode along the cobbled road. At one corner she was only a block from the cottage where Harriet and Jeremy were surely alone now. Vianna hurried past, trying not to think about the two lovers locked in each other's arms. Not until she reached the sail loft did she realize where she was heading. A few yards away the rope walk stretched its great length toward the lighthouse at the tip of the point. Already the odor of tar and hemp smote her, evoking that curious excitement the place held for her. With slower step, she made her way to it. What a fool she'd been to refuse to meet Tom here! What had she to fear? Tomorrow he would be gone. The thought that she would now never see him again brought an acute sadness. Tonight was a night of endings. Tears sprang to her eyes until, blinded, she halted in the shadow of the rope walk until she could see once more. Before her eyes could clear, she heard a step in the sand nearby.

"So you came after all. I hoped you might change your mind."

She whirled and there was Tom, familiar-looking again in an open-necked white shirt and lightweight trousers. "Oh, Tom!" she cried, flinging herself into his arms, weeping as if her heart would break.

"What is it?" he asked, and when she couldn't reply, he held her tenderly, murmuring comforting sounds against her hair until she quieted.

"I'm sorry," she said, sniffing, and accepted the handkerchief he offered her. "I don't know what's the matter with me tonight. I couldn't sleep and decided to take a walk. I didn't realize I was coming here until I got to Uncle Isaac's loft. Even then I didn't expect to find you here. I thought you understood I wouldn't meet you."

"I understood, but I came anyway on the chance you might change your mind." With a gentle finger, he wiped a tear she had missed.

She smiled tremulously. "I'm glad." The light cast by the stars and the moon was unusually bright. She saw his answering smile clearly.

"I am, too," he said. "Do you still feel like walking?"

"Yes, let's go down to the point."

Hand in hand they strolled toward the lighthouse, whose eye winked rhythmically at them.

"You've never told me about your fiancé," Tom said. "What manner of man is he?"

Vianna didn't reply at once. She was in no mood to think about Eban tonight. "He's older than I in years," she began reluctantly, "and even older in his attitudes. He has led a harsh life, and it made a man of him when he was scarce a boy." She recounted the major events of Eban's life. "He has decided he wants to be a whaler, and he will be given his own ship when he returns from the West Indies. It's being completed now, over in the shipyard."

"He must be a very good seaman if he's being given command of a ship."

"My father sailed with him once and thought him the finest first mate he'd ever seen, and Eban was a very young man at the time."

"You must be very proud of him."

Vianna looked at the white tower looming up ahead

of them, her hand very still within his. "Eban is an unusual person."

Tom gazed down at her. "I never doubted it for a moment. I knew he must be exceptional to have won you."

They were silent until Tom said, "The life of a whaler's wife surely is a lonely one, isn't it?"

"I know my mother misses my father dreadfully at times. She tries to hide it, but I can tell. It is something we take for granted, however. No girl raised in a whaling port expects anything different if she sets her heart on a man who hunts whales for a living, be he common sailor or officer."

"Did you never dream of marrying a man who could share your fireside every night?"

Again Vianna was slow to reply. "Every girl has her dreams," she admitted, then turned the conversation into a safer channel. "And what of Tom Fulton? You've been overly modest and have said little about yourself."

He laughed. "If I've said little, it's because there is little to tell. I am one of thirteen children, fitting into the middle someplace. My father is a shoemaker, and although he was given all the orders he could handle, so many mouths to feed are a pitiful drain on a man's purse. In our house there was too little food, too little space, and too much snarling over the little of each there was. I ran away when I was twelve, and I doubt that I was ever missed. I begged a job at a livery barn, sleeping in one of the stalls and eating meals with the owner and his wife."

"You slept in a stall?" Vianna asked, horrified.

Tom grinned down at her. "It wasn't as bad as it sounds. I had never had that much space to myself. At home we'd slept four to a bed. Nor had I ever had any privacy before. I thought I was living like a king."

They had reached the lighthouse and halted at its base. A short distance away the waves hissed on the shingle as they were pulled back into the bay. Both shingle and foam were silver against the dark water.

"But after a while I tired of mucking out stables. I apprenticed myself to a harness maker. That lasted a year. I've tried my hand at a variety of jobs and haven't found any that can hold me for long. I've seen a lot of my home state and have cherished my freedom to pick up and move on whenever the urge hits me."

"Do you never want to settle down?"

"I hadn't given it any thought until this past week. Observing Jeremy and Harriet has shown me it has its advantages," he said wryly. "However, I'm sure it will be some time before I'm ready to take on a wife and family. My father's hapless situation is still too vivid in my mind."

"Perhaps it would not be like that with you."

He shrugged. "Who can tell? I like the feeling that I am in control of my life and not a victim of capricious fate." He turned her to face him, putting his arms around her. "And so, Vianna Chadwick, you now know the life history of one Tom Fulton, a man who considers his visit to Govans Harbor, Massachusetts, one of the brightest episodes in that history." One hand smoothed her hair, then cupped her cheek. "I'll never forget you," he said softly, and kissed her.

Nor would she forget him, she thought, as for the last time she experienced the shivery sensation his lips unfailingly sent rippling through her body. A melting warmth seemed to dissolve her bones, and she leaned against him. He withdrew his lips from her clinging ones, blazing a path of kisses across her jaw, under her ear, down to the hollow of her throat. And he didn't stop there. One hand cupped a breast, lifting it, forcing it partway out of the square neckline of her dress, so that his mouth could savor the soft mound of flesh. The pleasure the caress brought her was almost too exquisite to be borne. She gave a little sob and passed trembling hands over his crisp chestnut hair.

"You are so beautiful," he breathed, claiming her mouth once more, crushing it with a hunger that she matched with equal intensity. His hands kneaded her back, moving down slowly, then arching her body to meet his. His male hardness, thrusting against her, brought a fiery torment that demanded to be satisfied. Lifted to a height of passion she had never experienced before, she writhed in his arms, seeking the fulfillment that she craved.

Together they sank to the ground at the base of the lighthouse, where they lay side by side, clinging desperately, unable to bear even an instant's separation of their mouths and bodies. A gasp was torn from Vianna as Tom's hand began to stroke her bare thigh. She stiffened, pulling her lips from his.

"Do you want me to stop?" he whispered hoarsely.

Her senses, clamoring for release from this exquisite torment, screamed, "No!" On the other hand, her moral training had been stern, uncompromising. As a result, her whispered yes was a reflex. Yet it was Tom's arms that were the first to loosen. He sat up and took a deep breath, releasing it in a rasping sigh. Getting to his feet, he said, "I'll be back in a minute."

Vianna, sitting with her back against the lighthouse, watched him walk down to where the waves washed the shingle. Scooping up some of the cold water in his hands, he splashed it on his face. He did this several times while Vianna rearranged her clothing and fought the raging emotions that shook her.

After a while Tom came slowly back to her. He seemed very tall standing above her, his head and neck dark above his white shirt. "I think you'd better go home," he said gently.

She nodded. He held out a hand and pulled her to her feet. He ran his hands up and down her arms once, then let her go. "Good-bye, Vianna."

Her eyes strained through the darkness to see his handsome face one last time. "Good-bye," she murmured. As she walked away, the lump in her throat began to dissolve into tears. Blinded, she collided with the corner of the rope walk. From there she made her way with difficulty to the sail loft, fighting the urge to run back and fling herself into Tom's arms. Ahead, the lamps along Front Street were transformed into great globs of light by her tears. The passion of a few minutes before had drained away, leaving a vast sorrow.

Her mother heard her come up the stairs. "Do you feel better, dear?"

"Much better. I'll be able to sleep now. Good night, Mother."

"Good night. Sleep well."

She slept hardly at all. Her reply had been aimed only at setting at ease her mother's anxieties. Vianna did not feel better. She felt different. Something had happened out there in the dark in Tom's arms. Lying in bed, she pondered it. The desire that had nearly swept her beyond the threshold of chastity was only a part of it. Now that it had cooled, she was aware of an enormous loneliness. The thought that she would never see Tom again was almost too painful to be borne. He had come to mean more to her in this past week than she had been aware. His image rose before her—the lean, broad-shouldered power of his body; his chestnut hair, so crisp beneath her fingers; those curved, sensuous lips; the smoky gray eyes whose direct look could set her atremble. "Tom, oh, Tom, I love you!" Her eyes flew open in astonishment, and she repeated the words slowly—"I love you"—and knew it was true. She stared at the sharply pitched ceiling above her. The familiarity of her room, viewed through the soft darkness, contrasted peculiarly with the transformation she suddenly sensed in herself. How had all this happened without her knowledge? All this time she had attributed her attraction to him to the physical responses he created in her. She had failed to recognize the growing emotional involvement until that moment when she had bid him good-bye. For a short time everything she had always wanted had been within her grasp, and she hadn't realized it!

If only you loved me! her heart cried out. *I would break my engagement to Eban without a second thought. I wouldn't care a whit for the gossip and scandal, if I could spend the rest of my life with you!*

She turned on her stomach, molding her body to the feather bed as if it were Tom, moving her face against the pillow and moaning softly. It had finally happened. She had fallen passionately in love, but there was to be no living happily ever after with the man of her dreams. She would never see him again.

"How am I going to live without you?" she cried silently, and gripped with an overwhelming sense of loss, she began to weep.

5

There was no sunrise the next morning, at least none that was visible. Fat gray clouds filled the sky, building toward a rain. The gloom outside matched Vianna's dark mood. It had been nearly dawn before she fell asleep, and when she awakened the clock downstairs was striking seven o'clock. Yet the heaviness in her body was not so much the result of physical fatigue as of despondency. The one thing she wanted more than anything else in the world, the one thing that would give her life the completeness every woman sought, was unobtainable. Tom could never be hers. She had begun to suspect that life as Eban's wife would lack essential elements; now she knew it could be no more than second best. It no longer mattered whether it was Eban she married or someone else. The joy of living with the man she loved with an intensity that went beyond anything she had ever dreamed would be denied her.

Lassitude kept her in bed far beyond her usual rising time. There was nothing to get up for. Harriet wouldn't want to see her today. It was too unpleasant to be outside now that it had begun to rain. Gone was the expectation of seeing Tom that had brought her bounding out of bed each morning for the past week. All the brightness had faded from her life, leaving her bereft and desolated.

Her mother finally came upstairs to check on her. "Aren't you feeling well?" she asked, stepping inside the bedroom when she saw that Vianna was awake. Her soft, plump face was worried.

"I'm not sick. I just didn't feel like getting up."

Mary Chadwick sat on the edge of the bed and felt her daughter's forehead. Her hand was warm and reddened from washing dishes and smelled of soap. "You don't seem to have a fever." She studied Vianna for a moment before advising her gently, "Be happy for Harriet, and remember that she loves you just as much as she ever did. In a day or two you'll be visiting back and forth like always. And once you are married yourself, you won't feel that she has left you. You'll understand that one love doesn't cancel out another."

Sighing, Vianna turned her eyes toward the gray, rain-streaked window. "I don't know whether I want to get married."

There followed a shocked silence, broken by Mary Chadwick's explosive, "Of course you do! You saw how happy your cousin was yesterday. Don't you want to feel like that?"

"I don't expect to be that happy."

"Why not?"

"I don't love Eban."

"That's nonsense." Agitated, the older woman shifted the weight of her stout body, causing the bed to bounce. "You're upset and unhappy. The world looks black to you this morning, but nothing has changed since yesterday. Of course you love Eban."

Nothing had changed? Vianna wondered what her mother would say if she told her that she had discovered overnight what love was and that her feeling for Eban did not resemble the real thing in the least.

"You'll feel better once you've had a hot breakfast," Mary Chadwick insisted. "Get dressed now and come downstairs. After you've eaten, we'll write a letter to your father, telling him all about the wedding."

"There is no whaler leaving soon to take it to him," Vianna said listlessly, pulling at a thread in the quilt that covered her.

"We'll write now, while it's fresh in our minds, and send it when we can. It will be like talking to him. It will cheer you up. Come along now. Get dressed while I fix you something to eat."

Her mother's prescription did not work, but Vianna received a pleasant surprise when Jeremy stopped in for a minute on his way back to the cooperage after lunch to tell her that Harriet wanted her to come over that afternoon.

"What did I tell you?" Mary Chadwick exclaimed, her relief evident. Vianna's dark mood had persisted despite all she had done to dispel it.

Donning a lightweight hooded cape, Vianna made her way through the steady rain to the cottage that was now home to her cousin. Painted yellow, with late-blooming purple irises on either side of the front step, it exuded a charm that was appropriate for a newly married couple who were madly in love. The romantic impression it offered served to remind Vianna of what she had lost, further lowering her spirits. Nevertheless, she greeted her cousin brightly, noting the glow that surrounded Harriet. Was it her imagination, Vianna wondered, or was her cousin's red hair actually shinier today? There was no doubting the extra light in her eyes or the new softness in her mouth.

"You seemed so sad last night when you left," Harriet remarked, hugging her, "that I wanted you to come over today so that you could see that nothing has changed."

There it was again, that phrase. The whole world had turned upside down, yet nobody was aware of it. She didn't intend to cast any shadows over Harriet's joy, however. "I thought you'd want to be alone a few days," she remarked, hugging her cousin back.

"I'm not used to all this silence and solitude," Harriet said, gesturing around the living room with its starched curtains and patchwork cushions on its maple chairs. The fire in the small brick fireplace baked away the dampness of the day. "It's all right as long as

Jeremy is here, but the minute he walks out the door I feel lonesome. Sit down. I'll make us some tea."

Vianna hung her dripping cape on a peg beside the door before seating herself at the table that was half the size of the one in the Sawtells' home. "I don't suppose you saw Tom before he left this morning."

"He said his good-byes last night. The Philadelphia packet leaves so early, you know." Harriet swung the steaming teakettle out of the fire and poured boiling water into her brand-new teapot. She held up the brown pot with its gold tracings. "Pretty, isn't it? You are having the very first cup of tea I've made in it."

"It would have been nice if he had stayed here. I'm a little surprised he didn't. He seemed so interested in our town."

"He might as well have." Harriet set out two cups and saucers, also new. "He didn't have anything in particular drawing him back to Pennsylvania. Jeremy said he sounded restless, as if he were really looking for a change. He was a lot of fun, wasn't he?"

Vianna nodded, and despite her attempts to prevent it, her mouth trembled. Unable to speak, she sat there with downcast eyes, under Harriet's thoughtful scrutiny. Her cousin took a chair beside her, and reaching out to touch her, said, "What's wrong, Vi? You came in here looking as wan as if you'd lost your best friend, and it isn't just because I'm married now, is it?" Her hand tightened on Vianna's shoulder as the thought hit her. "Has it got something to do with Tom?"

With one hand shielding her crumpling face, Vianna nodded. "I love him," she explained brokenly. "I didn't realize it until after we'd said good-bye last night. And now he's gone and I'll never see him again." She burst into tears.

Harriet digested this arresting bit of news, then asked, "You're sure? I mean, he's awfully handsome and nice and fun to be with. Maybe you just liked him a lot."

Vianna shook her head, which was still bent to hide

her face. "It's more than a liking. I've never felt like this before. Being with him does funny things to me, and now that he's gone I want to die."

"Does he feel the same way about you?"

"I guess not. If he had, he'd never have gone away. Oh, Harriet, I'm sorry to act like this. I didn't want to spoil your happiness by telling you my troubles."

"Dear Vi, what's a best friend for if not to confide in? I just wish I could do or say something that would make you feel better, but I'm at a loss." Harriet pondered her cousin's problem for a little while. As Vianna dried her tears, she asked, "What about Eban and your wedding? Will you go through with it?"

Vianna shrugged. "Why not? I'll never love anyone but Tom. I can't have him, so I might as well go ahead and marry Eban. No one will know the truth except you and me."

"What an awful thing to happen," Harriet said sympathetically.

"Awful, but wonderful, too." Vianna gave her cousin a shaky smile. "Ever since you fell in love with Jeremy, I've wanted to be in love, too. I wanted to feel all those new things I could see you were feeling. Well, now I have. I was too much a fool to realize it at the time, but at least I've had the experience and I'll have sweet memories to recall for the rest of my life."

She spent the afternoon with Harriet, sipping tea, talking about Tom, drawing some comfort from the ability to share confidences with her cousin up to a point. She understood now how, once you fell in love, there were things you kept secret even from your best friend. "I feel older than I did yesterday," she told Harriet.

"I know. Falling in love will turn you overnight from a child into a woman."

There was a knock at the door. Harriet got up to answer it.

"Is Vianna here?"

Setting her cup down with a crash, Vianna leaped to

her feet and turned toward the voice. There was Tom, coming from out of the rain into the keeping room. Despite the protection his hat gave, his lean cheeks were wet. Water ran from his jaw down his brown throat. If it had been up to her to speak in that first instant, she would have given herself away, but fortunately Harriet was quick with a surprised greeting as she invited Tom in. "We thought you left this morning. Here, give me your wet coat. We were just having tea. Sit down and let me pour you a cup."

Vianna recovered herself, and as Tom took a chair across the table and grinned at her, she said with a casualness that hid her fluttering emotions, "Were your ears burning? We've been talking about you."

"Anything you dare repeat to my face?"

"Actually, you came off rather well. Didn't he, Harriet?"

The new Mrs. Jeremy Walters set a cup and saucer before Tom and poured him some tea. "Better than you deserve, probably," she told Tom teasingly. "Now tell us what you're still doing here. Does Jeremy know?"

"I stopped at the cooperage to tell him, and I stopped at your house, Vianna, to tell you. Your mother said you were over here."

Whatever his news was, he had wanted to tell her at once. Vianna sat down once more, weak in the knees.

"I decided last night to stay in Govans Harbor. I've been going around town looking for a job. You'll never guess where I finally found one." His eyes were filled with laughter as he gazed into Vianna's, pausing before announcing, "At the rope walk."

Heat flooded Vianna's face. Harriet's glance went from her to Tom, then she said to him, "Would you like for me to disappear for a few minutes?"

"Jeremy married a smart woman. Thanks, Harriet."

She replied softly, "I've been there myself. Call me when you're ready for company once more." She left the room.

Tom turned back to Vianna. "Are you glad I'm staying?"

"Yes."

He cocked an eyebrow at her. "That's all? Just yes?" He was looking at her intently. "Last night led me to believe maybe I had good reason to stay here. Was I wrong? I've fallen in love with you, Vianna. I hoped you had with me."

"Oh, Tom!" It was all she could say for a moment. She gazed at the handsome face that had become so clear to her, letting her eyes rest on each of his features—the chestnut hair, the broad brow, the straight wedge of a nose, the sharply sculpted mouth. Drawing a ragged breath, she looked deeply into his gray eyes and said, "I do love you. I've spent the most miserable night and day I ever wish to spend. I thought I'd never see you again."

With a hoarse exclamation, he came to his feet. She was there to meet him, going into his eager arms and meeting his lips with such force that she tasted blood. Easing the pressure, he moved his lips slowly over hers, seeking, tasting, savoring, sending such delight through her body as she had never expected to feel again. His hands were possessing her in a way that made her pull back breathlessly at last and remind him, "Harriet didn't really disappear, you know. She's in the next room."

He groaned. "I know." He stole a few more caresses, nevertheless, before pushing her gently back down into her chair. He sat opposite her, clasping both of her hands across the table. "I've rented Jeremy's old room at his folks' house. In a month I'll have the money to rent us a little cottage like this, and we can be married. How does that sound?"

Vianna closed her eyes in ecstasy. "Like paradise." She sobered almost at once. "I'll tell my mother tonight. It will be difficult." She recalled her mother's agitated reaction that very morning when she had announced gloomily that she didn't love Eban. "She's going to be shocked. The whole town will be. Breaking engagements just isn't done, you know."

"You won't let her talk you out of it, will you?" Tom kissed her fingers.

Leaning across the table toward his lips, she murmured, "Do you really believe she could?"

Vianna didn't part from Tom until late that afternoon. They had announced their plans to Harriet, who was delighted and supportive. She promised to do all she could to help them. When Vianna finally returned home, Mary Chadwick was tatting lace to adorn some pieces of her daughter's trousseau. One of the lamps in the parlor had been lit to drive away the darkness of the rainy afternoon, and the steamy odor of clam chowder filled the house.

"Well, dear, did you and Harriet have a nice visit?" Her daughter's return brought life back into the lonely house, and Mary Chadwick greeted her with an affectionate smile, letting her tatting fall into her lap.

"We did. Harriet is so happy, and so am I." Vianna pulled a footstool close to her mother's chair and said, "I've got something to tell you. You aren't going to like it at first, but I want you to remember that what has happened has made me happier than I've ever been in my whole life. Will you remember that, Mother?"

The older woman's expression turned grave. "Tom Fulton was here looking for you this afternoon. I thought he was supposed to leave early this morning. Does this news of yours have anything to do with him?"

"Everything." Fingering the vivid silk scarf that draped the lamp table, Vianna revealed all that a daughter can reveal to her mother about a lover. "I thought I would never see him again. That's why I was so unhappy this morning. I didn't know he felt the same about me until he came to Harriet's this afternoon. He's found a job at the rope walk, and a month from now we can afford to get married."

"What about Eban? You're going to let him come home in two months to find you married? Without any warning?" Mary Chadwick's voice carried a strong note of disapproval that marked an even deeper emotion— fear. With her daughter wed to Eban Stanbro, she had envisioned a future that would differ little from the past. Vianna's presence in Govans Harbor would be assured for the remainder of Mary Chadwick's days. She would never be separated physically or emotionally from this child of hers whom she loved more than anyone else in the world, more even than her husband. But if Vianna married Tom Fulton, all of this might change. He was not a native son of Govans Harbor, and the ease with with he switched jobs was ominous because it indicated he might do so again, next time taking Vianna away from her to live who knew where. The very thought of losing her daughter struck terror into Mary Chadwick's loving heart.

"If I could let Eban know, I would," Vianna said, "but there's no way I can get word to him. There are no more ships going to the West Indies."

"Vianna, that is cruel. I am disappointed in you. I thought I had raised you to be considerate of other people's feelings." Mary Chadwick's distress revealed itself in the nervous way she worried the strip of white lace that lay in her ample lap.

"I realize Eban will be hurt, but I don't think he is going to be as hurt as you believe he will be. Eban is not a loving person. His pride will be injured, but not his heart."

"You're such a child!" Unable to sit still any longer, Mary Chadwick threw her tatting on the lamp table and got to her feet. She walked to the rain-streaked window and looked out toward the harbor. "You speak so knowingly, but what can you know of the human heart and its pain?" Her voice had risen. "And what makes you think Eban is not a loving person? I never heard such nonsense. He may be stiff and undemonstrative, but that is not unusual in a man." Her shoulders twitched beneath her gray cotton dress. "I dare not even imagine how this Tom Fulton expresses his feelings for you."

At the accusation that she was a child and therefore knew nothing, Vianna had bridled, but she took even stronger offense at this last remark of her mother's. "Tom kisses me in a way that leaves me no doubt that he loves me. Is there anything wrong with that?"

"Vianna, I don't want to hear about it!" Mary Chadwick spoke more sharply to her daughter than she ever had in her life. "I have tried so hard to bring you up to be a decent girl, and when you accepted Eban's proposal, I thought I had succeeded. He was exactly the kind of man I would have chosen for you if I had done the choosing. From the remarks you've made about him and about this Tom Fulton, I can see I've failed to instill in you the morals every decent woman should cherish."

As a matter of fact, her mother had never mentioned sex to her. Her only instructions had been to let no man touch her body until after she was married. What enlightenment Vianna had received was from Harriet, whose mother was more open about the subject than Mary Chadwick was. Her observation of her cousin's romance with Jeremy had expanded her knowledge, and falling in love with Tom had finally given her firsthand experience with this most secret and mysterious of human relationships. She had never considered the subject sinful, but wasn't that what her mother was intimating? How could she regard as wrong something that Vianna was discovering was the most awesome emotion a man and a woman could share? Had her mother conceived her believing all the while that she was doing something unclean? Vianna felt slightly ill. Or did Mary Chadwick believe that sex was permissible for herself but not for her child? "It seems we are both discovering things about one another today we never knew before," Vianna said quietly.

"I don't know what you mean." Mary Chadwick

turned determinedly from the window. "But this I do know. You aren't marrying this Tom Fulton until I've written to your father and you receive his permission to marry him." This was the only weapon she had with which to stop Vianna, and she thanked God it was a powerful one. She couldn't believe her daughter would marry without first informing Samuel.

"That will take months!" Vianna cried. "Perhaps even a year!"

"All the better. Maybe you'll come to your senses in that time." Mary Chadwick sensed victory.

A month earlier Vianna would have retorted in the heat of the anger that was sweeping her, but she was no longer the total child her mother believed her to be. The past week, particularly the last twenty-four hours, had started her on the road to maturity. Rising and walking to the far end of the room, she struggled to gain command of her tongue and her emotions. Before she spoke, she had come to a decision. "I won't wait for a reply from Father, but I do agree that letting Eban return to find me already married to someone else is much too cruel. I'll wait until he comes back and break the news as gently as possible. I hope that will meet with your approval, Mother, and that you will then give Tom and me your blessing."

Mary Chadwick stared at her daughter, bewilderment suffusing her fair, plump face. She had been defeated. "What has come over you? What has become of my little girl?" Her eyes filled with tears, and her mouth was trembling.

Vianna went to her, drawing her into her arms as if the older woman were the child. "Your little girl is growing up, as Nature intended," she said gently. "If you want what's best for me, you won't try to hold me back."

"I don't know, I don't know," Mary Chadwick murmured brokenly. "I wish your father were here."

*　　*　　*

Tom was not happy about having to wait an extra month before they were married, yet he agreed. "I'll be able to save a little more money, but it will be torture waiting all those weeks to possess you." He groaned and covered her mouth with his own.

The familiar fire burst into flame inside her, but she withdrew from his arms. It was a warm evening and still light enough that anyone glancing toward the lighthouse could see them. Vianna had no intention of letting things get out of hand as they had night before last when they had been in that very spot. "I'll see to it you remain a gentleman," she told him.

Brave words. And impossible to live up to.

Mary Chadwick was so cool toward Tom that they spent little time at the house. They visited Harriet and Jeremy as often as was possible without intruding. They went for walks about the town and on the beach.

It was early one evening while they were at the beach that Vianna's resolve collapsed. She had purposely not called Tom's attention to the cave on their previous walks along the shore, suspecting that the prospect of the total privacy it offered would be a lure he could not resist. The tide so far had aided her, being too high those other times to permit access to the cave.

They had walked to the beach and then sat in the sand for a while, talking. Vianna was reminded of the picnic of several weeks ago when she had sat in almost this same spot with Eban, Harriet, and Jeremy. She recalled how vexed she had been with Eban for his stuffiness, how frustrated she had become watching the two lovers exchange their hot glances and trying in turn to thaw her fiancé's icy emotions. How things had changed! And in so short a time.

She sighed happily, running her fingers through Tom's rust-colored hair as he lay with his head in her lap. "I cringe at the thought of the kind of life I'd have endured if you hadn't come to Govans Harbor when you did."

He picked up her other hand, which had been lying

on his chest, and kissed each fingertip. "My coming here was just as lucky for me. You don't know how much I'm looking forward to having a home of my own with you in it. I was so afraid of ending up trapped by too many mouths to feed like my father that I didn't admit to myself how tired I was of drifting and living in a single room wherever I went."

"We are sure to have babies," she warned him.

He grinned up at her. "Given the fact that you set me on fire if you're so much as in the same room with me, it is inevitable."

"You won't mind?"

He sat up and pushed her gently back onto the sand, bending over her and declaring, "Making love to you will be worth any price I have to pay." His lips barely touched hers, then moved lightly over her face, touching her eyelids, her forehead, her mouth again. The butterfly touch made her flesh tingle. She permitted him to continue his path of kisses down her throat to her breast, where his lips burned through the fabric of her summer dress. She lay still, letting herself enjoy the delicious sensation up to the point where she could barely restrain herself from pressing his head deeply into her breast, then stopped him. "We'd better go for a walk," she said softly, and struggled to sit up.

Tom sighed. "I've never walked so much with a girl in my life. In two months my legs will be worn down to nubbins." Despite his protest, however, he got to his feet and pulled her up, too.

As they started off, Vianna asked, "If you didn't walk with those other girls, what did you do?" She twined her arm with his, holding tightly to his hand, unable to bear total physical separation from him.

"Played tick-tack-toe or read poetry to them."

"A likely story," she commented dryly. "I don't have to ask if there were a lot of them. You know too well how and where to kiss me. You've obviously had a lot of experience." Her still-pounding heart was a warning reminder of this.

"And aren't you glad?" he teased.

"Very." Her smile was bemused, her mouth soft from desire that filled her body like warm honey.

"See that cave up there? The tide has always been too high to get up to it before. Let's go take a look and see what's inside."

Vianna held back. "I know what's up there. Moss, old shells, and lots of privacy. I don't think I should go with you."

"I promise you I'll behave like a perfect gentleman."

"It's myself I don't trust, not you."

Their glances met and held for several breathless seconds. "My passionate little virgin," Tom said softly. Then, winking roguishly, he declared with reassuring firmness, "Don't worry. I won't let you seduce me. Come on."

They climbed the outcropping of rough, tawny rock to the ledge that jutted like a porch in front of the gaping opening. The cave itself was not more than seven feet above the beach. Vianna hadn't been in it since the previous summer. Only during extremely violent storms did the waves reach this high, so there was seldom anything of special interest to be found in it. That had never discouraged a feeling of imminent discovery as she and Harriet had climbed up here as children, however. As Vianna reached it now and cast her eyes around the interior, she saw only the usual litter of shells and fish skeletons, remnants of meals the gulls had carried up. The cavern was fairly broad and deep but low, forcing them to bend over sharply as they entered. The last storm had occurred weeks earlier, and they found the floor and walls dry except near the opening, where the spray reached. Moss thinly furred the rock here; within, the floor was silted with fine sand.

Tom crouched down and picked up an unusually large quahog shell. "It took some gull to fly up here with this in its beak."

"Back in the days when Harriet and I played here,

we'd have used that for a dinner plate. You have no
idea how many pretend meals we prepared and ate in
this cave." Vianna rubbed a finger over the violet portion of the shell as she crouched beside him.

He kissed the tip of her nose. "I'll bet you were an
adorable child."

"Of course."

"An angel, too, I suppose."

"Always."

"Then what were you doing playing in this cave?
Don't tell me you weren't ordered not to because of the
tide."

She made a face at him. "Maybe my halo slipped
now and then."

He laughed and sat down, facing the mouth of the
cave, as he leaned back on his elbows. "Did you ever
come here with a boyfriend?"

"Never." She sat down beside him, straightening her
long skirt over her outstretched legs.

He glanced sideways at her. "I find that hard to
believe."

"So do I, now that I think of it. Maybe it's because
I didn't have a serious boyfriend. I did all my flirting
at the rope walk."

"I'm your first serious boyfriend?" Tom asked,
then replied to his own question as he remembered.
"That's right. You didn't know how to kiss a man until
I came along, did you?" He chuckled. "You learned
fast."

"I was always a quick study in subjects that interested me."

"Good, because there is still more to the subject than
I've taught you, you know."

"I know that all too well," Vianna replied in a small
voice. The sight of Tom's lean body stretched out beside her was disturbing. Her defenses were dangerously
weakened by the love for him that had grown daily
and by the desire for him that had grown apace, fueled
by the caresses they shared in the rare moments they

managed to be alone. If only they didn't have to wait to be married! They could have been man and wife at this very moment, free to enjoy this secret, private place overlooking the sea, free to surrender to this clamoring hunger for each other that she, for her part, was so weary of fighting. "We'd better go," she declared. "Every minute we spend here increases your danger." Her attempt at a light tone was a dismal failure, sabotaged by the force of the emotions surging through her. She got up, moving so quickly that she struck her head against the low ceiling of the cave. The blow and the pain sat her back down again, hand to her head. "Ouch! Ooohhh!"

"Are you all right? You could have knocked yourself out." Tom gathered her into his arms. "Let me kiss it and make it well."

Her face was against his throat. The heat from his body rose from the open neck of his checkered shirt; curly dark hairs peeped out of that same opening. Beneath her lips his blood pulsed strongly through a vein. The pain in her head faded beneath the stubbornly unquenchable desire that conquered her last fragments of will. Her lips began to move, forging a path of burning kisses up his neck and across his jaw. Then, with a sob of surrender, she laid her mouth on his. Just for an instant he responded, then, taking her by the arms, he forced her away from him. "I'll take you home." His voice was hoarse.

"I don't want to go," she whispered.

"I promised you I wouldn't let anything happen if we came up here."

Her lips continued to move compulsively over his face and throat as she murmured, "I love you. Oh, Tom, I love you so much."

He took a deep, ragged breath, letting it out slowly. "We weren't going to make it, anyway. Waiting, I mean. It might as well be now." He pulled her close again. Their mouths fused savagely.

For Vianna there was no holding back this time, no

internal censor warning, "This far and no further!" Their caresses mounted quickly in intensity, their bodies straining for union. There was one brief moment of pain, scarcely felt so swiftly was it followed by an ecstasy greater than anything Vianna had ever imagined. Even that grew, carrying her to impossible heights until at last the universe seemed to explode, sending her spiraling through space with Tom's arms bringing her to a safe landing.

When reality had knit itself back together, Tom raised up slightly to smile down at her. "My beloved," he said softly.

She smiled blissfully back at him.

"Any regrets?" he whispered.

"Yes," she replied. Seeing the wounded expression on his face, she added swiftly, "Not for reasons you might be imagining." Reaching up, she ran a loving finger over every feature of his face. "I wanted to satisfy myself that I could behave responsibly, no matter what the temptation. I was an impulsive fool when I agreed to marry Eban merely because Harriet was in love and I was determined to be in love, too. It terrifies me to think what I almost got myself into. I wanted to feel that I could act coolly and sensibly from now on, but I failed. That's what I meant when I said I had regrets. Outside of that, I have none at all. It was beautiful," she concluded, caressing his lips with her finger.

He kissed her finger, then smiled down at her. "Don't consider this a defeat. Passion has conquered the strongest of men and women."

"I can understand why." She kissed him with a tenderness beyond the power of words to express. "For better or for worse, I am yours forever now."

6

If surrendering to her desire for Tom was a defeat, Vianna felt no more regret once it had taken place. Sharing her body with him seemed so right, so natural, that she did not berate herself for being weak-willed or irresponsible. Once she had tasted the ecstasy to be found in Tom's ultimate embrace, she no longer fought her need for it. They made love whenever and wherever they were able to find the privacy to do so. The cave was their favorite trysting place, and they used it whenever the tide gave them access to it. The intimacy they now shared made the waiting for Eban's return not easier, as Vianna had expected at first, but more tedious. She felt so much a part of Tom as a result of their lovemaking that she was restless and discontented whenever she was separated from him. She observed Harriet as she bustled about her cottage, cooking for Jeremy, washing and ironing his clothes, keeping the house comfortable for him, and knew that if she could do these things for Tom, she wouldn't mind those hours while he was at work and not at her side.

Eban's new ship, to be called the *Trident,* was nearly completed and loomed large enough to be seen in the shipyard from almost any point in Govans Harbor. When he returned, the vessel would be christened and brought around to the wharf to be readied for its first voyage. Vianna was glad Eban would be commanding a whaler. It would insure his being away from Govans Harbor most of the time, saving herself and him much embarrassment. As a matter of fact, by the time he returned from his first voyage, she and Tom would have been married three years or more, and the broken engagement would be little more than a faint memory.

Two things occurred on Friday, August twelfth, 1848. Eban's ship was arriving in the harbor from the West Indies, and Vianna had decided for certain that she was carrying Tom's child. She had not revealed her suspicions about the baby to Tom, fearing he would not be at all pleased at the prospect of starting a family. She remembered well his dread of being burdened with too many children, as his father was. But now that she was sure of her condition, she had to tell him. She considered Eban's arrival fortunate, indeed, because she and Tom could be married without further delay.

As soon as it was known that the *Andover* was arriving from the West Indies, Mary Chadwick extracted a promise from her daughter that she would say nothing of Tom to Eban that first night, that she would give herself at the very least that much time to reevaluate Eban. It was plain to Vianna that her mother was hoping desperately that she would change her mind at the last minute and not break the engagement. Vianna agreed reluctantly. Time was important now that she knew she was pregnant. Yet it might be kinder not to hit Eban with the news on his first night at home. She managed to catch Tom as he left the rope walk at noon to tell him of Eban's arrival and warn him not to come to the house until eleven o'clock that night.

It was midafternoon before the *Andover* eased up to its berth beside the company warehouse. A large crowd had gathered to greet her and watch the docking. Vianna dawdled at home, using the excuse that her freshly shampooed hair was still wet and urging a fussing Mary Chadwick to go on without her, promising to be at the dock by the time the *Andover* tied up there.

She arrived just as the vessel was being made fast. Susannah Baker was among the crowd waiting there. Vianna had avoided Eban's sister as much as possible the last two months. Susannah couldn't have failed to know she and Tom were seeing each other. The town was too small to keep anything like that hidden, but no one except Jeremy, Harriet, and Mary Chadwick knew that she and Tom planned to get married. She had sworn Harriet and Jeremy to secrecy, and Mary Chadwick would have never so much as hinted to anyone that her daughter planned to break her engagement to Eban.

Susannah Baker's smile was less warm than usual when Vianna arrived at the dock. The fact that she wasn't standing beside Mary Chadwick was another indication that she had enough knowledge of Tom and Vianna to put a strain on the relationship with the Chadwicks, both mother and daughter.

"I didn't think you were going to make it." There was both irritation and relief in Mary Chadwick's voice as Vianna arrived. "There's Eban, see? Beside the main hatch. Susannah spoke to me, but that was all. Oh, Vianna, I do so hope you will get this wild notion out of your head and marry Eban after all!" She spoke softly so no one would overhear. "Things are going to be so awkward if you break your engagement. The embarrassment! I can't bear to think of it. And Susannah will never be friendly again." Mary Chadwick's plump face bore lines of tension.

Vianna noticed many of the spectators were shooting curious glances her way. Well, let them look. She didn't care what anyone thought. She just thanked her lucky stars that she had discovered what a mistake she was about to make before it was too late.

As she absorbed the curious glances, she was afraid suddenly that someone would tell Eban that she had been seeing Tom regularly before she informed him of it tomorrow night. She voiced her fear to her mother immediately. "I think I should tell him tonight and not wait. It would be awful for him to hear it from someone else."

Mary Chadwick said slowly, "Susannah wouldn't tell him. She wouldn't want to hurt him."

"She wouldn't, but there are probably others who would. You know how malicious some people can be, and although Eban is respected here, he is not especially liked. Someone might take great pleasure in informing him that his fiancée has been keeping company with another man."

"I suppose there are people who would be that cruel," Mary Chadwick said in distress. "I did so want you to spend an evening with him first, though. You are rushing things so, and if you would just give yourself time——"

Vianna interrupted. "Invite him over for supper as you planned, and that will give me all the time I need to reconsider."

There was no time to say more. Eban was coming off the ship. As he came down the gangway, his sister rushed forward to greet him. Vianna hung back until finally Eban, seeing her over Susannah's shoulder, said, "Vianna, how well you are looking," and came forward to kiss her chastely on the cheek.

As he greeted her mother, Vianna studied him and wondered how she could have imagined she would ever love him. She had forgotten with what irritating precision he spoke. The gaunt harshness of his face gave him a forbidding look; there wasn't a hint of physical attractiveness in his tall, shapeless body; and nothing in his glance or his kiss showed him to be any more stirred at the sight of her than at the sight of his sister. Once again she felt a rush of joyful relief that she had met Tom just in time to avoid making the disastrous mistake of marrying Eban.

She felt that relief so strongly during supper that she was able to endure Eban's stuffiness with tolerance, even pity. What an arid emotional life he would have, married or single. There was scarcely a trace of human warmth in the man.

As Vianna helped her mother with the supper dishes

while Eban smoked a pipe in the parlor, Mary Chadwick asked wistfully, "I don't suppose you've changed your mind?"

"It would have been a dreadful mistake for me to have married Eban, Mother. I know now I could never have been happy with him. Be glad for me, not sad."

"But Eban is such a fine man!" The remark held the intimation that Tom was not.

Vianna held her temper, replying calmly, "So is Tom, as you will find out if you'll only try." She didn't dare even imagine what her mother's reaction would be if she informed her that she could not marry Eban now because she was carrying Tom's child, but this was a revelation she would never have to make. She and Tom would be married immediately, and her mother would find out about the baby in due course.

Mary Chadwick sighed. "I'm going over to visit Mercy. I don't want to be here when you tell him, and he certainly won't want to have to face me when he takes his leave. Poor man."

After her mother had said good night to Eban and left the house, Vianna sat down in her mother's rocker, returning Eban's smile.

"Well, my dear, what have you been doing while I was gone?" he asked. "Planning our wedding, I'm sure." He relit his pipe, which had gone out while he was speaking to Mary Chadwick. The sun had not set, and the light from the window fell on the right side of his face, accentuating the groove that ran from his nose down past the corner of his thin mouth.

"It has been a very eventful two months," Vianna began. "Something has happened that is going to change the future for both of us."

The gaze from his deep-set gray eyes sharpened. "And what is that?"

Vianna paused a moment, letting him prepare himself. "I have met someone, a man I have come to love so deeply that I cannot marry you."

He froze. With his pipe held in one hand, he sat

and stared at her, absolutely unmoving, for so long that Vianna continued with her explanation.

"His name is Tom Fulton. He was Jeremy's best man. That's how we met. He was living in Pennsylvania, but he chose to stay here. He is staying with Jeremy's parents and has taken a job at the rope walk."

Eban's paralysis left him gradually. He looked at his pipe, then tapped it jerkily against the ashtray that sat on the table at his elbow.

"I thought Susannah was acting queerly." His voice was hoarse. "She knows about this, I presume?"

"I'm sure she knows I've been seeing Tom. No one except my mother, Harriet, and Jeremy know we plan to be married."

With his little finger, Eban pressed down the unburned tobacco still in his pipe. "What does your father say about this?"

"I have not heard from him. I wrote him a letter a month ago, but there is almost no chance that he has received it, and even if he has, you know how long his reply might take to reach me."

"Well, then, aren't you being a bit hasty? You cannot marry this other person without your father's consent." His characteristic dogmatic tone was evidence that he was recovering from the shock he'd received.

"I'll be seventeen next week. I don't need my father's consent, and with him a world away, it isn't convenient to wait for it. I hope for his blessing when he is able to send it."

"Surely your mother does not condone this rash behavior. I can't believe she would let you marry without your father's permission. It simply isn't proper."

"For her sake, I must tell you that she is most unhappy that I am breaking my engagement to you."

"Yet you persist in your determination to do so?" he asked sharply. "Vianna, what has got into you? You were always far too impulsive, but you were never defiant. What has this person done to you?"

"His name is Tom Fulton," she reminded him pointedly, "and he's done nothing to me except to make me happier than I dreamed it was possible to be. If I am being defiant, it is because I have the right to marry whom I choose, whether it pleases anyone else or not."

The rebuke he was prepared to give her died on his lips as he seemed to recall something. "This Fulton wouldn't have red hair, would he?"

"Tom's hair is more chestnut-colored than red."

"I saw him at the tavern late this afternoon, drinking with the other men from the rope walk. Why, he's just a boy! And I didn't like his behavior. Much too cocky."

Vianna felt a spurt of anger. "Tom is twenty-two, and it isn't necessary that you approve of his behavior."

"But he has no prospects! A job at the rope walk? What does that pay? Surely you don't want to marry someone of so low a station in life." His deeply furrowed face assumed an even grimmer aspect than it normally had. "Vianna, you are too young to know your own mind. If you marry this person, you will ruin your life."

"You are wrong," Vianna retorted. "I have come to see clearly these past two months that I made a serious mistake when I said I would marry you. I have done you grave harm, and for that I am deeply sorry, but I cannot allow you to speak disparagingly of Tom. He is a fine man, and his station in life is of no importance to me, because I love him and want nothing more than to live out the whole of my life with him."

"Love him!" Eban banged his pipe in a loud tattoo in the ashtray. "Having seen him, I can imagine what emotion you are confusing with love. He is the type who has only one thought in his mind where women are concerned and by looks and behavior can persuade a girl to forget all decency and decorum. He's a scoundrel, and if you had any sense, you'd recognize it."

Holding her anger in check, Vianna stood up. "I will not tolerate your insults to Tom. I wish you to leave."

Outraged at being ordered out by her, Eban took his time getting up. Icily furious, he said, "I will not let you humiliate me like this, Vianna. I will speak to your mother. Together we will prevent your marrying this young wastrel."

This further insult was too much. "Tom is not a wastrel," she cried. "He is ten times the man you are, Eban Stanbro. And I thank God I discovered what a real man was before it was too late!"

"What are you saying?" He grabbed her arm and shook her. "I won't be compared with a worthless young lecher who is more animal than human."

With her free hand Vianna slapped him with all her might. "How dare you speak of Tom like that! You with ice water in your veins! You call that human?" She struggled to free herself from his bruising grip.

Eban shook her again, thundering, "Once we are married, you will pay for this outburst!"

"We are *not* getting married! Can't you get that through your head? It is Tom I love, Tom's child I am carrying, and Tom whom I will be marrying!"

At the mention of the baby, Eban released her, shoving her away from him, his face contorted with revulsion. "Vile! Unclean! I suspected that you possessed shameful tendencies, and I was prepared to curb them and make a decent woman of you. I would not have you to wife now if you were the last woman in the world, you sinful creature!" With an exclamation of disgust, he whirled and strode out of the parlor as if fleeing something noxious.

Shuddering, Vianna sank back into the rocker. My God, what a fate she had escaped! Cold sweat popped out on her brow at the thought of what she had almost let herself in for as Eban's wife.

She was still sitting there, rocking and thinking, when her mother returned from the Sawtells. It had grown dark, but Vianna hadn't bothered to light a lamp. The slowly gathering darkness had been soothing. The emotional turmoil of her confrontation with

Eban had died, leaving her with the clarity of mind to plan exactly how she would tell Tom about the baby when he arrived later that night.

"How did Eban take it?" Mary Chadwick asked, lighting the table lamp.

"Not well. Here, Mother, take your rocker." Vianna changed to the chair in which Eban had been sitting. Her nose wrinkled with distaste at the smell of his pipe tobacco in the ashtray at her elbow. "He was angry and threatening, free with insults toward Tom, whom he remembered seeing at the tavern earlier. When I asked him to leave, he became even more insulting. I've been sitting here ever since, thanking my lucky stars that I decided not to marry him. I would never have been happy with such a man."

Mary Chadwick sighed. "I think you are wrong, but there's nothing more I can say or do. I was so hoping that you would reconsider once you had seen him again."

"I asked Tom to come here at eleven o'clock to-night. I'll tell him the engagement is broken and we can make our wedding plans." Vianna spoke with a certainty she didn't altogether feel. Despite Tom's declaration that, loving her as he did, babies were inevitable and a price he was willing to pay, she didn't know what to expect when she broke the news to him that she was pregnant.

"When word gets around," Mary Chadwick said disconsolately, "tongues are going to wag. And I don't suppose Susannah and Eban will ever speak to us again."

"They may not speak to me, but I'm sure they will still be friendly toward you. I told Eban you did not approve of my breaking our engagement."

Pleasantly surprised at this unexpected news, Mary Chadwick said, "That was thoughtful of you, dear. It will make things so much easier, I hope. And now I suppose I must accept the inevitable and try to become fond of Tom."

"It will not be at all difficult, Mother, as you will see."

Indeed her mother's greeting to Tom when he arrived was less stiff than her manner had been previously. She offered to make him coffee, which he graciously declined. "Then I'll leave the two of you alone. I realize you have much to discuss. Good night, dear." She kissed her daughter, said good night to Tom, and went upstairs to bed.

Vianna pulled Tom into the parlor and closed the door. "It's done," she said exultantly. "I've broken off with Eban. He refused to accept it at first, but I convinced him my decision was irrevocable."

He caught her in his arms. "There's nothing to stop us from getting married right away, then." His lean, handsome face shone with eagerness, his smoky eyes with a desire that told her he wanted her then and there.

"Nothing. And the sooner the better," she added somewhat nervously.

"Amen to that," he breathed, and pressed a burning kiss upon her lips.

How she longed to lose herself in the sweet rapture his body could give her, but this was not the place, nor was it the time. She must tell him. Dragging her crushed lips reluctantly away from his, she murmured, "It is not only because of this that we must wed quickly." She leaned back in order to look directly into his face. "I am with child," she said softly.

The news fell on him like a blow. She saw him flinch, then grow pale. He licked his lips before asking hoarsely, "Are you sure?"

"I am now. I've suspected it for more than two weeks. There can no longer be any doubt." His shock had been greater than she had anticipated. She regarded him anxiously. "You aren't at all happy about it, are you?"

He grimaced. "I knew it was inevitable, but I didn't expect it to come so quickly." When he saw that her eyes were filling with tears, he kissed her gently and said, "Don't worry, sweetheart. I'll love the baby, because it's yours. I need a little time to get used to the idea, that's all. You've had two weeks to accustom yourself to it."

"We can't delay the wedding too long," Vianna reminded him in a tremulous voice.

"Who's talking about delaying it? How soon can you be ready?" He was smiling now.

"I can be ready Saturday." All anxiety fled her. She spoke in an excited rush. "I've been sitting here tonight thinking about it. I'll wear the blue and silver dress I wore to Harriet's wedding. We'll have a supper like Harriet and Jeremy had, and pretty much the same people will be invited."

Tom grinned. "I think I can survive that. I'll go see Hiram Worley. He and his wife have been sorting through his mother's things since she died and must have her house about ready to rent now. Maybe we could rent it furnished."

"Oh, Tom, that would be lovely."

"I've had my eye on that place for several weeks, but I couldn't say anything to Hiram without giving away our plans." He caught her close again, burying his face in her hair. "Once the door of that house closes on us, I'm not letting you off the place for a week."

She moved her hands over the hard, broad expanse of his back, murmuring, "You'll get no argument from me about that."

Prevented by Mary Chadwick's presence upstairs from making love, they rationed their kisses and restrained their caresses, eschewing the sofa and sitting in separate chairs to discuss their plans for the future. It was long after midnight when Tom finally left. "Tomorrow evening we'll go to our cave," he murmured as he finally pulled his lips from hers.

Heart pounding, her body straining against his, she whispered, "Come for me right after supper."

"I will." He drew away from her with an effort and left.

With everything settled, free from all anxiety, Vianna fell asleep at once and slept far past her usual waking time the next morning. In fact, it was the sound of her mother's opening and closing the front door below her open window that awakened her. Recalling that she and Tom were now free to marry, she sighed and turned over, a smile on her face. Only three more days now. And with Harriet's wedding still so fresh in her and her mother's memory, the preparations for her own would not require a great deal of planning.

The door closed and her mother came upstairs. "I'm awake," Vianna called, adding cheerfully, "finally."

"Tom stayed awfully late last night." On this note of disapproval, Mary Chadwick appeared and came into the room. "I found this letter for you lying on the hall floor. Someone slipped it under the door. I don't know when. I didn't notice it when I came downstairs this morning, but I suppose I could have missed it."

Sitting up in bed, Vianna took the well-folded piece of paper from her mother and opened it. It was handwriting she had never seen before. Glancing quickly at the signature, she saw it was from Tom. *Dear Vianna,* she read silently. *I am leaving. You will know why. There is no use trying to find me. I'm sorry, but I've decided marriage is not for me.* It was signed merely, "Tom."

A heavy pain began to fill Vianna's chest, but she read the brief message once more, unwilling to believe what her eyes had told her. They had told her correctly, however. Tom was gone. He had fled because of the baby. "No," she moaned, falling back on her pillow as the steeply pitched ceiling suddenly whirled around her. "He loved me!" she gasped. "I know he did!" The pain in her chest swelled. "No, no, no," she cried, over and over again, twisting her head from side to side, trying to deny that this horrible thing had happened.

Alarmed, Mary Chadwick pulled the sheet of paper from her daughter's limp hand and read the message. "The scoundrel! How could he do this to you!" She gathered Vianna up against her warm, ample bosom and rocked her as if she were a child. "There, there, dear, I know it seems like the end of the world at this moment, but it isn't, and in a day or two you'll be able to see that he did you the biggest favor of your life by deserting you now. What if he had waited until you were married to do it?"

"He loved me!" Vianna sobbed.

Carefully, her mother said, "In his way, maybe he did, but if he isn't capable of any greater love than that, you don't want him for a husband."

"But I do! Oh, Mother, I loved him so!" Nausea rose in her, and her mother held her head over the washbasin as she was sick. It's the baby, Vianna thought. What am I going to do? The thought of being with child had not worried her, knowing that she and Tom were to be married before anyone need find out. All that had changed. There would be no wedding, and soon the whole town would learn that she was pregnant. Worst of all, her mother would either have to be told or be left to find out as her condition became obvious. Given her mother's disgust toward sex, Vianna could imagine her shock. Until now the love Vianna had received from her had been total and unreserved. But the baby might change that, Vianna thought, and never had her mother's tender ministrations and comforting arms moved her so deeply as now when there was danger that part of that love might die.

Prostrated by emotional shock and nausea, Vianna was not able to leave her bed that day. So great was her agony that she tried over and over again to alter reality, imagining that Tom changed his mind and came back, rushing up to her room to catch her in his arms and declare that he couldn't bear to leave her after all, that it was all right about the baby, and that they would be married as planned because he couldn't live without her.

This fantasy gave her a few moments of relief each time she played it over, but always at the end awareness of her real situation returned abruptly as she felt the sweat-drenched pillow beneath her cheek and the heat that was building in her bedroom. Moaning, she would turn over, feeling the pain of loss in every cell of her body. Never to see the look in his smoky eyes that could send that flash of delicious weakness through her, never again to feel his lips or the rapture in the uniting of his body with hers. How could she bear it? Having known all those things, how could she find any meaning in life ever again? She wanted to die.

Mary Chadwick went after Harriet and brought her to Vianna, hoping she could console her daughter.

"I can't believe Tom would do such a thing!" Harriet cried, sitting beside Vianna on the bed and holding her hand. "He seemed to love you so much!" Her freckled face was clouded with distress. She had obviously come in a hurry. Her red hair was uncombed, and the bodice of her green dress was spotted where hot grease had apparently popped on it. The hot air in the bedroom brought beads of sweat to her brow.

"He did love me," Vianna insisted brokenly. She would never believe any different.

"Then why did he skip town when the way was finally clear to marry you? Your mother said you broke your engagement last night as you had planned and that Tom had come to see you later. What did Tom say?"

"He acted as relieved and happy as I was. We set our wedding date for Saturday, and he was going to see Hiram Worley about renting his mother's house."

Puzzled, Harriet said, "It makes no sense."

It would if you knew about the baby, Vianna told her cousin silently, but she couldn't bring herself to reveal this to Harriet. She hadn't been ashamed of the fact before. She was now. Tom's betrayal had turned their once beautiful relationship into something sordid.

Harriet reread Tom's note, then asked thoughtfully, "Do you suppose he left on the *Antilla* when it sailed this morning? That would explain his saying it was no use trying to find him."

"He would never sign on a whaler, or any other ship for that matter," Vianna said dully. "He said more than once that going to sea was not for him."

"I stopped at Jeremy's folks' place on the way over to see if his mother had any idea where Tom had gone. She said she heard him come in late last night and then leave again. She supposed she'd been asleep when he came back a second time, but when he didn't appear for breakfast this morning, she checked his room and found him and all his things gone. She didn't know what to think until I told her about his note to you. He paid his room and board in advance, so at least he didn't leave owing the Walters money." Harriet lifted her skirt to dry her perspiring face.

"If he left last night, he might have walked to Reedsport and caught the packet for New York or anywhere to the south. Anywhere but Philadelphia," Vianna added bitterly. "He'd know that Pennsylvania would be the first place I'd check if I wanted to trace him."

"Trace him? Why would you want to do that?" Not knowing about the baby, Harriet was puzzled about why a girl would want to trace a man who obviously didn't want to have any more to do with her.

"I don't, of course. I can't think why he'd be afraid I would," Vianna said with as much indignation as she could muster. The baby was a secret she must keep as long as it was possible to do so.

"You're better off without him," Harriet declared stoutly.

If only you knew the whole story, Vianna cried out in silent despair.

By noon the next day, her mother had persuaded her to get dressed and come downstairs. "You'll never get over this lying in bed, dear."

Vianna knew she was right, and besides, the mortifying predicament in which Tom had left her had to be thought out. She had discovered that keeping to her bed was an attempt to escape reality. What was urgently necessary was to face it and try to come to terms with her problem.

Her mother had gone upstairs to take a nap after their noon meal, and Vianna was sitting in the parlor, rocking and staring out the window toward the harbor, when Eban passed in front of the window. A moment later the knocker sounded.

The last person in the world she wanted to see was Eban! She wouldn't answer. She'd pretend there was no one at home.

The knocker sounded again, louder this time.

"Vianna, are you downstairs?" her mother called. "There's someone at the door."

Eban would have heard. There was no way she could pretend any longer that there was no one inside the house. "Yes, I'll get it, Mother." It was all she could do to lift herself out of the rocker and force her legs to take her to the door. She paused an instant, marshaling what little physical strength she possessed, before opening the door and facing Eban.

"Good afternoon, Vianna." There was a gentle note in his voice she had never heard before. His gaunt, furrowed face was as grim as ever, but his mouth seemed less rigid, his deep-set eyes definitely softer. There was no sign of the rage he had felt toward her as he left her night before last. "May I speak with you?" he asked.

She hesitated. "I'm not feeling well, Eban."

"I'm sure you're not. I've heard what has happened, and I realize what an unfortunate position that has left you in. I've been doing a lot of thinking and believe that perhaps I can offer help."

"I don't see how that would be possible," she replied wearily. Why didn't he leave? She didn't want his sympathy, and the sound of his careful, precise manner of speaking was too irritating to be borne today.

"Please. Just give me ten minutes of your time. Then I'll go if you wish me to."

"All right," she agreed reluctantly, stepping aside to admit him.

At the sound of the closing door, Mary Chadwick called down, "Who was it, dear?"

"It's Eban. He has come to speak with me."

A surprised silence was the only response the older woman made to this announcement. Vianna walked ahead of Eban into the parlor, inviting him to sit down while she sank gratefully once again into the rocker, then waited for him to begin.

He sat very straight, his forearms on the arms of the chair, his hands gripping the ends, suddenly tense, his tone almost pleading as he spoke. "I'm willing to forget everything that was said night before last, pretend it never happened. If you are willing, also, we can go ahead and be married as we had planned."

Her mouth fell open in surprise. She hadn't known what to expect from his visit, but she hadn't suspected this. For a moment she could not think how to reply. Her first instinct had been to exclaim, "No! Never!" However, his surprising kindness and generosity deserved a more tactful answer. "Eban, I . . . Do you realize what you are proposing? You have not forgotten my, ah, condition, have you?"

He reddened. "That is the main reason I dared hope that you might reconsider marrying me. How many people know about the baby?"

"Just you, Tom, and I."

He nodded. "That is even better than I had hoped. We could be married, you could accompany me on my voyage, we could put into Lahaina for the baby's birth, and when we returned to Govans Harbor in three or four years, no one here would know that the child was not mine."

Vianna absently ran a forefinger across a small jade elephant that stood on the table beside her, while her mind raced. Here was a way out of her predicament that had not occurred to her. Neither she nor her parents would have to bear the shame of her baby's being born out of wedlock. Nor would the child be branded illegitimate. But to consent to be Eban's wife! The prospect sent a ripple of distaste sweeping through her. After having loved Tom and been loved by him, she could not tolerate the thought of being intimate with Eban. Before she met Tom, she had only her uninformed imagination to build a picture of what it would be like to be made love to by Eban. Now that she had experienced the act of love, the idea of performing it with Eban filled her with repugnance.

"I would love the child as if it were my own," Eban told her, breaking the silence.

Noting the softness in his normally uncompromising gaze, Vianna wondered if she had misjudged him. Was he less cold and uncaring than she had believed him to be? "You've taken me completely by surprise," she told him. "Your offer is incredibly generous, but I need more time to consider it."

"Of course. I learned this morning that I will be sailing on August thirtieth, so you will want to keep that in mind." He stood up. "I will leave you to think about it, then." Hesitating for a moment, he finally said, with the embarrassment of a man not given to emotional expression, "I do love you, Vianna. I want you to know that. I will be a good husband to you." He broke off awkwardly, then left the room quickly and let himself out of the house.

Vianna watched for him to pass the parlor window, wanting to view this man from a new perspective. She caught only a swift glimpse, but she saw the gaunt face and big body, the dark wavy hair, the forward thrust of the head. An unattractive man, but there was about him a sense of power and solidity, attributes that at this moment in her life she found very reassuring. She would always be safe and secure as Eban's wife. These factors had never entered into her dreams of marriage in those days when she was fantasizing about her still-unknown future husband and the life she would lead with him. She had sought romance, yearned for it, spent hours each day dreaming about it. Then Tom had appeared on the scene, Romance with a capital R, and what had all that excitement and rapture brought her except betrayal and humiliation? Romance was ashes in her mouth.

She heard her mother coming down the stairs, and a minute later Mary Chadwick came into the room, buttoning her bodice, her gray-blond hair a bit mussed. "What did Eban want, dear?"

"He still wants me to marry him," Vianna replied, a note of incredulity in her voice.

Mary Chadwick's hand paused over her buttons. Somewhat breathlessly she asked, "What did you tell him?"

"That I would think about it and give him an answer later."

"Oh, my dear, I am so happy you didn't refuse him outright!" The older woman sat down on the edge of a chair, hands in her lap, buttons forgotten. "He's such a fine man, and I would so like to see you marry him." When her daughter remained silent, she asked, "When is he due to sail?"

"On August thirtieth. He wants me to go with him."

One of Mary Chadwick's hands rose once again to fumble with a button. The news that her daughter might leave her for three or four years was most unwelcome. One of the reasons she had approved so heartily of Vianna's marriage to Eban was that his long absences would make it possible for them to continue their close relationship. "Would you want to do that?" she asked slowly.

"It would be the best possible way to forget Tom."

"I suppose it would." And there was always the possibility that she will be as poor a sailor as I was, Mary Chadwick was thinking. Or that she will get with child and come home to have it. There was little possibility that they would be separated for long. One couldn't raise a family on a whaling ship. Besides, seeing her daughter married to a man like Eban, especially after the close call she'd had with this wastrel Tom Fulton, would be worth some temporary separation. She could rest easy that her child's future was in responsible hands. "If you decide that you will marry him after all, don't worry about wedding preparations. I've planned this wedding in my mind a dozen times. You can leave everything to me."

"Thank you, Mother. That will be a big help, because I never gave my marriage to Eban much thought. But I'll want a very simple wedding if I decide to marry him."

"All right, dear."

Within three days Vianna had come to the conclusion that marriage to Eban was the best of the choices, all of them poor, that were left open to her. She accepted his proposal.

7

As Vianna stood on the gently pitching deck of the *Trident* and watched Govans Harbor recede as they piled on more canvas and sailed out into Cape Cod Bay, she wiped away the tears that kept spilling out of her eyes, and fought for control. She knew if she gave way to her grief, she would sob like a child. Saying good-bye to her mother had nearly torn the heart out of her. An occasional night spent at the Sawtells' had been the longest period of separation from her mother she had ever experienced. Mary Chadwick's loving presence had created a cocoon of security that had not been ruptured in all of Vianna's seventeen years. With each dip of the ship the silken thread unwound now, leaving Vianna exposed to a new existence in which she felt defenseless and unutterably lonely.

The early afternoon sun was hot, burning through the lavender bonnet that shaded her face and matched the dress she and her mother had quickly made for the wedding. She could not bring herself to wear the blue and silver dress she had planned to wear when she married Tom. She hadn't even packed it, leaving it hidden from sight in the small closet under the eaves in her bedroom.

Behind her, in the pen built aft of the booby hatch, the clucking of the hens was incongruously homelike. They, together with the sow and her family of six who shared the pen, would provide the captain's mess with eggs and fresh meat for several months.

The bay was a brilliant green, broken by whitecaps,

as the *Trident* headed toward the Atlantic. Keeping pace with her was the small sailboat that would return the pilot to Govans Harbor. Brand new, sparkling with her fresh white coat and black masts, the *Trident* cut through the waves as sleekly as a clipper, or so it seemed to Vianna. She had been aboard her father's ship many times, but only when it was docked. A whaling ship was to a clipper ship as a stout matron was to a slender girl, but as Vianna watched Govans Harbor slip farther and farther behind her, she thought that surely a clipper couldn't sail any faster than the *Trident* was sailing.

Next to the farewell to her mother, the parting from Harriet had been the most difficult. Her cousin's freckled face had collapsed and tears had streamed down her cheeks as she hugged her and cried, "Oh, Vi, I'm going to miss you so awfully!"

Vianna had hugged back, hiding her face in Harriet's red hair and saying nothing, knowing if she tried to speak she would break down.

Jeremy's brotherly kiss resulted in a rush of affection greater than any she had felt for him before. Aunt Mercy had tears in her eyes, but her voice was steady as she said, "God go with you, child." Uncle Isaac's voice had been surprisingly hoarse as he bid her goodbye.

Nathaniel's emotions of the moment were on a different plane. "I don't see why I couldn't have gone with you. Maybe I'm not twelve yet, but that shouldn't make any difference if I'm with you and Eban. I'd have made a good cabin boy for you."

"Maybe next time, Cap," she murmured. Eban had gently refused Nathaniel's plea, supported by Aunt Mercy and Uncle Isaac. He had explained to the boy that with his wife aboard, he would not be needing anyone to look after his quarters.

Joseph kissed her shyly, saying, "Don't forget that Bobby Howard will be aboard. He'd appreciate a few words from you now and then."

Vianna was well aware that the captain seldom if ever deigned to speak to a common seaman and that the forecastle, where the crew lived, and the quarter-deck, where the officers were housed, were two separate worlds. She wasn't sure that Eban would approve of her exchanging a few friendly words with the ship's chandler's son, even if he and Vianna had known one another all their lives. Bobby was also Joseph's best friend, and because this was his first voyage, he was certain to be lonely.

"I won't forget." It was only half a promise, but the best that Vianna could do under the circumstances.

Susannah Baker's kiss was warm. All was forgiven now that Vianna had married her brother after all. Even saying good-bye to Kermit Baker was like saying farewell to an old friend, although until that moment Vianna had felt she scarcely knew this quiet, reserved man.

When she at last turned to her mother, she saw a face as white as her own must have been. As they embraced, neither could speak. Vianna clung to the soft, plump body that had offered haven and comfort for every hurt from a skinned elbow to the anguished good-byes she bade her father each time he embarked on a new voyage. As the wife now of a man she did not love, with the frightening prospect of bearing a child ahead of her, she needed her mother more than ever, and it was all she could do to keep from crying out, "I can't leave, Mother! I just can't! Please make it possible for me to stay here with you!" But it was precisely because of the baby that she must separate herself from her mother and go with Eban to the other side of the world.

She kissed the soft, pale cheek, nodding as her mother murmured brokenly, "Send me a letter every chance you get. I'll be thinking of you every day."

In a voice that shook as if she were riding over a cobbled street, Vianna said, "I will, and I'll be thinking of you, too."

Neither could articulate that saddest of all words, "Good-bye." Their arms loosened little by little until finally, with enormous effort, Vianna turned away blindly and let Eban lead her up the gangway and onto the ship. Standing at the taffrail as the *Trident* moved out of the harbor, she waved and tried to smile. After a few minutes it did not matter that her smile wavered, because she was no longer close enough that those left on the dock could see her that clearly.

Despite the fact that she had turned seventeen a week ago, had loved a man and conceived his child, and had been deserted by him and known the depths of a despair that only a woman could know, at this moment she felt like a child and lonelier than she had thought it possible to feel. She stood all alone at the rail. Eban's presence at her side might have been a comfort, but he was behind her on the quarterdeck, watching every move the ship made, even though the pilot was taking the vessel out of the harbor.

She had become Mrs. Eban Stanbro three hours earlier in a small ceremony in her home with only the immediate families present. After a light lunch they had all come down to the dock to see the bride and groom off.

Mrs. Eban Stanbro. Vianna did not care for the sound of it, nor was she able to see her marriage as anything but a last resort. The one bright spot in the miserable situation in which she found herself was Eban's love for her. It had continued to surprise her during the dark days she had just lived through. Although it was expressed awkwardly, its existence was beyond doubt and hinted at a depth of emotion she hadn't believed him capable of. It revealed a humility she would never have suspected he possessed, either. How he must love her to have still wanted to marry her after the wound she had dealt him, and knowing she had got herself with child out of wedlock! Surely they could build a marriage on something as enduring as that.

Her house and the other buildings along Front Street were no longer distinguishable, presenting only a light streak against a background of the town's trees. Her mother had probably left the dock and returned home. I'd give anything if I could be with her this moment in our parlor, watching her plump hands fly as she tatted, Vianna thought. Oh, Mother, I miss you already! A fresh sob rose in her throat as she strained her eyes to make out their house, but it was no use. The distance was too great.

The small sailboat accompanying the *Trident* was signaled to pull alongside. It looked no bigger than a moth beside the fat whaler. Vianna watched as the pilot shook hands with Eban and climbed down the Jacob's ladder to board the boat. As it turned away from the *Trident* with a snap of its canvas and sailed back toward Govans Harbor, Vianna felt the last link with home break. Her world for the next three or four years would be this ship, her life proscribed by its dimensions and its routine and by a husband she had only a few hours earlier vowed to obey. A ship's captain ruled as absolute monarch on his vessel. Vianna suspected that Eban, despite his love for her, would demand the same unquestioning obedience from her that he expected from his crew. With leaden spirits Vianna turned away from the now blurry landmass. Eban was standing beside the helmsman, hands clasped behind his back, gazing forward past the coils of rope, the hatches, the three masts toward the forecastle, observing the crew, which had been ordered by the first mate to begin stowing the anchors and spare spars. He seemed oblivious to her presence on the quarterdeck, and his expression was so stern and forbidding that she did not want to risk speaking to him for fear of earning a rebuff for disturbing him, so she went down the companionway into the cabin.

Eban had brought her aboard the previous week to show her the ship and the cabin that would be home to her for the next several years. The accommodations were generous for a whaling ship. The day cabin was eight feet wide and twelve feet long. Farthest aft was a built-in sofa. A few feet in front of it was the captain's desk. In one forward corner was a chair and space for the small stove that would be set up when they hunted northern whale grounds. The door leading to the companionway and the officers' mess was at the opposite corner. Light was provided by three windows behind the sofa. Opening off the day cabin on the starboard side was the sleeping cabin. The bed was built against the bulkhead on one side and stood only two feet away from the wall on the other. At the foot of the bed was a washstand with cupboard underneath. Between it and the water closet was a deck-to-ceiling clothes cupboard. There was a porthole in the bulkhead near the head of the bed, another over the washstand.

It was to the sleeping cabin that Vianna went, swiftly and directly, to fling herself down upon the bed and give way to the sobs she had heretofore managed to hold in check. She wept with abandon, knowing she would not be heard. *I can't bear it,* she thought. *I will die of loneliness before the end of the voyage.*

But once all her tears had been shed, she was able to think what she might do to change her situation. Lying there, soothed by the slight pitching motion of the ship, she decided that as soon as the baby was a few months old, she would ask Eban to let her return home. If some people suspected the child was older than the age she gave, let them. They would never know for sure. She could even say it had been born prematurely. None of that would matter. She would be home again, among her loved ones, even in her old room. Eban could buy or build them a house when he returned. Until then she would live with her mother.

Meantime there was a good chance that they would encounter her father's ship at one of the whaling ports or hunting grounds. How happy she would be to see him! It was possible that she might see a lot of him if their ships hunted the same areas.

The prospect of seeing her father and returning to Govans Harbor was so comforting that she fell into an exhausted sleep so deep that when someone shook her shoulder, she had some difficulty awakening.

"Vianna, it's time for supper!" The voice and the grip on her shoulder were rough.

She sat up groggily. Eban was standing in the narrow space beside the bed, a queer look on his dour face. "I'll tidy up and be out in a minute," she assured him.

"Hurry. The officers will be coming down."

There was no water in the pitcher, so she could not wash, but she smoothed her hair, straightened her clothes, and went out to eat her first meal aboard the *Trident*.

The captain's mess was just forward of the day cabin. Opening off it on the larboard side were doors to the companionway, to the first mate's cabin, and to the cabin shared by the second and third mates. In the larboard corner was a door leading to the steerage cabin where the harpooners lived. At the forward corner on the starboard side was the door to the steward's pantry. The table, with its built-up edge to prevent plates from sliding off in rough weather and the benches running along each side of it, provided the only furniture in the mess. All were bolted to the deck. Directly overhead was a skylight.

Eban was pacing from day cabin to mess, his expression thunderous as she came out of the sleeping cabin. "Mr. Vickers will be down any minute."

"I'm sorry to be late, Eban." She hurried into the mess and sat where he silently indicated, which put her opposite him, at the head of the table. They were no sooner seated than the steward came through the pantry door bearing a platter full of beef and vegetables, which he placed before Eban.

John Colby's many years at sea had left him bent with rheumatism and no longer able to serve in any capacity except steward. He bobbed his bald head at

Vianna, greeting her with a mumbled "Ma'am" before retreating to his pantry again.

He was reappearing with the bread and coffee when Abner Vickers, the first mate, arrived. He paused as if waiting for Eban to introduce him to Vianna, but when no introduction was forthcoming, he greeted her with a polite, "Good evening, ma'am," and took his seat beside Eban. He was a stocky man, thick through the chest and neck, with a missing front tooth. His long dark hair was caught in a band of blue cloth at the back of his neck.

Eban was silently serving the three of them when the second and third mates appeared, a few minutes apart. George McAndrews, the second mate, was a thin young man with a pleasant face, but Vianna took an instant dislike to Mason Orne, the other mate. His body and skull were apelike, and his hands were covered with black hair. McAndrews gave her a warm smile as he took his place; Orne's small black eyes stared at her briefly before he sat down without so much as a silent nod.

Eban served each one without speaking, motioning for them to pass him their plates. Throughout the entire meal he said nothing. Vianna found the silence intolerably awkward. Once she tried to initiate a conversation by remarking about the fine weather, but Eban froze any response that might have been made with a glare around the table that terminated with her and was so venomous Vianna quailed. Losing what little appetite she had, she wondered what had put him in such a black mood. The officers ate quickly and excused themselves. Much to her relief, Eban followed them without so much as a glance at her.

She got up slowly and went into the day cabin, where she selected a book from the shelves behind the sofa and tried to read. It was a copy of Hawthorne's *Twice-Told Tales,* which she had never read despite the fact it had been around the house for a number of years. Her mother had insisted she take it and several others, declaring that she would need something to help her pass the long days aboard ship, and reminding her these books could be traded for different ones whenever she found a captain who was also looking for fresh reading material.

She carried the book to the chair and opened it. Through the bulkhead behind her, she heard the harpooners taking their turn in the mess. Free of the intimidating presence of their captain, they obviously enjoyed their meal. Vianna listened wistfully to the bantering tone of their voices and to their laughter.

Try as she might, she could not concentrate on the story she began, even after the harpooners left the mess. She had been dreading her wedding night from the moment she'd got up that morning. Tension began building inside her, heightened by the knowledge that Eban was in such a dudgeon.

It had grown dark by the time he returned to the cabin. Vianna had lighted a candle in its holder on the bulkhead above her chair when she heard footsteps coming down the companionway. She hoped it was one of the mates, but it was Eban. He entered the day cabin without glancing at her and went to his desk, where he lit a candle and began, ostensibly, to study a chart, but after a few minutes Vianna felt his eyes on her and looked up to find him staring at her. Her heart skipped a beat. His weather-cured face was flushed, his rage unmistakable. Was it her with whom he was angry? But why? Surely her slight tardiness for supper had not been such a serious matter.

Too frightened to say anything, she dropped her eyes and pretended to read again, but she continued to feel his baleful glare upon her. Two or three surreptitious checks confirmed that he had not taken his eyes from her.

After an hour of this, she could bear it no longer. "Why are you angry with me, Eban?" she asked timidly.

For a dreadfully long time he continued to glare at her without replying. When he did, his voice was hoarse and he sounded as if he were choking. "Slut! Whore! Don't try to deceive me. Ever since we boarded the ship, you've been parading yourself, trying to seduce me."

She sat stunned by his incredible accusation. "I have done no such thing!"

"You lie! You think you can enslave me with your body and escape your punishment, but you are wrong!" He jumped to his feet and hurled himself across the short distance that separated them, his face black with rage.

Vianna saw the blow coming and tried to duck it, but she was imprisoned by the chair. His hand caught the side of her head so hard that for an instant the cabin went black. Before she recovered, another blow to the head followed. Instinctively, she tried to escape, pushing herself up out of the chair, only to be driven back into it by another clout. Covering her head with her arms, she cried, "Eban, for God's sake, stop! I have done nothing!"

"Nothing?" he screamed. "You whore around, humiliate me, and say you have done nothing?" He continued to rain blows about her head and shoulders.

Propelled by terror, Vianna kicked and clawed her way past Eban's heavy body and made for the companionway, but he caught her at the cabin door and pullled her back, ripping her dress off one shoulder in the struggle. With a hoarse cry, he reached for her breast, which was now visible beneath the thin fabric of her summer shift. Grasping it cruelly, he made animallike sounds, then with both hands tore her dress from her body with three powerful jerks. He knocked her to the deck and began pulling off his pants. When Vianna scrambled to her knees and tried to regain her feet, he kicked her. She fell back. Immediately, he flung himself upon her. The next instant she felt a fiery pain as he entered her. She screamed and tried to roll away, but he was too heavy. In five thrusts he reached his climax, jerking and groaning atop her.

With a smothered cry of revulsion, Vianna was able to push him off. She rose painfully, her groin on fire. Her one thought was to flee. Once more she made for the companionway, and once more Eban caught her before she got out of the cabin. He was sobbing, his gaunt face contorted with hate, as he began to beat her again.

"She-devil! You tricked me! You've smeared me with your foulness!" Naked from the waist down, he was using his arms, fists, the flat of his hands as weapons to pummel her. She stumbled backward, trying to avoid the blows. His fist caught her jaw, and oblivion provided her with a means of escape.

Regaining consciousness a few minutes later, she found herself on the deck of the cabin. Eban was gone. Her body felt as if it were one vast bruise. Groggily she managed to sit up. The candlelit cabin swam before her eyes. She sat very still for a while, then, physically aching, emotionally numbed, she managed to stand up and make her way unsteadily to the sleeping cabin. Removing the tattered remains of her dress, she longed for water with which to wash herself. Not only was her groin still burning, but in addition she felt defiled. Eban's bestial taking of her had borne no resemblance to the act of love she had experienced with Tom.

Hysteria threatened to sweep over her. She struggled to hold it at bay. They were only a few hours out of Govans Harbor. Maybe Eban would take her back. Their marriage had been a mistake. He must have believed he had forgiven her for breaking their engagement and wounding his pride, but he hadn't. He despised her. They could never manage to live together for three or four years in the tiny enclosed world of the *Trident*. It was not too late for him to take her back home.

Once the solution had occurred to her, she couldn't wait for him to return to the cabin so that she could broach the subject. She pulled herself off the bed, threw her cloak over her nightgown, and went stiffly up the companionway. As she stepped out on the deck she was struck for an instant by the beauty of the night. Overhead, through the sails, she could see the stars, looking so much closer and more numerous than they had from the land, and off to larboard the moon shone with serene purity. How incongruous that a night that had produced such horror for her should be so beautiful!

The man at the helm murmured a polite greeting.

"Where is Captain Stanbro?" she asked. She wondered how much he had heard of the violent scene that had taken place below.

"Taking some exercise, ma'am. He was up by the mainmast a minute ago."

Vianna thanked him and went forward. She found Eban standing at the larboard rail, smoking his pipe and staring at the wide silver streak the moon painted on the water. Roughened by the choppy water, the streak had the appearance of hammered pewter. He started visibly when she came up to him. "Get below!" he ordered, his voice tight.

She had approached him trembling inside, but his command killed her fear, replacing it with an icy steadiness. "Don't use that tone with me. I'm not one of your common seamen."

"I said get below!" he hissed, threateningly.

"Or you'll what? Hit me and let all the watch see you do it?" She glanced pointedly around. The crewmen on watch were plainly visible. The deck was too small to provide much privacy, even at night. If they kept their voices low enough, however, they could not be heard. "I've come to ask you to take me back home. You won't waste more than a day or two of time, and we can tell everyone that I get seasick even in calm water and can't go with you."

"I'm not taking you home." He jammed his pipe back in his mouth and stared off across the water.

"But why? Our marriage was a mistake. You can't deny that now. You don't love me. It would be folly for us to try to live together for three or four years on this ship. It will be like a prison for both of us."

He blew a large puff of smoke slowly into the darkness. "Our marriage was not a mistake."

She regarded his profile, dour-looking even in silhouette, and was swept by hatred so intense it thickened her voice as she said, "Surely after what you have just done to me you aren't going to claim that you love me?"

He gave an ugly laugh. "I played that role to perfection, didn't I? Everyone saw me as the besotted fiancé who was willing to take you back despite the humiliation you had dealt me." He puffed on his pipe a few times to keep it going. "Well, I got what I wanted, and making a fool of myself was worth it. You're going to pay for humiliating me, and you're going to learn that immorality does not go unpunished, either."

Appalled, she asked, "You mean you married me so you could punish me?"

He turned a ghastly smile upon her. "For the rest of your life, Vianna."

She stared at him, her eyes wide. He couldn't be serious! Through stiff lips, she begged, "Take me back home, Eban, please."

"For the rest of your life," he repeated, then started aft, leaving her alone.

She steadied herself against the rail, feeling faint. It had all been pretense on his part, a diabolical plan to marry her so that he could wreak vengeance on her for rejecting him in favor of Tom. A shudder shook her aching body. She was trapped, a virtual prisoner of a man who could do anything he wanted to her. Eban reigned supreme here. No one dared question his behavior or challenge his decisions. What crewman would risk his captain's ire by protesting Eban's treatment of his wife? Aware of her complete helplessness, she made her way dully back to the cabin. She hung up her cloak and got into bed, pulling the covers over her shivering body.

When Eban came down sometime later, Vianna tensed, pretending to be asleep. He came in, used the water closet, and undressed. Watching him warily all the while through slitted lids, she was swept by revulsion at the sight of his white, lumpy body. A moment later he blew out the candle he had placed on the washstand and got into bed beside her. Lying there still as death, Vianna waited for an assault of one kind or another. None came. He turned his back to her and a moment later began to snore.

Sleep, when it finally came to her, was more like the loss of consciousness she had experienced following Eban's blow to her jaw than normal repose.

Awakening the next morning, she would have believed the beatings and rape had been a nightmare, had it not been for the pain that suffused her body. The place beside her was empty. On the bulkhead opposite the porthole above her head, a circle of sunshine lit the painted boards. Behind the bulkhead at the head of the bed she heard the steward stirring in his pantry. Uninterested in breakfast, too weak and listless to leave the bed, she didn't get up, and Eban didn't call her.

She lay there suffering an acute case of homesickness. What wouldn't she give to be magically transported back to Govans Harbor! If only she were lying in her own bed, listening to her mother fixing breakfast downstairs. At the thought of her mother, her breath caught on a dry sob. She longed to be able to bury her face against that warm bosom, feel those loving arms around her, and hear that soft voice assuring her that everything was going to be all right and she no longer had anything to fear. She rubbed her cheek against the pillow in an agony of despair. Those days were gone forever, and the future looked so black she wanted to die. Her throat ached with unshed tears, but she discovered that she was too miserable to weep. *I want to go home,* she cried silently, knowing it was not possible.

Later she heard Eban enter the day cabin. A rustle of paper told her he was at his desk. He did not come into the sleeping cabin until shortly before noon. He was coatless, his checkered shirt with its wide collar was well starched, and his canvas pants were loose about his hips and legs. His expression when he looked at her was remote. "Get dressed and fetch some fresh water so that I can wash before dinner."

That was all. He turned and went back to his desk.

Vianna sensed that she should not tarry. The task of getting out of bed wrenched several groans from her. She went to the clothes cupboard and pulled down the first dress her hand encountered. Dressing was a painful ordeal that she accomplished as quickly as possible. The scrimshaw combs that she always wore in her hair had fallen out during her struggle with Eban. She went into the day cabin to retrieve them and found them lying on the floor near the chair she had been occupying. Eban did not look up. As she picked them up, she asked quietly, "Where do I go to fill the pitcher?"

"To the scuttlebutt. From now on, see to it I always have fresh water to wash with." He delivered the instructions still without looking at her.

She returned to the sleeping cabin, combed her hair at the mirror above the washstand, and left to fetch the water. As she stepped on deck, she noted that most of the sails had been set to take advantage of the fair wind. The *Trident* was rushing away from the North American coast as fast as it could go, holding to a southeastern course that would bring it within a month to Cape St. Roque, the easternmost tip of South America. It would be another month or more after that before they would round Cape Horn and run any chance of meeting her father. For a moment she felt faint with terror at what those two months might hold. Her stagger backward against the housing of the companionway drew an apprehensive look from the man at the helm only a few feet away. "Careful, ma'am! It takes time to get used to a rolling deck."

She thanked him and made her way forward, past the booby hatch, past the mainmast, past the brick tryworks that would reduce the whale blubber to valuable oil, all the way to the foremast, where she found the barrel of fresh water beside the forecastle hatch, aware every step of the way of the curious glances of the watch who were unaccustomed to seeing a woman aboard, especially one who invaded the crew's section of the ship on an errand usually performed by a cabin boy. Vianna wondered if any hint of what happened last night in the cabin had filtered up to the forecastle. It was possible that the mates who had not had the watch might have heard something. More than likely they had not suspected the truth even if they had. They might have attributed the commotion to the shocked struggle of a virgin bride against the sexual advances of her new husband.

As she reached the scuttlebutt, one of the crew drew apart from the small group working near the windlass. "I'll fill that pitcher for you, ma'am." It was Bobby Howard, her cousin Joseph's good friend.

The ship chandler's son was well on the way to being a good-sized man, broad through the chest, long of leg. A square jaw and curly blond hair lent him an attractiveness that could not fail to win him any feminine heart he set out to conquer once he returned to Govans Harbor. At home he had addressed her as Vianna. They were, after all, only a year apart in age and had known each other all their lives. The distance that separated the quarterdeck from the forecastle was far greater than the one hundred feet of deck between them, however, and Bobby Howard had already learned that protocol demanded that he now address her as "Ma'am."

"Thank you, Bobby." The sight of a familiar face was cheering. "How do you like the life of a sailor so far?" she asked as he dipped water from the barrel.

"I scarcely know a jib from a mainsail, but I'm learning fast. Mr. Orne is quick with a kick if you don't understand a command or are slow to obey."

The brutality of the apelike third mate came as no surprise to Vianna.

"We're sure to have some rough weather one of these days, and then I'll see how good a sailor I am." As he grinned at her, a voice roared, "Back to work, Howard! This ain't no blasted tea party! Jump!"

"Aye, aye, sir!" Bobby Howard thrust the full pitcher into Vianna's hands, banged the top back down on the barrel, and sprang to his task.

Mason Orne was heading for the forecastle, probably to reinforce his verbal command with another kick, when Vianna passed him on her way back to the cabin. His small dark eyes looked through her as if she didn't exist. Poor Bobby, she thought. How unfortunate to have drawn this third mate's watch his first time at sea. If Eban continued to beat her, the two of them would have more in common than their hometown.

When she received no beating that day or the next, she began to be encouraged. Eban's attitude toward her was that of a master toward a servant. He ignored her except when he wanted something.

Eban scarcely even looked at her for the first two days after he thrashed and raped her. On the third night she caught him staring at her as she read in the day cabin. Her blood ran cold, and she didn't comprehend a word of what she read for the next hour. However, when they went to bed he lay beside her without touching her, as usual.

His stares became more frequent during the next few days, but not once did he lay a hand on her. His baleful glares frightened her, but when they did not lead to any further violence, Vianna allowed herself to hope that he had decided not to beat her any more.

They had been married exactly one week when, upon retiring, he did not begin snoring soon after as he invariably did. It was obvious from his rapid breathing that he was still awake. Vianna lay very still, trying not to call attention to herself, hoping that his sleep-lessness had nothing to do with her. Suddenly he gave a gasping groan, hurling himself upon her and tearing at her nightgown.

Trying to capture his hands, Vianna exclaimed, "Eban, there's no need to force me! I won't refuse you."

This brought not a change of tactics on his part, but a string of epithets as his hands grew so cruel she cried out and tried to evade them. It was impossible. Pinned beneath his body, she clawed at his head, his shoulders. Oblivious to her raking nails, he forced her thighs apart and lunged into her. She screamed. The next moment it was over. His orgasm paralyzed him briefly. Seeing her chance, Vianna shoved him off her and scrambled out of the bed to fumble in the dark for a light. The candle she found on the washstand, the matches on Eban's desk. As the day cabin sprang to light, she saw Eban standing in the door in his nightshirt, his face livid with rage and scratched by her nails. He was not alone in his fury, however. "We are going to talk, Eban," Vianna declared. "I will not be abused in this way."

"Vile creature!" He spat the words at her. "You deserve every blow. You are depraved. You know I would not befoul myself with you so long as I'm in control of my senses." He started for her. "So you flaunt your body before me until I lose all reason!"

The instant he started toward her, Vianna ran for the door. She made it to the foot of the companionway outside the day cabin before he caught up with her and pulled her back. She screamed. "Help, someone! Please!" He dragged her into the cabin, slamming the door shut behind him. A kick in the backside drove her facedown onto the deck. She screamed again. Another kick caught her in the ribs. Such blows held no satisfaction for Eban, however. He wanted to feel her flesh smash beneath his hands. He hauled her to her feet and set about pummeling her in every area of her body. Vianna had not left off screaming, realizing she was powerless to protect herself against his superior strength and knowing her only chance of rescue lay in attracting the attention of one of the mates. Their cabins were only a few yards away.

She was blocking blows to her face with her arms when someone knocked on the door. "Help me, please!" she screamed. Eban paid no attention to the knocking, grunting with sadistic pleasure each time his blows connected with her flesh.

"Captain! Open up!"

Ducking and weaving, Vianna continued to scream.

"Open up, Captain, or I'm coming in!"

With a curse, Eban lunged for the door and flung it open. George McAndrews, the second mate, stood there, a frightened but determined look on his thin, boyish face. Vianna screamed, "Get me out of here!" and tried to push past Eban, but his doughy body effectively blocked her.

At the apparition of Eban in his nightshirt, his face crisscrossed with scratches, and Vianna looking like a madwoman with her hair flying wildly about her head, the expression on George McAndrews's face turned to one of horror. Whatever exclamation it was he made was drowned out by Eban's roar, "Mr. Vickers!"

The words were scarcely out of his mouth before the first mate emerged from his cabin, his dark hair freed from the blue band that usually secured it. "Aye, sir." It was obvious he had heard the whole thing but had chosen not to interfere.

"Put this man in irons!" Eban bellowed. "He is to be flogged in the morning!"

"Aye, sir. Come along," he said firmly to McAndrews.

"But he's beating her," the second mate protested, "just as he must have been doing before!"

"It's none of our affair," Abner Vickers said gruffly. Grasping the second mate's arm, he led him, still protesting, up the companionway.

Eban slammed the door, turning to confront Vianna

with a murderous glare. "The next time you scream or call for help, I'll have *you* flogged. There is no way you can escape your punishment. Now go to bed. Get out of my sight."

She obeyed because she had no choice. She was a prisoner of a jailer whose strength she couldn't match. But physical strength wasn't everything. Next time he came at her, she would be prepared.

While she lay sleepless, she planned her defense. A knife was the smallest, most easily hidden weapon she could think of. Also the most effective. Tomorrow she would steal one from the steward's pantry. When at last Eban came to bed, she squeezed herself against the bulkhead to avoid any contact with him, hatred like a sickness in her stomach.

8

George McAndrews was flogged the following morning as Eban had ordered. Vianna was forced to stand beside Eban on the quarterdeck and watch the poor wretch's raw flesh quiver beneath the lashes delivered by the first mate. The entire crew had been mustered to witness it. By then everyone knew what had happened, and as they listened to the screams that finally tore their way out of the second mate's throat, they absorbed the message they were meant to receive. Anyone who interfered with the captain's personal affairs could expect the same punishment.

Vianna tried to tune out the cries and blind herself to the cruel spectacle that made her own painfully bruised ribs and buttocks trivial in comparison. When McAndrews was led, sobbing, to the forecastle hatch, Eban announced to the crew that the second mate was relieved of his rank and would henceforth serve as a common seaman. Mason Orne was elevated from third to second mate and Devin Farley, an experienced seaman, was appointed to take Orne's former office. At the conclusion of this grim ceremony, the first mate ordered the watch on duty to work and dismissed the other two. Eban set out for a stroll about the quarterdeck. Vianna assumed that she, too, was dismissed, and went below. She made straight for the sleeping cabin, made the bed, then sat down upon it, listening to the sounds the steward made on the other side of the bulkhead as he cleaned up the remains of breakfast in his pantry and prepared for dinner.

It was some time before the sounds ceased. When they did, Vianna waited for a little while before heading for the mess. She was stopped at the cabin door by the sound of voices and some thumps. George McAndrews's gear was being moved out, and the new third mate's gear was being moved into the cabin shared by the two lesser mates. When all grew quiet again, Vianna opened the door cautiously and stepped into the mess. The door to the companionway was open, as was that to Mr. Vickers's cabin. The first mate, however, was not in it. The door to the other cabin was closed. Vianna hurried toward the pantry, determination stronger by far than her fear of having her errand discovered.

The pantry, like the galley up on the main deck, was incredibly small. Accustomed to her mother's kitchen and the even larger one at the Sawtells', Vianna marveled that anyone could cook in and serve a meal from these tiny spaces. Finding a knife was easy. She opened the only drawer there was, and there, among the table silver, were the sharp knives. She took the smallest one, hid it in the folds of her skirt, and left the pantry. Still no one in sight. She had nearly reached the cabin when the door to the second and third mates' cabin was thrown open and Mason Orne's apelike bulk loomed within it. Whether he had heard her and was curious to see who was moving about the mess or whether he was on his way somewhere she could not tell. He gave her his usual hostile stare. Either he disliked all women or he disliked having a woman aboard ship. It could not be any personal antagonism, because they had been complete strangers until they met at the supper table the first night at sea.

Vianna said dryly, "Congratulations, Mr. Orne, on your promotion."

Less inclined than ever to show her even minimum respect now that he was aware of Eban's abuse of her, he made no reply, watching malevolently as she opened the door to the day cabin and disappeared inside.

Shrugging off the second mate's unfriendly behavior, Vianna hid the knife in one of her shoes that sat at the bottom of the clothes cupboard in the sleeping cabin. That task completed, she closed the cupboard door and took a deep breath. Next time Eban felt the urge to thrash and rape her, the odds would be a bit more even.

By late afternoon all thought of defending herself had fled. Earlier the breeze had increased, the ship had lain over to it, and even Vianna, who had escaped the depressing confines of the cabin to take some exercise on the main deck, could see that the clouds contained wind. She wondered if she and Bobby Howard were going to have a chance to see whether they were good sailors or not. When spray began to fly over the forecastle, Mr. Vickers ordered the royal halyards to be sent over to windward and the mizzen royal furled.

Giving up her walk, Vianna made for the cabin. As she passed the galley, the cook was already preparing supper, a sure sign he was expecting rough seas.

During the customary silent supper in the officers' mess, Vianna heard the mate on watch shout an order above the wind to take in the royals. By the time the meal was over, the plates were sliding about the table and Vianna's stomach was queasy. Within the hour she had lost her supper and was still making regular visits to the water closet. Finally, too sick to get up and go to it, she set the washbasin beside the bed and lay in abject misery as the ship pitched into the heavy head sea, which struck the bow so hard she could hear the thunderous blows where she lay in the stern. The ship worked hard, groaning and creaking, while the wind roared through the rigging. There was a constant shout of orders from the deck. All hands had been called up. Eban was on the quarterdeck, piloting his vessel by means of orders given to the first mate, who passed them to the crew.

The storm with its driving rain lasted for two days. In all that time Vianna made no attempt to get out of bed. Even had she not been ill, she doubted that she could have stayed on her feet with the ship pitching and rolling so violently.

During the third night the wind went down. Eban, who had taken sleep in snatches on the sofa, came to bed and was asleep almost immediately. Vianna lay awake, enjoying the relief of possessing a steady stomach once more. However, when she saw the huge chunk of salt beef and ship biscuit the steward set out for breakfast the next morning, her budding appetite was dampened.

The steward noticed her wary look at the salty beef. "Best thing in the world for the stomach, ma'am, after a bout of seasickness."

Eban shot him a threatening look, and John Colby shuffled arthritically back to his pantry.

Vianna discovered that the steward was right. She felt like a new woman after downing some of the leathery beef and one or two hard biscuits. In fact, she asked John Colby later in the morning for another piece of the salt beef and gnawed on it the rest of the day.

On her walk that morning around the deck, she encountered Bobby Howard, who, with the rest of the watch, was replacing some of the standing rigging that had been weakened by the strains put upon it during the storm. The new third mate had Bobby's watch now, and it was plain from the way he issued his orders that he was not the brutal taskmaster Mason Orne was. Vianna greeted Bobby with a smile, asking, "How did you weather the gale?"

He grinned through the beginnings of a blond beard. "Badly, ma'am. I've never been so sick. But cook told me that beef and biscuit would put me right again, and it has." He sobered. "And you, ma'am? How are you faring?"

Suddenly her throat tightened and she could only shake her head in reply.

His eyes flashed with impotent rage. "You can be sure I'll be sending a letter home the first chance I get."

"Yes, do that." Maybe it would bring help. "I'm sure my letters will be censored."

Putting aside protocol for the moment and speaking as one who had known her all her life, he said, "I wish there were more I could do for you, Vianna."

"Thanks, Bobby. It's a comfort to have you on this ship." She'd have liked to talk with him longer, but it wouldn't do to test the tolerance of the new third mate too far. She moved on.

Within a week, Eban's desire had built to the point of explosion again. Vianna saw it coming—the stares, the increased hostility. She braced herself and waited, determined to fight him off this time with the aid of the hidden knife.

His passion erupted one night, and with it his fury. She was reading in the cabin, and he had been on deck ever since supper. She heard him coming down the companionway, and a moment later he came striding into the cabin, slamming the door behind him. He made for her, emitting a curious growling sound that articulated finally in the words, "Damn your eyes!"

By that time she was out of her chair and scrambling in the clothes cupboard for the knife. But where was it? She shook the shoe she had hidden it in. Not there. She shook the other. Not there, either. She managed to shake the extra pair of Eban's shoes that sat there, too, before he reached her and yanked her to her feet by her hair. Jerking her head from side to side with such force that the world spun around her, he snarled, "You thought to escape your punishment by attacking me, did you? Do you take me for a fool? You try anything like that again and I'll have you keelhauled like some mutinous seaman!"

She struck out as well as she could with hands and feet as he raped her, then beat her in a fury over his own weakness. The damage she did to him was as nothing compared to the punishment he dealt out to her. When his rage at last abated, he threw her back down on the bed and towered menacingly over her.

"Remember what I said. I will have you flogged, keel-hauled, or anything else I wish if you attempt another attack on me. And it will afford me the greatest of pleasure." Delivered of that threat, he shoved her over against the bulkhead, took his place in bed beside her, and dropped immediately off to sleep.

Unable to bear his nearness, Vianna got up, took an extra blanket from the drawer underneath the bed, and moved to the sofa. There was no doubt that Eban had the power to do anything to her he pleased so long as she was on this ship, and now that the crew had seen what would happen to any one of them who tried to interfere where she was concerned, she couldn't count on any of them to come to her defense. The knife had seemed like a good idea, but what if she had managed to wound him? She shuddered at the thought of what his punishment of her might have been. Killing him had never been her intention, but she realized that if she resorted a second time to using a weapon, she'd have to. Otherwise there would be no escaping his terrible retribution. Dear God, she could kill no one, not even Eban! There had to be some other way.

When Eban found her on the sofa the next morning, he said nothing, and from then on she did not lie in the bed except when he raped her or when he was absent from the cabin.

It was clear to Vianna that there was no haven, no hope of rescue for her on board Eban's ship. She would have to get off it. Eban had said he would take her to Lahaina so she could have her baby in the hospital there, but that was months in the future. The thought of the beatings she would have to endure if she waited that long was intolerable. Sooner or later Eban would have to put into some port for fresh water and provisions. She might be able to escape then, or perhaps gamming would offer her an opportunity. This exchange of visits to one another's ships by captains among the whaling fleet provided them with a fairly active social life, as well as a means of exchanging news of home, of other vessels, or of the movements of the whales. Since leaving Govans Harbor, Eban had deliberately avoided other ships. If one was sighted on the horizon, he ordered the *Trident*'s course changed. Yet he could not evade them forever. Once they rounded Cape Horn and began hunting the whale grounds, they would encounter other whaling vessels. It was unthinkable that a captain would refuse to gam. Eban could not do so without arousing suspicions. Of course he could make excuses for not inviting other captains aboard his ship, thus preventing any contact between herself and them, and she fully expected him to do this. He would visit the other ships instead. But in order to gam, whalers drew close to one another and lay to while one captain was rowed to the other ship for a visit. Once the *Trident* was within shouting distance of a vessel, Vianna meant to scream for help and beg its captain for sanctuary.

She was napping one day after dinner when she was awakened by a pounding at the door. She hurried to it and upon opening it found the carpenter on the other side with a small supply of tools at his feet. "I thought someone was knocking," she said in surprise. Then, noticing the man's sheepish expression, she inquired, "What are you doing?"

The carpenter, whom everyone called "Chips," was approaching middle age. He was a tall, thin man with knobby hands. Vianna had never seen him without the knitted blue wool cap on his head. "Captain's orders, ma'am. I'm to put this bolt on the door." He pointed to a contraption of wood and metal he must have made at his bench aft of the tryworks and was now installing.

"Whatever for?" Vianna asked, although a suspicion was beginning to dawn on her.

The carpenter ducked his head and replied, "You'll have to ask the captain, ma'am."

"I certainly will." She brushed past him and went immediately up to the main deck. She found Eban at the carpenter's bench, smoking his pipe and idly examining the assorted tools that lay about. "Why are you having a bolt put on the cabin door?" she demanded.

He picked up a drill and tested the sharpness of the bit. "I would think that would be obvious."

"Beating me is not enough, is that it? You're going to keep me locked up in the cabin, too?"

"Not all of the time." The breeze carried the smoke from his pipe back into Vianna's face. She didn't think she would be able to tolerate the smell of a pipe again if she ever got off this ship. He dropped the bit and pushed some other tools around testily. "You cannot be trusted. I will not have you trying to escape when we meet another ship."

"Trusted! You make it sound as if I would be committing some crime if I tried to escape being beaten and raped by you."

"Shut your mouth!" He peered around as if afraid someone might have overheard.

"Why? Everyone aboard knows you beat me." She glanced sharply at him. "Or is it the rape you don't want them to know about? That's it, isn't it? You don't want anyone on board knowing you are intimate with me. My God, Eban, you are sick!"

He raised his hand as if to strike her with the wrench he held. His face was purple.

"Captain, there's a school of porpoise up ahead. Oh, I'm sorry, sir, I thought you were alone." It was Mr. Vickers, and he knew very well Vianna was with Eban. She had seen him coming toward them from the stern. He had spoken up to save her from the blow Eban was about to deliver. "I thought we might put out some lines and catch some for supper, sir."

"Go ahead," Eban growled. He threw the wrench back on the worktable. When the first mate had moved out of earshot, he declared with barely contained fury, "It's you who are sick, sick with corruption! Any moral man would be ashamed to have been seduced by a woman like you. But I won't be again, so you needn't try." He spun on his heel and strode away from her.

She stared after him. How could his mind have grown so twisted? She recalled his prudish behavior during their courtship. There had been something wrong with him even then, just as she suspected. Her rejection of him, her love affair with Tom, had apparently heightened his revulsion of his own sexual appetite because it was focused on a woman he considered depraved. One could have pitied him if he weren't such a monster.

With the bolt attached to the outside of the cabin door, Vianna knew she would be locked in the minute they came upon another vessel. She wouldn't be able to plead for help; she would never even see another captain. But everyone else aboard the *Trident* would. After considering the matter for a few days, she decided to ask Bobby Howard to help her.

Except when pursuing whales, a captain and his first mate were seldom, if ever, absent from the ship at the same time. That meant one of the other mate's boats would be used to row Eban to gam with another captain. As part of the third mate's watch, Bobby was assigned to his boat. Sooner or later it would take its turn carrying Eban on his social call, its crew also going aboard to visit their counterparts in the forecastle of the other vessel. She approached Bobby with her plan as soon as she had it carefully thought out. He was just coming down from the lookout when she came up on deck that morning. There was little chance a whale would be sighted before they rounded the Horn and entered the Pacific; nevertheless, lookouts were posted on every whaler almost as soon as a ship left its home port.

Vianna headed for the scuttlebutt, pitcher in hand, certain that Bobby would come up to speak to her. In fact, he was there before her, getting a drink. They were nearing the equator, and it was very hot. He scratched his blond beard as if it itched. The remainder of the watch were working far enough away at their tasks that Vianna was assured of some privacy for her talk with the ship chandler's son, who greeted her warmly and offered to fill the pitcher for her.

Despite the new third mate's more lenient attitude toward his watch, Vianna knew she must waste no time. Nor did she want to arouse anyone's suspicions that this conversation was anything more than her usual exchange of friendly words with the boy from her hometown.

"I intend to get off this ship, but I'll need help," she began at once. "I have figured out a way with almost no risk. Can I count on you?"

He spilled most of the water down the sides of the pitcher as he tipped the dipper, even forgetting to address her as "Ma'am" in his agitation. "You know I'd help you if I could, Vianna, but I daren't. I'd be flogged for sure."

"Only if someone found out, and they won't, I promise you that. There's no way anyone will be able to connect you with the plan I've figured out." She glanced around the deck. No one was nearby. The mate was aft, talking to the helmsman, and Eban was in the cargo hold with Mr. Vickers. "I'll give you a note, which you will conceal. The first time you row Eban to gam with another captain, take it with you. Leave it in the forecastle of the other vessel, to be found after you've rowed him back to the *Trident*."

Bobby Howard dipped more water up slowly. "Captain Stanbro will know the note had to be carried by one of us who rowed him over."

"But he won't know *which* one. And he can't afford to flog all of you, because you would be in no condition then to man your boat in case a whale was sighted."

He finished filling the pitcher before he said anything. "I'd like to help, but . . . let me think on it for a while." His blue eyes, made vivid by the tropical sun, were troubled within his bearded face.

"Of course. No one knows better than I what I'm asking." She took the pitcher from him and made her way back to the cabin.

Less than a week later, after a particularly bad beating by Eban had left Vianna with a black eye, Bobby Howard motioned her forward of the tryworks as she took her morning exercise on deck. Hidden from the sight of anyone on the quarterdeck, he said, "I'll help you." He avoided looking directly at her, obviously embarrassed by the sight of her bruised eye.

Vianna was certain it was that grim evidence of her plight that had convinced him to take the risk. Gratefully she said, "Someday, somehow, I'll repay you. Here's the note." She had written it immediately after asking Bobby for help and had carried it with her ever since, in case he agreed to her plan. The message read, *Dear Captain, I believe my husband has gone mad. He beats me with such regularity and cruelty that I fear for the life of my unborn child. Should you think it is I who am mad, consider the fact that he will not invite you aboard his ship. He would not give me the opportunity to plead for your help in person. I must get off this ship. Please help me!* She had signed it *Vianna Chadwick Stanbro,* realizing that if it were read by someone who knew her father it would lend a bit more credibility to the astounding message.

She handed the tightly folded piece of paper to Bobby Howard after checking carefully to make certain no one was watching. "When my father hears what you have done for me, he'll do everything he can to advance you in your career with the fleet."

He palmed the note swiftly and then casually scratched his beard as if nothing had happened. His voice was grim, however, as he said, "I could not stand idly by any longer and see you so badly treated." Touching his cap, he turned away and headed for the forecastle.

The *Trident* was drawing very near Cape Horn when

one morning at dawn everyone was surprised to hear the shout, "Ship ahoy!"

Vianna, on the sofa, heard Eban come instantly awake with a furious curse. It was clear what had happened. The lookout must have fallen asleep and another vessel had come up to the *Trident* during the night and was now so close it would be impossible to avoid it. Someone would pay dearly for this negligence that, with luck, would provide a chance for her to escape.

With her breath coming fast and shallow, Vianna kept to the sofa as Eban, his suspenders flopping as he buttoned his shirt, emerged from the sleeping cabin and ran past her. When Vianna heard the bolt drop, she got up and began to dress, praying that the ship would be a whaler, that Eban would be forced to gam, and that the third mate's boat would be the one that rowed him over. She heard Eban, trumpet to mouth, identify himself, and holding her breath, she listened for the reply.

"The *Contest* of New Bedford, Captain Loper, fifty-two months out, twenty-one hundred barrels. Homeward bound!"

Vianna let out a small cry. A whaler it was! On its way to a home port only a short distance from Govans Harbor! *Dear God, let me go with it!*

She could see nothing from either the stern windows over the sofa or from the portholes in the sleeping cabin; but wearing a path between the two, she was at last rewarded by the sight of the other whaler. Through the porthole she saw the *Contest,* lying to off the starboard beam of the *Trident,* looking much like a derelict after more than four years' absence from home. Long rust streaks ran down her sides, and the boats, hanging from their davits, were wanting paint. All hands were topside to greet the *Trident,* their clothes so ragged and patched it was hard to see the original pattern or shape of a shirt or jacket. Yet the most graceful clipper ship couldn't have offered a more delightful appearance to Vianna's eyes.

"I am sorry I cannot invite you aboard, Captain," Eban was shouting. "My wife is accompanying me on this voyage, and she is unwell."

Vianna heard this remark with some surprise. She had known Eban would make some excuse to prevent any other captain from boarding the *Trident,* but she hadn't expected this one. She had assumed he would make no mention of her at all in those situations where he could not avoid gamming.

"My sympathy to your wife, sir, and have your men row you over here. We'll have breakfast together."

"Thank you, Captain."

Vianna bit a knuckle, waiting.

"Mr. Farley, I'll be taking your boat."

She closed her eyes, unable to believe her good fortune. Bobby Howard would be going to the *Contest.* Her note would be delivered. Surely her rescue was only a few hours away! "Collect the mail, Mr. Vickers. I'll be taking that to Captain Loper."

Vianna hadn't tried to write to anyone back home. She knew Eban would not permit her to send a letter that told the truth about her situation, and she couldn't bring herself to write cheerfully as if there were nothing wrong. Eban would not be carrying any letters of hers across to the other ship to be taken to Govans Harbor, but how about letters from the crew? He couldn't censor everyone's letters. She wasn't sure how it could help her if word got back to Govans Harbor about how she was being treated. Yet it would make her feel better to think someone knew.

Eban came below to finish dressing. He pulled Vianna into the sleeping cabin with him, where he could keep an eye on her and prevent her from running up to the deck.

"Are you going to allow me to go to breakfast, or do you plan to keep me locked in?" she asked coolly, watching him pull on his socks and shoes.

For a reply he pounded on the bulkhead that separated the sleeping cabin from the steward's pantry. "Steward!"

"Aye, Captain!"

"Bring Mrs. Stanbro some breakfast. I want it in five minutes."

"Aye, aye, sir!"

It was coffee, cold salt beef, and biscuit. John Colby apologized when he carried it in and set it on the desk. "It's all I could get together in five minutes." His movements were stiff and slow.

"Thank you," Vianna said. "It will do nicely."

Eban followed him out, dropping the bolt into place.

There was nothing to be done but wait. She hadn't really wanted food, but she had discovered that ship biscuit was very good to quiet the queasiness she had in her stomach every morning. Gnawing one, she paced the cabin, too nervous to remain still. Overhead she heard the boat being lowered. The two ships had drifted slightly, and the *Contest* was not visible at the moment. She kept watching, and after a time it swung into view again. By this time Vianna could see the boat. Eban stood of necessity, all the seats being occupied by the oarsmen and the boat steerer. It was a precarious position, for even a calm sea rocks a small boat, yet Eban kept his hands in his pockets, holding to nothing, balancing himself on his straddled legs. Vianna's interest was not in him. It was in Bobby Howard, his broad shoulders reaching forward, then laying back, as he pulled at his oar. Although it was October, it was springtime here in the southern latitudes and he was hatless, his blond hair and beard setting him apart from the rest of the boat crew. Would he leave the note, or would his courage desert him at the last moment? As that thought struck her, Vianna clasped her hands and cried softly, "Please, Bobby! Please!"

She remained at the porthole, watching as Eban and then the crew climbed the Jacob's ladder to the deck of the *Contest*. From what she could see of Captain Loper at this distance, he was a short, rotund man with a salt-and-pepper beard. He had dressed for the occasion and wore a white shirt, tie, and vest beneath his dark jacket. He shook hands with Eban and led him to the cabin. Vianna's eyes followed Bobby Howard as the boat crew were welcomed aboard by the men of the *Contest*. He and the others wandered with interest about the deck, stopping at the scuttlebutt to quench their thirst after the row over, and after a while they were led down to the forecastle for breakfast.

To her dismay, they emerged again after only a few minutes, kids full of salt beef and biscuit in their hands. Obviously they had elected to eat on deck rather than in the forecastle, which was probably stuffy and hot. Had Bobby had time to hide her note? Vianna could make him out easily, sitting on a coil of rope among a group of fellow seamen. She had no doubt that sooner or later the conversation would get around to her. Crews always compared ships and officers. Eban's abuse of her would be a prime bit of gossip to exchange. The *Trident*'s boat crew would feel no restraint about this topic, knowing what was said in the forecastle would never reach Captain Loper. The only thing that would reach him was the note addressed to "Captain" that Bobby Howard had already placed or would secretly place in the crew's quarters. When it was found, it would be delivered to the first mate, who in turn would take it to the captain.

For the next two hours Vianna stood at the porthole or, when the *Contest* drifted out of her sight, paced the cabin. When the cabin grew hot, she threw open the windows, wishing she could open the door to get a cross breeze. She heard Mr. Vickers and Mason Orne come to breakfast, and after them the harpooners. On the *Trident* the daily routine was unbroken.

At last Vianna saw Bobby Howard and the others go over the side and take their places in the whaleboat. Because the *Contest* had been out of Vianna's sight at times, she had no idea whether Bobby had returned to the forecastle on some excuse or not. Eban emerged from the cabin with Captain Loper and stood talking with him for a few minutes before descending to the boat. At once the crew laid to their oars and began to pull him back to the *Trident*. This time Vianna's eyes were not on the boat. They were fixed on the *Contest,* where canvas blossomed swiftly as the ship started for home once again.

Find it! Find it quickly, Vianna prayed. More sail was made, and the vessel's speed increased. Eban no sooner set foot on his own deck than Mr. Vickers sang out the order to make sail. Within thirty minutes the *Contest* was far beyond hailing distance.

Apparently feeling it was safe to let Vianna out of the cabin, Eban came below and unlocked the door. As he entered, she asked, "Had Captain Loper any news of my father?"

"None." Without so much as a glance at her, he threw his coat on the sofa and sat down at his desk.

"But he's been hunting the whale grounds for four years! Surely he's seen my father."

He pulled a chart from the drawer and made no answer. Vianna knew he was lying. In fact she suspected that he'd made a point of finding out where Samuel Chadwick might be so that he could avoid him, but that wouldn't matter, *if* her ruse worked.

She went up on deck and stood at the taffrail, watching the receding *Contest*. Soon now, she urged it silently. She also kept an eye forward, watching Bobby Howard. When she caught sight of him repairing some running rigging at the mainmast, she strolled toward him.

"Good morning, Bobby."

"Good day, ma'am." That, with a faint nod, was all she got. He seemed absorbed in his work.

She made a complete round of the deck, hoping he would give her some sign the second time around that he had accomplished his mission, but when he saw her approaching, he left his task and moved to the other side of the ship to exchange a few words with the mate. It was obvious that he did not want to talk to her, for what reason she could not be sure. She hoped that it was because now that the deed was done, he was playing it safe and avoiding all contact with her. A knot of anxiety formed within her, however. His behavior could be due to the fact that he had changed his mind about helping her and had not delivered the note after all.

She remained on deck, standing in the shade beneath the flat roof that sheltered the helm and the aft portion of the quarterdeck, watching the *Contest* growing smaller and smaller. Surely someone had found her note by now! Why weren't they turning around?

She had to tear herself away to go to dinner, not wanting Eban to develop any suspicions, but as soon as she was finished, she returned to the deck, using the warmth of the cabin as an excuse.

By midafternoon the *Contest* was barely visible on the horizon, and Vianna was certain something had gone wrong. Disappointment was like a drug in her veins, dragging at her, robbing her even of the strength to stand at the rail any longer. She returned to the cabin to find Eban still poring over his charts, probably planning a hunting route that would prevent the *Trident* from meeting her father's ship.

Among the things she had brought on this voyage was a bolt of flannel for baby clothes and diapers. She pulled it out of the drawer beneath the bed and carried it to the mess, where she unrolled it on the table and began cutting some diapers to be hemmed. In her low state of mind, this simple, uncomplicated sewing task was all she had the energy to tackle. Soon, however, she would have to make some gowns for the baby.

She was nearly finished hemming the first one when the cry "Sail ho!" made her jerk. Putting her pricked finger to her mouth, she looked up to see Eban shove away from his desk, glowering at this second unwelcome intrusion of the day.

"Where away?" came the mate's query.

"Astern of us, sir," came the reply from the masthead. "It's the *Contest*. She's turning to come up on us again."

This bit of news drew a curse from Eban. "What the———" He glanced sharply at Vianna as if a sudden thought struck him, but he said nothing and went swiftly up to the deck. Vianna flew to the cabin window. She could see nothing. She ran to the porthole. The sea was empty. Either the *Contest* was off to larboard or it was so far behind them that only the lookout, from his perch high above the deck, could see it.

"Call all hands, Mr. Vickers!" Eban bellowed. "I want this ship in full sail in ten minutes!"

"Aye, aye, sir!"

"Oh, no!" Vianna wailed softly. The *Contest,* filled almost to bursting with its cargo of whale oil, could never catch the still empty *Trident,* even if it, too, put up all its sails. The fact that the other ship was turning to come up to the *Trident* could mean only one thing. Her message had been found and delivered to Captain Loper, and he was coming to rescue her. But he would never make it. When it became evident to him that Eban was running from him, he would give up the chase and turn back toward home.

The temptation to go up on deck and watch the race was almost too strong to deny, yet Vianna realized she must act as if she knew nothing of the *Contest*'s reasons for wanting to come up again to the *Trident*. Eban might suspect the reason had something to do with her, but he could not be sure. She didn't want to give her ruse away, because she would try it again at the first opportunity, providing Bobby Howard would help her a second time. So she remained in the cabin, watching from the windows. A ripple of joy went through her when at last the *Contest* hove into sight.

She cheered it on silently, her muscles as taut as if she were actually pulling it toward her. But although the other ship carried full sail, too, the wind was fair and the *Trident* was lighter by tons, and after two hours, Captain Loper apparently realized the futility of continuing the pursuit. Straining her eyes, Vianna saw the topsails taken in; these were followed by others, and the *Contest* fell back. Within minutes she had dropped below the horizon.

It was over. She had failed. She would remain a prisoner on the *Trident* for who knew how long. Vianna went slowly back to her sewing, awash in hopelessness, but well aware that when Eban came down to supper shortly, he must notice nothing amiss.

She was the object of many pointed stares from Eban that night and the next day. She ignored him, going coolly about her sewing and the rest of her daily routine. It pleased her to see him uncertain about something, especially as concerned her.

When the cry, "Sail ho!" came again the next afternoon, her first feeling was one of anguish that she hadn't gotten another note to Bobby Howard. She hadn't dared risk it. Then the thought occurred to her that maybe the *Contest* had managed to overtake them after all.

"Where away?"

"Two points off the starboard beam."

That couldn't be the *Contest*. Vianna ran to the sleeping cabin, and through the porthole she saw a clipper ship, long and slim, a vision of immaculate whiteness at this distance. Not for the first time Vianna wondered why a man would choose whaling when he could sail on a clipper ship and make it to California quick as a wink, unload, take on new cargo, and be back home in a few months. For clipper ships, even trips to China were short compared to the voyages of whaling ships.

Taking advantage of the fair wind, the clipper was flying under full sail. The *Trident* could not outrun her, but there would be no need. There would be no gamming between the whaler and this merchantman. They belonged to two different worlds. The clippers had been built when gold was discovered in California and speed was their goal, not oil. If this clipper deigned to recognize the presence of the fat, inelegant *Trident,* it would be for an exchange of trumpeted greetings, no more.

As the other ship drew closer, it did appear that they would pass near enough to exchange greetings. Vianna started for the door. Maybe she could slip up on deck without being seen and signal the clipper somehow! She couldn't let it get away without at least making an attempt to communicate her plight! Someone was running down the companionway. She made a dash for the door and collided with Mason Orne.

"No, you don't," he growled, catching her in a crushing grip and trying to push her back into the cabin.

Vianna fought him. It was like struggling with a gorilla, and just as futile. He hurled her through the door, sending her staggering against the desk. Behind her, the door banged closed and the bolt dropped in its slot.

Cursing the second mate for the brute that he was, Vianna ran back to the porthole in the sleeping cabin. Thank heaven Eban hadn't fixed the windows so they couldn't be opened!

The clipper flew across the water toward them. In no time Vianna could read the name, *Starfire,* painted in black letters along her sharply pointed bow. Officers and crew lined the rail, looking as neat as if they had left their home port only hours before. Come closer, she urged them. She couldn't make them hear her if they passed the *Trident* at too great a distance.

"Ship ahoy!" the clipper captain shouted, his voice magnified by a speaking trumpet.

Vianna's eyes scanned the rail. Yes, there he was, holding the trumpet to his mouth.

"The *Starfire* of Boston, Captain Tucker, twenty-two days out. Request permission to come aboard."

Vianna's eyes widened. What on earth!

"The *Trident* of Govans Harbor, Captain Stanbro, fifty-three days out and clean." Eban was stalling. The clipper captain would not be interested in whether he had taken any oil yet, and it was obviously unnecessary to identify himself or his ship, Vianna thought. Captain Tucker knew who he was, and his desire to come aboard was so extraordinary that he had to know there was something wrong on the *Trident*. Vianna's mind made the connection swiftly. The *Contest* had spoken to the *Starfire* as they passed, asking the clipper to do what it had been unable to—catch the *Trident* and investigate.

"My profound regrets," Eban continued, "but I cannot offer you the hospitality of my ship, because of a grave personal problem."

"Would that problem pertain to your wife, sir? A message written by Mrs. Stanbro was delivered to Captain Loper of the *Contest,* asking for help to be taken off your ship."

"My wife is with child," came Eban's reply, "and it has addled her mind."

Vianna gasped. What a lie! She put her face in the open porthole and screamed, "Help me! Get me off this ship! It is my husband who is mad, not me!"

The vessels were too far apart. Vianna's face could not be seen at the small round opening. Nor could her voice carry across the distance between them without a speaking trumpet. Frantically she sought for another means of communication. She ripped a case from a pillow and, thrusting her arm through the porthole, she waved it vigorously.

"I'd like to come aboard and speak with her, Captain Stanbro."

"You will not take my word? You insult me, sir, and you shall not board my vessel."

Vianna waved the white flag wildly, bruising her

arm against the steel rim of the porthole but oblivious
to the pain. Captain Tucker or someone aboard his
ship had to see her signal! They mustn't let Eban bluff
his way out of this situation!

"Captain Stanbro, someone is signaling from a stern
porthole. I must insist you let me come aboard your
ship."

Encouraged, Vianna tried to signal more vigorously.

"Be off with you!" Eban roared. "Let me get about
my business. My owners have hired me to catch whales,
not to stand about discussing the condition of my poor,
mad wife! Mr. Vickers, furl the royals."

"No!" Vianna cried. The effect of this order would
reduce the speed of the *Trident,* increasing the distance
between the two ships and cutting off communication.
She couldn't let the *Starfire* get away! Pulling in her
arm, Vianna dropped the pillowcase and dashed to the
cabin door, pushing against it with all her might. She
had to get out! She couldn't let the clipper sail away!
Sobbing with frustration, she beat upon the door,
screaming for John Colby, for anyone, to let her out.
Rescue was so close. If only she could get back on deck,
she'd throw herself in the water and try to swim to the
Starfire.

The door refused to budge. The chair was bolted to
the floor. She couldn't use it as a battering ram. She
ran back to the sleeping cabin and stood on the bed,
but there was no use trying to squeeze through the
porthole. It was much too small. Just in the few minutes she had been at the door, the *Trident* had fallen
so far behind the *Starfire* that Vianna could no longer
see the clipper. Her captain would not take in sail.
Her owners counted on a quick turnaround in cargo for
their investment. At any rate, Captain Tucker had done
all he could. Boarding the *Trident* by force would be
an act of piracy, no matter what the reason.

Vianna sank to the bed, sobbing wildly. Escape had
been so near! She might not get another chance! She
would die on this ship! And so would her baby!

She was still lying there crying when Eban burst into the cabin. "Whore! Slut! You tried to trick me again, did you?" Something came down across her back with such stinging force that she screamed. Twisting and rolling away, she saw a three-foot length of black whalebone in Eban's hand. He was flipping the flexible bone with such force that it sang as it whipped through the air.

The beating that followed was far worse than any she had received so far. Her screams fell to moans as her strength ebbed. When at last he left off, panting and wheezing above her, she was barely conscious. Apparently this was strictly punishment for her escape attempt, because he did not rape her, leaving her instead and going back up on deck.

It was several days before she recovered enough to go topside. When she did, she carried a new note and slipped it to Bobby Howard, who accepted it grimly when he saw the bruises on her face and neck.

Eban, however, managed to evade every ship that poked a sail above the horizon. Two weeks after their encounter with the *Starfire,* they arrived at Cape Horn. The weather had worsened as they drew near this treacherous spot where the Atlantic and Pacific winds and waters met, then calmed for two days, giving them a quiet Sunday. On Monday morning the wind was light, but by noon it had freshened, and shortly before sundown, Vianna heard the cry, "All hands ahoy!" A moment later one of the crew yelled, "Here comes Cape Horn!" She had been dreading this most dangerous stretch of the voyage, yet she went up on deck to see what they were heading into.

She found the crew hauling down and clewing up as a large black cloud rolled toward them from the southwest. She stood at the bulwarks amidships, staying out of the way, watching the men at their work, until the sea became so heavy that the bow was plunging into it. By the time she had made her way aft to the quarterdeck, the whole forward part of the vessel was awash with water. As she went down the companionway, she felt the ship straining against the head sea and heard the order shouted to double-reef the topsails. The next moment a squall of sleet and hail struck, clattering on the deck over her head and peppering the stern and starboard windows. The deck of the cabin began to pitch so sharply that Vianna wondered how the men could retain their balance as they worked. She couldn't. She was hurtled from one end of the cabin to the other until she reached the sleeping cabin, where she lay down. Despite the fact that her head was first below her feet, then above them, she did not get seasick. Her stomach had become accustomed to constant movement, apparently even violent motion.

The storm raged all night. Vianna kept to the bed, and when Eban came down, he slept on the couch fully clothed. Just after sunrise the next morning, the wind went down. Going up on deck for a few breaths of fresh air, Vianna found it covered with several inches of snow. With the abatement of the wind the sails were hoisted again, and the ship stood up to her course.

Early that afternoon the wind freshened once more, turned into a gale, and they had a repeat of the past twenty-four hours, but with the storm raging even more ferociously. In fact, the ship creaked and groaned as if it were being pulled apart, frightening Vianna to the point where she started up the companionway to seek reassurance from Eban. That he might be furious with her for bothering him while he fought to prevent his ship from being sunk didn't deter her. She *had* to know that they would survive.

As she pushed open the hatch door, sleet stung her face. Staggering, she pulled her cloak more tightly about her. Eban was standing with the first mate beside the helmsman, protected only a bit by the narrow roof running from the cabin across to the galley and bosun's locker on the starboard side. "Are we going down?" Vianna cried.

Eban was shouting to Mr. Vickers, and if he heard or saw her, he gave no sign. As the bow dived deeply into a huge sea, Mr. Vickers, holding to the binnacle with his legs spread wide apart, yelled, "Let them cut it loose, sir. I don't think a man can hang on out there."

The argument must have started before Vianna reached the deck, because Eban bellowed, "Give him the order or I'll send you out there to do it!"

The first mate rubbed the back of his neck as if in great anguish. "Howard, lay out there and furl the jib!"

Several of the crew turned toward the quarterdeck to make sure they had heard correctly. Bobby Howard, his head covered by an oiled cap, his blond beard running water, was clinging to a shroud, struggling with some sleet-coated rigging. When he heard the order, he too looked aft. In the premature twilight created by the storm, his face went as yellow as his beard. Beyond him, Vianna saw the bow of the ship bury itself in the sea again. The bowsprit, to which Bobby Howard had been ordered, disappeared deep into the ugly water and with it the sail he was being sent to furl. Yet sailors did not disobey orders. It was a matter of pride to them to perform the most dangerous of tasks without so much as a grumble, and if it resulted in a close brush with death, they carried on as if it weren't worth commenting upon.

Yet Vianna sensed that this was different. Why had Eban designated Bobby specifically for this perilous job? Did he suspect something? Know something? Surely it wasn't possible he had found out that Bobby was a partner in her conspiracy to escape the *Trident*. She quelled the urge to cry out a protest to Eban, realizing that if he had a suspicion that would confirm it. Besides, she was too unknowledgeable about the technical workings of a ship, despite the fact that she was a captain's daughter, to know for certain that Eban was giving Bobby Howard a command that was impossible to execute.

They all watched, eyes squinted against the driving sleet, as Bobby went forward, his body bent against the wind. The rest of the crew followed, and as the ship chandler's son sprang between the knightheads out upon the bowsprit, they hauled the jib down. The great triangular sail went flying off to leeward, whipping against Bobby, whose feet were on the footropes. Vianna could see him holding on desperately to the spar in an effort not to be thrown off the boom.

"Keep her off," Mr. Vickers warned the helmsman. "Haul down the staysail!" he yelled to the crew. "Quick! All hands! Save the boom."

Amid the mad rush to keep the boom from snapping, the *Trident* plunged once more into a huge sea. The boom, the bowsprit, and Bobby Howard disappeared as the wave paused high above their heads then came crashing down, with a volume of water that threatened to wash everything overboard. The men in the lee scuppers were in water up to their waists. Vianna clung to the doorframe of the companionway, speechless with terror, unable to believe the rest of the ship would not follow the bow into the sea, never to rise again. But the water rolled on under the ship, letting the bow rise. With all eyes riveted on it, they watched the bowsprit rise slowly, tearing itself loose from the sea until at last it was free. The slender pointed beam of wood thrust itself cleanly into the air. Its stark emptiness brought a cry from nearly every throat. Gone was the staysail and gone, too, was the scrap of humanity that had only moments before clung so bravely to the bowsprit.

"Man overboard!" came the cry from every fellow crewman.

Mr. Vickers nearly knocked Eban off his feet as he

whirled and ran to the stern to drop the life buoy, a long slender cask attached to a rope. Like dry leaves blown before a wintry wind, the crew flew aft, lining the bulwarks and the taffrail in search of some sign of Bobby Howard. Vianna pushed past a stony Eban to join Mr. Vickers and two others at the taffrail. The line paid out slowly, drawn by the cask, which in turn was drawn by the ship that made but little headway against the heavy sea. Every soul on the *Trident* except Eban and the man at the helm watched the gray, heaving sea in intense silence. Finally Mr. Vickers shouted to Eban, "No sign, sir. We must circle."

Eban's reply was firm. "Maintain course!" he told the helmsman in a shout meant to be heard by everyone aboard.

"But, sir, he may still surface!" Mr. Vickers's anguish was shared by all the men.

As for Vianna, she could keep quiet no longer. She staggered over the rolling deck to where Eban stood, grabbed both his arms, and shook him as hard as her poor balance would permit. "Eban!" she screamed. "We've got to stay here and look for him! You can't just let him die!"

Scarcely moving under her attempts to shake him, he gave her a smile, one of pure evil, and said so only she could hear, "I can do anything I please on my ship." With his smile and the light burning in his deepset gray eyes, he looked like Satan himself. "A similar fate awaits anyone else you persuade to help you escape."

Horrified, Vianna let her hands drop away from his arms.

Although a captain had absolute power over his ship and everyone on it, in extreme cases charges could be brought against him. Seldom was he ever found guilty of misusing his power, but a charge of murder, even though he was likely to be found innocent, would not look good on his record. For the benefit of the crew and, Vianna suspected, to protect himself from the possibility of any charge being brought against him later, he said more loudly, "To circle in these seas would be to risk sending this ship to the bottom. I dare not. Mr. Vickers, finish furling that stay-sail!"

The first mate ordered the crew back to work. They went sullenly. Perhaps there was fear in them as well as rage. Some may have suspected why Eban sent Bobby Howard out on the bowsprit to almost certain death. Those who had no idea why it was done would see Eban simply as a heartless master. No matter which of the two groups they fell into, every member of the crew would be thinking that he, too, could be sent to his death at the whim of this cruel captain.

Vianna remained at the taffrail long after everyone else had given up hope. The life buoy had been pulled back in and secured, but she couldn't tear herself away, watching the ship's wake until her eyes burned. Somewhere behind the thick black clouds the sun was setting, taking with it what little light there was. At last, her body bruised by the rail, her legs trembling wearily from the effort to balance herself, Vianna went below.

Once inside the cabin, she slowly removed her cloak and hung it against the bulkhead of the sleeping compartment to dry. Sinking down upon the edge of the bed, she stared sightlessly at the dripping garment. Bobby Howard was gone. Just like that. His life snuffed out swiftly as a candle flame, and all because he had tried to help her. It was incredible, yet horribly believable. She couldn't erase the memory of Eban's expression when he declared with smug, almost gleeful, satisfaction that he could do anything he pleased and get away with it.

She shuddered and wrapped her arms around herself as the icy breath of evil chilled her. Her need to escape the *Trident* was even more urgent now. If ever Eban tired of beating her and raping her and sought a fresh form of punishment, he might kill her. She could not ask anyone else to risk his life by helping her. She would have to do it solely through her own efforts.

She hadn't an idea how.

9

─────────────────────────────

They needed fresh water badly, and the provisions for the officers' mess had been so depleted that at least half the time now the fare at the captain's table was the same salt beef and biscuit diet the forecastle lived on. Yet as the *Trident* moved up the west coast of South America, Eban refused to put in at either Más Afuera or St. Ambrose Island. Hunting was very good. Since leaving the Cape behind them, they had taken twenty whales. Meanwhile, Eban had skillfully avoided contact with the several whalers they had seen. He was sailing these hunting grounds with such élan that Vianna was convinced Captain Loper of the *Contest* had given him specific information on the whereabouts of her father's ship, leaving Eban feeling very safe for the time being. Encountering the *Majestic* could be disastrous for him. There was no way of knowing whether word had reached Samuel Chadwick by letter or by another ship that his daughter was accompanying her new husband on his voyage. If it had, Vianna's father would be searching for the *Trident*. Even if he had not learned of it, avoiding other vessels would not always be possible, and if the *Majestic* should come upon them unexpectedly, as the *Contest* had done, Eban would be trapped. It was obvious from the way he was moving freely about that there wasn't any danger of this happening at present.

Vianna had still not come up with any plan of escape, although she thought about it constantly. It was on her mind one afternoon as she sat alone in the cabin, sewing a flannel gown for the baby. They were close to the equator, and because of the torrid heat, she had left the door open to get a breeze through. When a knock came at the door, a quick glance showed her the steward standing there. Puzzled by what might have brought him, she nonetheless smiled and invited him in.

John Colby's faded cotton shirt and trousers were clean but wrinkled from their launderings in salt water. His bent posture gave Vianna a twinge in her back, reminding her of the constant rheumatic pain he must be suffering. He came close to the plain, varnished desk and spoke across it as she lay her sewing in her lap.

"I've just learned from one of the lads that we've changed course. We're heading due west. That means we're going to the Marquesas for water, ma'am."

"I've heard my father speak of them," Vianna said, wondering why he had come to tell her this. "He seldom puts in there, though. Not many ships do, do they?"

"Most ships have likely reprovisioned at one of the South American ports or one of the other islands by the time they hit the Marquesas, but now and then hunting will be so good near there that a ship will cruise those waters for weeks and reprovision before it heads north." He paused. "I've known of men to desert their ship in the Marquesas and sign on the next one that showed up."

Was he suggesting she escape when they arrived there? Vianna dropped her eyes to the small garment in her lap, thinking rapidly. Would it be possible? "Are there docks there?"

"No, ma'am. The water gets too shallow for anything but boats. We'll likely anchor out a mile or two."

Vianna tapped her thimbled finger thoughtfully on the leather sofa cushion. "Are the natives friendly?" Some of the Pacific Islanders were not. They had even been known to attack the poorly armed whalers, despite the false gunports most whalers had painted on their sides to deceive any would-be aggressors.

John Colby's dark eyes crinkled. "That's putting it mildly, ma'am. They'll put out in their boats and swarm all over this ship, stealing and trading and begging." He added pointedly, "There will be a lot of going and coming in our boats and theirs between ship and shore."

She fielded his direct gaze. "I see."

"There's only one thing, ma'am."

"Yes?"

"Those natives don't allow no women in their boats. It's taboo."

She absorbed that bit of information before observing dryly, "That must be rather inconvenient for the women."

"It for sure is that. If they want to go from one bay to the next, they've got to go by foot. If they want to visit a ship like the *Trident,* they've got to hitch a ride in a whaleboat." He gazed through the stern window above her left shoulder and remarked with studied casualness, "If a woman wanted to, she could probably put on some sailor clothes and fool 'em."

Vianna picked up the tiny flannel gown and pulled the needle from the spot where she had secured it. "If a woman had a good enough reason to want to fool anyone, I believe that might work."

"I could even get her the clothes."

Vianna took a few tiny stitches before saying, "That would be a gallant gesture, Mr. Colby, but if she were caught you would probably find yourself in even more trouble than she was. I'm sure she would prefer to manage by herself."

There was a pause, then he said, "Well, ma'am, I just thought you'd like to know where we're heading. I'd best be getting supper ready." He started for the door.

"I appreciate it, Mr. Colby. Thank you."

"You're welcome, ma'am."

When he was gone, her hands dropped to her lap, her sewing forgotten. How long did she have to work out a plan? She hadn't thought to ask. John Colby had offered a good idea. Could she carry it off? Excitement rippled through her at the thought of setting foot on land once more. She was convinced that if she could just manage that, Eban could never capture her. She would hide too well, and when another ship put in there, she would beg a ride to wherever it was going. Eventually she would find one that was returning to the United States. If there were a ship already in the harbor, her escape would be more difficult, because Eban would be sure to keep her locked in the cabin. In that case, reluctant as she was to do it, she would have to ask John Colby's help. He would have to throw the bolt for her. Her biggest problem, however, would be to leave the ship without being seen.

She mulled over the possibilities during the succeeding week. The crew worked around the clock more than once during that period. When a whale was brought back to the ship, work began on it immediately. There was no break except for meals until all the blubber had been reduced to oil. Vianna's restlessness was such that she went often to the main deck to watch the process. She found the activity of the crew a welcome diversion from wrestling with the problems her escape presented. Invariably she returned to the cabin mentally refreshed.

There was another reason she watched the cutting in of the whales. She discovered it as the crew began to process their second whale. The long, narrow cutting stage had been lowered over the side. The first and second mates had taken their places upon it and were severing the head from the rest of the body with their long-handled cutting spades. When it was free and hanging from chains that had been rove through it, the mates began to remove the blanket of blubber from the corpse. A preliminary cut was made, and the huge hook on the cutting tackle was thrust through it. Then, as the cutting spades made diagonal slices through the hide, the hook was heaved upward, stripping away the blubber as one might peel an apple.

It was while observing this process that it occurred to Vianna that this was what her father had been doing all these years and was very likely doing this minute. The thought brought him so close to her that tears suddenly stung her eyes. Yet the thought was enormously encouraging. It gave the possibility of encountering his ship an immediacy it hadn't had before. Beyond that she felt comforted to realize that outside this present nightmare she was living, she had a father and mother whose love existed even as she stood on this deck. She had come to feel so alone these past months. How good it was to remember that she was not!

After that she spent much of her time on deck, watching the crew lower the strips of blubber through the main hatch to the upper hold, where it was cut into smaller chunks and sent back up to the try-pots, where it was rendered like pork fat. The resultant oil was poured into casks to be stored in the lower hold.

The only process she could not observe was the retrieval of the oil in the whale's head. As soon as all the blubber had been peeled from the body, the carcass was set adrift, and the head, which until then had hung suspended from a block and tackle over the ship's side, was brought aboard. It was so large it could not be lowered to the blubber room; in fact, its size and weight were so great it could crush a man to death by jamming him against a bulwark. To prevent such an accident, it was securely lashed to prevent its sliding about on deck as the ship rolled. The upper part of the head of the sperm whale, or the case, was a reservoir holding pure spermaceti, the most prized of all whale oil, used for making candles or as fuel for lamps. The strange white liquid congealed when it was exposed to the air but became liquid again when heated. This precious substance was bailed out of the head by a member of the crew who stripped naked before descending into the cavity. At this stage of the process Vianna went reluctantly below.

One hot and very still day, as she was watching the mates on the cutting stage slicing the blubber off an especially large sperm whale, she felt a queer flutter in her stomach. Instinctively she put her hand to it, and when she felt her swollen abdomen, she realized what it was. The baby! Until that moment, even though she carried it in her body, it had not seemed real to her, but here it was alive and moving and separated from her hand by only an inch of flesh. A secret smile curved her mouth. The men at their work, the half-peeled carcass of the whale, the still, green water—all faded from her sight as her vision turned inward. She left the rail and went to the cabin to be alone with her baby.

She went to the sleeping cabin, where she could not be seen by anyone passing through the mess, and placed both hands upon her abdomen, the knowing smile on her lips. Tom's child. The thought of Tom brought bittersweet pain. She loved him still, would always love him. Loving and being loved by him had been the most glorious experience of her life. His child would be a living memento of that experience. *Nothing,* she thought fiercely, *and no one is going to harm our child.* Since she was defenseless against Eban as long as she was aboard the *Trident,* her escape in the Marquesas had to succeed.

She went out into the day cabin and sat down in the chair. The ship was lying to during the cutting-in process, and the sea was so calm that the horizon, as she viewed it through one of the stern windows, was a straight line. Involving John Colby or any crew member in an escape attempt again was unthinkable. For that reason she could not disguise herself in any of their clothing, even if she could manage to steal some from the forecastle. Using some of Eban's clothes was out of the question, too. He would spot them instantly. There was only one place she could get an outfit that would disguise her adequately and without incriminating anyone else—the slops. Somehow she had to break into the tween-deck ship's store and get some new sailor clothes. The slop casks were stowed along the starboard side of the blubber room. That the casks were locked was certain. That meant she'd have to acquire the keys somehow. She wasn't sure where they would be.

Rising out of the chair, she went swiftly to the desk and searched it. What was this? To the rear of the drawer she had opened was a stack of letters tied with a string. She flipped through them. They had been written by the crew and bore the addresses of family or friends. Here was Bobby Howard's, addressed to his father and mother! This was the mail Eban was supposed to have taken with him when he gammed with Captain Loper of the *Contest*. He had made sure no word of his brutal treatment of her would get back to Govans Harbor.

She wasn't surprised. Just angry. There were relatives waiting hungrily for word from their sailor sons, husbands, fathers. She knew well the longing for mail from absent loved ones. There was no way she could see that these letters reached their destinations, yet she pulled Bobby Howard's from the stack, and taking one of her books down from the shelf behind the sofa, she hid the letter between the pages. Eban never read. It would be safe there, and maybe someday she could send or give it to Mr. and Mrs. Howard. This last communication was all that would return to them of their son. She ran her hand over the letter sadly, then closed the book and replaced it on the shelf.

Resuming her search of the desk, she found in the top right-hand drawer, a ring with a dozen or so keys attached. Bearing no numbers or tags, they told her nothing. However, they were the only keys in the desk, and she had never noticed Eban carrying any in his pockets. Yet even if they were the right keys, how could she get into the ship's store without being seen? There were several ways to get to the blubber room or the tween deck; but entering it from the main or fore hatches on deck would attract too much attention. So would going down into the forecastle and going into the tween deck from there. The closest way for her was to go through the mess, into the steerage, and through its door into the blubber room. The main problem with that means was getting through the steerage without being seen. There was no way of knowing when the harpooners' cabin might be empty or how long it would remain so.

Vianna's head came up, and she stared through the cabin door into the corner of the mess where the door to the steerage was located. It was closed, as it had been all through the voyage because of her presence on the ship, providing the harpooners with total privacy and preventing any embarrassment of her by their rough talk and manners. It must be hot in there today without a cross breeze, she thought idly, then remembered that all the crew were occupied with cutting in. The steerage was probably empty this very minute. She started to get to her feet, then sat down again. The blubber room wasn't. Men were busy there, cutting the thick "blankets" of blubber into "horse pieces" that would fit in the try-pots.

She drummed her fingers thoughtfully against the varnished desk top, still so new it bore no scratches. The best time to enter the tween deck was when the boats had been lowered to chase whales. All the mates and harpooners would be gone, as would all the crew except for the shipkeepers, and they would be on deck. She leaned back in the chair. Yes, she could get into the slops without being seen then. She opened the drawer to examine the keys once more. If they did indeed fit the locks on the stores, she could acquire the disguise she would need to sneak off the ship in the Marquesas.

It seemed to be a foolproof plan—except that no more whales were sighted. Hunting had been so good it never occured to Vianna that they wouldn't go on killing them as regularly as they had been the past ten days. But the whale being processed the day Vianna decided on her plan was the last. Meanwhile, they sailed inexorably nearer the Marquesas.

Realizing she was running out of time, Vianna sought frantically for another method of getting the outfit she needed. There were clothes as nearby as the mates' berths, but they, like Eban, would be sure to recognize them if they saw them being worn by someone else. Besides, she didn't want any blame to fall on Mr. Vickers or Mr. Farley. Mason Orne she didn't care about, but he was so squat and apelike she doubted she could make his clothes fit her, unless it was a shirt. One of his would probably conceal her swollen abdomen very well. That possibility gave her another idea. Why couldn't she take a shirt from him, pants from Mr. Farley, who was short and slender, and a hat from Mr. Vickers? This last item would likely be instantly recognized by its owner, but she would find some way of changing its appearance. As for shoes, she would need none. The crew had gone barefoot ever since they entered tropical waters. A stain of some kind would hide the soft whiteness of her feet.

Acquiring these items might not be too difficult. From the cabin she could keep a watch on the mates' quarters to see when they were absent. Mr. Vickers was nearly always on deck. The other cabin was shared by the second and third mates, and finding a time when they were both on deck would be trickier.

At this point she realized that each of the mates would miss at once any item of their scanty wardrobes that disappeared. They would suspect theft immediately and be on the lookout for those stolen garments. She would have to be very lucky indeed not to be noticed when she appeared on deck in her purloined clothing. It wasn't hard to imagine Mason Orne's delight in catching the thief, and his pleasure would be trebled when he discovered he had foiled her escape attempt.

So, what was she to do? She tried to recall everything John Colby had told her about what to expect when they reached the Marquesas. When she remembered his amused reply to her question as to whether the natives were friendly, she thought she might have found a solution. "They'll swarm all over this ship, stealing and trading and begging," he had said. All the officers would most certainly be on deck, keeping an eye on things, if that were the case. She could wait until that very moment to steal the clothes and make her escape. The confusion would be a big factor in her favor.

She would have preferred breaking into the slops and getting what she needed, because it would have reduced the chances of attracting the attention of the mates who might recognize their missing garments, but days passed without sighting a whale. Her anxiety and frustration grew.

"Land ho!" came the cry from the lookouts late one afternoon.

Vianna was sewing listlessly in the cabin, awaiting the call to supper. She had been working on the baby's layette merely to delude Eban into thinking she was planning on using it here on the ship, knowing all the time that she could take none of it with her when she escaped. At the shout from the lookout, the sewing fell into her lap, forgotten. That would be the Marquesas Islands! Laying the tiny blue flannel garment aside, she went up on the deck. Eban was on the quarterdeck, peering off to larboard. She followed his eyes and saw the low ridge of land rising only a few inches above the horizon.

She felt suddenly nervous. The time was near. "What land is that?" she asked of Eban, pretending ignorance.

"The Marquesas Islands," he replied coldly and without looking at her.

"Will we be putting in there?"

The glance he shot her now was full of suspicion. "Why should it matter to you?" His face was fully bearded after more than three months at sea, the deep furrows from his nose to the corners of his mouth hidden. The hairy covering over the lower part of his face served to emphasize the long, narrow nose and the deep-set eyes that regarded her so chillingly.

"I do so long for a drink of sweet water," she replied innocently. "The water we've been drinking is scarcely palatable. Will we be going in?"

"Yes," he admitted grudgingly, and turning his back on her, he went over to speak to the man at the helm.

Vianna stood there a few minutes longer, gazing at the bit of land on the horizon. They would reach it during the night and either anchor or lay off and on, going in tomorrow morning. Until then, she could do nothing and must hide her growing nervousness from Eban.

Sitting in the cabin that night pretending to read taxed all of her powers of deception, but she decided sewing would be worse, so she kept to her book. She gave a furtive sigh of relief when Eban went to bed early. She made up her bed on the sofa as she had been doing for weeks and gratefully extinguished the lamp. Darkness did not bring sleep, but it did bring privacy to toss and turn and give vent to her restlessness.

She was dressed and on deck the next morning at dawn, and there off to larboard lay an island almost near enough to touch, so lushly green it looked like a velvet pincushion. Vianna had never seen anything so beautiful in her life. Solid land! Only the sight of Govans Harbor could have thrilled her more. Adding to its beauty was the emptiness of the harbor. Not a ship to be seen! Instead of being locked in the cabin, she would be free to move about the ship and carry out the details of her escape plan. She would have preferred to observe the activities that were to come for a day to discover the best means and time to leave the ship. She knew from hearing her father tell of his stops to take on fresh water and food that it took several days to accomplish the task. Eban was too devious and unpredictable, however, for her to rely on that probability. It would be just like him to take on only as much as could be brought aboard in one day and then sail off again. She could not risk waiting. Her escape attempt must be made this very day.

Eban came up on deck and conferred with the mate on watch, who then gave the order to up anchor and enter the harbor. As they sailed in, Vianna studied the place. A native village of around one hundred thatched bamboo huts ringed the harbor, which was small and too shallow to permit the *Trident* to move in any closer than several hundred yards. There were no slips or jetties, just a sandy beach already thickly populated with natives and canoes waiting for the ship to come within rowing distance. Behind the cleared space that the village occupied was jungle, climbing up a low range of mountains. Surely she could conceal herself well enough in that to evade the search Eban would most certainly put out for her once he discovered she was gone. As she studied the thick green rain forest, she decided with a spurt of fear that the biggest danger would lie in the possibility that she would get lost and never find her way out again. That, however, was a risk she would face when the time came. Her immediate problem was to get off the ship.

The *Trident* moved smoothly into the harbor. The nearer it drew to shore, the more details Vianna could make out. Although the huts appeared to be located haphazardly about the village site, she noticed that there were wide paths linking them together. At the center was a long rectangular building, also made of bamboo, but much larger than any of the other structures. Vianna was deciding it was probably a meeting-house or a holy place when the humans on the beach came into focus. But were they human? A shiver ran down her spine. The brown, naked bodies of the men were hideously tattooed. They looked like a species of scaly creatures spawned in the dank jungle behind them. They presented such a ferocious appearance that Vianna could not believe John Colby had been correct when he assured her they were friendly. Could she trust her life to savages like these if she were lucky enough to reach their village? Another ship might not arrive for months. Would she still be alive? These natives looked as if they could tear her to pieces with their teeth!

As she stared at them in horror, her determination to escape faltered. She would be leaving a known terror for one that was unknown. At the moment Eban's brutality seemed preferable to putting her life into the hands of these savages. Perhaps she should wait and make her escape at another time, in another port.

Before the *Trident* had dropped her anchors, canoes were already gliding through the brilliant blue water toward her, manned by the tattooed natives. Their excited chatter, an alien sound bearing no resemblance to the English language, floated across the water to Vianna.

The watch that was about to come on duty brought their tea and beef and biscuit breakfast up on deck to eat while they feasted their eyes on the first land they'd seen since leaving Govans Harbor. When they saw that most of the canoes carried fruits and vegetables, they saved their sea fare to trade for the fresh food.

The moment the *Trident* dropped anchor, one canoe separated from the rest and came forward. Larger than the others, it was crewed by eight men. Exactly in the center, on a low, flower-decorated throne, sat an old, shrunken man. Above a loincloth made of plaited leaves, his tattooed brown skin hung in folds. His wiry hair stood out like a silvery halo around his wrinkled face.

Observing all this from the quarterdeck, Eban ordered guards stationed at all the hatches and had the Jacob's ladder put over the side. When he went forward to greet the native who was obviously the chief, Vianna followed discreetly behind. It was easy for her to remain inconspicuous, because the crew were all clustered amidships, where the ladder had been dropped.

John Colby, who must have been looking for her, moved up to her side.

"They don't look at all friendly," she whispered to him doubtfully.

Unlike many of the crew, the steward had not let his beard grow, and his pasty face looked even unhealthier this morning, fresh from the razor as it was. Vianna had often wondered why he continued to shave every morning, suspecting that his twisted hands must have been especially painful at that time of the day. Nevertheless, she was glad he did. His appearance when he served their meals was never anything except neat and clean.

At her doubtful remark about the natives, his dark eyes brightened with amusement. "They do look fierce, don't they? But don't let that fool you. They're friendly as puppies and can be just as big a nuisance."

Despite his age, the chief scrambled easily up the ladder to the deck, where he landed with a huge grin and the proud announcement, "Me Chief Wanoo."

Eban didn't step forward to separate himself from the rest of the crew, but his authoritative tone accomplished that when he declared, "I am Captain Stanbro. I am in need of fresh water, and I wish to trade for wood and food."

Chief Wanoo nodded, still grinning. His teeth were surprisingly white and strong. "We have," he replied confidently. "Much wood. Many pigs and chickens. You say how many you like. We catch. For now my men have food in canoes for trade." Without waiting for permission for them to board, he turned and shouted something at the hovering canoes. The brown-skinned crews moved in on the *Trident* like a swarm of bees, covering the deck as if it were a hive, offering bananas, coconuts, pineapples, and strange fruits Vianna had never seen before.

Suddenly one of the natives discovered Vianna. He let out a loud trill of surprise that drew his fellow tribesmen. As they all jostled for a look at her, she was grateful for John Colby's presence at her side. Their faces would have been frightening even without the disfiguring tattoo marks. Their brown eyes, surrounded by whites that were not white at all but tan, gleamed with a wild light, and jutting brow bones gave them a perpetual scowl.

At her elbow John Colby said, "You may be the first white woman some of them have seen. Not many captains' wives travel with their husbands."

Her blond hair was a source of wonder to them. Vianna steeled herself as they reached out brown hands to touch it, murmuring among themselves about this strange-looking woman. When one of them tugged at one of the scrimshaw combs in her hair, she stepped back quickly, and John Colby said in a scolding tone, "No savva that." They accepted the restriction without argument, contenting themselves with feeling the fabric of her dress and staring grinningly at her. One thrust a banana at her, and this set off a mass demonstration of their generosity. Her arms were soon so full of fruit she could accept no more. Smiling, she thanked them and sat down on the main hatch to enjoy a breakfast of the first fresh fruit she had tasted in weeks. After watching her eat with great interest for a while, they gradually drifted away to trade their wares with the crew for shirts and hats and salt beef. Eban and Chief Wanoo had disappeared, probably to discuss the details of their substantial trade. John Colby went off, too, to engage in some bargaining of his own.

While Vianna nibbled the fruit, she surveyed the scene before her with sharp interest. So far as she could see, every member of the *Trident*'s crew was on deck. She had no trouble locating the mates. All three of them were topside, mingling with the natives. Eban's whereabouts were soon revealed, when he appeared in the companionway door leading to the cabin and summoned the first mate. He was obviously conducting his business with Chief Wanoo in the cabin; it would be impossible at the moment for her to procure the items of clothing she needed from the mates' cabins.

When she finished her breakfast, she stood at the bulwark, gazing sharply at the beach. A throng of women and children had been left there to enjoy the novelty of the whaler from afar. It seemed John Colby had been correct about the taboo against women in canoes. Not a one had been brought to the ship. That meant she must disguise herself very carefully if she were to make it to shore. She would have to go in one of the canoes. Trying to sneak ashore in one of the whaleboats that would be going to the beach to bring off supplies would never work. She would be recognized immediately, and she couldn't count on all six of the crew wanting to risk certain punishment if Eban discovered they had been a party to her trick. How was she going to board one of the canoes without calling attention to herself? Even dressed as a sailor, she'd stick out like a sore thumb in the midst of all those naked, tattooed bodies.

She soon saw that it could be done. The men who were not on watch were eager to set foot on land and began to hitch rides in the canoes as one by one they returned to the beach. The natives were eager to show off their newly acquired hats, shirts, trousers, and whatever other items they had traded for to the women. They wore their new clothes, but none of them was interested in a complete outfit. One would be wearing a hat, another a shirt, still another a pair of duck pants, although trousers were not a popular item. Two or three seamen could be accommodated in one canoe. She would attract the attention of no one on the ship if she boarded one of the native boats. Her problem would be hiding the fact that she was a woman from the savages.

Eban, Chief Wanoo, and Mr. Vickers emerged from the cabin after about an hour. The chief was smoking a new pipe, obviously a gift from Eban. The ship carried a supply of pipes, tobacco, beads, and other items to trade to Pacific island natives for fresh provisions.

Walking with great dignity now, Chief Wanoo made his way to the ladder and descended to his canoe. Mr. Vickers and Eban bid him farewell and then huddled together on the quarterdeck, discussing, Vianna presumed, the task of bringing the provisions from the beach to the *Trident*. The other two mates were on deck in plain sight. Casually Vianna slipped past Eban and the first mate and went below.

At the bottom of the companionway she paused. Before her the mess stood empty. To her left were the two mates' cabins. Beyond them in the corner was the door to the steerage. It was closed. So was the door to Mr. Vickers's cabin; she tried it and found it unlocked. She entered quickly, pulling the door shut behind her. The narrow space in which she found herself contained a built-in desk in the forward end with a straight chair. Hooks on the bulkhead held a few clothes, among them Mr. Vickers's rain gear. His berth ran the length of the cabin along the bulkhead. Beneath it was a sea chest. She had already decided to obtain her hat from Mr. Vickers. Should he happen to recognize it and take a good look at the face it hid, he was almost certain to say nothing. Vianna was convinced that she had his full sympathy. She was taking no chances, however. She meant to disguise each piece of clothing in some way so that it would not be immediately recognizable.

A palm hat, rather the worse for wear, hung atop a canvas jacket. She swept it from its hook and hurried out, closing the door behind her.

The cabin next door was almost identical to the one she just left, except that it contained an upper and lower berth and no desk. Here, too, clothing hung against the bulkheads on hooks. It was easy to identify Mason Orne's shirts. Despite the fact that he was a short man, his gorilla chest required a very large shirt. She picked a worn, striped one from the two that were obviously his. From the third mate she took a pair of duck pants. She could roll up the legs, and as for the waist fitting, she presumed her pregnancy would take care of that.

She hesitated, listening, before she sped out of the second cabin and made for her own. Once in her quarters, she went to the sleeping cabin and stuffed the hat in the drawer beneath the bed. Then she cut a piece off the tail of the shirt and another from the bottom of one of the trouser legs and set about sewing these patches on—that from the pants to the elbow of the shirt, the one from the shirt to the knee of the pants. It seemed a sufficient disguise. Neither man would recognize his garment if it bore an unfamiliar patch. She simply basted them on, hid them beneath the bed, took the hat to the desk, splashed some ink across the crown, and it was done. Replacing the hat in the drawer beneath the bed, she sat down to catch her breath. She had her sailor outfit. Some watered ink could be rubbed on her feet and face to hide their whiteness when the time came to leave. She knew it had to be soon. By afternoon the whaleboats would be engaged in bringing supplies from the beach, and with most of the men busy at this task, any crew member aboard a native canoe would be conspicuous.

Vianna returned to the deck. It was as she hoped. Some of the canoes that had gone back to the beach were returning, filled again with fresh fruit. One was getting ready to leave the *Trident*. John Colby and the carpenter were hitching a ride in it.

"Can I bring you anything, ma'am?" the steward asked before descending the ladder.

"That's very kind of you, but I can't think of anything."

"I'll keep my eyes open so that I can give you a good account of the village."

With suggestions as to where she might hide, Vianna surmised. "Yes, I'd appreciate that."

Giving her a nod, John Colby began a rather stiff descent into the waiting canoe. The carpenter was already aboard. As soon as the steward was safely seated, the natives pushed away from the ship and began their row for the beach. Vianna watched. Both crew members were wearing palm hats, and by the time the canoe was a few lengths away, she could not have identified the two men. Even more encouraging was the fact that some of the natives, too, were wearing hats. Two others were wearing newly acquired shirts over their tattooed chests. She would not stand out at all once she got aboard a canoe. Her most dangerous moments would be when she emerged from the cabin, crossed the deck, and descended the ladder. There were still two canoes tied up to the ship. She surveyed the deck from the empty quarterdeck. The dozen islanders still on board were in the forepart of the vessel, dickering with the seamen for knives, kerchiefs, braces, any of the small store of possessions the sailors were willing to trade for shell necklaces, carved boxes, or whatever the natives had to offer. Eban and Mr. Vickers were on the opposite side of the vessel, inspecting one of the whaleboats that had been repaired by the carpenter after the last whale pursuit. The third mate was nowhere to be seen. Vianna assumed he was one of the crewmen who were now on the beach or on their way there.

The canoes that were returning to the *Trident* would arrive in a few minutes. There would be a great deal of confusion as the natives swarmed aboard once more. Vianna bit her lip. It seemed a good time to arrive on deck in her disguise. But how long would she have to stand around waiting for a canoe to leave? As she contemplated her chances, she saw Eban and the first mate go down the main hatch. She guessed that they were going down to see to the trade items that would be paid to Chief Wanoo for the provisions Eban had ordered. If that were the case, they would be occupied below for a considerable time.

Her chances for escape might never be better. Vianna glanced forward, hoping she could see some indication that at least one group of natives were about to leave, but they were all still engrossed in the pleasurable business of trade. She hesitated, indecisive for only a minute, then headed for the cabin.

She stripped off her clothes quickly and donned the shirt and pants. It was the first time in her life she'd worn a pair of trousers. She felt naked, having her legs thus exposed instead of hidden by a long skirt and petticoats. With her scrimshaw combs she pinned her blond hair high on top of her head and set the stained palm hat over it. Even with the mass of hair filling the crown, it fit loosely. All the better, she decided, because it came down low over her eyes and hid her face well. She poured a bit of water in the tin cup that sat on the washstand, carried it to the desk, where she darkened it with a bit of ink, and returned to the sleeping cabin to rub the stain on her feet below the rolled-up pants and on her face and neck. Looking into the mirror, she could not recognize herself. But did she look like a man? She was sure anyone giving her a second look would penetrate her disguise. Somehow she'd have to evade any second looks.

She sent one last glance around the cabin. She could take none of her personal possessions except the combs in her hair. Not that it mattered. Nothing was more important than her freedom. With hands gripping the sides of the doorway, she took a deep breath. Then, heart beginning to pound wildly, she made for the companionway. If Eban chose that moment to come down, her escape attempt would be aborted instantly and violently. The stairway was blessedly empty when she reached it. Not daring to let herself be trapped there, she took the steps two at a time, then paused breathlessly at the top. Through the open door she could see no one on the quarterdeck. Now that they were anchored, there was no need to keep a man at the helm. Gathering herself together, she eased out on deck and slipped around the corner to stand near the rail on the larboard side. There wasn't a soul nearby. All the activity was forward and on the starboard side, and in the next moment further activity erupted as the arriving canoes were tied up and the native crews swarmed aboard. Attempting to be as invisible as possible, she sauntered cautiously toward the gangway where the ladder hung. The deck was so hot it burned the soles of her feet. Clad in her strange costume, she felt as if every eye were on her, but she went unnoticed in the general confusion. The two canoes that had been tied to the ladder before she changed clothes were still there. The newcomers were tied to the other side of the ladder. Behind her was the mainmast. She placed herself aft of it, out of sight of those in the forepart of the ship. A few feet away Eban's heavy voice came up through the main hatch from the blubber room. It was muted, however, which meant he was not directly beneath it and therefore not coming up. She prayed he would remain below until she was well away from the ship.

Never good at waiting, she stood for what seemed like an hour, growing more and more tense as she listened to the sound of Eban's voice drifting up the hatch. Hurry, she urged the islanders silently. My luck won't hold forever. With the sun almost directly overhead here so near the equator, there was no shade to stand in. She lifted one foot then the other from the hot deck.

"Start bringing them up after dinner." Eban's voice was so loud and near, she jumped. He was coming up! Vianna cast around for a better hiding place. Where better than on the fringes of the bargaining throng around the forecastle?

Just as she was about to dart away from the mast, Eban's voice drifted up to her again, but this time he was moving away from the hatch. He wasn't coming up after all! Vianna expelled her breath in a little grunt of relief. At the same time, some natives separated from the crowd and moved toward the gangway, chattering and examining their newly acquired possessions, some of which they were wearing.

The moment had come! Vianna strolled toward the gangway, head well down. She reached there when they did. Without letting them get a good look at her face, she pointed downward toward the canoes, then toward the beach. Her mouth was so dry she couldn't have spoken if she had wanted to, and of course she had no intention of giving herself away with her woman's voice.

The natives nodded, one sweeping his arm grandly toward the beach. He was the one who scrambled down the ladder first. Vianna crowded in and went down next, afraid her awkwardness on the ladder might be apparent enough to arouse some suspicion and therefore not wanting a big audience below her.

The canoe bobbed sharply as she stepped into it, throwing her off balance. Fortunately she came to rest on one of the thwarts as gracefully as if she had been seating herself in a wobbly canoe all her life. Forcing herself to go loose so that she could roll with the craft as the other islanders stepped aboard, she kept her head down and waited for them to take their seats and cast off. Every nerve in her body was singing. She didn't dare look up to see if anyone was watching from the rail.

Chattering ceaselessly in their strange-sounding language, they untied the canoe and pushed off, their chest and arm muscles rippling beneath their brown, tattooed skin. Facing forward as they all were, Vianna did not have to continue concealing her face. The four men in front of her were too busy paddling to look back at her, and the two behind her were seeing nothing but a vague shape within well-worn sailor clothes. Yet she couldn't really feel safe until she was hidden in the jungle behind the village.

The canoe cut through the brilliant blue-green surf

as smoothly as a cutting spade through blubber. Fear began to give way to excitement as Vianna saw the stretch of water between herself and the *Trident* rapidly widen. This was the first time she'd been separated from the ship since she boarded it in Govans Harbor on her wedding day. She recalled the lack of emotion with which she had viewed the *Trident* as it rode in its slip in the harbor the last week before her marriage. She had been too benumbed from the shock of losing Tom to feel much of anything. No such numbness dulled her emotions today. As she gazed at the fat white ship, dangling its whaleboats like earrings, she experienced such revulsion her stomach heaved and she swallowed swiftly to steady it.

It was when she was swallowing a second time that a gust of wind tore the palm hat from her head and sent it tumbling through the air to her left. It happened so swiftly that her grab for it was much too tardy. Behind her a screech nearly rent her eardrums; it was followed by a second one, and the next thing she knew she was being beaten over the head with the paddles of the two islanders who had been sitting behind her. Their screeches had alerted their colleagues, who left off paddling to look aft to see what was happening. Vianna had a glimpse of four dark, wild faces staring in horror at her; the two nearest her also began beating her with their paddles. Trying to protect her now-exposed blond head from the blows, she cowered, arms raised, and screamed, "No savva that," as she had heard John Colby scold them earlier that day for touching her hair. This time they did not desist. Among the furious words yelled at her, she heard one repeatedly that sounded like "taboo." Arms grasped her, lifting her from the thwart. She fought savagely, but she hadn't a chance. She felt herself sailing through the air and saw the water beneath her. Her landing was surprisingly soft. She surfaced at once and started swimming toward the beach. It was a long way away, but her chances of making it were much better than her chances would be if she headed back to the ship.

The irate natives were not through with her, however. A paddle came crashing down squarely on top of her head. For an instant she felt pain, then nothing as she lost consciousness.

The next thing she knew, she was lying on her back in the water. Someone's arm was across her chest, crushing her breasts painfully. Groggily, she began to struggle.

"Don't fight me, Mrs. Stanbro, or we'll both drown."

Vianna recognized the voice. It was George McAndrews. She relaxed. His first attempt at rescuing her from Eban had failed, but now they were out here in the water alone, with no one to interfere. He would get her to the beach safely. She relaxed. Her head hurt dreadfully. She slipped into unconsciousness again.

When she awoke, she knew at once where she was. As the familiar surroundings of the day cabin registered on her mind, she screamed, "No, no!" and tried to sit up, but the pain in her skull smote her with such violence she fell back onto the sofa. What was she doing here? Why hadn't McAndrews taken her to the beach? She began to cry weakly.

Her scream had been heard. Eban suddenly appeared above her, smiling, but it was such an evil smile that she shuddered. "You see, Vianna, God is on my side. I am His instrument of punishment. You will never escape me."

Vianna stared up into the face of her husband, glowing with the sick light of fanaticism.

"You have committed a despicable sin." His voice was thick with revulsion. "Only through chastisement can you be cleansed. God has assigned that task to me. He will not take you from me until your purification is completed. Your attempts to escape, just like your attempts to corrupt me, will fail. The Devil is in you," he declared in a rising voice, "but the power of God will prevail!"

His thundering pronouncement ricocheted from side to side inside her throbbing skull. She closed her eyes against the pain and to shut out the sight of Eban's terrifying face. There was no longer any doubt about it. He was utterly mad.

10

For the remainder of the *Trident*'s stay in the Marquesas, Vianna was kept locked in the cabin. Making a prisoner of her was unnecessary. The concussion she had suffered when one of the islanders struck her on the head with his paddle kept her groggy for twenty-four hours. At the end of that time, the ship upped anchor and sailed away.

John Colby brought her broth made from one of the chickens with which the officers' mess had been provisioned. He also brought her news.

"George McAndrews jumped ship. He hasn't been seen since he swam out to save you and brought you back aboard."

Vianna had pushed herself up into a sitting position when the steward came in. Her head still hurt, and the room tilted several times before it steadied for her. "Why didn't he take me to the beach instead of bringing me back here?" she asked in despair as she took the bowl of broth from the desk. The rich fragrance of the soup and the yellow circles of fat floating on top were almost too much for her stomach for the moment. "We'd have both been safe then."

Shoving a plate of biscuit toward her with a gnarled hand, John Colby explained, "George weren't a good swimmer. He couldn't have made it to shore with you. He barely made it back to the ship. You was a dead weight."

"He must have known he was signing his death warrant to come in after me. No wonder he deserted. I'm glad he managed to get away." Vianna took a spoonful of the broth and found it tasted surprisingly good.

"We all heard your screams. When the captain saw what it was all about, he just stood there watching those savages beat you and throw you in the sea. We all waited, hoping he'd give an order to someone to go in after you. But he didn't. When you went down after that hit on the head, George dove in." The steward turned apologetic. "I'd have done it myself, ma'am, but I'm so stove up I knew I couldn't do you no good."

Vianna let her spoon rest in the bowl and gave him a weak smile. "I'm glad you didn't try. You're the only friend I have left on this ship."

He nodded and said bitterly, "There are better swimmers aboard than George was. They could have dove in for you, but I guess none of them wanted to bring trouble on themselves."

"After what happened to Bobby Howard, I can't blame them. I didn't want to involve any of you, anyway. I'm sorry about George McAndrews. He's come to a great deal of grief because of me."

For the first time since he came into the room, a smile flitted across John Colby's pasty face. "I wouldn't feel too bad about him, ma'am. Leastways not because of his jumping ship. He'll find a berth on another one, and it's bound to be a happier ship than this 'un. Once he tells his story, he might even be signed on as a mate again."

"I hope so." Vianna sipped some more soup thoughtfully. "Where are we heading now?"

"To the New Zealand whaling grounds."

"New Zealand!" Vianna exclaimed in dismay. "We're so close to the Sandwich Islands! I hoped—I mean I thought we'd probably work our way to Lahaina." Undaunted by her failure to escape in the Marquesas, she was determined to try again when they reached Lahaina. Because there was a small colony of Americans there—businessmen, whalers, whalers' wives, missionaries—Eban would keep her closely confined, but one way or another, she would break free and find sanctuary in the colony.

"There's no need to go there, ma'am. Not now that we've got provisions. And we don't have enough oil to turn over to our agent there." He peered at her sharply with his dark eyes. "I can let you know as soon as I hear we're heading up there. It should be our next stop."

"Yes, please. It is very important to me."

"I understand, ma'am. You can count on me."

By the time the *Trident* reached the New Zealand whale grounds, Vianna was five months pregnant and fearing more and more for her baby. How long could it survive those beatings? The larger she grew, the more awkward she became at defending herself. She tried to give as good as she got, but the few scratches and bruises she was able to inflict on Eban left him unfazed. He was so consumed by rage and passion during those episodes that Vianna was sure he wasn't even aware of his wounds until afterward. Then he ignored them. And her. His lack of attention to her had never been based on indifference, but on arrogant contempt. If he thought she found such treatment humiliating, he was mistaken. The view of her that he harbored in that sick mind of his mattered not at all. Even the physical pain she suffered as a result of his beatings caused her less distress now than her burgeoning anxiety over the safety of her baby. In the event it survived the regular assaults on her body, would Eban get her to Lahaina before it was born? When he had asked her to marry him the second time, suggesting she accompany him when he sailed, he told her she could have her baby in Lahaina. She had counted on that, even after he exposed himself as such a monster. She hadn't expected him to permit her to walk off the ship and enter the hospital there, but she continued to believe he would make up some story and bring the doctor aboard to attend to her. Now that her time was drawing nearer, she began to wonder if she could trust him to take her there.

One afternoon as he sat over his charts at the desk, she bit off a thread on the last of a pile of diapers she'd been hemming. She'd been steeling herself to introduce the subject for the last thirty minutes. "Eban, will we be in Lahaina in time for the birth of the baby?"

"I doubt it." Although he didn't bother to raise his eyes from the charts, his reply was calm. The subject of the baby had not, apparently, fired his rage as Vianna had expected. Yet that was small consolation.

In dismay she cried, "But you must! It is my first child! I will need a doctor."

"I will be your doctor."

Vianna stared at the still lowered head. Horror began to rise within her like water in a leaking boat. "You know nothing about delivering babies," she said faintly. "How can you attend me?"

He glanced up and smiled through his black beard. "I will see that you don't die."

The smile as well as his statement sent a chill through her. "What about my baby?" she asked slowly.

He continued to smile, and the sight was so frightening she would rather have had him glare at her. "I will take care of it."

She gave a choked cry. "You mean to kill it!"

"God does not want it to live."

"Eban, that would be murder! God would never ask you to do that!"

"God does not condone sin. Sinners must be punished."

"But the baby is innocent!"

"It is the fruit of your sin and therefore corrupt." The calmness with which he continued to speak was grotesque.

Trembling uncontrollably, Vianna nevertheless tried to speak as calmly as he. "Eban, I'm sure you've misunderstood God's commands. I beg you to speak with

Him again and ask Him if He truly means for you to kill my baby."

Her presumption that he could be wrong broke through his calm. "There's no need for that," he said stiffly. "I did not misunderstand." He turned his attention back to his charts, ending the discussion.

Vianna heaved her heavy body from her chair and flung herself toward the desk, protesting wildly, "You can't do this! God did not tell you to murder my baby! It's your own desire to punish me that is behind it all, but it you who will be punished. Your sin will far outweigh mine. You will burn in Hell if you kill my baby!"

He glanced up, asking lazily, "Are you trying to frighten me, Vianna? You are wasting your time. It is you who will be consigned to Hell, not I. You've so befouled yourself with lust that you would never be permitted to enter Heaven."

"I loved Tom!" she cried. "If I had not waited for your ship to return as my mother asked me to do, Tom and I would have been married. It was only because I was trying to spare your feelings that our child was conceived out of wedlock."

Eban grimaced with distaste. "Don't put the blame on me, Vianna. I did not push you into that man's embrace. You went into it of your own free will." The image that this conjured up in his mind destroyed his unearthly tranquility. His cheeks and brow, all that was visible of his face above his beard, reddened and he rasped, "Harlot! Fornicator! You aren't fit to be a mother!" Rising out of his chair, he struck her across the face. "You had your filthy pleasure!" he thundered. "Now you will pay for it!"

He beat her until he was gasping for breath, then went up on deck. Vianna pulled herself off the floor, moaning, and staggered to the bed. She fell across it and lay unmoving. Her physical pain was nothing compared to her panic. Her baby was doomed unless she could get off this ship before it was born! There were no islands down here. Other ships, perhaps, but her chances of rescue from that quarter were so slim since her previous attempt at a similar escape that she could find little hope in that idea. Dear God, was there nothing she could do to save her baby?

One day after they had been cruising the New Zealand grounds for about a month, Vianna realized that she could get free of Eban without any effort on her part. She was very slow at recognizing the possibility, however.

"There she blows!" came the cry from one of the mastheads one morning. "There, there! She blows!"

"Where away?"

"Two points forward the weather beam, about two miles off. A school of them!"

Vianna was on deck, taking her exercise. The sun was warm, the breeze cool, and the air clear as clean glass. Just as she reached the bulwark to look for the whales off the weather beam, the lookouts cried out in unison, "There go the flukes!"

Eban shouted, "Time, Mr. Vickers! Time!"

The first mate sang out the exact minute.

The sperm whale yielded the greatest amount of oil of any of the species of this leviathan, and was therefore the prime target of the whale hunters. When its distance from a ship prevented the lookouts from identifying it by its superior size, they timed its blows, which came with undeviating regularity. In this case, however, the whales had dived, leaving the hunters uncertain whether these were sperm or whether this was a school of some other type of whale.

At the first shout from the masthead, the watches below rushed up on deck. While the boatsteerers placed the tubs of whale line in the boats, Eban ordered the ship kept away from the wind and then shouted, "Lower four boats."

It was the first time he had ordered his own boat lowered. Up to that point, three boats had been all that were needed, but the school of whales they had just sighted was the largest they had so far come upon.

"Hoist and swing!" the first mate called out.

The boats that hung from their cranes on either side of the *Trident* were now lowered with a mate in the stern and the harpooner in the bow of each. Eban took his place in the stern of the fourth boat. The other four crewmen slid down the lines that still held the smaller craft to the ship. After setting the single sail, they took up the long oars, the boats were set free, and they pushed away from the ship's hull to go after the whales.

The knitted red cap of Emore, the harpooner in Eban's boat, was the only bit of color to stand out against the green water as the boats pulled rapidly away. Behind Vianna, who watched from the rail, the *Trident* was peculiarly empty. Only the carpenter, the sailmaker, the steward, and the cook remained aboard as shipkeepers. John Colby was at the helm, his bent body curved over the wheel. The cook was stationed in the mainmast head lookout, and the other two worked the sails to keep the *Trident* away from the wind.

The cook, a small, wizened man with a high-pitched voice, sang out, "There they are! Off the starboard boat, but the crew can't see them from where they're sitting!"

Nor could Vianna see the whales from where she stood, but moments later, in the area the cook indicated, the water erupted in the low, bushy spouts of the sperm whale. Instantly the boats swung their sails and went off in pursuit. By now the four craft were indistinguishable from one another, but Vianna could still see the crimson spot that was the hat of the harpooner on Eban's boat. Even from her vantage point she was able to see with what speed the boats took off, using both sail and oars.

"A bit more, men!" the cook cried to the boat crews, encouraging them even though they couldn't hear him. "Pull, pull! Crack your backbones! There's a hump! Give it to him, Walker! He's fast! There's the second harpoon. They've got him!"

Behind her Vianna heard John Colby's shout of triumph.

"Aye, go for it, captain." The cook continued his chatter of encouragement.

Vianna watched the splotch of scarlet rise in the boat, and a moment later the cook cried, "He's fast! And another! Yes, both harpoons in him. There he goes!"

The whale took off, pulling Eban's boat with him. The sail collapsed, the mast snapped by the tremendous speed of the wounded sea monster. His course took him across the bow of the *Trident* and, although they were two miles away, Vianna could see the boat tearing through the water.

"They're off on a Nantucket sleighride," the cook shouted down to the steward. "Mark their course. The other harpooners missed their mark. They've fastened to Mr. Vickers's whale."

Vianna was not interested in the other three boats or the whale they were preparing to tow back to the ship. She was watching Eban's boat fly through the water, growing smaller every moment. In no time it was out of sight. One thought had begun to burn in her brain. It was not unusual for a whaleboat, taken for a Nantucket sleighride, never to be seen again.

Gazing at the now empty horizon, Vianna pressed a trembling hand to her throat. Dear God, could it be possible that her problem would be solved in this way? She wondered why she hadn't thought about something like this happening before. Chasing whales was such dangerous business that seldom was a voyage completed without loss of life or serious injury to one or more of the crew. Captains did not join every chase and therefore the incidence of such accidents among them was low, but the possibility existed nonetheless. She closed her eyes and moaned softly. *Please, God!*

John Colby held the *Trident* in position while the three boats set about the Herculean task of towing the enormous whale back to the mother ship. By the time the creature had died from the thrust of the mate's lance in its lung, he had towed the boat several miles further away from the *Trident*. That distance was now retraced with painful slowness. Meantime, there was no sign of Eban's boat.

It was late afternoon before the whale was secured along the ship's side and the boats hoisted back aboard. When the first mate noticed that Eban was not there, he questioned John Colby.

"He and his crew were taken on a Nantucket sleigh-ride. Didn't you see it?" The steward had surrendered the helm to another crew member and was examining the enormous corpse that lay in the water on the starboard side of the ship.

Mr. Vickers responded angrily, "Why didn't you inform me at once? I saw nothing. We were too busy taking our whale. Which direction?" When John Colby told him, he called for the glass and searched the horizon. "How long since you lost sight of the boat?"

"Shortly after noon, sir."

"No sign since?"

"No, sir."

"We must cut loose the whale and go in search of them."

John Colby cleared his throat, staring hard at the first mate. "This whale looks to yield better than one hundred barrels."

Vianna had remained on deck all day, gnawing a bit of salt beef and some biscuit, since the cook's ship-keeping duties had kept him out of the galley. She was near enough to read the glance that passed between the steward and the first mate. John Colby's concern had nothing to do with oil. He was trying to create time for Mr. Vickers to consider the situation. The steward obviously regarded Eban's disappearance as the work of a merciful fate, a deliverance that should be accepted as a gift, and he was hoping the mate would see it that way, too. That was exactly how Vianna viewed it. She stepped forward.

"Mr. Vickers, may I speak with you in private?"

"Of course, ma'am."

She led the way aft, down the companionway and into the cabin, followed, she was sure, by every pair of eyes on the ship. Suddenly realizing how tired she was from being on her feet all day, she sat down on the sofa and motioned toward the chair in the corner. "Please sit down, Mr. Vickers."

"If it's all the same to you, Mrs. Stanbro, I'd as soon stand."

She nodded and gazed steadily up at the stocky first mate. "My husband is insane. He has already killed once, as you know. Bobby Howard's death was no accident. Now he plans to kill my baby when it is born." When the first mate started to protest his disbelief, she held up her hand and rushed through her explanation. "He has told me this. He does not plan to go to Lahaina when my time comes so that I can have a doctor attend me. He says he will deliver the baby himself."

Beads of sweat formed on the mate's upper lip. "That does not mean he plans to kill your baby."

"He does! He told me so. He said that God does not want it to live."

An incredulous shaking of his head sent his clubbed hair, secured by its blue riband, sweeping from shoulder to shoulder. "Ma'am, I cannot believe the captain would kill his own child."

Vianna's face flushed but she didn't drop her eyes. "It is not his child. That is the trouble."

It was the first mate who cast his eyes down at this revelation. Sweat began to bead his brow as well as his lip.

Vianna went on. "He believes he has been commanded by God to punish me. That's why he's been beating me. That's part of the reason he plans to kill my baby when it's born, although he claims God does not want it to live because it is the fruit of my sin and therefore corrupt. Those are his very words, Mr. Vickers. Surely you can see that he is completely mad."

The mate's stocky body twitched. "Even if he is, I don't see that there is anything I can do."

"You don't have to set off in search of his boat."

His breath came hissing out from between his clenched teeth as if he'd been holding part of it back, anticipating her proposal. "I can't do that. If he's still alive out there someplace, it would be the same as murder."

"So would going out to find him so that he can kill my baby when it's born."

The mate wiped the sweat from his upper lip with a knuckle, unable to counter her argument.

Vianna went on in a quiet voice that nonetheless sacrificed no note of urgency. "I will share the responsibility. Neither of us will ever know for certain that he wasn't already dead when we made the decision. If you're worried about some of the crew making accusations against you later, you could pretend to search, perhaps in a different area from the one John Colby has indicated. I doubt though that any of the crew would be sorry that Eban could not be found. They must fear him after watching him send Bobby Howard to certain death." She thought he paled slightly at this reminder. "There would be an investigation, of course, but I would testify that I was satisfied that you had done everything you could to find my husband. My word as his wife would surely quiet any suspicion that you had not searched adequately for him."

"I'm afraid there would be a lot of suspicion when people learned how he had treated you. And it will become common knowledge, ma'am, once we return to Govans Harbor. There isn't a man aboard who doesn't know of his cruelty toward you."

"All the more reason, then, that none of the crew

would cause any trouble if you made a less than thorough search."

A short silence followed. Sweat trickled from Abner Vickers's brow down his temple and into his eye. He blinked and dried his whole face on the sleeve of his shirt. Breaking the silence at last, he asked, "Do you realize what you are proposing, Mrs. Stanbro? Can you live the rest of your life with this on your conscience?"

Vianna closed her eyes and replied in a faint voice, "I will never know but that he was already dead when we had this discussion. I believe I can live with my conscience given that uncertainty. On the other hand, if he returns alive and kills my baby, I think I shall go mad."

She heard him move, and when she opened her eyes, she saw that he was pacing back and forth in front of the desk, one hand rubbing the side of his face. After what seemed a very long time, he halted, his face clearly showing the strain of the choice he had been forced to make. "There are five other men in the captain's boat. If it were not for them, perhaps I could do as you wish. God knows you have sufficient reason not to want your husband found. But I can't let five innocent men die without making a good search for them. I'm sorry, ma'am."

Vianna sagged against the sofa cushion. She had forgotten about the others in Eban's boat in her desperate desire to make the most of this opportunity to break free of Eban that had so unexpectedly presented itself. She could not live with their deaths on her conscience. "You are right, of course," she told the first mate quietly. "I had forgotten about the crewmen."

Vickers gave an audible sigh of relief. "Then I'll get the search started at once, ma'am." He left quickly. She heard him take the stairs two at a time.

Vianna's head fell back against the sofa. Was this really she, Vianna Chadwick, wishing for a man's death, even trying to bring it about? It was a relief in a way to have Abner Vickers refuse to go along with her suggestion. Yet it left the problem of her baby's survival still unsolved. All she could do was to hope and pray that Eban's boat would not be found.

They had to beat their way against an unfavorable wind. The steward served supper, bringing Vianna's into the cabin at her request. It began to grow dark, and still there was nothing for the lookouts to report. Lanterns were hung from the masts to catch the eye of any survivors. Soon after nine o'clock fog moved in, enveloping the ship. Mr. Vickers ordered the sails furled and the *Trident* lay to, waiting for the fog to lift.

"Otherwise we might miss them," he explained to Vianna, "or even run them down."

The silence on the ship that night was uncanny. There was none of the usual hiss of water past the hull, no orders called out to set this sail or reef that one, no snapping of canvas in the wind. Even the normal creaks in the rigging were muffled by the fog, and the vessel lay so still it left off groaning as it did when it worked.

The effect of this unnatural silence was to cause Vianna to strain for any sound that might indicate they had come upon Eban's whaleboat. Twice she left her bed and, covered by her cloak, went up on deck to peer futilely through the fog that was so thick she could barely see the water directly below the bulwark.

Two hours after sunup the next morning, the fog had burned off and Mr. Vickers ordered the sails to be set. This time the wind was fair and they moved swiftly over the waves. Vianna haunted the deck, peering first from the starboard side, then the larboard, from stern and from bow.

About noon the first mate ordered the ship turned, and they began to circle. It was only an hour later that the lookout on the foremast called out, "Three points off the larboard bow! I can't make out what it is."

As the *Trident* headed in that direction, Vianna went

to the bow. At first she could see nothing, being on a lower level than the lookout, but after a while she, too, could make out a tiny smudge against the horizon. By that time the lookouts could identify it.

"It's an overturned boat! I see some men clinging to it!"

Vianna's heart began to race. There was a rush to the rail by the crew, all of whom were on deck. John Colby came up to her. He still wore the apron he had worn while serving dinner. With one gnarled hand he rubbed an aching shoulder, giving her a gentle nod, then stood beside her in supportive silence as the *Trident* moved toward her stray boat.

Mr. Vickers put the glass to his eye frequently in an effort to see how many survivors clung to the boat and who they were, but the ship was still too far away to make out any details.

"The boat's been stove," a lookout called out finally. "Only part of it's afloat."

The sun on the water was so bright that Vianna's straining eyes soon blurred. "Mr. Vickers, may I use the glass for a few minutes?"

"Of course, ma'am."

Vianna raised the long spyglass, moving it slowly until she had it focused on the broken whaleboat. She could make out some round shapes that must be heads, but because of the distance they all ran together. She kept the spyglass, and the first mate made no attempt to reclaim it, relying on the lookouts in the three mastheads for his information.

The glass was heavy, but Vianna rested her arms only for an instant now and then, so great was her anxiety to discover what her fate would be—a continuation of the nightmare she had known for the past six months, or freedom.

Gradually the heads began to come into focus, showing separately against the partial hull of the overturned boat. She scanned them swiftly. "I see only three survivors, Mr. Vickers," she said, a tremor in her voice. Eban was not among them.

The chief mate called up to the lookouts, "Are there any men on the far side of the boat?"

The answer did not come at once as the men in the crow's nests sought a glimpse of the hidden side of the hull. "Can't see, sir," came one reply that was echoed by the other lookouts.

A wave of dizziness swept over Vianna. She closed her eyes and gripped the rail to steady herself. The spyglass would have fallen to the deck if John Colby hadn't caught it. He yelled to someone. "Bring Mrs. Stanbro some water. Be quick about it!"

The next thing she knew the dipper was eased into her hand and guided to her mouth. The water tasted of the oak barrel from which it came, but its coolness revived her. "Thank you," she murmured.

"There are two more men on the other side of the boat," one lookout called. "Yes, that's right. Five in all. No sign of the sixth. I don't see Emore's red cap."

That meant little. The harpooner's cap could very well have been lost when he was thrown into the water.

Mr. Vickers left the quarterdeck and came down to where Vianna stood, near the starboard gangway. "If the lookouts in the main masthead had the glass, ma'am, they could likely identify the survivors."

And then she would know whether she had been released from the horror of Eban's retribution, or whether she was doomed to go on living the nightmare. Suddenly she was frightened. She preferred uncertainty to the awful knowledge that her punishment would continue.

"It might be good news, Mrs. Stanbro." It was John Colby, breaking through her thoughts with the hopeful reminder. She nodded slowly at him, understanding his unspoken message, and gave up the glass to the first mate, who sent a man aloft to give it to a lookout.

With the steward standing protectively beside her,

Vianna chewed her lip and waited. Her heart beat wildly. It was the longest few minutes of her life.

"There's Jefferson," the lookout yelled down. "And Keller." He paused. "They're all there except Emore. No sign of him."

Everything inside Vianna seemed to stop. She refused to believe it.

"You're sure Captain Stanbro is there?" Mr. Vickers demanded.

"Yes, sir. No mistaking him."

A small sob escaped Vianna. She slumped. John Colby's rheumatic arm went around her waist, surprisingly strong. "I'll take you to the cabin."

Her legs would scarcely support her. The steward half-carried her down the stairs. He led her to the sofa, where she lay down, eyes closed. "I'll be back in just a minute," he told her.

Vianna's heart had slowed to a painful thump. Why couldn't it have been Eban who was lost? So far as she knew, the harpooner, Emore, was a harmless man who killed only whales. Why had his life been taken while that of an insane murderer like Eban was spared?

"Drink this, Mrs. Stanbro."

The cup she sipped from held straight rum. She choked, pushing it away.

"You'd best drink it down, ma'am. It will restore your strength."

"No," she whispered. She didn't want her strength restored. She wanted to die. "My husband plans to kill my baby when it is born. There is nothing to stop him now."

The steward sucked in his breath. "Are you sure, ma'am?"

"He told me so. He's gone completely insane. He believes God has commanded him to do it." She began to weep silently.

John Colby stood beside the sofa, not speaking, for some time. Then he said firmly, "God won't let the captain kill your baby. He will be stopped one way or another. You can count on that, ma'am."

"I wish I could believe that."

"I don't have one single doubt about it."

Vianna opened her eyes and looked up at him. He was gazing at her intently. "Trust me," he urged.

The emphasis he put on those two words puzzled her. Whatever could he mean? Persuaded, she nodded.

"Drink this, then," he said gently and placed one of her hands around the cup. "You're a young woman, and once all this is behind you, you'll find you have lots to live for."

She would have everything to live for if he was right and God would see to it that Eban was prevented from murdering her baby. Raising Tom's child and loving it was all she asked of life now. The desire to live flickered and began to grow. Bringing the cup to her lips, she drank the fiery liquid down to the last drop.

11

Eban was not chastened by his close brush with death. He was, if anything, even more vengeful toward her, Vianna thought, as if he realized he might be cheated by fate of his pleasurable punishment of her and therefore wanted to crowd as much of it into their time together as possible.

Soon after they resumed the hunt, the weather turned bad, a circumstance Vianna welcomed at first because it kept Eban so busy that he didn't have time to think about her.

One gale would scarcely blow itself out before another hit. It was impossible to take any exercise on deck during these storms, and sometimes the vessel pitched so violently that she lay down upon the bed and remained there, fearful that if she tried to move around or even sit in a chair, she'd be thrown to the floor.

A particularly violent gale buffeted them about for three days. Exhausted by the constant jerking of her body this way and that for so long a time, Vianna was sleeping heavily the third night when she began to dream that the ship was sinking. Her ears filled with the sound of rushing waters. Panic brought her awake, only to realize that it wasn't just a dream. Water was pouring into the ship! She sat up, frantically searching the desk for the matches and calling out to Eban in the sleeping cabin, "Eban, we're going down!"

Before the words were out of her mouth, she heard his feet hit the floor. He was across the day cabin and at the door by the time she had the candle lit. She wondered how he could have moved so swiftly and so surely with the ship bucking like a wild horse. Beneath his striped flannel nightshirt his milk-white legs and feet were swept with water as he flung open the door to the mess. With one long stride he was back to the desk, grabbing the light from Vianna's hand. A moment later he was bellowing for Mr. Vickers. "Go tell Mr. Farley that last sea broke the skylight, and send the steward to clean up this water."

"Aye, aye, sir!"

As Eban came back into the cabin, the bow rose sharply, sending more water from the mess over the sill and across the deck as far as the sofa. The vessel hung there on the crest of that sea for a long moment, then the bow dropped as the stern rose and the door banged closed of its own accord. "Get this water mopped up in here," Eban barked at Vianna and went back to bed.

For three weeks they were tossed by gales. If they were fortunate enough to have a calm day or two in between them and managed to take a whale, it sometimes had to be cut loose from the ship before the cutting in was complete because of rising winds and seas.

If they encountered any other ships during this period, Vianna did not learn of it. In the few hours she was able to spend on the main deck, she saw none. It wouldn't have mattered, in any event. The seas were much too rough to have permitted gamming. She had not given up the idea of getting aboard another ship somehow. She wondered if that wasn't what John Colby was more or less promising when he had urged her to trust him. The bad weather was eating up what little time she and the steward had left. She realized that even if she managed to escape to another ship, that vessel might not get her to Lahaina in time for her to have her baby there. The thought of giving birth with no one in attendance except a strange captain and his crew, none of whom surely would have had any experience with such a process, struck terror into her heart, but to a much lesser degree than the thought of remaining on the *Trident* and letting Eban attend her.

At last the storms abated and they were favored with a stretch of good weather. Hunting was resumed, so successfully that the cargo hold began to fill rapidly with casks of oil and spermaceti.

It was during the cutting in of a large right whale, a species whose oil was of an inferior quality but which yielded a great quantity of valuable whalebone, that Eban fell sick. She recognized his step coming down the companionway that afternoon and didn't bother to look up from the book she was reading when he entered the cabin. Halfway across the floor, however, he suddenly bent over, clutching his stomach. She looked up then and saw that his face was white as a sail and beaded with sweat. Trying unsuccessfully to smother a groan, he rushed to the water closet. When he emerged a few minutes later, he went directly to the bed and lay down. Knowing he would demand attention if he wanted it, Vianna returned to her book. She couldn't bear to work on the baby's layette any more. Superstitiously she felt that if she completed it, she would never get to use it. These last weeks of her pregnancy were rushing by so fast that she was grasping at anything, even magic, to protect her baby.

A little while later she heard Eban vomiting into the washbasin, which he must have set beside the bed. He was scarcely finished when she heard him gasping through gritted teeth, and he dashed for the water closet again. When he came out he yelled at her, "Bring me the medicine chest!"

She went at once to the drawer beneath the sofa where the ship's supply of drugs and remedies was kept and took the box to him. "Fetch me a cup of water and a spoon."

She went to get a spoon from the steward's pantry and found John Colby sitting in the narrow space on a small box, arms folded across his chest and smoking a pipe. She thought he looked less pasty than he usually did. When he started to struggle painfully to his feet, she bade him remain seated.

"Sick, is he?" he remarked when she explained the errand she was on.

"In great pain, too, I think," Vianna added. "What do you suppose it could be?"

"Maybe he et something that disagreed with him." He spoke loudly, as if he wanted Eban, on the other side of the bulkhead, to hear him.

It was then that Vianna noticed that John Colby's eyes were unnaturally bright. "Perhaps that's it," she agreed absently, taking the spoon he handed her and returning to Eban. She poured water from the pitcher into the cup that always sat on the washstand and took it to him.

He poured some powder from a large jar into the cup, stirred it until it dissolved, then began cautiously to drink it. "Put it back," he told Vianna, motioning toward the medicine chest. He kept the jar of powder and set it on the floor within his reach. As she was replacing the box in the drawer beneath the sofa, she heard him begin to vomit into the washbasin again. It didn't sound as if he were going to be able to keep any of the powder down.

Vianna went back to her chair and picked up her book, but she couldn't read. An incredible possibility had lodged in her mind. Had John Colby poisoned Eban? He was experiencing some sort of excitement. His unusual color and the brightness of his eyes were evidence of that. Was this what he had been promising when he assured her that Eban would be stopped one way or another from killing her baby?

"Vianna!" Eban's bellow had lost a great deal of its volume.

She went to the door of the sleeping cabin.

Eban cast a baleful look at her. "How are you feeling?"

She wasn't deceived into believing his interest contained any actual concern for her state of health. "I feel all right."

"Get Mr. Vickers down here."

She went topside and found the first mate checking some new halyards some of the crew had just finished replacing. "My husband is ill. He wishes to speak to you in the cabin."

He followed her back and said, "Yes, captain?"

Eban had drawn himself up to sit on the edge of the bed when the first mate entered. His face, what was visible above his beard, was bloodless, as were his lips. His voice was reedy as he asked, "Are any of the officers sick?"

"None that I know of, sir."

"Well, find out for sure and report back here."

"Aye, aye, sir!"

Vianna was no sooner back in her chair than Eban made for the water closet where she heard him groaning and gasping for a very long time. He was still in there when Mr. Vickers returned and spoke to him through the closed door of the toilet.

"No one else is sick, sir."

"They're not?" Thin as Eban's voice was, it was easy to hear the surprise in it.

"No, sir."

"Well, if anyone else gets sick, let me know at once, do you hear?"

"Aye, sir."

"That's all, Mr. Vickers."

"Aye, sir."

Vianna ran a finger along the spine of her book pensively. She, Eban, and the officers had eaten porpoise sausage, boiled potatoes, and onions at their noon meal. Their dessert had been fresh pineapple left from the supply procured in the Marquesas. They had all drunk tea from the same pot. In fact, everything had come from the same platter or pot except the pineapple. John Colby had brought that out in individual dishes. The opportunity had existed for the steward to poison

Eban. If he had indeed done it, did he mean to kill Eban or merely make him so ill he would head for Lahaina and a doctor?

Your imagination is running wild, she scolded herself. Eban was dreadfully sick, though, much more so than anyone she had ever seen, and more so than a mere stomach upset would be responsible for. If it were not poison, the cause was some very serious ailment that, if it did not kill him, might force him to take the ship to Lahaina.

At the end of an hour, not having heard further from Mr. Vickers, Eban sent Vianna for him again. The report was the same. No one else had been taken ill. By this time Eban was too sick to sit up, and after he had dismissed the mate, he glared up at Vianna from his pillow. "You've poisoned me," he declared weakly.

Her eyes widened in surprise and she gaped at him. "I've done no such thing!"

Her astonishment over his accusation was so unfeigned that not even Eban could doubt her. "If it wasn't you, it had to be the steward."

"That's nonsense, Eban! You haven't been poisoned. You've eaten something that has disagreed with you."

"Nothing ever disagrees with me except bad fish, and if there had been something wrong with that sausage, the rest of you would have fallen sick, too."

"Then there surely is something seriously wrong inside you, and you should get to a doctor as soon as possible."

Snarling, he said, "That's what you're hoping for, isn't it?" A cramp hit him, doubling him up and wringing a tortured moan from him. When he could speak, he said, "Send the steward to see me." Weak as he was, he could still bark.

Vianna found John Colby still in the steward's pantry, sitting on the small box. "He wants to see you. He believes you have poisoned him," she warned.

"He does, does he?" He had gotten to his feet,

wavering on undependable knees and unable for the moment even to straighten to his usual stoop. His voice revealed neither surprise nor fear at her announcement. Without further comment he shuffled behind her and went to the door of the sleeping cabin. "You wanted to see me, captain?"

"What did you put in my food? Out with it, man. There's no use of your denying it. I know you've poisoned me, and I want to know what you used. There may be something I can take to counteract it." He pointed a threatening finger at the steward. "Tell me or I'll have you keelhauled."

"I never poisoned you, captain," John Colby declared firmly. "Not intentionally, anyway. There might have been something wrong with the sausage, but if there was I didn't know about it."

"You're lying. The sausage didn't poison me, you did. If it had been the fish, everyone who ate it would have got sick."

"It doesn't always happen that way. Some stomachs are just a mite more sensitive to some things. If the fish was just a tad off, it might not have bothered the others who et it."

Another cramp hit Eban, sending him rolling about the bed in agony. When it subsided, his voice broke on a sob as he cried thinly, "Blast you, Colby! Tell me what you've dosed me with or I'll call Mr. Vickers down this minute and order him to keelhaul you."

"I can't tell you what I don't know, captain."

"Vianna, get Mr. Vickers!"

She had been standing to one side of John Colby, out of Eban's sight, listening, wishing she could see the steward's face. But perhaps it was not giving away any more than was his voice. Perhaps he was telling the truth. On the other hand, admitting he poisoned Eban would not have saved him from punishment. Either way, he was going to die. A man of his age and in his rheumatic condition couldn't survive being hauled across the keel of the ship. She did not know how

Eban would order it done. Hauling John Colby from bow to stern would likely drown him. If it were to be from one side of the ship to the other, the immersion in the cold water would do him in if the scraping across the barnacle-encrusted hull didn't.

She made no response to Eban's demand that she fetch the first mate. Instead she crept noiselessly out of the cabin and up the companionway in search of Mr. Vickers. She spied him immediately just going into the bosun's locker across the deck from the companionway door. She crossed behind the helmsman and entered the small storage area that smelled strongly of oakum and hemp. "Mr. Vickers, John Colby is in serious trouble. The captain believes he has poisoned him and is going to have him keelhauled. Some of us who ate the same food will have to pretend we have sickened, too."

At the word keelhauled, the chief mate sucked in his breath. Before he could say a word, John Colby came up to the doorway and said to Vickers, "The captain wants to see you right now." His pasty color had returned.

Vianna's eyes went to the mate and she said in a rush, "Delay a moment or two. I'm going to be sick." She crossed back to the companionway, pulling a handkerchief from the pocket of her dress. When she had descended to the cabin, she pressed it to her mouth and, with a loud groan, rushed through the sleeping cabin to the water closet. Imitating the sounds she had heard Eban make in there, she pretended to be miserably sick, even going so far as to stick a finger down her throat to induce vomiting. When she emerged a few minutes later, she tried to look as shaky as possible. Eban regarded her curiously. "Whatever you've got, I've got, too," she said faintly, and patting her mouth with the handkerchief, she made for the sofa as if she couldn't wait to lie down.

She had no sooner stretched herself out there than

Mr. Vickers knocked. "The captain asked to see me, ma'am."

"Go on in, please," she urged feebly.

He went quickly across to the sleeping cabin and declared, "I hope I didn't keep you waiting, captain, but I've got three men up on deck who are most terrible sick."

"Who are they?"

"Mr. Hadley, sir, Walker, and Steele." The last two were harpooners who would have eaten the same food as was served in the captain's mess.

"I told you to report to me at once if any of the other officers got sick."

"I only found out about it a few minutes ago, sir. They thought they could carry on with their duties, but they're heaving and rolling around the deck in awful pain now."

"You're sure?"

"Yes, sir. I don't know when I've seen men so sick. What do you suppose it could be?"

There was definite relief in Eban's reply. "Something we ate, Mr. Vickers. Your turn is coming, and I can guarantee you the worst bellyache you've ever had in your life. That's all."

Dismissed, the first mate turned and on his way out exchanged a conspiratorial glance with Vianna, who decided it was time for another dramatic trip to the water closet and made a rush for it. When she came out, Eban was curled up in agony, oblivious to anything except his own suffering. Back on the sofa, Vianna considered the situation. Either Eban had actually been poisoned or he was seriously ill from natural causes. If he believed it was food poisoning, he would wait it out, expecting to get better soon. Left untreated, his ailment might very well prove fatal. She doubted there existed any antidote for whatever poison John Colby might have used, and if Eban's attack was caused by a bad appendix or something similar, he probably could not get to a doctor in time to save his life. They were weeks away from the Sandwich Islands, the only place in the whole Pacific where there was a hospital. If Eban survived this attack but remained ill, maybe he would make for Lahaina. For now, there was nothing she could do but wait and continue her pretense in order to save John Colby, innocent or guilty, from being keelhauled.

Eban remained deathly sick for three days. Continued diarrhea, vomiting, and pain brought periods of delirium, during which Vianna nursed him. At the end of those three days, his symptoms faded, leaving him lucid but wasted and spent. In the interval Vianna had decided that if he recovered, she would pretend she had not. Eban took such satisfaction in punishing her that she was convinced he did not want her to die. Her death would rob him of the pleasure of revenge. She hoped that if he believed she were in danger of dying, he would get her to a doctor in an attempt to keep her alive. It was the only chance remaining for her to save the life of her baby.

He did not seem concerned, however, when he learned from Mr. Vickers that, although the other officers had recovered from what he still believed to be food poisoning, Vianna had not. "How can you still be sick?" he demanded as, still too weak to be up and about, he lay and watched her emerge shakily from the water closet. "You were well enough to nurse me. I can remember you washing me."

Vianna made her eyelids appear very heavy and replied feebly, "I never did become as violently ill as you did. I've been able to get around a bit, but I can keep almost nothing on my stomach."

"Well, you'll get over it the same as I did. Tell the steward I'll be coming to the table for supper, and tell him to serve salt beef and biscuit. There's nothing better for settling a stomach."

Vianna went to find John Colby. He was up on deck, smoking his pipe and visiting up around the forecastle with some of the crew who were off watch. When she delivered the message, he took his pipe from his mouth and blew out a stream of smoke slowly. The breeze caught it, carrying it over his shoulder and away from her. "He's feeling better, then?" he asked.

The other three crewman waited for her reply with more than polite interest, she thought. "He seems fully recovered except that he's staggery as a newborn colt."

"I could bring him his supper if he feels like eating. There's no need for him to come to the mess until he's stronger."

Was he looking for another chance to poison Eban, now that his first attempt had failed? Or were she and Eban suspecting him of a deed he was not guilty of? The steward's pale, dark-eyed face told her nothing. "I'll suggest it to him,'" she replied, "but I'm sure he's already made up his mind to go to the table." Which meant that Vianna could not dine in the mess as she had been doing, not if she wanted to continue the pretense that she was still ill. "I'd appreciate it if you'd bring some broth to me in the cabin for my supper. I'm still not feeling well."

John Colby eyed her speculatively, then replied, "I'll bring you the broth, ma'am."

She thanked him and took a few turns around the deck, enjoying the fresh air and sun, before returning to the cabin to take up her role as invalid. Eban met the suggestion that he take his supper in the cabin with surly silence. Vianna shrugged inwardly and took her place on the sofa again, feigning lassitude.

The steward brought a bowl of broth and some biscuit to her while Eban and the other officers were eating. "I'm sorry you're still feeling poorly, Mrs. Stanbro."

In a voice that she hoped wouldn't be heard in the next room, she explained, "I'm all right, but I hope if I pretend to be sick enough, the captain will decide to take me to Lahaina. From some of the things he has said, I believe he wants to keep me alive. I'll need your help, John. You'll have to sneak some solid food to me when you can, because I'm going to induce vomiting each time after Eban knows I've eaten to make him think I can't keep any food down."

John Colby gave her an approving nod. "I hope it works, and you can count on me. It's the only way left, I guess, for me to lend a hand."

That enigmatic remark was the last hint she received from the steward that he might have tried to poison Eban. She never did know for certain, but she harbored the suspicion for as long as she lived.

For a week she deceived Eban into thinking she was still desperately ill. At the end of that time, she began to plead with him to set course for Lahaina and get her to a doctor. "The food poisoning was complicated by the fact that I'm carrying a child," she told him one night as he prepared for bed. She lay on the sofa, her face powdered with flour that John Colby had slipped in to her, the skin under her eyes smudged with a bit of ink. Much practice had made her skillful at speaking in a frail voice. "I can't go on like this for very much longer or I'll die."

He regarded her coldly as he unbuttoned his shirt. "You can't be as bad as you let on. You haven't lost any weight."

That had been something she couldn't do anything about except think up an explanation that sounded plausible. "What you see is the puffiness and bloat every pregnant woman develops. It will increase as my condition worsens. It's a very bad sign. Believe me, Eban, I know. I've heard my mother and Aunt Mercy whisper about these things." She was counting on his ignorance. As a man and as a bachelor until a few months ago, he would know nothing about pregnancy. "Please, I beg of you, get me to a doctor."

"Hunting is too good," he said brusquely. "I'm not going to leave here because you're too much of a molly-coddle to throw off a case of food poisoning. Pull yourself together and stop acting as if you've got one foot in your grave." Upon delivering that command, he left her and went to bed.

Determined not to give up, Vianna made a trip to the water closet to vomit every time Eban was present in the cabin. Most of her performance was merely sound effects, but after a few more days of this, she pretended to be too weak to go each time to the toilet, setting the washbasin beside the sofa and making sure there was a little water in there all the time so that Eban would believe she couldn't keep even water down. His recovery had been steady and he spent most of his time on deck, giving her plenty of opportunity to get up and move around, read, or eat the solid food John Colby sneaked in to her. She longed to go up on deck for some fresh air and exercise, but that was out of the question.

At the end of another week she was pretending to be much worse. Whenever Eban was below, she kept her eyes closed as if she were only partially conscious. The smudges beneath her eyes had been made darker, and a little of the ink applied to her lips gave them a blue look against her floured skin.

"Eban," she said at last, in a voice that sounded as if she were summoning her last measure of strength.

He had just entered; he paused beside the desk, glowering down at her.

"You must get me to a doctor," she whispered. She kept her lips stiff and her eyes closed.

"A doctor would give you the same powder you've been taking. There's nothing else to be done for an upset stomach."

"This is more than an upset stomach." She gazed imploringly up at him, saying piteously, "I'm dying, Eban. Surely you can see that it's true."

He stared at her for a long time. The grooves that started at each side of his thin nose and ran into his beard had deepened since his illness. They helped lend to his face the accusatory quality that she had seen in pictures of Biblical prophets. She let her eyelids fall, afraid he'd detect the lie she was acting out. It was not necessary to fake rapid, shallow breathing with him staring at her like that.

When at last he spoke, it was in that eerily calm tone he had used the day he told her he would kill her baby. "God would not want you to die. If you are dead, I can't punish you. I suppose I must take you to Lahaina." Almost as if he were sleepwalking, he turned and left the cabin.

With prickling scalp, Vianna listened to him go up on deck. Was he really going to change course for Lahaina? She waited tensely, scarcely daring to believe she was finally going to return to civilization, where she could surely manage to get away from Eban. During his illness he had behaved so normally that she had almost forgotten he was mad. Even in his periods of delirium he had sounded saner than he had just a moment ago. She rubbed the chill from her arms, then lay still again, waiting for her body to sense the ship's turn. Before it could, John Colby came limping with surprising speed down the stairs and into the cabin, his face alight.

"We're heading for Lahaina! The captain told the mate to get him there as quick as he can. No hunting along the way!"

Relief brought a sensation like sudden release from great pain. "We did it, John," Vianna exclaimed softly.

He grinned. "Yes, ma'am."

"I'll have to continue being sick, though. We'll have to carry on as we have been."

"Don't worry, Mrs. Stanbro. I'll see you're well fed. You've got to keep your strength up."

Indeed she did. Her time was so near, and she didn't want anything to happen to her baby now. They would both be safe soon. She didn't doubt for a minute that once she was in a doctor's hands, she would not only be delivered of her baby safely, she would also be able with the doctor's help to break free of Eban forever.

"How long will it take us to get to Lahaina?" she asked.

"About a month," the steward replied.

·· She laughed softly. It struck her that this was the first time she had laughed since she could remember. "A month is a long time to be sick, but I'll manage."

It wasn't easy. She found it tiresome to pretend so constantly. Her stomach grew sore from induced vomiting. She longed to be able to enjoy a real meal at leisure instead of bolting some food in the cabin while Eban was absent. The cabin! There were times when she couldn't stand its cramped space any longer and would rush to throw open a window, thrusting her head out to feel the wind and spray on her skin.

As they drew near the Islands that last week, her close confinement and all the pretense grew more irksome. Anticipation increased her restlessness, making it more difficult to act the role of invalid. To make matters worse, the weather was fair and warm. During that last week, she began to sneak up to the deck at night while Eban was asleep to take some exercise. She knew she had nothing to fear from the watch. The crew would not give her away to the captain and neither would Mr. Hadley. She never appeared on deck during Mason Orne's watch.

They were three days from Lahaina when she thought for a few panic-stricken minutes that she had been found out. "Where have you been?" Eban's voice came out of the dark at her as she crept back into the cabin from one of her night walks above.

For an instant she was too startled to speak. She could envision her whole deception crumbling. Fright gave to her voice a genuine faintness as, thinking swiftly, she said, "Oh, Eban, I had the most terrible dream," then collapsed as carefully as she could in the darkness at his feet.

Nothing happened. Eban remained silent, unmoving. Had he swallowed her little act, or was his rage building to the point of another beating? Vianna was steeling herself for a kick in the ribs when, with a curse, he swooped down, lifted her off the floor, and put her down on the sofa. By the faint light that came through the window above her, she saw his tall, nightshirted figure disappear into the sleeping cabin. She waited a few minutes, heart still pounding madly, before she pretended to regain consciousness, making slight movements and moaning softly. When no further sounds came from the sleeping cabin, she began to relax. What a fool she had been! From now on, she wouldn't move from the sofa except to visit the water closet. She would give her best performance to date as a wasting invalid during these last few days.

She told John Colby about her close call the next morning when he brought her second breakfast in to her. She had made sure Eban had seen and heard her losing her first breakfast. He was on deck now, however, and she applied herself hungrily to the fried potatoes and pork chops on the desk before her.

"I thought for a few minutes that all was lost," she told the steward. "How Eban discovered I was gone, I'll never know. He must have come into this cabin for some reason, though, and found the sofa empty." She chewed the crisp pork with relish. "I've never been so startled in my life as I was when his voice boomed out at me from the dark, demanding to know where I had been." She related to him how she had pretended to faint.

John Colby had looked upset ever since she began her account of her close call. Now he cautioned, "You've got to be more careful, ma'am. I sure wouldn't take any more midnight strolls if I was you. It wouldn't do to ruin everything when we're so close to Lahaina."

"Don't worry. I intend to——" Her voice trailed off as Eban appeared in the open cabin door.

He didn't come in. He just stood there, glaring murderously at her. Seeing the color drain from her face, John Colby turned around and froze. His movement drew Eban's attention away from Vianna. "Get out! I'll deal with you later." He strode into the room and made for the sleeping cabin. The steward exchanged an apprehensive look with Vianna, then shuffled out.

Eban reappeared, whipping the length of black whalebone back and forth through the air so fast it sang. Vianna hadn't seen it since the beating he gave her after he learned from the captain of the clipper that she had slipped a note to the captain of the *Contest*.

She lunged ponderously to her feet and tried to get to the door, but Eban cut her off, pushing her so hard that she fell sprawling backward on the sofa.

"You never tire of making a fool of me, do you?" he asked in a terrifyingly soft voice, making the black whip sing again. "I can't kill you, but I can make you wish for death." He brought the whip down across her swollen abdomen.

Vianna screamed and tried to push herself up, but she couldn't break through the flurry of blows that rained down upon her. She felt every one of them. She prayed for unconsciousness, but it wouldn't come. Eban did not quit until his breath was whistling in his throat. When he left her, she was too exhausted from her futile struggle to escape the singing black whip and too wracked with pain to move, although she felt blood running down her bare arm. Overhead she heard Mr. Vickers call out to the watch to make some sail changes. A few minutes later the shaft of sunlight that shone through the window above the washstand and onto the floor of the day cabin slowly shifted and disappeared. Vianna began to sob weakly. Eban was turning the ship. They would not be going to Lahaina.

As she lay in a haze of pain, she heard other sounds, unfamiliar orders, strange scrapings and thuds. After a while she realized what was happening. Eban was preparing to have John Colby keelhauled. Now and then she heard Eban's voice or that of Mr. Vickers. Beyond that, a sullen silence fell over the ship. Would the crew rebel against Eban's sadistic command? The ship was less than two days from the Islands. They could take it in and explain what had happened. They must know they would have her supportive testimony, too.

The preparations continued. Knowing nothing about this rare form of punishment, Vianna could not follow their progress by the orders she heard given. It was when she heard a great deal of activity immediately above her head on the afterdeck, followed by a splash, that she knew the command was being carried out, and in its worst form. John Colby was being pulled one hundred feet or more underwater from stern to bow. At least at this latitude the water was warm. If he didn't drown, perhaps he would survive.

With superhuman effort she dragged herself to her feet and made for the companionway. By the time she had managed to pull herself to the top of the steps, it was all over. Leaning against the hatch frame, she heard shouts from the bow.

"Hoist him up!"

"Easy now."

"Is he alive?"

"Pump the water out of him!"

Vianna didn't recognize any of the voices. They belonged to John Colby's fellow crewmen, who had been faced with the choice of aiding in this terrible punishment or committing a crime for which they could have been hanged.

The crowd in the bow was so big she couldn't see what was happening. Eban stood near the bulwark in a little area of space that the crew scrupulously avoided. Too weak to go to the bow or even make herself heard up there from where she stood, she croaked to the helmsman, "Find out if he's alive, please."

The man tore his eyes from her bloodied condition and shouted, "Will he live?"

It was the first mate who replied from somewhere within the huddle of men surrounding the steward. "He's starting to breathe."

"Thank God!" Her legs were trembling and threatening to give way. She made her way slowly back down to the cabin and collapsed on the sofa. She would never get free of Eban. Her baby would die; perhaps she would, too. But if John Colby lived, she would not have another man's death on her conscience.

A substitute steward informed her later that morning that John would be all right, but it would be several days before he would be able to resume his duties.

Vianna did not recover from her beating. Some of the pain faded, but after two days she began to feel almost as sick as she had previously pretended to be. When she became aware that the baby was no longer moving inside her womb, she was alarmed.

"I think you've killed my baby," she told Eban one morning, just barely managing to keep her voice under control. He was dressing and came to the door of the sleeping cabin, pulling his suspenders over his shoulders. Her announcement brought only a stony glance from him before he turned away to pour some water into the basin for a wash.

Maintaining her calm with great effort, Vianna went on. "I haven't felt any movement since you beat me the other day. There's definitely something wrong inside me. I began to feel sick yesterday. I feel much worse today."

Eban made a sound of disgust and said over his shoulder, "Stop it, Vianna! You should know by now you only waste your time trying to deceive me."

"That is not the case this time. I am really and truly sick, and I believe it's because the baby is dead inside me. If I don't give birth within a day or two, I'll die. I may die in any event. The baby is decaying inside my womb."

"And I must turn the ship around and take you to Lahaina?" Eban came back to the door to shoot her a contemptuous look. "You never give up, do you?"

Vianna bit her lip. How was she going to make him believe her? Struggling to keep her panic at bay, she said, "Ask God if I am deceiving you. You know He does not want me to die. He will tell you I am not lying."

Eban turned almost purple. "You're not going to make me appear a fool before God, too! If I hear another word out of you about going to Lahaina, I'll beat you again!" He whirled and plunged his face into the washbasin, snorting and splashing furiously.

Vianna turned her head toward the back of the sofa. The despairing movement sent a wave of sickness through her. She couldn't stand another beating, not so soon. She would wait a day, perhaps two, and try again. Or maybe by then she would be so sick she would not have to say a word. Eban could see for himself that this was not another attempt to deceive him.

Twenty-four hours later she went into labor. Even though the delivery was an easy one, she was out of her head much of the time. She did rouse, however, when she felt her body expel the baby. Opening her eyes, she saw Eban examining it at the foot of the bed. The awful odor alone was enough to tell her it was dead. Her wail of despair could scarcely be heard. "Tom," she cried, then fell into a coma.

12

Tom's name was on her lips when she opened her eyes. She had been talking to him. Where was he? He had been here in her room just a moment ago. Sunlight filtered in from the slatted blinds that covered the huge open windows to her left and at the foot of her bed. Her eyes opened wider. This wasn't her bedroom! It wasn't the ship's cabin, either! She turned her head and found a small white table beside the bed on her right. It held a pitcher and a glass, both sparkling clean. Her bed was narrow and plain and covered with a sheet and a light blue blanket. There was a strong smell of antiseptic in the air, mingling peculiarly with the fragrance of the brilliant red and yellow flowers blooming outside one window.

I'm in a hospital, Vianna told herself. But where? Is this Lahaina?

A girl appeared in the doorway to Vianna's right, drawn, Vianna guessed, by the murmuring she'd been doing as she regained consciousness. Brown-skinned, with long black hair and pretty features, she wore a long dress of vivid, flowered cotton and no shoes. She glided toward the bed, smiling. "You awake finally? I go get doctor."

"Wait. Where am I?"

"American Hospital. Lahaina."

Vianna closed her eyes in an ecstasy of relief. "Thank God." When she opened her eyes again, the girl was gliding silently out of the room in her bare feet.

She was alive! And out of Eban's clutches, at least

for the time being. Somehow she would make that condition permanent. She took stock of her physical condition. She was so weak that it took great effort to move her head or speak. Her body beneath the light blanket was very thin. She appeared taller than she remembered, but perhaps that was because it had been several months since she'd been able to lie on her back and see all the way to her toes. With a sense of emptiness, she recalled the baby. It had been a boy, something of Tom to hold in her arms, to love and cherish for the rest of her life. Now she had nothing left of him except memories. Tears spilled out of her eyes, running across her temples and into the pillow.

A small, gray-haired man in a white coat, moving with slow deliberation, came into the room. Behind his spectacles his eyes were sharp, but when he spoke, his voice was kind. "Well, Mrs. Stanbro, you've had us worried. How do you feel?"

"Weak. Other than that, I don't feel anything."

He smiled. "That's a good answer. I'm Dr. Young, and I've been taking care of you ever since your husband brought you in last Thursday."

"What day is today?"

"Friday. You've been here nine days, so you can understand why I'm so delighted that you've regained consciousness. Just let me check a few things." After a thorough and intimate examination that left her flushed with embarrassment, he announced, "It's a good thing you are as young as you are, Mrs. Stanbro. An older woman wouldn't have survived what you've been through."

She asked in surprise, "You know all about it?"

He raised his sharply angled eyebrows. "About the baby dying several days before it was born? Of course. Your husband told me how it was born while he was hurrying to get you to Lahaina."

"He lied," Vianna declared flatly.

The physician's face showed no change of expression.

"You're saying he lied about the baby's being born dead?"

He thought she was one of the women who, because they couldn't accept the loss of their baby, would insist that it was all a mistake or that someone was playing a horrible trick on them and keeping their baby away from them for some reason. "I know my baby was born dead," she said heavily. "I was conscious and I saw it. The ship was not hurrying toward Lahaina, though. It was sailing away from here." She related the whole story, groping for words when she came to the part about the baby. Doctor Young caught on at once. "The baby was Tom's?" he asked bluntly.

She nodded, unable to look at him, her eyes on her hands as they nervously twined and untwined on top of the light blanket.

"And then?" he prodded.

This time she spoke weakly but without pause, giving the full account of her experiences aboard the *Trident* that ended with the delivery of her dead baby. "Now that I'm off that ship, I'm never going back, but I'll need your help, doctor."

"There's nothing either of us can do while you are this weak, young lady. We'll talk about it again when you're stronger."

Vianna studied the empty smile in the pink face that was surprisingly smooth beneath the gray eyebrows and hair. "You don't believe a word I said," she declared dully.

"You did some wild raving in your delirium, Mrs. Stanbro. It will take you a few days to sort out reality from those hallucinations. Don't let them frighten you. Just remember they were merely bad dreams."

Earnestly, Vianna objected. "I don't know what I said while I was delirious. It may have had nothing at all to do with the ugly situation I'm in. I can assure you, however, that the story I've told you is true, every word of it. Surely you saw the bruises left on my body by Eban's last savage beating."

The doctor spoke as if to a disturbed child, gently but firmly. "You fell in your cabin while the ship was pitching in a storm, Mrs. Stanbro. That's the source of your bruises, not a beating, and the cause of your baby's being born dead."

"That's not true! Eban has been beating me regularly ever since we sailed from Govans Harbor. Any crewman on my husband's ship will verify it . . . anyone except possibly the second mate, Mr. Orne. He has disliked me from the day I came aboard." She raised one hand slightly in an imploring gesture. "Go talk to the crew. Please!"

Doctor Young took the hand and, patting it, said, "Don't agitate yourself. You'll only do yourself harm. A serene mental condition is as necessary to your recovery as rest and nourishing food."

Her voice rising, she protested, "I won't have any peace of mind until I have your promise to prevent my husband from taking me back aboard his ship!"

He patted her hand again, then laid it gently at her side. "We'll talk about it later. I'll have some food brought in to you, and you must eat it whether you're hungry or not. The more you eat, the quicker you'll regain your strength."

Vianna sighed wearily. She hadn't expected it to be easy, but she hadn't expected to be as weak and helpless as a baby, either. Doctor Young's admonition about eating hadn't been necessary. She was determined to regain her health and strength as fast as she could.

When the native girl came in, she bore not only a bowl with a spoon in it but also a large red flower in a gourd vase. "I thought you like," she said, smiling, as she set it on the bedside table.

"It's beautiful." Vianna was touched by her thoughtfulness. "Thank you." In the starkly furnished room the scarlet blossom was as showy as a Fourth of July rocket. "What is its name?"

"Hibiscus. Will last all day without water. See." The girl shook the vase to demonstrate its emptiness.

"Incredible, and it's quite the loveliest thing I've ever seen."

The girl pulled up a small white chair from the corner and gestured toward the profusion of flowers growing outside the window at the end of the room. "Those hibiscus, too."

Vianna looked at the bowl of oatmeal the girl was preparing to feed her. "What time of day is it?" She was certain by the look of the sunshine outside that it was not morning.

"Is two hours past midday."

"What is your name?"

"Maile," the girl replied shyly.

She doesn't look any older than I am, Vianna thought. "How long have you worked here in the hospital, Maile?"

"Two years. I went to missionary school. I learn English there. Doctor Young teach me to nurse." She spooned the heavily sugared porridge and cream into Vianna's mouth with graceful brown hands.

"Do you like taking care of sick people?"

Maile declared matter-of-factly, "It make me feel good. Is nice to help people."

"Are you married?"

The girl ducked her dark head. "No, but I marry soon. His name is Kekoa." Her voice was soft.

"Does he work here?"

"No, he fisherman. He sell fish to hospital and to *haoles.*"

Vianna repeated the unfamiliar word. *"Haoles?"*

"White people. The boardinghouses for whalers and wives buy from Kekoa. Missionaries. Even American consul say his fish freshest and best," Maile informed Vianna proudly. She nodded approvingly as Vianna accepted the last spoonful of oatmeal. "You eat good. Will make husband very happy when he come tonight and doctor tells him. We afraid you die."

"Has my husband been coming every night?"

Maile nodded. "He very worried."

Worried that she would die and he'd be robbed of the pleasure of beating her. Worried, too, that she would regain consciousness and betray him to the doctor. What would he do when he found out she had done that very thing? She had no doubt he would counter her story in some way, probably with the same explanation he had presented to Captains Loper and Tucker. The situation was altogether different now, however. Would a doctor accept his implication that pregnancy, or even the death of her baby, had addled her mind? Doctor Young's initial response to her tale had not been encouraging, but there would be time to bring him around to believing her eventually, she hoped.

The conversation with the doctor and the simple task of eating had exhausted her. When Maile left, Vianna closed her eyes, and for a little while her mind was as empty as the bowl Maile had carried away. As she began to feel once again the lightness of her body, grief moved back into her heart. She had never felt so empty, so physically bereft. Now that she did not have Tom's child, she had nothing. She wept quietly, then slept.

When she awakened to the sound of rich laughter and voices speaking in a strange tongue outside the window to her left, and saw the brilliant hibiscus through the slatted blinds of the window at the end of her room, the sorrow that weighed upon her lifted a bit, lightened by the sensation of freedom. Gone was the oppressive presence of Eban, the feeling of being confined in a prison at the mercy of a brutal jailer. Hope, a dark and desperate emotion for so long, glowed fresh and alive. She would get back home to Govans Harbor! She knew it! Nothing and no one would ever get her back aboard the *Trident*. In the next two weeks, perhaps longer, that it took her to return to good health, she could find a means of revealing Eban for the madman he was and obtaining the protection of someone who would keep him away from her. Doctor Young was the most convenient candidate for this, and when he came in to check her before leaving the hospital for the day, she followed up on her earlier request that he confirm the truth of her story by checking with the crew of the *Trident*.

In reply to her query, the doctor said he had not. "I've been in surgery," he explained. The pink face that had appeared so smooth when she saw him a few hours ago was drawn with fatigue and tension now. He wore a fresh white coat.

"Will you go to the *Trident* tomorrow?" she persisted.

He pulled up the small, white, wooden chair and sat down beside her bed, sighing. "Tomorrow you will recognize your hallucinations for what they were, and then there will be no need for me to go to your husband's ship."

"And if I don't, will you do as I ask? You said a serene mental condition was essential to my recovery. Don't you think humoring me in this case should be part of your treatment?"

He laughed. "You are a very cunning young lady. I'll wager that you almost always manage to get what you want."

"You are so wrong, doctor." Her voice broke slightly. The two things she had wanted more than anything else in the world—Tom and his child—she had lost. "My life depends upon your believing my story, and I promise you that if you make no effort to test the truth of it, I won't get well. I'll refuse to eat, and I'll do anything else I can to make sure I have to be kept here and away from my husband."

Somewhere up the hall a man began to cough. She had heard that sound once before in her life. Her mother's only brother had died of consumption. Vianna had been very young at the time, but she had never forgotten how he had sounded as he coughed his life away.

Dr. Young waited until the hospital grew quiet again before remarking, "A hospital is a dreary place, my dear, sometimes even for those of us who work in it. I think that after you've been here a couple of weeks, you'll be only too happy to leave."

Now it was Vianna's turn to laugh, but there was no mirth in it. "Compared to the hell I've escaped, doctor, your hospital is as gay as a picnic. I could spend the rest of my life here and feel myself lucky. However, I don't plan to stay here forever. I want to return to my home in Govans Harbor, Massachusetts. Are there any ships in the harbor that are returning to the United States?"

"I don't know. I'm afraid I don't pay any attention to the ships that go in and out of here, except when a crewman from one of them is brought in for treatment."

"You could find out if you'd go to the wharf tomorrow to visit the *Trident*."

Laughter wiped away the weariness and strain from his face. "You are persistent, aren't you?"

"When you talk to the crew of the *Trident*, you'll understand why."

Still looking amused, he stood up and replaced the chair in its corner. "With spirit like yours, Mrs. Stanbro, your recovery is inevitable. I must get on to some other patients whose prognosis is not so cheerful or so certain. Eat a good supper tonight, and by morning your head will be clear and you can pester me about something else."

"Doctor, are you ever wrong?"

"Sometimes."

"Good. If you admit to that, then I can go on hoping you'll believe my story one of these days."

He smiled at her. "Good night, young lady. I'll see you in the morning."

It wasn't Maile who brought her supper. The new

nurse was about twenty years older than Maile, nearly six feet tall, and must have weighed several hundred pounds, without being fat. "Is nice see you awake. My name Hali." Her black hair was cut shorter than the younger nurse's had been, and there was nothing shy about her. She gave Vianna a warm smile as she set the supper tray on the bedside table and drew her up on her pillows.

"I can feed myself tonight," Vianna said, brushing her loose blond hair back from her face.

"In morning, maybe. Not tonight," Hali said firmly, knocking the top off of a soft-boiled egg and thrusting a spoonful of it into Vianna's mouth.

Vianna permitted herself to be treated like a sick child, and by the time all the egg and fresh fruit had been eaten, she was so tired that she saw the wisdom of Hali's imperious refusal to allow her to eat by herself. She also found that despite the older nurse's authoritative manner, she was warm and friendly, and after living in a totally masculine world for eight months, Vianna took great pleasure in her company.

In fact, when supper was over and Vianna had rested, she felt almost like the girl she had once been in that other lifetime in Govans Harbor. The pleasant interlude was brief, however. As she lay listening to the strange and beautiful birdcalls that came through the now-closed windows, she became aware of familiar footsteps coming down the hall toward her room. There was no mistaking them. Her thin body tensed, and when Eban came into the room she continued to gaze through the blinds.

"So you're awake," he said brusquely.

She made no comment.

"Does the doctor know you've regained consciousness?"

He was fishing. He wanted to know if she had spilled the whole ugly tale to Doctor Young. Vianna settled more deeply into her pillows. Let him wonder. He would get no information out of her.

"Vianna, I asked you a question!"

She continued to gaze through the slatted blinds. The angle of the sun's rays on the grass beyond the narrow arcade outside the window told her it was about to set.

"Answer me, you whore, or I'll——"

Rage sent adrenaline shooting through her. She flung her head around and demanded, "Or you'll what? Beat me? Go ahead, Eban. Let them all see what a beast you are!"

For an instant, she thought he would. He took a step forward, hands reaching for her. Unfortunately, he got himself under control just in time. Shaking with repressed fury, he loomed over her and warned hoarsely, "Just wait until I get you back aboard the ship."

"Get out, Eban! Leave or I'll begin screaming and tell the nurse you struck me."

His face became so gorged with blood she expected him to fall to the floor in a fit of apoplexy. Strange grunting sounds welled up from his heaving chest. Then he whirled on his heel and strode from the room.

The sun had set now. The last remaining rays were gone. As Vianna peered into the gathering dusk, she felt exhilarated. She wasn't a helpless victim any longer. While she was in the hospital, Eban couldn't touch her. On the contrary, he was going to have to play the role of devoted husband. At this thought she knew a moment's anxiety. More than anyone here in the Islands, she knew what a skillful actor he was. Hadn't he deceived them all back in Govans Harbor, pretending to be the forgiving, loving fiancé who still wanted to marry her despite her rejection of him? She was not the sole witness to the type of husband he had shown himself to be, however. There were more than twenty men on the *Trident* who could back up her story. If they would. And if someone would take the trouble to question them.

These were only faint shadows on her present situation. She had a large chunk of time ahead of her in which she could convince someone to prevent Eban from making a prisoner of her once again.

She slept well that night. Maile brought her breakfast, and soon afterward Doctor Young came in.

"Well, young lady, how are you feeling this morning?" His smooth pink face was freshly shaved, his gray hair neatly brushed. His eyebrows formed such perfect inverted V's that she wondered if he had used a razor on them, too.

"Quite well. So far I've eaten everything the nurses have brought me. So far," she repeated with emphasis.

"Still threatening, are you?"

"My head is even clearer than it was yesterday. If you had been here last night when Eban visited me, you'd have seen and heard for yourself that I haven't been merely imagining that my husband is a monster. He almost lost control of himself and struck me. I was hoping he would. I'd have had a fresh bruise as proof to show you this morning."

His response to this was a noncommittal "Hmmm" as he lifted her wrist and began counting her pulse. His examination took several minutes, during which Vianna said nothing more. She wanted his full attention when she pressed her case.

"You seem a trifle stronger," he said at last, "but there's no need to contemplate starving yourself—at least not just yet. Your recovery is going to be slow enough to please even you."

"You're not trying to divert me from carrying out my threat, are you, doctor?"

The flatness of his no was convincing. "You were filled with infection when you were brought in here, Mrs. Stanbro. You haven't got rid of all of it. Your body is laboring to throw it off, and it needs all the help it can get."

"If you would promise me I'd never have to go aboard the *Trident* again, I'd recover so fast it would astound you."

Doctor Young shook his smooth head. "My dear,

I'm only a physician. How could I promise you anything of the sort?"

"By discovering that what I've told you is true and declaring, as my physician, that you can't allow me to accompany my husband on the remainder of his voyage."

"Your husband is a fine man," Doctor Young said reproachfully. "His concern over your condition while we waited to see if you would recover couldn't have been greater."

"I can imagine how well he played his role of anxious husband. You should have seen his performance back home when we resumed our wedding plans." Vianna sighed. "Don't let him fool you. If you'll keep as sharp an eye out for his hypocrisy as you do for physical symptoms in a patient, you'll realize there's something wrong with the man."

The physician smiled. "I can promise that."

Vianna brightened. "That's a start."

"Meantime, young lady, you continue to eat what we bring in to you and give your system all the help you can to flush these poisons from your body."

"Yes, doctor," she agreed meekly.

"I'll see you again this afternoon."

As it turned out, he came in just as she was finishing her noon meal. Maile had allowed her to feed herself and had gone off to wait on other patients. The tray still lay across Vianna's middle, but she had slid down carefully beneath it so that she could get her head lower. It had a tendency to lightness when she raised it. As a matter of fact, her whole body reminded her that she was still filled with infection when she sat up. The faint nausea had left her, and she was feeling much steadier when she saw Doctor Young enter her room with that slow, deliberate tread of his. He was frowning and he looked thoughtful. "John Colby was in a little while ago, asking how you were. He's been in several times this past week. He was very happy to hear you were recovering."

"He's a dear man. The best friend I had on the ship. In fact, Eban had him keelhauled for helping me deceive Eban into bringing me here a few weeks ago."

The doctor looked startled. "Keelhauled? I didn't know whaling captains used that form of punishment."

Vianna captured his gaze and held it. "I told you my husband was a monster."

Doctor Young didn't pull his eyes away from hers. He met them steadily, saying nothing for a few moments. "I told Colby you were making fair progress except you still couldn't separate delirium from reality, and went on to tell him briefly what you told me about Captain Stanbro."

Vianna suddenly went very still.

"He confirmed everything."

Vianna inquired faintly, "Did you believe him?"

"The man's manner was so earnest I couldn't doubt him. Besides, I gave him only part of the story you gave me. He was able to fill in the rest, and it corroborated your account."

She could have shouted for joy. Eagerly she asked, "Will you help me, then?"

"I can keep you here in the hospital as long as possible. Other than that, I don't see that there is anything I can do."

"Tell the police! Tell the company agent! There must be someone who can restrain Eban from carrying me off again."

Doctor Young sighed, pulled up the chair, and sat down. "What would I tell them? That your husband has been beating you? That's no crime, my dear. They might agree it was an unfortunate situation, but they wouldn't interfere in a marital problem."

"He'd have to kill me before it would be considered a crime, is that it?" Vianna asked bitterly.

"Something like that."

"He did kill Bobby Howard. And he tried to kill John Colby."

"Can you prove that?" Doctor Young declared

sadly, "The only crime a captain can commit that he might be brought up on charges for is losing his ship through poor seamanship. In matters pertaining to his crew he has carte blanche."

"There must be something you can do," Vianna said desperately.

"The American consul might help you. You could write him a letter, describing your situation and asking for his protection until you are well enough to return to the United States."

Hope sprang to life again in Vianna. "Would you write the letter for me? My hands are so weak and shaky I couldn't write legibly. I could dictate it to you."

"It's the least I can do."

"Can we do it now?"

He smiled. "Of course. I'll go get what I need."

The letter was hand-delivered to the consul that very afternoon. Vianna expected a reply the next day. It didn't come. In fact, she waited three days, chafing at the delay, being warned by Doctor Young not to excite herself, and enduring the regular evening visits from Eban. During these visits she ignored him for the most part, but now that the doctor was enlisted as an ally, she made no attempt to provoke him into an attack on her. She had endured all of his beatings she was going to—she hoped.

On the fourth day Maile brought her the letter she'd been waiting for. Tearing it open with fingers made strong for the moment by her excitement, she scanned it swiftly, then let out a moan.

Maile had started to leave. She halted in the doorway and looked back, a slender figure in her long green dress. Her pretty face was filling with concern. "Is bad news?"

"Yes," Vianna whispered. "Is Doctor Young here?"

"He gone see sick baby. He come back later."

"Will you ask him to come see me as soon as he returns?"

"Yes." Maile came closer, regarding Vianna anxiously. "You be all right?"

Vianna nodded wearily. "I'm just angry and disappointed, that's all."

"I send doctor right away when he get back," Maile promised, and she glided out.

Vianna started at the beginning of the letter. It was long, apologetic, and sympathetic, and the message could have been conveyed in a single sentence. The American consul was deeply sorry, but he had no authority to intervene in difficulties between a man and his wife. Difficulties! He could dismiss Eban's brutal treatment of her with that inadequate word? With wrathful indignation Vianna crumpled the heavy paper into a ball. It appeared that Eban, as her husband, had as much power over her as he did as captain over his crew. No one was willing to challenge him.

She was concentrating so hard in her attempt to find a new source of help that she didn't hear the quiet knock at her door. Staring sightlessly through the slatted blinds at the green and gold afternoon, she heard someone call, "Mrs. Stanbro?"

Turning her head, she saw two women standing in the doorway. They looked like Americans. In fact, in their calico dresses with scrimshaw brooches they looked so much like the whalers' wives back home in Govans Harbor that she experienced a rush of affection as strong as if she were acquainted with them. "May we come in?" the older one asked.

"Please do." Vianna smiled at them as they came forward.

The one who had spoken was about her mother's age, with the same plump, matronly body. Her hair was dark, however, instead of blond. Her cheerful nature was mirrored in her face and in her gray eyes.

The younger woman was extremely thin, almost to the point of emaciation. Her dark hair had a lifeless look, and her nose and cheeks were sprinkled with freckles although she, like her companion, wore a bonnet to protect her face from the sun.

"I'm Emily Carver," the older woman said, "and this is Florence Aubrey. Our husbands are whaling captains, too, and of course we heard by way of the grapevine immediately that you had been brought into Lahaina aboard your husband's ship, desperately ill. We were so relieved to hear a few days ago that you would recover." She paused and said tentatively, "I hope that we haven't come too soon."

"I'm beginning to feel much better," Vianna told her, "and I can't tell you how good you ladies look to me. You make me feel as if I'm back home in Govans Harbor." She gestured toward the corner. "I'm afraid there is only one chair."

At that moment Maile appeared, carrying a chair identical to the one already in the room. Silent but beaming, she set it down next to the bed, pulled the other one forward, and glided out. "Thank you, Maile," Vianna called after her. To her visitors she declared, "She takes such good care of me."

"Some of the native girls are decent," Florence Aubrey admitted grudgingly, lowering herself into one chair and sitting as primly as her drooping shoulders would permit.

Emily Carver settled much more comfortably onto her chair and said, "We had the pleasure of meeting your father a month ago."

"My father was here? And only a month ago? Oh, how I wish I'd been here then! Where is he now, do you know?"

"He's making straight for home with a full cargo."

"We missed him by so little," Vianna said in a small voice. Tears pricked her eyes. "I was so hoping to see him."

"He expressed the same wish to see you. A merchantman had dropped mail off here several weeks before your father arrived, and there was a letter waiting for him from your mother informing him of your marriage and that you were accompanying your new husband on his first voyage as master of his own ship. He spoke well of his new son-in-law. You appear to be a very fortunate young woman, my dear." Emily Carver hastened to add, "I realize your present sorrow is a heavy burden to bear. I, too, lost a child, a little girl two years old. It was many years ago and I have had other children, but I still feel the loss."

Florence Aubrey declared, "You are young. You will have other children, too."

Vianna dropped her eyes and nodded painfully. *But I wanted this one,* she told the other woman silently. As for having others, she couldn't think of anything more horrible than becoming pregnant by Eban. He must never be allowed to reclaim her as his wife. She wondered if these whalers' wives could be convinced that Eban was mad and be drafted as allies who would prevent him from taking her back aboard his ship. It was unfortunate that her father, ignorant of the truth, had been so free with his admiration of Eban.

"We've not met your husband," Emily Carver told her. "He spends much of his time here with you, we have heard, and the rest of the time on his ship."

It did not surprise Vianna that Eban was avoiding the small colony of Americans in Lahaina. He had never been a sociable person, and besides, the less contact he had with them, the less likely they were to find out the true state of affairs between Eban and her. She wondered if any rumors of the truth had arisen from the *Trident*'s crew. Some of them undoubtedly would tell tales of Eban's brutality while drinking with crews from other ships in Lahaina's taverns. If they had, perhaps it would not be so difficult to convince the women she needed protection from him.

"My husband spends very little time here," she began, feeling her way and watching their expressions closely. "He comes for a few minutes each night to see me. That is all."

"Oh," said Emily Carver, clearly disconcerted. Her

companion said nothing, but she fixed her eyes curiously on Vianna.

"Eban does not always tell the truth."

Neither of the women made any response to this, but Emily Carver began to look uncomfortable.

"The truth of the matter is, he beat me so badly that he caused the death of my baby and almost killed me." Vianna delivered this information in a quiet voice, watching them intently.

"Now, my dear, you shouldn't say such things!" The admonition exploded from Emily Carver. She glanced in embarrassment at her friend. Florence Aubrey returned the glance, but instead of exhibiting embarrassment, she nodded as if the two of them shared some secret knowledge.

Turning to Vianna, the younger woman said sternly, "Mrs. Stanbro, you shouldn't say such things about your husband. When you are feeling better, you will realize they are not true."

Suspicion flickered in Vianna. Slowly she said, "My husband had told you my illness addled my mind, is that it?"

Emily Carver hurried to say reassuringly, "It's nothing to worry about, child. You've been through enough to unbalance any woman, but things will straighten out for you in due time."

Vianna sighed and closed her eyes. It would be futile to try to convince them that it was Eban who was mad, not she.

"Your husband is having a very difficult time, too. You should not forget that," Emily Carver reminded her gently. "His grief over the baby together with his anxiety over you has been a great burden. And he's having the usual problems, besides, with his crew. Two of them have deserted, and he is trying to find replacements."

"It's wicked, that's what it is!" Florence Aubrey's voice dripped disgust.

Vianna opened her eyes and gazed at the flushed,

emaciated face of the younger woman. "What is wicked?"

Florence Aubrey twitched her drooping shoulders. "The way these sailors take up with the native girls. The girls help them run off and hide in the jungle, where they live like savages!"

"Would you know the names of the two men who deserted from the *Trident?*"

Florence Aubrey sniffed, "The steward for one, and I understand he's an old man. One would think he'd be past such things."

Vianna experienced a rush of gladness at the news about John Colby and leapt to the defense of this man who had been her friend and had risked so much to help her. "Mr. Colby's desertion would not have been for immoral reasons. My husband tried once to kill him and failed. He would undoubtedly try again. Mr. Colby is only trying to stay alive."

Florence Aubrey and Emily Carver exchanged another knowing look, then the older woman said easily, "We're tiring you, Mrs. Stanbro. We will be going. If we can do anything to help you, anything at all, just send a message. We are boarding at Mr. Stratton's. We're expecting our husbands any day now and will be here as long as they are in port." She gave Vianna a warm smile. "Good-bye, my dear. I hope your recovery is speedy and complete."

Florence Aubrey's farewell was a nod and a thin smile.

After they left, Vianna lay there thinking about John Colby's escape into the jungle of Maui. She was delighted for him and wondered if he meant to live out the remainder of his life here or if he would surface after a time and sign on another ship. Whatever his choice, she wished him the best. She also wished she knew how he had engineered his disappearance.

She listened to the soft slap of Maile's bare feet somewhere up the hall. Native girls, Florence Aubrey had said. Would Maile know anything about that? If there were ways of hiding deserting sailors from the law, perhaps the same means could be used to hide her until Eban's ship sailed. She dismissed Florence Aubrey's other remark about running away to the jungle to live like savages. From her acquaintance with Maile and Hali, and after observing and listening to the Sandwich Islanders who frequently passed her windows, even though they usually spoke in their native tongue, she couldn't believe that they were savages. Vianna decided she would not be afraid to trust her life to them. On the contrary, it was the thought of being taken back to the *Trident* and once more becoming the victim of the savagery of her supposedly civilized husband that terrified her.

"You asleep?" Maile asked softly, coming to the door. Vianna waved her in. "I was lying here wondering about something." She watched the girl's graceful movements as she returned the one chair to the corner. "How do sailors who desert their ships manage to drop so completely from sight?" There was no doubt about it. Maile's hand paused on the chair and her eyes evaded Vianna's as she went to tighten the blanket at the foot of the bed. "I have a very good reason for asking, Maile. Has Doctor Young told you how my husband beats me?"

"Beats you?" Maile looked up, shocked.

He obviously hadn't told her. "He killed my baby," Vianna declared, and told the girl about the beatings without revealing the reasons for Eban's brutality. By the time she had finished, distress had erased all traces of the happy expression Maile normally wore on her lovely brown face. Shaking her head slowly in horror, she gasped something in her native tongue.

"I would rather die than go back on that ship," Vianna said. "I would like to run away like the sailors do, but I don't know how."

"Is not hard for sailors to run away into jungle. They tough. Not used to soft life like *haole* lady."

"I could be tough if only I had someone to show me the way."

"You sick. Is very hard journey. You might die."

"I'm getting better every day. Soon I'll be strong enough that my husband will take me back to his ship where he can beat me some more. I must be gone from here before then."

Maile drifted thoughtfully to the extra chair, placing her hands on its back. "Doctor Young very good man. He help you."

Vianna explained about her attempts to enlist the aid of the doctor and of the American consul. "They are not going to help me." She held out a hand appealingly to Maile, who came forward and placed her hand in Vianna's. "You and your people are the only hope I have left."

Maile stared at the floor in irresolute silence for so long that Vianna cleared her throat to remind the young nurse that she was there. The girl raised her head slowly and said, "I ask Kekoa. Is secret, though. You must say nothing to anyone, not even doctor."

Vianna squeezed her hand and exclaimed softly, "Not a word!"

The opportunity to help someone brought the smile back to Maile's face. "I tell you tomorrow."

"Thank you," Vianna whispered, beaming. As Maile left with the extra chair, she clasped her hands tightly over her chest, scarcely daring to believe she'd finally found someone willing to help her escape Eban.

13

To Vianna's surprise, Eban visited her shortly after her conversation with Maile. He had never come to see her in the afternoon before. She soon found out why.

"I've talked to the doctor," he growled. "He says you're coming along as well as can be expected, but you won't be strong enough to leave for several weeks. You aren't malingering, are you?" From out of his bearded face came a glare that pressed her into the pillow. "If I find out you are deliberately slowing your recovery, I'll have you transferred to the ship immediately."

Vianna fought to hide her consternation, replying calmly, "I'm eating every bite of food they bring me. The doctor must have told you that. What more can I do?"

"Your deceitful nature would find some way if one were to be found." The intensity of his glare did not diminish.

She sent him a look that expressed her loathing, then turned her head toward the window. A native gardener was working in the round flower bed that graced the front lawn of the hospital, his naked brown chest gleaming in the sun.

"It was clear from Doctor Young's attitude that you have told him about our marriage, making me out to be the villain, of course, and you the innocent party."

Because it was imperative that Eban suspect no one of lending her aid, she said with genuine bitterness,

"He will do nothing. He says he won't interfere in a man's treatment of his wife."

"I had counted on that," Eban said, adding with smug ruthlessness, "I can treat you any way I please."

The truth of that statement had been brought home to her twice in the last few days. She had never before realized what complete power a husband had over his wife. In the marriages among her own family that power had been exercised with such a gentle hand that she wasn't aware of its existence.

"You've made sure I will get no sympathy from the rest of the Americans on the island, too, haven't you? Two whalers' wives came to see me today. You've made them believe I'm crazy."

With a trace of amusement, as much as he was capable of, Eban observed, "They were most distressed to hear it."

Trying for the right combination of anger and hopelessness, Vianna sighed, "So you've eliminated any source of help I might appeal to. I hope you're satisfied."

"I have a mission to carry out. I will let nothing interfere with that," he declared in righteous tones.

"Well, you'd better allow me to recover fully then before you drag me back aboard your ship, or you'll find yourself beating a corpse."

"I'll wait a reasonable time, but my company expects me to hunt whales. Recovered or not, you will sail with me when I'm ready to leave."

He went out, going up the hall with that stride Vianna had come to know and fear.

When the doctor came in for his late afternoon call on her, she showed him the reply she'd received from the American consul. "I'm not surprised," he said. He seemed relieved, too, that the official had taken the same position he had. "I am sorry, though, that there isn't more that we can do."

"Just keep me here as long as you can," Vianna told him.

He gave the letter back to her and jammed his hands forcefully into the pockets of his white coat. "I've already taken steps to assure that. Your husband talked to me this afternoon about you and I warned him your recovery would be slow and would require a great deal of medication and bed rest."

"I hope he'll heed you. He informed me today that he would wait a reasonable time and then it would be out of the hospital for me and back to the ship."

Doctor Young's sharp eyebrows drew down in a frown. "I'll be as persuasive as possible. Now let's see how you are really doing, young lady."

It had been an eventful day, and Vianna fell asleep shortly after supper. She awakened once in the night to the sound of a baby crying somewhere in the hospital. Her loss came back to her like a sudden onset of pain, and she wept. Only when she turned her thoughts to the possibility that she might break free of Eban with Maile's help could she go back to sleep.

She was awake early, waiting impatiently for Maile to bring breakfast. By the time the young nurse arrived, Vianna was in a ferment from anticipation. Her eyes fastened on the girl the moment she glided into the room, trying to read in her expression the answer to the question that had been beating in her brain for the last two hours. Maile wore her usual smile, brilliant as her flowered dress. "*Aloha.*"

"Good morning. I thought you'd never come."

Maile asked in surprise, "I late?"

"No, no, it's just that you were going to tell me something today. You haven't forgotten, have you?"

Maile set the tray on the table while she propped Vianna up in bed. "I speak to Kekoa," she said reassuringly.

"Well," Vianna prodded when she didn't continue.

Holding a finger to her lips, Maile glided silently to the door, peered up the hall, and satisfied no one was near enough to overhear, she came back and announced in a low voice, "Kekoa say can be arranged——"

Vianna interruped with a choked cry.

"——but very hard journey and must wait until you are well."

"We don't dare wait that long! My husband will carry me off before then. He was here yesterday and said he would wait only so long and no longer."

Maile digested this while she placed the tray across Vianna's lap. Studying her patient's pale face, she declared, "You still sick. Cannot leave hospital yet."

"Not yet, but maybe in a week."

"I not think so."

"Ask the doctor. You needn't tell him I want to leave then. You'll know how to find out."

"I try."

Maile's report of the doctor's opinion was discouraging. Although Doctor Young had not indicated it to Vianna, he was not at all pleased with the pace of her recovery. He confided to Maile that the infection that had brought her close to death was stubbornly resisting treatment.

"Is wrong I tell you this," Maile admitted unhappily, "but you in such hurry to go, and I have to tell you why you no can. Not yet."

"When?" Vianna inquired urgently. "Did the doctor say when he thought I'd be back to normal?"

Maile shook her head. "He not know. Say it will be long time, though."

In one way it was good news, Vianna consoled herself in the days that followed. Neither she nor Doctor Young would have to try to deceive Eban about her condition. She had to admit that she still felt quite ill, especially when she got up to use the chamber pot. As long as she lay quietly, with her head low on the pillows and her zeal to escape Eban flowing like fire through her veins, she could almost believe her good health had returned.

Contemplating her escape occupied most of her waking thoughts. It was what she turned her mind to when memories of Tom or grief over the loss of their baby threatened to overwhelm her. She sensed that the depression brought on by letting her mind dwell on these things would slow her physical recovery.

It occurred to her one day that if she wasn't going back to the *Trident,* there were personal belongings she would never see again—jewelry, clothes, toilet articles. Asking Eban to bring them to her would be folly; his suspicions would be immediately aroused. But there was one thing she could ask for in all reasonableness— the scrimshaw combs her father had made for her. Of all the items she would be leaving behind, those were the most precious to her.

"My hair hangs in my face when they sit me up to eat," she told him the next time he came. "I would appreciate it if you'd bring my combs so that I can fasten it back out of my way."

He made no reply, and although she reminded him twice, he never brought them.

She had been hospitalized two weeks when Eban began to grumble and accuse her of pretending to still be sick. Vianna denied it. "Ask the doctor. He knows more about my condition than I do, but I can tell you most positively that my head still swims whenever I try to stand up. In fact, I'm not allowed to use the chamber pot unless one of the nurses is here to steady me and make sure I don't fall."

"I intend to talk to the doctor tomorrow," Eban declared.

The degree of his impatience was made disconcertingly clear when he arrived the next morning while the doctor was conducting his daily examination of Vianna. Without preamble, he demanded to know when he could take Vianna back to the ship.

The frost that suddenly formed in Doctor Young's sharp blue eyes told Vianna how annoyed he was at the unapologetic interruption and at Eban's churlish tone. Nonetheless, he answered civilly enough. "Your wife won't be well enough to leave the hospital for at least two weeks. I can't guarantee that her health will permit my dismissing her even then."

"And I can't permit her the luxury of such a lengthy convalescence," Eban declared. Whether because of the heat in Lahaina or because of some unfathomable reason of vanity, Eban had visited a barber that morning and had his beard shaved off and his dark hair trimmed short. The full force of his cruelty, unleashed in these last nine months, had surfaced for all the world to see in the bare face—the thin mouth turned down at the corners, the nose with the dark, flaring nostrils, the harsh grooves that ran down his hollow cheeks. Once merely forbidding, his aspect had grown fiercely vengeful. "I've been hired to catch whales," he said gruffly. "Every day I'm tied up in port, my employers lose money. I'll remain in Lahaina one more week, then I intend to sail, and my wife will accompany me."

"Unless you want to condemn Mrs. Stanbro to lifelong invalidism, you should not remove her from here that soon."

Eban fixed the doctor with a hostile stare. "I think you're exaggerating."

"Are you questioning my professional judgment?"

"No, I'm accusing you of uniting with my wife in a scheme to keep her here as long as possible. She's proven herself to be a liar and a cheat, and she's been very successful in enlisting the aid of several other men to help her evade her marriage vow of obedience to her husband."

Anger deepened the pinkness of Doctor Young's smooth face, and his voice, though carefully controlled, was cold as he replied, "My decision is based on my patient's well-being, sir, and I tell you now that she can't endure any of your savage beatings in her present condition."

Eban stiffened. "The way I treat my wife is none of your business!"

"Anything that affects her physical or mental con-

'dition is my business, and I'm warning you that if you persist in your brutal treatment of her, you'll kill her!"

"Brutal!" Eban roared. "If you knew what kind of woman she is, you'd not be so free with your condemnation. She's bewitched you with her female wiles just like she did the others! I won't have you touching her anymore. I'm taking her back to the ship in the morning. I'd take her now if the vessel wasn't being smoked. Prepare a supply of medications and a list of instructions as to how I'm to give them, and have them ready when I come for her in the morning!" He stalked out.

Panic brought Vianna to a sitting position, head swimming, vision blurring. "You can't let him take me away in the morning! Please, doctor, isn't there some way you can put him off?"

Flushed with fury, Doctor Young shook his head in an agony of helplessness. "He has a right to take you out of here any time he pleases. There's no way to prevent that except through persuasion, and Captain Stanbro is beyond the reach of reason. I'm afraid I'll have to do as he says and prepare to dismiss you tomorrow."

Vianna sank back on her pillow. For a moment she thought she would faint. If Maile's fiancé could not get her out of here before morning, she was doomed.

"I can't tell you how sorry I am, Mrs. Stanbro," the doctor said, obviously deeply distressed. "Maybe if I hadn't lost my temper and warned him not to beat you, he would have left you here."

As the room steadied, Vianna said feebly, "Will you ask Maile to come in?"

"Of course." He left at once, and Maile came hurrying in only moments later.

"You sick?" she asked, coming directly to the bed.

"No," Vianna replied. She managed to speak firmly, knowing it was imperative now that she fake as much strength as possible. She recounted to the girl what had just transpired between Eban and Doctor Young. "I must get out of here tonight," she concluded. "Tell Kekoa it must be arranged!"

Maile shook her head vigorously. "Too soon for you. Too soon for Kekoa. Not possible."

"If Eban gets me back on that ship, he'll beat me until I die!"

The native girl gave a soft cry of horror. "He evil man, I know. I hear him yelling at doctor when he in here." She took a hard look at Vianna. "You still sick, I know, but I guess better you make journey into mountains than go on ship again. I tell Kekoa." Her face fell. "He out in boat fishing. I not know where."

Panic rose to the surface in Vianna again. "Can't you send someone to hunt for him? Surely you know the places he's likely to be."

"I try. I send message to hurry up plan." Her anxious expression was not reassuring as she sped out of the room on bare feet.

Vianna broke out in a cold sweat. What if Kekoa could not be found? A clammy trickle ran down her ribs. Was she destined never to escape from Eban?

An hour later she heard a commotion up the hall. Doctor Young's voice was protesting to someone about something, but she wasn't able to make out what it was. Then someone was coming down the hall, accompanied by the doctor, whose slow tread she had come to recognize. Vianna barely restrained a gasp when Mason Orne, the second mate, came shambling in like an aggressive gorilla. She gathered the blanket up around her shoulders as his simian eyes swept over her and the room. Behind his squat, thick body, she spied Doctor Young, clearly outraged at this rude invasion. Brushing past Orne, he informed Vianna caustically, "Your husband seems to think you might take flight, my dear, and has sent someone to guard you and make certain you are here when he comes for you in the morning."

Vianna stifled a groan of dismay. Had Eban suspected something, or was he only remembering her other escape attempts?

Mason Orne shuffled toward the chair in the corner, lifted it in his long hairy arms, and carried it without a word to the hall, where he could be heard setting it down and settling heavily into it.

"This is incredible," the physician said slowly. He stared at Vianna, a strange expression on his face. After a moment, he patted her hand and said firmly, "He can't do this." Without explaining or elaborating, he left her.

In the light of Doctor Young's remark, Vianna expected Mason Orne to be ejected from the hospital, but as the day wore on, she continued to hear him outside the door, breathing in that loud, snuffling manner that used to irritate her so at meals in the captain's mess. Even providing Kekoa or someone else came for her, how could they get her past the second mate? Eban had chosen well when he designated Orne to guard her. No one else on the *Trident* would serve him so loyally or so viciously. What a stroke of good luck it was for her that the ship was being fumigated today! Her hands crumpled the top of the blanket anxiously. If only Maile would bring her some word!

Not until dinnertime did she see Maile again. Mason Orne let her pass without a word, and she came in bearing the food tray. "More food," she said brightly and rather loudly. "Must eat, Mrs. Stanbro, so you get strong."

Eyes on the door, Vianna asked, also rather loudly, "What have you brought me?"

"Roast pork and yams." Maile leaned toward her ear as she placed the tray across Vianna's chest and whispered, "We take you out tonight late."

Blissful gratitude washed over Vianna. "Thank you," she sighed.

"You like?" Maile asked for the second mate's benefit.

"Very much." She pointed to the door and mouthed, "What about him?"

Doubt clouded the girl's face. "I tell Kekoa," she whispered. "You eat good," she said aloud. "I be back later."

Obeying Maile's injunction to eat well was not easy. Excitement put butterflies in Vianna's stomach, and delicious as the roast pork was, she had to force it down. Eventually she managed to eat every bite, knowing it was important that she give her meager strength as much of a boost as possible for the ordeal that lay ahead of her.

She had been finished with her dinner for a little while when she heard Mason Orne demand, "You there. Bring me a tray of that there roast pork."

Maile's soft voice replied, "No more. Only enough for patients and me."

"There must be something left. Bring it here."

"None left," Maile repeated.

Orne made a sound of disgust. "You're lying, you brown-skinned bitch. Where's the doctor?"

"He go home to eat."

"Goddamn it, how do I go about getting some food in this place?"

"I not know." Maile came into Vianna's room, and the instant she was out of Orne's sight an impish grin spread over her face and she rolled her eyes toward the hall.

Vianna didn't have a chance to return the grin. Mason Orne barged in without an apology or a knock. He must have been able to see the gardener working in the flowers from where he sat in the hall, because he went straight to the window and called out, "Hey, *kanaka!*"

Through the blinds Vianna saw the gardener straighten and look around. Mason Orne searched and found the cord that raised the blind, and he yanked it up. "Over here."

The native ambled over, a big man wearing a brilliant cotton skirtlike garment that left his well-muscled chest and legs bare. "Can you get me something to eat? I'll pay."

The *kanaka* looked around thoughtfully. "No place around here."

From behind Mason Orne, Maile was shaking her head vigorously. The gardener caught her signal, hesitated, then said, "I bring my dinner, but too late. I already eat it, else I give you some. No pay."

The second mate cursed. "There must be someplace around here you could get something for me!"

"Mango tree here," the gardener said, pointing to a corner of the lawn. "You want ripe mango, I find you one."

His appetite whetted by the smell of the roast pork, Mason Orne snorted in vexation. "All right. Bring me three or four."

Maile remained in the room until Orne had his fruit and had returned to the hall. "I go with you tonight. Doctor say you no go alone." Her voice was no more than a murmur.

"The doctor?" Vianna whispered in surprise.

"He no want your husband to have you anymore. He know about Kekoa and others who take sailors into mountains, so he ask me. I say plan already made. He say good, I must go to nurse you."

So that's what Doctor Young had meant when he said, "He can't do this," after Eban had sent Mason Orne to stand guard over her. He had finally become convinced that, at least in this case, he had a duty to protect a wife from her husband. "Oh, Maile, you don't know how happy I am that you're going with me! You said it would be a hard trip, and no one knows better than I how weak I still am."

Maile flashed her radiant smile. "I happy, too. Have never been with Kekoa on journey like this."

She was looking upon it as an exciting adventure, Vianna reflected. She herself viewed it much more soberly, but it was encouraging to know that Doctor

Young knew of the plan and approved, even though he was concerned enough about her condition that he was sending Maile with her.

Maile picked up the tray from the bed and murmured, "I see you again tonight late."

"I'll be waiting."

The hours crawled by. Vianna tried to force herself to sleep but succeeded only in napping briefly. Nonetheless, she lay quietly, willing herself to manufacture strength for the flight into the jungle.

Eban came back to the hospital that night. She heard his step coming down the hall and heard him say, "Anything to report, Mr. Orne?"

"Nothing, sir. Only the day nurse and the doctor and the old nurse who came to work a little while ago have gone into the room."

"Well, look sharp! I don't trust any of them. Can you stay awake tonight?"

"I can go days without sleep, sir. Have many a time going round the Horn. But I need food, captain. I ain't had nothing but some fruit to eat since I left the ship this morning."

"I brought you some salt beef."

Mason Orne's response revealed the only hint of humanity Vianna had ever seen him display. "Thank 'ee, captain," he exclaimed gratefully. "Them mangoes I et are roiling around inside me like heavy seas, but this beef will put my belly right again."

"I'll be back first thing in the morning to get my wife. As soon as she's aboard, we'll sail."

"Might I ask where we're going, sir?"

"North to Kodiak."

"It'll be good to feel a rolling deck under my feet again."

"Good night, Mr. Orne."

"Good night and thank 'ee again, captain."

Vianna listened to Eban's departing footsteps in surprise. He wasn't coming in to see her! She felt as if she had been given a gift. She snuggled deeper into her pillows. If nothing went wrong, she had seen the last of him. Forever and ever, she hoped, but if ever he did enter her life again, it would be in Govans Harbor, where she would have the protection of family and friends.

Maile had said they would come for her late tonight. Not knowing what she meant by late, Vianna couldn't sleep. Hali came in about eight o'clock to give her the day's last dose of medicine, which she took every four hours.

"How you feel?" the big woman asked. Her face shone like dark, polished wood as she stood at the bedside, holding a glass of water in which the powder had been mixed.

"Weak, and I'm getting tired of it."

"Must be patient," Hali declared firmly. Her voice came big and strong from the thick throat that rose from the low, round neck of her colorful dress. "Medicine time." A powerful arm encircled Vianna's shoulders and raised her so that she could drink. When Vianna made a face after downing the bitter stuff, Hali chuckled. "Is good for you, anyway. You good girl." She blew out the lamp she had lighted earlier in the evening. "Sleep time."

"Good night, Hali."

After she was gone, soft light filtered in through the open doorway from the hall lamps. Outside, the moon shone brightly on the flower beds. The hospital was quiet except for Mason Orne's loud breathing. Courting sleep, Vianna turned her thoughts to home and the people she loved. It was spring in Govans Harbor. Daffodils would be blooming on the south side of the house, and her mother would be brushing and cleaning heavy winter clothes that would be folded into chests and sprinkled with mothballs. The sun would begin to fill the parlor in the afternoon where her mother would sit with her tatting or a book. The image of Mary Chadwick in the parlor, her plump body relaxed against the chair back, sent a wave of homesickness through

Vianna, but it was followed almost at once by the ex-
ultant thought that within a short time she would be
on her way back to Govans Harbor. As soon as it was
safe to come down out of the mountains, she would
return to Lahaina and take the first ship going back
to the United States. Contemplating this loving picture
of her mother, Vianna drifted into a light sleep.

She came awake at once when Hali's big form cut
off the light from the door. The nurse made for the
bed with her stately tread, carrying a small night lamp.
"Is time," she whispered, bending close. "You scream."

Vianna stared up blankly at the broad dark face.

"Kekoa ready," Hali repeated impatiently. "Scream.
Now."

What Hali commanded, one did. Vianna filled her
lungs and let out a screech that must have reached every
corner in the hospital. She was rewarded by an approving grin from Hali, who bent over her, hiding her from
Mason Orne, who came bursting into the room and
stopped just inside the doorway to cast about for the
meaning of the disturbance. Over Hali's shoulder,
Vianna saw a silhouetted form slip up behind the mate
and hit him with a short club. Orne dropped like an
anchor. The next moment two men hurried in, carrying what looked like a long pole. Maile was behind
them. "This Kekoa," she said without bothering with
a greeting.

Vianna's glance quickly took in a handsome young
man with curly dark hair and a beautiful body.

"And this Boki."

The second man was older, but his muscular torso
had given up nothing to age.

The long pole turned out to be two poles with
heavy cloth strung between to form a stretcher. Hali
and Maile slid Vianna swiftly from bed to stretcher,
which was then shouldered by the two men, one at her
head, the other at her feet.

"*Aloha,*" Hali said with a warm smile.

"*Aloha* and *mahalo,*" Vianna said gratefully.

Swaying gently in her sling, she was carried swiftly down the hallway, which she was seeing for the first time, past darkened doorways, and out a wide front entrance that had been left open. As Maile passed the desk that faced the entrance, she swept up a knapsack with a wide loop that she slipped over her head, leaving the bundle to swing beneath her right arm at her waist.

No one spoke as the small party hurried through the moonlit night. Vianna did not know their immediate destination and did not ask. She shared the sense of urgency the others obviously felt. Mason Orne might regain consciousness at any moment and would waste no time sounding an alarm. He would get no help from Hali. Vianna almost wished she could witness the confrontation between the big woman and the second mate. Orne would head for the *Trident* in a fury to report to Eban. She had no doubt that he would notify the authorities and a search would begin for her.

They wound through streets of native huts where only a dog's bark now and then broke the silence. The men moved at a trot, and the shock of their feet hitting the earth passed up through their shoulders to the poles from which Vianna's sling was suspended, jarring her. After a half hour of this, she was relieved to see a palm-studded beach ahead, where a fishing boat waited. There were two other men beside it, who greeted Kekoa and Boki in their own language.

Vianna was lifted aboard, the poles resting on the thwarts, leaving her to hang an inch or two from the bottom of the boat. Maile sat at her head. The boat was shoved into the surf, and the men paddled furiously to get it far enough from the beach so that the waves wouldn't take it back in. After a short spell of this, two of them hoisted a sail. The breeze caught it, and they glided silently over the moonlit water.

Sweet relief mixed with fatigue sent Vianna into a peaceful sleep. When she awakened, it was beginning to grow light at the horizon, and the boat was approaching another palm-studded beach, this one narrower. There was no sign of habitation here, and a few hundred feet back from the water's edge the palms were engulfed by jungle, which rose gradually to mountain peaks, still black against the fading darkness.

Vianna was laid gently on the sand while the others, including Maile, pulled and tugged at the boat until they had it beached. With machetes the men hacked enough palm fronds to camouflage it. By that time the eastern sky was a vivid pink.

"We get into jungle, then we eat," Maile told her.

Vianna nodded as she was picked up again, and they headed into what looked to be a sold wall of vegetation. Once through the wall, however, a path ate its way through the heavy growth. Single file they followed it, and after a half hour or so the ground began to rise and the breathing of the men who carried her grew loud. The only other sounds to be heard were a few birds awakened by the sunlight that was beginning to touch the tops of the tallest trees.

They rested briefly, eating a breakfast of cold pork, yams, and breadfruit from the tree under which they sat. From her knapsack, Maile took a bottle and mixed some of the powder it held with water from a gourd. "Doctor send plenty medicine," she said. "He tell me take good care of you."

Vianna smiled tiredly and took the draught. "I'm not worried. I know I'm in good hands."

When they resumed their journey, she fell asleep.

14

———————————

The trek through the mountainous jungle took them
two days. Progress would have been difficult without
any burden to carry. Vianna pitied the four men, who,
though they took turns carrying her, nevertheless grew
very tired. She wondered how she could ever repay
them. When she brought up the subject during a rest
stop the first day, Maile and Kekoa assured her no
payment was necessary, but she pondered the matter
as they moved through the jungle. She had no money,
but her father would doubtless be back here in a year.
He could see that they were rewarded for their efforts to
save her.

The jungle was a beautiful place. Now and then
they entered a valley and the peaks surrounding them
were solid with rain forest, the greenness broken here
and there by a tree covered with red blossoms. Within
the jungle itself there were flowers in abundance,
stunningly vivid.

On the second day, however, Vianna grew less aware
of her surroundings. The constant jar and swing of her
body was fatiguing. She began to suffer from dizziness
that upset her stomach so much she couldn't keep anything down, not even the medicine Maile faithfully
administered.

Late the second afternoon they halted. Kekoa took
a conch shell from a leather bag and climbed the
tallest tree in the area. Once at the top, he blew into
the conch, sending the weird, moaning cry out over the
jungle. Within half an hour, six men appeared from

257

the direction in which Vianna's party had been heading.
After joyful greetings and much happy laughter, two
of the new arrivals shouldered Vianna's sling, and they
all set off again. In a short time they came out upon
a valley laid out in a patchwork of neat fields. At the
far end lay a small village of bamboo and thatch huts.
Smoke from cooking fires wreathed up into the darken-
ing sky. The sun, although an hour or two from setting,
had sunk behind the mountains that ringed the valley,
and the air was growing cool.

Maile smiled down at Vianna. "We almost there."

Too weak to speak, Vianna responded with a faint
smile.

They went down to a narrow stream that cut through
the center of the valley, following it up to the edge of a
pool of the clearest water Vianna had ever seen. Above
it was a smaller pool. Both were fed by a waterfall
dropping out of the jungle-covered slope above. The
small caravan veered slightly away from the pool, following a path bordered on either side by sweet potato
and melon patches that led up to the edge of the village.
By this time the small caravan had been joined by a
group of children who covered Vianna with friendly
stares. Their excited chatter was the most noise Vianna
had heard since she left the *Trident*.

The thatched huts were scattered haphazardly around
the village, although what was obviously the main path
cut a fairly regular swath among them, ending at the
rear of the village where a building, four or five times
the size of the huts but also constructed from bamboo
and with a thatched roof, stood. Some distance beyond
it, the ground began to rise again in a gradual slope
that sharpened eventually into another jungle-clad
mountain.

The caravan halted at the second hut it came to.
Here a big woman, even more massive than Hali, and
a man even bigger than she came forward, welcoming
her in their native tongue and smiling. Kekoa said,

"This is Wakea and Iolani, his wife. You stay with them. Maile, too. They no speak English."

Vianna's smile, though weak, was warm. *"Aloha,"* she said. She was taken into their hut and carefully laid on a woven mat at one side of the rather dark interior. There were no windows, and the only light came through the wide, low doorway. From her mat Vianna could see the cooking fire outside with a small pig roasting over it. At any other time the smell of the browning meat would have made her mouth water, but she felt desperately tired and ill. With a feeling of deep dismay, she acknowledged to herself that she hadn't felt this sick since awakening in the hospital in Lahaina.

"You rest now," Maile told her, covering her with a blanket sewn with colorful bird feathers. "I give you food and medicine later."

Vianna needed no urging. Beneath the mat lay a pile of large green leaves, forming a soft bed. She closed her eyes and fell soundly asleep.

She was awakened at dawn by the crowing of a rooster and the grunting of pigs somewhere nearby. On the other side of the hut, Wakea and Iolani were stirring on their mats. Behind her head she heard someone else stirring. It was Maile, who snuggled deeper beneath her blanket and grew still again. She must be exhausted, too, Vianna thought. As for herself, she felt slightly better, but she was familiar enough with illness now to realize that the journey into the mountains had cost her much of the gains she had made in the hospital.

Iolani sat up, yawning, and glanced immediately at her guest. When she saw that Vianna was awake, she smiled hugely. After getting to her feet with a gracefulness amazing in one so large, she padded outside to stir up the coals of last night's fire. Her movements brought Wakea fully awake and, rising to his feet, he sent Vianna a warm smile, too, before following his wife out of the hut. A short while later Iolani reappeared with slices of peeled fruit in a gourd bowl. Offering them to Vianna, she said cheerfully, "Papaya."

The narrow yellow crescents, dripping juice, looked good to Vianna. *"Mahalo,"* she said, rising on one elbow and reaching for one. As the interior of the hut suddenly whirled around her, her hand missed the bowl and fell to the blanket. Iolani made a sympathetic sound and pushed her gently back down upon the mat. Placing the bowl near Vianna's head, she said something and gestured, indicating to Vianna that she try eating while lying down. This proved to be a better arrangement. The first bite was greeted by a queasy stomach that gradually steadied and welcomed the fruit.

Watching her, Iolani nodded encouragingly and said something in an approving tone.

Maile awakened and from her mat asked sleepily, "How you feel, Mrs. Stanbro?"

"Very shaky, but better than I did last night."

"I give you medicine after you eat."

Iolani, towering over them both, spoke at length in her native tongue.

When she was finished, Maile translated. "She say you have very sad story. I tell her last night. Often hear sad stories from sailors, Iolani say, but yours most sad. She think captains of ships very mean. No understand why any man go to work on ships. Think they must all be like a Mr. Fully who was here not too long ago. He was knocked on head one night in town and when he wake up, he on ship out to sea."

"Shanghaied," Vianna observed. "Some captains get their crews that way, but not whaling captains. Tell Iolani I agree with her. I don't understand how any man could choose the life of a sailor."

At the end of her first week in the village, Vianna was discouraged with her progress. It didn't seem to her she had gained as rapidly as she had her first week of consciousness in the hospital. Life was pleasant here in the village, and everyone was kindness itself, but now that Eban no longer stood as a malevolent barrier between her and home, she was desperately impatient to return to Govans Harbor. She ate well and Maile administered her medicine religiously, but she remained weak and felt absolutely wretched.

Before Kekoa, Boki, and the other two men who had brought Vianna to the village returned to Lahaina, Vianna asked Kekoa if he knew anything about John Colby and where he might be.

"He taken not so far away from Lahaina." He and Maile sat beneath a breadfruit tree that grew between the hut belonging to Wakea and his nearest neighbor. Vianna was carried out there each morning to lie all day on a bed of leaves where the sun could filter down softly on her and where she could watch the leisurely life of the village flow around her. The villagers were friendly and curious, bringing her a gift of a flower or an especially ripe fruit, sometimes a fragrant *lei* to wear around her neck. Maile was sitting close to Kekoa, a graceful hand lying on his brown thigh. She was so obviously in love with him, and Vianna could understand why. He was strikingly handsome, with curly black hair and smooth, even features.

"This village," Kekoa explained further, "used only for sailors someone want bad. No one find here. Other sailors, like John Colby, not hunted for much. Easy to hide them close to Lahaina."

"I wonder if Eban is still hunting for me."

"I find out and send message. We go tomorrow morning."

Maile's spirits were low for a few days after her fiancé left, but she gradually brightened back up, and Vianna realized how much she depended on the girl's cheerfulness to keep her own spirits up.

Kekoa and the others had been gone less than a week when two more natives arrived with another fugitive. Jervis Robbins was a young man who had signed on a merchantman in Boston, been singled out for brutal treatment by the first mate, and had taken his revenge when they reached Lahaina, beating the mate in a tavern brawl and hiding out for three days before finding someone who would lead him into the mountains. They also brought news of Eban. He had the law out combing the whole of Lahaina for Vianna, maintaining she had been kidnapped and he wasn't sailing until she had been found. He had tried to implicate Doctor Young, but he couldn't persuade anyone that the physician had had anything to do with Vianna's disappearance.

The news that Eban was still in Lahaina quieted Vianna's impatience to leave to a certain extent. It would be folly for her to go back there until he and the *Trident* had sailed away.

Jervis Robbins spent a lot of time visiting with her, delighted to have found another American in the village.

"Will you go back to sea?" Vianna asked one afternoon as they talked beneath the breadfruit tree. She was able to sit up for short periods now and was leaning back against the tree trunk. From this vantage point on the edge of the village she could see the whole of the valley spread before her, bisected by the stream that flowed from the lower of the two pools beneath the waterfall. The pools were hidden by trees, but there were no trees bordering the stream. Fields grew right down to its banks on either side. It was shallow enough to wade easily, and she could see Wakea in the field that she now knew was his, hoeing some rows of corn and melons.

"I don't know whether I want to go back to sea or not," Jervis Robbins replied. "If they'd feed us something besides salt beef, it wouldn't be so bad, but eating that stuff three times a day, seven days a week, I got so I could hardly swallow it." His thin face and spare body looked as if he had managed to eat only enough of the sailor food to stay alive. It was hard for Vianna to picture him giving any man a beating such as the one he was supposed to have given his first mate.

"They tell me it's a healthy diet if you can get hold of some fruit now and then to prevent scurvy," he continued, "but I got so I'd dream at night I was back home eating my mother's chicken and dumplings and apple pie."

He was eating a mango at that very moment. It occurred to Vianna that she had never seen him without some bit of food in his hands. Observing his hands as they peeled the thick, rosy skin back from the center pulp, she noticed for the first time how large they were in proportion to the rest of him. Perhaps they were the reason he had acquitted himself so well in his fight with his former first mate.

"I traded for a book on the California goldfields with one of my shipmates. I've a mind to go there when I get back to Lahaina. Sounds like a man could make a fortune in no time with a little luck." He chewed a large mouthful of sweet, stringy fruit. "There's men out there that's made money just by finding gold, then selling their claims. They wind up being rich men without hardly doin' a lick of work."

Vianna couldn't believe it was that easy, but she enjoyed listening to Robbins talk about California. When he found out she was genuinely interested, he carried the book around in a pocket and read to her a bit each day, showing her the maps of the different goldfields and contemplating the possibilities of each.

After Vianna had been in the village for two weeks, she wondered why these rootless men who were brought here ever left. Food was obtained from the jungle and the fields with very little expenditure of effort. With a few chickens and hogs, a man could eat very well. And if the life-style lacked some of the comforts of a more advanced society, she thought it would be far preferable to the harsh and crowded conditions on board a ship. The climate was nearly perfect. Showers were frequent but brief, giving way easily to the sunshine again, and the temperature was never too hot or too cool. The ideal living conditions might account for the perpetually cheerful nature of the *kanakas,* Vianna decided.

Kanaka was a Hawaiian word that meant "man" or "human being," Maile told her. The people of her islands applied it to the peoples from all the South Sea islands. Vianna was somewhat surprised. She had believed it to be a derogatory term applied to the Sandwich Islanders by white people.

One day she noticed that the bottle of medicine Maile was measuring out for her was almost empty. The possibility of running out of the drugs Doctor Young had sent, when she was still so far from being fully recovered, was alarming. "Are all the bottles that nearly empty?" she asked in dismay.

"You no worry," Maile replied, stirring the powder into the water in a small gourd. "When gone, I give you *kanaka* medicine."

Vianna dropped her eyes quickly to hide from Maile the sudden fear she felt. Not for the world would she have her friend know that she had no faith in native remedies. But how could they be as effective as the modern medicines of a civilized society? If she had to rely on them, she might never fully regain her health.

"Couldn't you send a message to Doctor Young and have him send some more?" she asked, unable to conceal all of her doubt.

"Not necessary," Maile said, bringing her the gourd. "Our medicine good. You be surprised how good."

Vianna remained unconvinced and made up her mind that she would send an order to Doctor Young the first time someone left for Lahaina. When Maile gave her the first dose of a native remedy two days later, she thought wryly that if unpleasant taste had anything to do with curative powers, this *kanaka* medicine would be as effective as Doctor Young's had been.

Jervis Robbins had been in the village for a couple of weeks when he informed her he'd made up his mind to go to California. "I'll go back to Lahaina as soon as I can get someone to take me there. Sooner or later

I'll find a ship that's going up there and will sign me on." He grinned. "Then it's the goldfields for me, and when I've got a pan full of nuggets, I might go back to Boston and start up a shipping company of my own."

By the time he left, Vianna had made some progress and decided she didn't need any more medicine from Doctor Young. Iolani had made her a long blue dress out of one of her own, and Wakea had carved her two combs out of lovely dark wood. She was no longer confined to bed. She walked to the lower of the two pools beneath the waterfall for her daily bath now. True, it took her all morning to walk there, rest, bathe, rest, and walk back the quarter of a mile to the village, but it was a great improvement over her condition when she'd arrived here. Encouraged by this, she began to talk of returning to Lahaina.

"Eban is surely gone by now, and I might be able to catch a ship for home. There's no medicine in the world that would do me more good than the knowledge that I was on my way back to my family."

"You get sick again," Maile warned her. "You no think of going back to Lahaina until you strong enough to walk back."

"Oh, Maile, that will be forever!"

Maile shook her head. "You get well fast now. You see."

She did not exaggerate. Incredibly, Vianna was much stronger within a week. When she had made the trek to the pool one morning, bathed, and returned all within an hour, Vianna exclaimed, "I believe your medicine is better than Doctor Young's!"

Maile chuckled. "I try to tell him that many times. He no believe. He believe *haole* medicine best."

They were sitting beneath the breadfruit tree, eating some of the fruit that had dropped to the ground. Maile forgot her fruit for the moment. "Kekoa say Mr. Fully sick man, too, when they bring him here. Mostly sickness of the mind. He very unhappy. Made his body sick, too. But after two weeks of Iolani's medicine, he better."

Vianna finished her fruit and wiped her fingers on the thick grass. "He was the sailor who was shanghaied, wasn't he?"

"He no sailor. Never sail before. Never want to sail, but bad man make him write note to girl saying he no marry her because she going to have baby. Then bad man hit him on head, and when he wake up, he on ship out to sea."

Vianna turned her head slowly and stared at Maile, who halted in the act of taking another bite of fruit and asked swiftly, "You all right?"

Vianna licked her lips and asked in a strangled voice, "This Mr. Fully. Is that his real name?" She cleared her throat. "Could his name have been Fulton?"

Maile didn't take the time to ask her why she wanted to know. "Iolani!" she called out. When the big woman emerged from the hut, Maile rattled off some questions to her.

Iolani replied, nodding. Among the unfamiliar words that formed her answers, Vianna easily made out the name "Tom Fulton." Feeling suddenly faint, she leaned back against the tree.

Maile put a steadying hand on her shoulder. "Lay down. You too pale."

Vianna's hand closed convulsively over Maile's. "Tell me. Was his name Fulton?"

"Tom Fulton. Everyone call him Mr. Fully here because Fulton too hard to say." She tried to press Vianna into a prone position, but Vianna's joyful expression stayed her hand.

"That's the man I told you about," Vianna said excitedly. "The man I loved, whose baby I lost. I thought he ran away because he didn't want the baby!" With wide, glistening eyes, she begged, "Tell me again about Tom's being forced to write that note."

Maile relayed her request to Iolani, who gave her

brief account of Tom's story. It tallied almost word for word with what Maile had said.

Vianna's head had stopped spinning and she sat up, thinking swiftly. "It was Eban! I know it was Eban who forced Tom to write that note to me. I don't know how he did it, but a monster like him would find a way. And then he knocked Tom out and put him aboard the ship—it was the *Antilla*—yes, I remember it leaving that morning. Oh, Maile!" she cried, throwing her arms around her nurse and friend, "Tom still loves me and wants me, wherever he is!"

But where was he?

"Ask Iolani if she knows where he went when he left here."

After another consultation with the huge woman, Maile said, "He talk of nothing but going back to girl he loved. He sign on ship going to America."

It was almost too much happiness for Vianna to absorb all at once. She felt dazed, aware that an idiotic smile was stretching her face. "He loves me!" She whispered it over and over again. By now Maile was sharing her joy, glowing as Vianna suspected she herself must be. Even Iolani was beaming as she joined them beneath the tree, commenting excitedly in her own tongue, as she towered over them.

Vianna's bemusement gave way shortly to the realization that she had to communicate with Tom. Upon his arrival in Govans Harbor he'd be hit with the devastating news that she had married Eban and gone off on a three- or four-year voyage. For all he or anyone back there knew, she was now and forever Mrs. Eban Stanbro. She had to get a letter to him, explaining everything and telling him she would be returning to Govans Harbor just as soon as possible.

After an hour's hunt Iolani brought her the stub of a pencil and an ancient sheet of paper retrieved from a trunk a seaman had left in the village years ago. As Vianna settled back against the tree and began with the words *Dearest Tom,* tears stung her eyes. She had never expected to speak or write those words again. Inexpressible joy swept through her again as she contemplated the beautiful knowledge that Tom still loved her, had in fact never stopped loving her. That he cherished her this very day no less than he had during that heavenly summer in Govans Harbor was a thought that brought such intense happiness that she began to weep silently. After a few moments, she impatiently brushed away the tears so that she could see to write the letter she couldn't wait to send Tom. She began her tale and the words flowed, so many of them that she had to write smaller and smaller in order to squeeze them all onto that one sheet of paper.

Wakea himself took the letter to Lahaina, leaving that very afternoon. Through Maile, Vianna asked him to inquire if Eban were still there and if any ships in the harbor were returning to America and when. He promised to find out and return at once.

He was back in four and a half days. Eban and the *Trident* were gone, he said, but all of Lahaina was on the lookout for Vianna, including the agent of the company that owned the *Trident*. Eban had changed his story, explaining that her mind had become unbalanced by the loss of her baby and he now believed that she probably had not been kidnapped but had either wandered away or run away. He had gone off to do some more whale hunting but would return in a few weeks, and he requested that if she was found she be held under guard in the fort until he came back.

For a moment Vianna was engulfed in a wave of spiritual fatigue. How much longer was she going to have to struggle against Eban's insane despotism? Wakea's next words were cheering, however. A ship was leaving for the United States the day he reached Lahaina and her letter to Tom left with it. For a second Vianna felt a flash of disappointment that she couldn't have sailed on the same ship, but Wakea had more news. Another vessel, the *Marengo*, was in port and would be returning to America in about two weeks.

"I've got to be there." Vianna's glance swept the circle of faces—Maile's, Wakea's, and Iolani's—as they sat near the fire that evening, eating supper. It was already dark, but the flames cast sufficient light that she could read their expressions. She expected an argument but got none.

"You wait one more week, then you be plenty strong enough," Maile told her. "Maybe carry you anyway to make sure you not get too tired."

"I don't want to be carried. I'll walk."

She did walk, and she got terribly tired, but it was simple fatigue, not the kind that resulted from ill health. Vianna was delighted to discover that she was, as far as she could tell, as good as new, thanks mostly to the *kanaka* medicine. At least her recovery hadn't picked up speed until she had run out of Doctor Young's medicine. She even enjoyed the trek that took them directly back to Lahaina instead of to the bay where Kekoa's boat had landed the night of her escape. The path was not hard to follow, and the exotic beauty of the jungle was a source of unending wonder to her.

As they broke through the trees on the slope above Lahaina, she saw the whaling port spread out below her, a small town fronting on a great blue and white harbor.

"Marengo," Wakea said, pointing. He and another man had brought Maile and her out of the mountains.

Vianna followed his pointing finger and saw a merchantman anchored out to the left side of the harbor, its bare masts looking pencil-thin at this distance. What luck! A whaler might hunt on its way back to its home port, but a merchantman would be fully loaded and would head straight for home. This was the first look she'd had at Lahaina, and her vantage point couldn't have been better. It was easy to see why this huge, quiet harbor had grown into the famous whaling port that it was.

Wakea did not take her all the way into town. They

halted at a cluster of huts on the outskirts. The particular hut he led her to was overflowing with people—a young couple, their three small children, and a withered old woman. The young couple and the children greeted Wakea, Maile, and the other man with shouts of friendship. The old woman looked on, nodding and smiling toothlessly.

"This is Kalani and his wife, Hina," Maile said. "This is Gramma." Everyone laughed delightedly at this English word. "And this is John, Luke, and Mary." Another burst of laughter resulted from Vianna's look of surprise. "Kalani and Hina Christians. Use Bible names for children."

Vianna and Maile were shown to an empty hut next door, where they would sleep. They would be eating with Kalani and his family, however.

"You don't have to stay with me any longer," Vianna told Maile. "These people speak English, and I'm sure you must be anxious to go back to your family."

"I go see them. Tell them I'm back, but I stay with you until you leave. You need help maybe till then."

Yes, she needed someone to find out when the *Marengo* was sailing and to buy passage for her on the ship. There was also the problem of finding the money to buy that ticket. This was a problem she did not think her *kanaka* friends could help her with.

Maile went almost at once to visit her parents and let them know she was back in Lahaina. She didn't return until early evening. It had begun to rain, and Vianna was taking supper with Kalani's family in his hut. Maile, who had already eaten, sat with them on the beaten earth floor and told them she had stopped by the hospital to tell Doctor Young she would be able to go back to work in a week or so.

"He very happy you strong and not sick anymore." She grinned. "I tell him it was *kanaka* medicine did it, not his."

"I'm inclined to agree," Vianna declared.

"Doctor Young say he lend you any money you need to get home."

Vianna, who had been eating a piece of roast chicken, let out a small cry. "The dear man! I was wondering how I would pay for my passage."

"He also send two letters. They came for you morning after we took you away. He say nothing and keep them for you." Maile pulled two envelopes from the neck of her dress.

Vianna almost grabbed them out of her friend's hands in her eagerness to see if one was from Tom. With acute disappointment she saw they were from her mother and Harriet. She ripped open the letter from her mother and scanned it. No mention of Tom. Harriet's, however, yielded what she sought. The opening paragraph told her everyone was well and they missed her and hadn't heard from her yet and that Harriet was going to have a baby in August. That was this month! The date on the letter was May fourteenth.

I don't know how to tell you this, Harriet began, *and perhaps I shouldn't. But I keep remembering how you suffered when you thought Tom had deserted you. He showed up a month ago with the wildest story you ever heard.*

There followed an account of the part of the story that Vianna had learned from Maile and Iolani.

I can't believe Eban would do such a thing, Harriet continued. *No one else believes it, either, not even Jeremy. He says Tom came from a very poor family and that Tom had always sworn he wouldn't get married and saddle himself with a dozen kids. He thinks Tom panicked and ran away to avoid marrying you, then had second thoughts and came back with this wild story about being shanghaied. Tom is putting on quite an act, though. He went straight to Bert Gerber and demanded he do something, but Bert has watched all Govans Harbor kids grow up for the last thirty years and not commit any crimes more serious than stealing apples. Tom's story was not only fantastic, but*

*Tom is a stranger. Bert sent him away with the threat
that if he didn't stop slandering Eban, he was going to
throw him in jail.*

*Tom didn't have any better luck when he went to see
the owners of the* Trident. *He demanded they order
Eban home to stand charges of assault and battery,
kidnapping, and more. They thought Tom was crazy.
I think maybe he is, too, or was in the end. He went
raging around town like a madman, drinking and fighting. Finally he even turned against you. He told Jeremy
and me that he guessed he shouldn't have been surprised that you up and married Eban after he left. He
said you were nothing but an impulsive child and probably hadn't ever really loved him. Really, I was glad
when he left town. He told Jeremy he was going to
California to hunt for gold and he was never coming
back.*

*I'm telling you all this hoping it will ease your heart
in case you're still pining for Tom, because it is clear
now that he's a drifter and a liar who would always be
able to come up with some excuse, no matter how
wild, for his irresponsible behavior. It should make you
humbly grateful that you ended up married to a good,
steady man like Eban.*

Vianna dropped the letter and covered her face with
her hands, murmuring, "Oh, no! No!" Just when she
thought that she and Tom would be reunited, she was
told he was gone forever. What was the matter with
those people in Govans Harbor? Couldn't they see that
Tom was telling them the truth?

She felt a hand on her shoulder and was aware that
Maile was saying something to her, but all she could
hear were those words of Harriet's, . . . *going to
California to hunt for gold and he was never coming
back.* If only he had waited just a few more months!
Why had he gone off in such a hurry? She could understand how crazy with frustration he must have been
when he couldn't get anyone to believe his story, but

why had he turned against her? That had been so unfair!

Anger swept away her despair. She became conscious of her surroundings, of Maile's hand patting her shoulder and her soft voice making comforting sounds. She took her hands away from her face. The whole family was watching her anxiously. The children looked frightened, and Gramma's lips were nervously moving in and out over her toothless gums.

Vianna managed a faint smile. "I'm all right," she assured them. "There was bad news in the letter, but I'm all right. I want to be by myself and think."

As she got to her feet, Maile reminded her, "It is raining."

Vianna nodded, asking, "Kalani, may I wear your cape?"

His dark eyes swept her, and then, deciding she was indeed all right, he said gently, "Is there by door."

She took the cape made from large overlapping leaves, threw it around her, tying it at the throat, and went out into the wet dusk. The cool, wet air felt good on her anger-flushed face.

Nothing but an impulsive child who had probably never loved him! A tongue of shame licked at her, and she began to walk faster. Perhaps she was impulsive, or at least she had been at one time. She had been trying to curb that impulsiveness, though, and Tom knew it. And to use that as a basis for his accusation that she had probably never really loved him was plain stupid. If he believed that, then he had never had any faith in her, and maybe she *was* lucky to have missed marrying him.

Her anger had built to the point where she was almost running, but this last thought brought her up so sharply she skidded on some wet leaves and nearly fell to the path that connected the scattered huts. She sought shelter under a spreading banyan tree and pressed a hand to her wet face. What was she thinking! She would marry Tom this very minute if it were pos-

sible. He had been angry and bitter, just as she had
been these past few minutes. He must have gone through
a horrible time from the moment he awoke on that out-
bound whaler. Then to manage to get back in eight
months and find her married, gone for three or four
years, and with no one to believe him or help him get
her back! Having known the depths of despair herself
during this past year, Vianna could imagine how he
must have felt.

Oh, Tom, we were torn from each other's arms by
the unspeakable cruelty of one person, and now mis-
understanding and bitterness are going to keep us apart
forever!

Tears joined the rain on her face as she sobbed
quietly. The dusk had deepened into darkness. Here
and there among the trees a doorway glowed orange
from the fire within. The only sound was the uneven
patter of the rain on the leaves. Once Vianna had
thought life would be almost perfect if she could return
to her mother, her childhood home, and her relatives
and friends. Discovering that Tom still loved and
wanted her had changed that. All that awaited her
back there was half a life. Without Tom or his child,
the years would crawl drearily by, arid and ill-spent.

"Why couldn't you have simply gone home to Pennsylvania instead of running off to California where I
can't find you?" she whispered.

Absently she wiped the tears and rain off of one
cheek. What was it Jervis Robbins had said about gold
seekers? Everyone makes for San Francisco sooner or
later to spend their gold dust. He was looking forward
to just getting off a ship in the fabulous city that had
sprung up when gold was discovered to the east of it.

Vianna watched a shadow pass across a lighted doorway, knowing that what she was thinking was reckless.
Nevertheless, her heart had begun to beat faster. If
Jervis Robbins was right, there was a chance she could
find Tom if she went to San Francisco. It would be no
problem to find a ship going there. Since gold had been

discovered, there was a steady stream of ships taking cargo to California. And here she was, practically in its front yard compared to the thousands of miles of Pacific and Atlantic waters that lay between her and Govans Harbor. She could catch a ship here in Lahaina and be in San Francisco in a few weeks, whereas it would take months to travel the distance to Massachusetts. Why shouldn't she give it a try? It was the only hope she had of ever seeing Tom again. She would always regret it if she didn't make this attempt. The opportunity was at her fingertips. All she had to do was reach out and take it.

Lips parted, she put out her hand.

15

Vianna approached the agent's office feeling as exposed as if she were naked. It was the first time she had emerged from hiding since being carried into the mountains. Emily Carver and Florence Aubrey were the only two people in Lahaina who would recognize her, yet the American colony was small, with everyone knowing nearly everyone else. As a stranger she would be highly visible.

Although the midmorning sun was warm, her hands were icy as she turned from the side street onto the wide, busy wharf. There were piles of barrels and cargo everywhere and wagons moving both from wharf to warehouse or warehouse to wharf. Facing this broad thoroughfare was a long line of buildings. Staying close to them and out of the traffic, she searched for the office she was seeking. There it was, almost halfway down the street. "Gunther and Cowley, John Arlington, agent," the sign read.

She had made her decision to go to San Francisco on Thursday night. Kalani went to the wharf the next day to see if there were any ships in port that would be heading for California. There had been one. The *Silver Cloud,* a merchantman, was leaving on Tuesday. Vianna sent Maile to Doctor Young with a message saying she would gratefully accept his offer of a loan to buy her passage, not to Govans Harbor, but to California. He arrived that night, not only with money but also with a valise containing a scanty wardrobe his wife had been able to put together for her.

He peered sharply at her, his face smooth and pink beneath his white hair. After a moment's scrutiny, his eyes crinkled warmly at the corners. "Yes, you're fine. I can see that. Better than fine. You've got a vital look about you."

They were seated on mats outside the hut. Kalani and his family had drifted away after welcoming the doctor. Only Maile remained, cutting small chunks of fresh coconut for them to nibble on. The cooking fire had died down, leaving mostly gray ashes. The sun had set, but the sky still held clouds painted gold.

"That vital look," Vianna told the physician, "results from the possibility that I may be able to put my life back together."

Doctor Young accepted a piece of coconut from Maile. "I wish you luck, my dear." There was a thread of doubt in his voice.

"You don't think I'll find Tom, do you?"

He chewed some of the sweet, oily meat and swallowed before answering. "It's a long chance, but worth it if for no other reason than that it has given you this glow of health. As a doctor, I rejoice in that, whatever the cause."

Kalani had booked passage for her on the *Silver Cloud* the next morning, pretending to be her servant and explaining that his mistress was ill with a toothache and couldn't attend to this task herself. He bought the ticket in the name of Mrs. Nathaniel Sawtell. It had afforded Vianna some amusement to reflect upon how excited her nephew would be if he knew he was a part of the intrigue to get her away from Lahaina.

There wasn't a trace of amusement in her as she made her way toward the office of Gunther and Cowley. Aware that her facial muscles were much too tense, she tried to relax them, smiling at the driver of a wagon loaded with barrels as he pulled over to avoid hitting another wagon in the crowded street. She was rewarded by a smile and a slight tip of his cap. The size of the wharf and the heavy traffic made Govans

Harbor seem like a sleepy village. No wonder Lahaina was compared to Nantucket or New Bedford.

By the time she reached the large overhanging sign identifying the company that owned the *Silver Cloud*, Vianna hoped she looked like a woman anticipating a reunion with her husband in San Francisco instead of the nervous fugitive she was.

Pushing open the door, she went in. The office was surprisingly small. It was lit by two windows, one on either side of the door, and held a desk and a few chairs. Behind the desk, on the rear wall, shelves had been built from floor to ceiling and were filled with a chaotic jumble of papers and files. Against one of the other walls stood a huge safe, so massive Vianna wondered how the wooden floor supported all that weight. The opposite wall was covered with framed paintings of ships.

The man seated at the desk glanced up as she entered. He was small; his brown suit looked too big for him, as did his high, starched collar. His black hair was parted precisely down the center of his scalp and combed back, leaving soft locks like wings on his forehead. Removing his glasses and rising to his feet, he said, "Good morning. May I help you?"

"I'm Mrs. Nathaniel Sawtell. I'm sailing on the *Silver Cloud* this noon."

"Ah, yes. The boat is waiting, Mrs. Sawtell. Is your luggage outside?"

"This valise is all the luggage I have."

John Arlington blinked at her, surprised.

Quickly, Vianna gave the explanation she had thought up to cover this situation should it arise. Smiling easily, she hoped, she said, "My husband has made a successful gold strike. He said not to burden myself with old clothes for this trip, promising to buy me a whole new wardrobe when I get to San Francisco."

"I see." He was regarding her with sharper attention than she'd have liked. "I mentioned to several of our countrymen and women here that you were taking the

Silver Cloud, and they said they had not had the pleasure of meeting you. They thought it strange you could have been in Lahaina without any of the American community making your acquaintance."

Vianna managed to maintain her smile. "I arrived from Honolulu only three days ago, and unfortunately I've been confined to bed ever since with a toothache. I've been staying with a Christianized native family whom I learned about from one of the missionaries on Oahu." Thank heaven she had created an entire biography for herself before coming out into the open. "I arrived in Honolulu about a week ago from Boston, not knowing anyone in the Islands. Happily, I've found you all to be most friendly and helpful."

Slightly discomfited at the possibility that he might be the one exception to this, the agent shuffled some papers on his desk, then said, "You're a lucky lady to have been promised a new wardrobe, Mrs. Sawtell. And you are probably in a hurry to get this journey started." He came around the desk and took her valise. "I'll escort you to the boat."

With a big inward sigh of relief, Vianna walked with him to a dock where several boats were tied up. Their crews lounged against a warehouse nearby. At the sight of the agent, six of them broke away from the group and took their places in one boat. To the bosun John Arlington said, "This is Mrs. Sawtell, your passenger." He pulled a folded sheet of paper from inside his coat. "Give this to Captain Weeks." After helping her into the boat, he wished her a safe voyage and stood watching them as they pulled away from the dock.

It took only a few minutes to reach the *Silver Cloud.* Vianna was welcomed aboard by the captain, a rather handsome man with dark curly sideburns. "Will we have to wait for the rest of your luggage, Mrs. Sawtell?" he asked, noting the light valise.

"There is no more, captain," she said, and repeated her story about the new wardrobe her husband would

gift her with. "I'm afraid you'll grow very tired of seeing my two dresses during our voyage, captain, but on
the other hand you won't have to find room to stow
my extra trunks."

"It will be a pleasure having you aboard, ma'am, no
matter what you wear." He regarded her pretty face
with its fresh glow of health with frank appreciation
and not a hint of suspicion.

Nonetheless, Vianna felt the tension drain out of her
body a few minutes later when the anchors were hauled
up and the ship began to glide out of the wide harbor.
What a difference from the last time she had sailed
out of a port! Already it seemed to have happened in
another lifetime, that heartrending farewell to her
mother and Harriet and the others. The present departure brought a sense of freedom so great she felt as if
she would burst. There was undeniably a touch of
sadness at leaving Maile and Doctor Young and the
others who had offered her immeasurable kindness, but
she meant to write to them and had the promises of
Maile and Doctor Young to write back. With her father
already on his way home, it was more than likely he
would have sailed again before a letter could arrive
there, so she had left a letter for him in Lahaina, telling him of her incredible experience and asking him to
repay Doctor Young and the others who helped her.
She wrote letters to her mother and Harriet, recount-
ing her experience to them, too, and telling them she
was going to California to try to find Tom. Their letters would be carried to Govans Harbor on the *Marengo*.

As she watched the island of Maui draw away from
the *Silver Cloud,* she gazed at the mountains, wondering where Wakea's village was. It had provided the
first step in her escape from Eban. This ship was the
final step. Please God, she would succeed in repairing
the ruin he had made of her life.

The voyage to California was swift and uneventful.
Captain Weeks's gallantry and conviviality made it seem

like a pleasure cruise. The contrast between this trip and the voyage she had suffered through on the *Trident* couldn't have been greater. But those months with Eban were in the past. She wouldn't think of them. Instead, she enjoyed each new day, regarding it as a gift and refusing to let herself think she might fail in her search for Tom.

When the *Silver Cloud* sailed into San Francisco Bay, Vianna stood at the rail, gazing at it in awe. She had lived on Cape Cod all her life and seen its harbors, but none of them could compare with the size and depth of this one. To starboard she saw the military garrison built on a hill, guarding the mouth of the harbor. Captain Weeks had informed her it was still known as the Presidio, a holdover from the days when this was Spanish territory. On the opposite side of the harbor the land was cut into several bays, which could accommodate large ships, the captain said. It was in that direction, up the Sacramento River, whose mouth Vianna couldn't see, that the goldfields lay. But this area could not hold her interest at the present moment. San Francisco was beginning to unfold before her eyes, and it was a city unlike anything she had ever seen.

"Is that all there is to it?" she asked finally after surveying the jumble of tents and shacks that staggered back from the waterfront and up the hills that overlooked the bay. "A sailor I talked to in Lahaina called it a fabulous city."

Captain Weeks laughed. "He was probably referring to the drinking and gambling and vice that one finds in San Francisco. Those three forms of entertainment comprise about ninety percent of the business that's done here." The breeze ruffled his curly dark hair, and he brushed a lock of it back off his forehead. Not for the first time on this voyage Vianna was aware of his virile handsomeness. There hadn't been even a hint of flirtation the two weeks they had shared the confines of the *Silver Cloud*. The captain was married and believed Vianna to be married, too, happily. Her thoughts

were so filled with the possibility of a reunion with
Tom that no man, no matter how attractive, could have
stirred her emotions. This didn't prevent either of them,
however, from appreciating the physical charms of the
other.

"Merchants are beginning to realize that there is
profit to be made from other forms of enterprise,"
Captain Weeks went on. "There have always been
those who sold picks and shovels and supplies to miners, but it has become evident to plenty of people that
the segment of the population engaged in the three
major businesses form a sizable group of potential customers for everything from clothes to mirrors and slop
jars. The town even boasts a newspaper. There are
several hotels, but I would recommend only one, the
Dayton House. But I forgot. You have no need of a
hotel. Your husband is waiting for you."

Vianna let that comment pass and gestured toward
the ship they were passing. It was anchored and the
decks were empty. "It looks deserted," she observed.

"It is. Many of these ships are," he said, waving a
hand around the crowded harbor. "They brought cargo
here and the crews jumped ship and disappeared into
the goldfields."

Three hours later, after having said good-bye to
Captain Weeks and been rowed ashore, Vianna found
San Francisco to be an even cruder place than it had
appeared from the deck of the *Silver Cloud*. There had
been no cabs at the dock, and she was forced to walk
to the Dayton House, a distance she calculated to be
about a mile, after inquiring about its location from
the bosun before she stepped ashore. In most places
there were no sidewalks, and she was obliged to make
her way up the streets, which were ankle deep in dust
and littered with horse droppings. The dearth of vehicles she had found at the dock did not exist here.
Horses, mules, wagons, and carriages created clouds
of dust that set her coughing and laid a film over her
dress. She was grateful for the hat Mrs. Young had

supplied. It had kept her hair, at least, from becoming befouled.

She stared in fascination at the many prospectors she saw in the streets, bearded men whose ages couldn't be discerned, clad in worn denim clothing, leading their mules up the street, refusing stubbornly to give way to the vehicles whose cursing drivers had to swing out around them.

It seemed as if every other doorway spewed forth music and loud laughter. Squeezed between the saloons were offices for assayers and lawyers, barber shops, butcher shops, and now and then a large frame building bearing the name Emporium or, more modestly, General Store. Here and there an enterprising entrepreneur had simply strung a canvas roof over the space between two frame buildings and set up business within. San Francisco was a raw, hastily assembled town that nevertheless was seething with vitality and promise. Its spirit infected Vianna, and by the time she arrived at the Dayton House, she was certain that somewhere in this lively town she would find Tom.

The hotel was a two-story building on a corner, its single coat of white paint already peeling off the green lumber siding. Not much space had been allotted to the lobby. It was as if the owner had begrudged the need for this area that could not be rented out and set aside only enough to hold a desk and a few square feet of space for a potential customer to stand. A stairway to the right of the desk led upstairs. On the other side of the room a hallway ran to the back of the building, and opening off it was a wide door through which Vianna could see the dining room. Accustomed to cramped spaces on a ship, she was not put off by its size, and she noted with approval and a measure of surprise that it was spotlessly clean, a miracle considering the dust outside. The clerk behind the desk greeted her with a friendly smile. He was young and pale and had a withered left arm. He asked rather apologetically for a week's rent in advance. When Vianna heard the sum he stated, her heart sank. Captain Weeks had warned her that everything was dreadfully expensive in San Francisco, but she hadn't been prepared for anything like this. Some of the money Doctor Young loaned her had been left after Kalani had paid for her ticket, but one week at the Dayton would deplete her finances alarmingly.

"If I find a cheaper place to stay, will my money be refunded?" she asked.

"Yes, ma'am, but I'm afraid you won't find any other place suitable for a respectable woman to stay."

Vianna bit her lip. "I can only hope then that my business here can be concluded quickly." Her search could begin this minute. "Do you know whether there's a man in San Francisco by the name of Tom Fulton?"

The young man thought for a moment, then shook his head. "I'm afraid not. That doesn't mean he might not be here. Men are going in and out of this town every day, either to or from the goldfields."

"I thought he might have stayed here."

"I'll check. We've only been in business six months." He flipped the hotel register to the first page. "It will only take a minute or two to run through the names of our guests." He was quick but thorough. "No, ma'am. There's no Tom Fulton on this list."

Vianna hadn't really expected that kind of luck. She registered as Miss Vianna Chadwick and would use that name henceforth, hoping to attract Tom's attention to her presence in San Francisco. The wedding ring Eban had given her was gone, thrown surreptitiously into the waters of the bay as she was rowed ashore from the *Silver Cloud*. With its disposal went the last vestige of her nightmarish union with Eban.

Begging a piece of stationery and pen and ink from the hotel clerk, she followed him down the hallway to room number four. The room was sparsely furnished with bed, commode, a wooden chair, and nothing but hooks along one wall for clothing, but it was as clean as the lobby had been. She unpacked her valise in ten minutes, then sat down with swelling heart to write to Tom. She did not bother to write a full explanation of all that had happened; that could be covered when they were reunited. Instead, she told him that Eban had tricked her, too, but that she had got free of him and was in San Francisco. "I've never stopped loving you, Tom, and my profound hope is that we can find each other again and start anew from that terrible moment when we were torn apart." She told him where she was staying and that she was starting out that very moment to search for him. She signed it, "Yours forever and ever, Vianna."

After addressing it to Tom in care of General Delivery, she went immediately back to the desk and asked directions to the post office and the newspaper office. The clerk informed her they were next door to each other about eight blocks away.

She found them easily, mailing the letter first and then placing a notice in the newspaper, stating that Vianna Chadwick of the Dayton House would appreciate any information on the whereabouts of Tom Fulton, formerly of Pennsylvania. The editor promised the notice would appear in the next issue of the weekly, which would be published on Thursday.

When she returned to the hotel, a stout, sour-faced woman had joined the young clerk behind the desk. It was obvious from her tone and the agitated way he was rubbing his withered arm that she had been berating him about something. The woman broke off as Vianna came in, raking her with critical eyes.

"This is Miss Chadwick, our new guest, Mother."

The proprietress of the hotel nodded, but her sour manner did not sweeten by so much as a drop. Apparently the Dayton House did so much business that the woman did not have to put herself out to be friendly. After spending eight months with Eban, Vianna's tolerance for persons with nasty dispositions was nil, but she needed information and she resisted the desire to turn her back on the woman and go straight to her room. Going up to the desk, she addressed the young man. "How would I go about finding someone who came out here to look for gold?"

Before her son could reply, the woman spoke up coldly and said, "Lookin' for a miner in the goldfields is like lookin' for a certain flea on a dog's back. Less'n you know what strike he's working."

Vianna said evenly, "I've heard that sooner or later a miner comes to San Francisco. I was hoping to find him here."

"What's his name?"

"Tom Fulton."

"What's he to you?"

Biting her tongue to keep from blurting out that it was none of her business, Vianna lied coolly. "He's my brother."

"Check the whorehouses."

"Mother!" The boy's face went scarlet as he shot Vianna an apologetic look.

Vianna felt a flush rise to her cheeks, too, and not all of it was caused by embarrassment.

The woman appeared perversely pleased at the effect her suggestion had had on the other two. She shrugged and added, "Every miner who comes in from the goldfields visits the bawdy houses. Talk to the girls. If your brother is especially handsome or rich or rough, they might remember him."

"As a matter of fact," Vianna declared serenely, "he is extraordinarily handsome, and by now, perhaps, very rich. Thank you for your good advice. I'll take it." As she headed for her room, she was rewarded by the look of disappointment that flashed across the woman's sour face. Once in her room, however, she threw her hat on the bed angrily. The old witch! She had been deliberately insulting. A respectable woman wouldn't be caught dead visiting a brothel for any reason. Nor would Tom.

Vianna stared at her hat on the narrow metal bed. Tom visit a brothel? She recalled his impatient ardor

before she had surrendered to him and his eagerness
for her body afterward. His robust sexual appetite
would send him in search of a woman wherever there
was one available. With a sting of jealousy, she conceded that he would be a regular customer of the San
Francisco brothels whenever he was in town. But inquiring for him herself in those places was out of the
question. The very idea made her whole body flame
with embarrassment. Whom could she ask to do this for
her? The only persons she knew even slightly in this
city were the clerk downstairs and his mother. Vianna
suspected the son would leap at any excuse that would
take him to a bawdy house, but he had never met
Tom and so knew nothing about what sort of person
he was or what he looked like. It would be as useless
to ask him to go as it would be to ask that old virago,
his mother, to do it.

That left no one except herself.

Vianna walked over to the single, narrow window
and looked out at the busy street. Through the thick
stream of traffic she could see the businesses on the
other side, housed in unpainted buildings for the most
part, a few of them in tents. She felt as if she had
arrived in a foreign country, far more alien than Maui
had been. Nothing here resembled the sturdy buildings
and tidy streets, the air of permanency and age, that
she had grown up with in Massachusetts. Back there
it was unthinkable that a decent woman would even
cast her eyes upon a house of ill repute. This was a
different world. And she was a far different person from
the one who sailed away from Govans Harbor. She was
willing to do *anything* to find Tom. She squared her
shoulders. Yes, even that.

She returned at once to the desk to find only the
clerk there. She asked matter-of-factly, "Can you tell
me how many brothels San Francisco has and where
they are located?"

He had been going through a pile of papers that
appeared to be receipts or invoices, a frown clouding

his pale face. At her question he looked up and blinked. "Surely you don't——"

She cut him off firmly. "Indeed I do. I haven't much time in which to find my . . . brother. My money is not going to last much more than a week. I've decided to take your mother's advice."

"I don't think she meant it as good advice," he said bitterly.

Vianna replied with some amusement, "I suspect you are right, but I've given it some thought and have decided it's a possibility I can't afford to overlook. I'd like to start immediately."

"You can't go unescorted!" He was plainly distressed. Indicating his withered left arm within its shortened shirt sleeve, he said, "I wouldn't be any good to you even if I could get away from here." He thought a moment. "You'll need a carriage, and if you'll wait until this evening, I think I can fix you up with a driver who will also make a good chaperone. He's an older man who works in a livery barn during the day and drives his own cab at night. His name is Vern Upton, and I'd trust him with my own sister," he vowed, adding shyly, "if I had a sister."

"That's very kind of you."

He blushed. "Not at all, miss. I'll have Vern call for you here after supper."

The old dragon who ran the Dayton House proved to be as good a cook as she was a housekeeper. When Vianna left the dining room that night, the son was watching for her. He called to her and introduced her to the man who was standing at the desk, hat in hand.

"This is Vernon Upton, Miss Chadwick."

As Vianna murmured politely, she took a good look at the man who was to drive her on her tour of San Francisco's houses of ill fame. He was tall and slender, most of his height being located above his belt. His legs were thin and bowed so sharply she thought he must have been put on a horse before he could walk. His jaw was as remarkably long as his upper torso.

Although he was middle-aged, he retained the appearance of a man one wouldn't want to pick a fight with. Vianna found him slightly intimidating until she heard the gentle manner in which he acknowledged their introduction.

"We have a big job ahead of us, miss," he said at once. "Shall we get started?"

"I'll just get my hat and shawl."

When she returned, he had left. "He's waiting outside in his carriage," the clerk told her. "I hope you find your brother." He broke off, flushing, and amended awkwardly, "That is . . . I mean . . . good luck, Miss Chadwick."

"Thank you," Vianna said with a smile. "I'll be the happiest person in the world if I find him."

The carriage and the team that drew it were a glossy black, both bespeaking meticulous care by their owner. When Mr. Upton handed her up into the vehicle, Vianna noted that the leather seat was completely free of dust, an impossible condition to maintain on San Francisco's streets. Whatever dust had collected during Mr. Upton's drive to the Dayton House had been whisked away upon his arrival there.

He took his place on the driver's seat and asked, "Are you ready?"

She took a deep breath, replied that she was, and they started off.

Their first stop was only a few blocks away. "This is the House of Gold," Vern Upton informed her. "The madam's name is Daisy Ranney."

Vianna eyed the tall wooden building with its balcony across the front of the second floor. Two flares stood before the fancy front door. From inside came the sound of loud, feminine laughter. For a moment her resolve melted. A man's laugh overrode the girl's. It reminded her of Tom, after they had made love and he was relaxed and content and was reminiscing about some of the pranks he and Jeremy used to pull. This particular laugh did not belong to Tom, but he might be behind that very door.

"Do I address this woman as Miss or Mrs. Ranney?" Vianna asked faintly.

Vern Upton jumped off the driver's seat and stood waiting to help her down. There was a hint of amusement in his voice as he replied, "I don't reckon you'd offend any madam if you called her Missus."

Vianna summoned her courage and put her hand in his. As she stepped to the ground, Upton said, "I'll be right out here waiting. If you run into any trouble at all, just yell."

The remark was meant to be reassuring, but it had the opposite effect. What lay behind that carved door? What was she walking into? Her courage faltered and she stood there, tempted to climb back into the carriage and ask to be driven back to the hotel. The man's laugh rang out again, so silky and unthreatening that she told herself she had nothing to fear. Before her courage failed her again, she marched up to the well-lit door and knocked.

The door was opened almost immediately by a woman with the most voluptuous figure Vianna had ever seen. Her face, beneath the piled black hair, was neither young nor pretty, but Vianna, observing the creamy breasts swelling up out of the neck of her red velvet gown, could see how she could arouse desire in men of any age.

Daisy Ranney's dark eyes swept the pretty young blond girl who stood on the doorstep, noting her nervousness and the tremor in her voice as she asked, "Are you Mrs. Ranney?"

"That's me. What can I do for you?"

"I'm looking for someone. His name is Tom Fulton. Do you know him?"

The woman's face had given nothing away from the moment she opened the door, despite her surprise at finding a girl there who looked as out of place as a horse in a parlor. Now, however, her expression became even more tightly closed. "One of the things we offer here is strict confidentiality. If you're having trouble with your husband, I suggest you wait until he comes home and have it out with him there. I don't want none of that kind of trouble in my place." She started to close the door.

"You don't understand! Tom isn't my husband, and I'm not here to make trouble."

Daisy Ranney paused. "What do want with him, then?"

"We were going to be married." Vianna's lips began to tremble. "But something awful happened and we were separated."

The voluptuous madam scrutinized her mercilessly. Then, apparently touched by the despair in Vianna's shaking voice, she said, "You'd better come in and tell me all about it." She stepped back and waited.

Vianna hesitated, peering warily past Daisy Ranney's naked, creamy shoulder.

"Well, come on. No one in here is going to lay a hand on you."

Stepping inside, Vianna could scarcely restrain a gasp of surprise. The plainness of the exterior of the House of Gold had given no hint of the opulence she found within. The foyer in which she stood and the parlor visible through the wide, draped doorway to her left boasted crystal chandeliers, red woolen carpets, and polished mahogany furniture. Laughter and the murmur of many voices came from the parlor, and Vianna caught a glimpse of a filmily clad girl before following Daisy Ranney as she turned right and went into a room that, although it was as elegantly furnished as the foyer and parlor, was unmistakably an office. She moved sensuously to her desk, inviting Vianna to sit down and indicating a low, armless chair upholstered in rose-colored satin.

"Now, Miss——"

"Chadwick."

"Tell me about this awful thing that happened to you

and your lover." She seated herself in a thronelike black chair, one ivory arm resting on the polished desk, her eyes as dark as the mahogany of which that piece of furniture was made.

Vianna took a ragged, nervous breath and began, skirting the embarrassing truth about her love affair with Tom and the fact that the baby she had carried was his.

"If he skipped out on you, aren't you wasting your time trying to find him?" Daisy Ranney interrupted.

"He didn't run away! He was tricked," Vianna declared, and went on to explain.

A few moments later, the older woman interrupted again. "This Eban risked killing his own child just to punish you?"

Vianna dropped her eyes. "Y-y-yes." She could feel Daisy Ranney's eyes boring into her bowed head.

"I see." And Vianna knew the madam understood everything, but with a delicacy she hadn't expected from a woman who ran a brothel, Daisy Ranney allowed the truth to remain unspoken. She listened silently from that moment on.

When Vianna completed her saga, Daisy Ranney observed, "That's the craziest story I ever heard in all my born days, and honey, I've heard some beauts."

Vianna exclaimed defensively, "It's true! Every word of it!"

"I'm sure it is, honey. Unfortunately for you and this Tom Fulton. I wish I could say I knew him, knew where he was, but I don't remember the name of every man who comes in here. They hit town for a few days, then disappear. I'll ask my girls, though. One of them may remember him." She got up. "You wait here. I'll tell them to come in, and you can describe your Tom to them."

They came to the office singly and in twos and threes, not overly pretty girls, but young and fresh, dressed in ruffled negligees and heavily made up. They listened to Vianna's description, reflected, then unanimously and sympathetically declared they could remember no man of that name or description.

"Sorry, honey," Daisy Ranney said from behind her desk when the last one trooped out. "But don't give up. There's seven more places like this one in town. He's sure to have turned up in one of them. That is, I mean——"

Vianna smiled and said quietly, "It's all right. I know Tom. That's why I'm here, and if I manage to find some trace of him in one of these places, I'll be the happiest woman in the world." She stepped away from the rose satin chair, holding out her hand. "I want to thank you, Mrs. Ranney. You've been kindness itself."

Chuckling, Daisy Ranney took her hand. "You probably came here expecting to be eaten alive. As you can see, we're not as bad as we've been painted."

"I'll testify to that any time." She squeezed the woman's hand and followed her to the front door.

"I'll keep my eyes and ears open, Miss Chadwick. I'll tell my girls to watch out for your Tom, too."

"I'd be most grateful. I'm staying at the Dayton House, in case you have any information for me."

When Vianna emerged from the House of Gold, Vern Upton jumped down from his seat and handed her in. "Any luck?"

"I'm afraid not. Take me to the next one." Vianna settled back, unencouraged but no longer dreading the task she had set herself to.

16

It was past midnight and Vianna was tired. She had visited four brothels without results. Each madam to whom she told her evasive story surmised the truth about her baby but showed the same tact Daisy Ranney had, sparing her the embarrassment of asking her outright if it was Tom's. At the end of each fruitless visit, she had urged the madam to contact her at the Dayton House if one of the girls remembered something or if Tom turned up. Slumped back against the black leather seat of the carriage, Vianna realized her night's task was much bigger than she had anticipated. It was also much pleasanter. She had found all the bawdy house proprietors to be as helpful as Daisy Ranney had been. When Vern Upton asked her after she left the fourth brothel if she didn't want to call it a night and resume her search the next night, she had said no, that she wanted to continue if he was willing.

"I reckon I can hold up if you can," he'd replied.

Vianna heard the raucous noise rising from the next brothel while they were still a block away.

"This is Ruby's," Upton announced as he pulled the horses up in front of it.

She surveyed the rough board exterior with as much trepidation as she'd felt upon approaching her first brothel. Without exception, all the others had had names with the word *gold* used somehow in them and had been two-story affairs. Vianna had come to expect uniformity, and the fact that this establishment resembled none of the others in any way was jarring.

Ruby's was all on one floor and was big as a livery barn, which it resembled, Vianna decided, with its square false front and wide double doors. It stood apart from the other buildings on the block. A hitching rail ran along all four sides of the building, and there was scarcely a space that wasn't filled with a horse, a mule, or a buggy. Flares on tall poles stood at each of the four corners, and some light leaked from windows located toward the back. The only windows in the front of the building were located above the double door. They were only about a foot high, but long, and made of randomly shaped pieces of colored glass.

"You want I should go with you?" Vern Upton asked as she hesitated before taking his hand and stepping down. "It's always been a wild place, but it's calmed down some the last two weeks. Ruby found a guy who could keep the peace."

Vianna was tempted to accept his offer to accompany her, but she shrank from the role of helpless female. After what she'd been through with Eban, she could surely handle any situation she found herself in. Couldn't she? Swallowing again, she assured Upton she wasn't afraid to go in alone, and she walked up the dirt path to the door.

Both doors were flung open at her knock, and she found herself staring up at a giant of a man. He was at least seven feet tall, probably more, and everything about him was oversized but in such fine proportion that he gave no impression of awkwardness despite his unusual size. His dark hair was thick and wavy and trimmed short. He was elegantly dressed in a tan suit, brown satin waistcoat, and brown boots. Lying behind the surface curiosity in his blue eyes was the deepest pain Vianna had ever observed in anyone's eyes.

"I'd like to see Ruby," she announced in a small voice.

"Would you follow me, please?" His voice was a surprise. She had expected a bass rumble. What came out was high-pitched and rather effeminate.

The barnlike structure was divided into several parlors, all as opulently furnished as she'd come to expect from her visits to the other brothels. Although their route led them through only one, she glimpsed the others in passing. They were crowded with men in rough miners' clothes being served drinks by girls in pastel satin negligees. The din was deafening, but the tone was the genial one of men having a good time. If this had been a wild place up until two weeks ago, as Vern Upton said, Vianna thought she could make a pretty good guess as to when this giant came to work here.

Vianna squirmed inwardly at the attention their passage through the room drew and was relieved when they entered an office so cluttered with furniture, paintings, and knickknacks that the small, plump woman behind the desk was almost invisible.

"A lady to see you, Ruby." The giant stepped aside to allow Vianna to enter.

There was plenty of ruby red velvet and silk in the room, but the woman herself did not look like a ruby. She was blond and blue-eyed, and the white arms emerging from the puffed sleeves of her blue gown were fat, the flesh beginning to hang loose with age. Eying Vianna skeptically, the woman said, "Come in and sit down."

As Vianna took the proffered chair, the giant quietly left. Still regarding her dubiously, Ruby asked, "What is it you want to see me about?"

When Vianna replied that she was looking for a man named Tom Fulton, she received the usual response of an instantly closed expression. "I don't want to make trouble for him," she explained quickly, and repeated her tale for the fifth time that night. The mask fell from Ruby's face halfway through it.

"Where's this son of a bitch Eban now, dearie?"

"Hunting whales in the Pacific, or me in Lahaina."

Ruby shoved back her chair. "Would you like a drink?" When Vianna declined, the other woman went to a small table in the corner beside her desk that held a decanter and glasses. "I hope you don't mind if I have one. I need a snort after hearing a story like that one." She poured some whiskey into a glass, downed it in one gulp, and poured another, which she held in her hand. "I sure wish I could say I knew this here Tom Fulton, but I don't. Let me ask my girls."

This investigation proved no more fruitful than the previous ones had. Fatigue and disappointment weighed heavily on Vianna as she rose to go. "You've been very kind to give me so much of your time."

"Don't mention it, dearie." Ruby's soft, loose face turned bitter. "I wish that son of a bitch Eban would turn up here. I'd sic X. on him."

"God forbid that he would come here!" Vianna shuddered, then recalled with relief, "He doesn't know I've come here, and I covered my tracks so well, he never will."

The giant entered at that moment. Addressing Vianna, he said in his strangely effeminate manner, "Some of the girls tell me you are looking for a man named Tom Fulton. I know someone who goes by that name, and the description fits, too."

Vianna caught the back of her chair. "Where is he?" she whispered.

"He went back to the goldfields. Until two weeks ago I worked at another place, and he was a regular caller there for a few weeks. He said someone had stolen his claim, and he had tried but couldn't get it back. He brought what gold he had in order to have a fling here before going back to hunt for another one."

Vianna's legs were trembling. "Do you know where he went?"

"No, but some of the girls might." For the second time Vianna noticed the dark melancholy that lay in the depths of his eyes. "He was a big favorite with them, if you'll pardon my saying so. He might have told one of them where he was heading."

Breathlessly, Vianna asked, "What was the name of the brothel? I must go there at once."

Ruby spoke up. "You're nearly out on your feet, dearie. Why don't you wait until tomorrow? It isn't as if he was here in town and you could hunt him up tonight."

The giant, who had also noticed her extreme weariness, suggested, "Why don't you let me go there tomorrow, talk to the girls, and see what I can find out? This may not even be the same man, but if it is, I can get the information as well as you could."

"X. has the right idea, dearie. You go home and get some sleep. You shouldn't be canvassing whorehouses, anyway. X. can report to you tomorrow."

Vianna hesitated. She was so close to finding Tom.

Ruby reminded her with rough gentleness, "He's back up in the mountains. You're not going to be reunited with him tonight, no matter what you find out."

Vianna gave in. "I'm staying at the Dayton House. Room number four."

X., the giant, said, "The girls sleep till noon. I'll report to you tomorrow afternoon, whether I find out anything or not."

Ruby patted her arm as she led her toward the door. "I sure hope this is the guy you're looking for, dearie. If I can be of any help to you, don't hesitate to ask."

Vianna thanked them both and followed X. back through the parlor to the front door. With his huge hand covering one of the knobs, he said, "I didn't get your name, miss."

"I'm Vianna Chadwick."

"I guess you heard Ruby call me X. The last name is Medrano."

"Good night, Mr. Medrano. And thank you again."

Vern Upton was dozing inside the cab and awoke sheepishly as she spoke to him. "You can take me back to my hotel, Mr. Upton. I may have found Tom. Mr. Medrano is going to find out more and report to me tomorrow."

"Well, now, I'm glad to hear it." He had scrambled down and was handing her in.

As they drove off, Vianna watched the light filtering out through the colored windows above the double doors. They reminded her of a church. Incongruous? Perhaps not. It was possible her prayers had been answered in that very place.

She slept late the next morning. Awakening once, she reminded herself there would be no word of Tom until afternoon, and she might as well pass the time sleeping. Her mind and body, exhausted by her long and eventful first day in San Francisco, embraced further sleep ardently.

She was awakened at noon by the proprietress, who Vern Upton had told her was Mrs. Dayton herself. "Are you all right in there?"

Vianna replied groggily that she was.

"You missed breakfast, and dinner's half over. If you want anything to eat, you'll have to look sharp. I stop serving in half an hour."

"All right, Mrs. Dayton. I'm getting up."

Once she sat down and began eating the ham and fresh biscuits, she was glad the old harridan had got her up. She discovered that she was starved, and the meal was just as tasty as her supper last night had been. It left her with time to kill afterward, though, and she couldn't leave the hotel. She would have liked to go to the desk and visit with Oscar Dayton, but he was laughing and joking with two men who were seated on the stairway that ran up the wall to the right of the desk. Slowly she made her way back to her room, where she pulled the wooden chair up to the window and sat gazing out upon the ceaseless activity of the street.

Twice she went to the desk and asked the time. Finally, about two-thirty, X. Medrano arrived. When he stepped across the threshold, her room suddenly shrank to the dimensions of a pantry. He wore the same tan suit he'd been wearing the night before, but his shirt was snowy fresh, and his waistcoat was of watered green silk. "Please sit down, Mr. Medrano," she said, indicating the chair.

An embryo of a smile moved across his broad face. "If I broke Mrs. Dayton's chair, we'd both be in for an awful scolding. I'll stand. You take it, miss."

Feeling as if the room were too small for both of them to stand up in, Vianna did as he suggested. Looking up, hands tightly clenched in her lap, she asked, "What did you find out?"

Another barely conceived smile filmed the sadness that seemed as much a part of his eyes as the blue color. "The girls remembered a Tom Fulton very well, and it appears certain from the things they said about him that he's the man you're looking for."

One of Vianna's hands fluttered to her face as X. Medrano continued. "The girls agreed that it was the American River he was heading for, too."

"I've got to go there," she said in a trembling voice. She had found him! She must get to him at once!

The giant settled into a more relaxed stance, putting most of his weight on one long leg and thrusting the other out at a slight angle. "There are packets running up and down the Sacramento, and you could take one of them to the mouth of the American, but it probably wouldn't do you any good. Fulton undoubtedly has gone up the river into the mountains."

"How did he get up there?"

"He probably went as far as Flume by stage, but from there on the only mode of transport is by mule or shanks' mare." He regarded her uneasily. "The American is a long river, and the country it runs through is as rough as it can get. You can't go up there," he warned earnestly, "if that's what you're thinking."

Vianna got up and went to the window. A cloud of dust hovered over the street, stirred up by the wheels and hooves and feet that were moving purposefully toward unknown destinations. "If I remained here, Mr.

Medrano, how long might I have to wait before Tom returned to San Francisco?"

He shifted his weight again and didn't reply at once. Finally he admitted, "From a few months to forever. Sometimes men go out there and are never heard from again. Some of them give up and go back East by the land route. Others just disappear."

Vianna turned to look at him. "Die, you mean."

He nodded. "And not all from natural causes or accident. Greed turns men mean, and there's nothing that makes a man greedier than the sight of gold."

Vianna left the window. She didn't feel like sitting down, but there seemed to be too little space for her in the room otherwise. Perching tautly on the edge of the bed, she said, "I've almost lost Tom twice. I'm not going to wait idly here and chance losing him again. I'm going up there and search for him."

The man clearly wanted to move about, but there was so little space for him to do it. He took a step and a half to his left, then a few steps to his right, which brought him up against the opposite wall, where her other dress and shawl hung from hooks. Rubbing his forehead so hard that the skin wrinkled, he said, "It's madness, if you'll pardon my saying so. The goldfields are a whole different world, and a man's world at that. The only women up there are—well, the girls you met at Ruby's are genteel ladies compared to those who go to the goldfields to ply their trade. There aren't even many of them. There's a little bit of law in Flume. They've elected a sheriff, anyway. Beyond that, there's no law along the rest of the river. A man can be shot for one poke of gold, and even if the identity of the murderer is known, nothing is done about it." He stopped and clenched his jaw a few times. "Dying is the least that could happen to a decent woman like you if you went out there."

"I could go as far as Flume. Tom might be known there. Maybe I could hire someone to carry a message to him."

Ruefully, he remarked, "You wouldn't stop there. It's plain you're bound and determined to find him. If there's no trace of him in Flume, you'll start out to look further for him."

She didn't deny it. Even if he hadn't exaggerated the dangers, she doubted that she could bear to be halted in her search for Tom when he was so near. He seemed so distressed by the thought of her exposing herself to the perils of the trip that she said cheerfully, "I may find him in Flume, and then I wouldn't have to look any further."

"I'll pray that you do, Miss Chadwick." He left, scarcely hearing her fervent thanks, genuinely upset because he hadn't been able to dissuade her from her rash project.

Vianna was not entirely without qualms as she paced her room, contemplating the mission she was setting herself. This was savage, unsettled country she would be going into, not at all like civilized New England. Inexperienced and consequently ill-equipped for such a challenge, she would be like a landlubber thrust onto a storm-tossed ship.

She noticed for the first time that the basin and pitcher on the commode were of a pattern similar to the set Eban had had on the *Trident*. The thought came to her that she had become rather skilled at surviving. A few minutes later she was out on the street, looking for a store that sold guidebooks and maps of the goldfields.

For the next three days she studied the book she bought. The maps it contained were intimidating, showing the goldfields in unrelievedly mountainous terrain to the east of the Sacramento Valley. The area surrounding the American River looked as rugged as the rest. Combing that region would be a formidable undertaking. She began to doubt that she could do it.

She was examining the maps with a feeling of despair one afternoon when someone knocked at her door. To her surprise, she found her visitor to be X. Medrano. "I was afraid you might already be gone," he said, relieved.

She invited him in and indicated the book that lay open on the bed. "I'm still in the planning stage, and I must admit I haven't made much progress."

His massive physical bulk, encased in a soft gray suit, seemed to fill the room to its corners. His glance took in the map showing on the book's pages. "You haven't changed your mind, I take it. You still intend going."

"I do, but I won't deny that I'm frightened."

He played with the thick gold watch chain that hung across the front of his ivory-colored, brocaded satin waistcoat. "Would you accept some company on your trip?"

Retreating from his overwhelming presence, Vianna took to the edge of the bed, perching there rather uneasily. "Who would want to accompany me?"

"I would."

Vianna picked up the book and pretended to look at it. "I'm afraid not, Mr. Medrano."

"Don't misunderstand, Miss Chadwick. I would be going only as your friend and protector."

"Why would you want to do that?" She tried to read the big face that loomed so far above her.

His expression was both shy and wistful. "I haven't been able to get you out of my mind. I couldn't stand to think of you heading for the goldfields alone. You need a protector, and no one could do that job better than I."

Astonished that she had had this kind of effect on this immense man, Vianna could think of nothing to say for a moment. He knew she was searching for a man she loved. Did he think that she would agree to a romantic interlude in the meantime? The idea was abhorrent to her, but she must not let him know that. Although his manner was mild, his emotions might be as overgrown as his body. He could break her in two if he got angry.

"But don't you see," she said gently, "that an arrangement like that isn't possible? It wouldn't do at all."

"Yes, miss, it would. You need have no fear of me. Our relationship would never be anything more than friendship." The full force of the pain that always lay hidden in his eyes hit her now. "I was gelded as a boy." As he made the pronouncement, his voice rose a little higher than usual. "You would be perfectly safe with me. Ask anyone in San Francisco. I'm known around town as the Eunuch."

Vianna could not think what to say. The man's anguish transmitted itself to her. She had never felt such pity for anyone.

X. Medrano broke the lengthy silence, his voice controlled now. "I know you think me a freak, but when I said you didn't have to be afraid of me, I meant that in every way. I learned years ago that violence was something I couldn't allow myself unless I wanted to leave a string of dead men behind me. I had my revenge on the fellows who did this to me. After that I settled down. Hardly anything riles me anymore." Again that ghost of a smile. "And anyone who wants trouble changes his mind the minute I show up, so wherever I go things stay pretty peaceable. That's why I think you ought to let me go with you."

"You'd leave your job and accompany me, knowing that my sole purpose is to find the man I love? Would it be worth it, Mr. Medrano?"

"Yes," he answered simply. "I've never felt this way about a woman before. I want to be with you and take care of you. I'm not exaggerating when I say I'm afraid that if you go up there alone, you'll never be heard from again. I'd go crazy back here thinking of all the things that could happen to you. Besides," he said, fingering his watch chain again, "I've been playing with the idea of going to the goldfields myself. If you find this man you're looking for, I might just stay and do some prospecting."

Vianna flipped the pages of the book a few times,

the sharp papery sound filling the silence. At last she said, "I take this as one of the greatest compliments I've ever received, but I'm afraid I'll have to give it a lot of thought before I can accept your offer to accompany me."

"I understand."

"I'll let you know my answer in a few days."

When he had gone, she remained as she had been, sitting on the edge of the bed, flipping the pages of the book absently. After a few minutes, she went out to the desk and found Oscar Dayton alone, leaning across it on his one good arm and staring dreamily out the clean front window. He straightened guiltily when she came up.

"Do you know the man who just left here?" Vianna asked.

"Everyone in San Francisco knows X. Medrano, Miss Chadwick."

Flushing slightly, Vianna asked, "Is it true that women have nothing to fear from him?"

He rubbed his withered left arm in embarrassment. "That's true."

"I see," she murmured, then turned and went thoughtfully back to her room.

17

The gold camp called Flume was swiftly developing into a town. A day's drive by stagecoach from the mouth of the American River, it was located just at the edge of the mountains. The small amount of gold the spot had yielded had been exhausted, but the residents were discovering that they could fill their pockets with gold without pan, pick, or shovel. They provided services and goods for the miners who passed through on their way to the goldfields farther up the river and for those who came back for supplies.

The town was the last outpost of civilization—if one used the term loosely—and on that mid-September evening when Vianna and X. Medrano got off the stage, the single street that comprised the business district rang with the noise that issued from the two brothels and three saloons that shared Main Street with the more prosaic business establishments. The noisiest of the saloons was the same type of structure Vianna had seen here and there in San Francisco. A canvas roof had been stretched across the space between a general store and the recorder's office, where claims were registered. The rear wall was also of canvas. The front was wide open, and as Vianna stepped down off the coach in front of the stage office, she could look across the street directly into it. A crude wooden bar ran along one side, and behind it, built upon the outside wall of the recorder's office, was the back bar, filled with liquor bottles. Kegs with square wooden tops served as tables that teetered on the uneven earthen floor. Other kegs and boxes substituted for chairs.

Two doors up the street from the stage office was a hotel, with a brothel next door. X. Medrano took Vianna's valise and his own and led her away from that one and back to the hotel at the end of Main Street. There was none of Mrs. Dayton's cleanliness here. The bare wooden floor of Vianna's room was stained with tobacco juice, and a few butts of old cigars, smashed by dirty boots, lay about. The commode was simply a box on which sat a metal pitcher and basin. The begrimed window was curtainless, and there were not even any pegs in the rough board walls on which to hang clothes. But it was the bed that caused Vianna the most dismay. The sheets looked as if they had come up the Sacramento River with the metal frame and hadn't been washed since.

She was regarding the linen with revulsion when X., whose room was next door, stuck his head in. "Looks like a mule's been sleeping there, doesn't it? Mine is the same way. I'll go see if I can coax some clean sheets and pillowcases out of the owner."

In five minutes the bedding in Vianna's room was being changed by a fat man who kept a wary eye on X., who lounged in the doorway, watching. Vianna reflected with some amusement that, given his overpowering presence, X. probably was a very successful persuader. Not for a single moment since leaving San Francisco had she regretted allowing him to accompany her. She was learning that he could be an extremely useful companion in many situations and was a congenial one at all times.

The purpose of her trip was always at the forefront of her mind. Her love for Tom was a living presence within her, unlike those terrible months aboard the *Trident* when she was preoccupied with efforts to save herself and her baby from Eban's unholy wrath. The closer she came to finding Tom, the fresher became her memories of him. One that returned to her again and again was of a hot July night. It had followed a week of summer rains that confined them to her mother's parlor each night, constraining them, making caresses impossible, silencing their expressions of love. Several nights Tom had tried to outwait Mary Chadwick, hoping for some moments alone with Vianna after the older woman went to bed, but she remained stubbornly in the parlor, tatting, saying little, putting a damper by her presence on the casual conversation they tried to maintain.

When at last the rain stopped, they leaped to the excuse of a walk when Tom called on her that evening. They headed by tacit agreement toward the beach, first with her hand on the crook of his elbow until they left the town behind them, then with arms around each other's waist, the physical contact after their long abstinence firing the flames of their desire. At the bottom of the path that put them on the beach and out of sight of even the outlying homes, Tom pulled her against him, and they kissed with a blind urgency that blotted out everything except their straining bodies and lips. It was still daylight, however, and although there was no one in sight at the moment, they couldn't make love in the open. Unable to break apart, they loosened their clasp on each other to free their hands to caress and touch while their mouths still moved voluptuously together.

After a few moments of this, their clamoring desire tore them apart and sent them hurrying toward the cave on trembling legs. That quick walk remained a blur in Vianna's mind. She had been conscious of nothing but the sweet tide of passion that broke over her in wave after wave, causing her breath to come quickly and her body to feel as if it were melting.

Once they had reached the cave and removed the necessary clothing, they filled their arms with each other, clinging and kissing. Their bodies fused almost immediately, their rapture heightened by their abstinence of the past week, every movement bringing gasps of exquisite pleasure. Their desire had built to such an intense degree before they reached the cave that it was over very quickly, and they lay smiling at each other as the thumping of their hearts gradually quieted.

This particular episode of their lovemaking stood out in Vianna's mind above all others. Since leaving San Francisco, the memory of it had come back to her many times, flooding her with aching need and an almost intolerable anxiety. She had to find Tom! She hoped desperately that she wouldn't have to search any farther than Flume, that he would be there or near there and they could be reunited at once.

As she watched the fat hotelkeeper pull the soiled sheets from her bed, she asked him if he knew a Tom Fulton, and described him.

He repeated the name, puffing from his exertions. "I don't believe I know him. But that don't mean he ain't been here. He might a stayed at the other hotel, or even slept out in the open if he didn't have money for a room. These miners get so they can sleep in a pouring rain with no more than a blanket to cover 'em." He unfolded a sheet that, though not exactly white, had been laundered. "Ask at the recorder's office or the saloons and—that is, any of the other places in town. Someone might have seen him around."

Vianna couldn't think about supper until they had asked around for Tom. X. took the three saloons, the two brothels, the livery barn, the blacksmith shop, and the barbershop. Vianna inquired at the other hotel, a café, the two general stores, the recorder's office, and the sheriff's office. The last place she found locked up. They met at the café next door to their hotel and compared notes. Not a soul they had questioned knew Tom or remembered seeing him around Flume. Vianna's disappointment was acute. She had been dreading the possibility of the trek up the American River. Unfortunately, it would have to be made.

"There's no use staying here," Vianna declared dejectedly as they were served a slab of steak with boiled potatoes and onions on the side. The café was un-plastered and unpainted, the chairs and tables crude affairs built of raw lumber, but it was reasonably clean. "I'd like to move on up the river tomorrow."

"Another order just like this," X. told the waiter before the man got away from the table. To Vianna he said, "Don't you want to rest a day or two? From here on the going will be rough. There's absolutely nothing up there. We'll have to take what supplies we need and buy mules to carry them."

Vianna's finances were nearing the vanishing point. She didn't intend paying another night's rent on a hotel room when there was nothing more to be learned in Flume. At the news that they would need mules for their trip up the river, she asked in alarm, "How much will a mule cost?"

"I inquired when I was in the livery barn and the owner said he could let me have two for fifty dollars apiece."

Vianna winced. "I don't have fifty dollars."

"Don't worry. I'll buy the mules. You use your money to buy your share of the supplies." The size of his bites would have choked a man of normal size, yet there was nothing gross about his table manners. "I'd advise you to buy a couple sets of men's pants and shirts. Boots, too. You won't be able to hike through these mountains in your dresses and those shoes."

She saw the wisdom in his advice, but that meant further expenditure of her dwindling money supply. However, she had no choice. She must find Tom, if it took every cent she possessed. "Let's buy what we need the first thing in the morning and get started."

She was facing the door and noticed the man who came in. He was almost burly, but not quite, to the point of stoutness. A black mustache curved down the corners of his mouth. On his head he wore a frayed straw hat and on his chest a sheriff's star. He was the one person she hadn't been able to find to ask about

Tom, and she was glad when she saw him survey the crowded café, then head for their table.

"I'm Buck Rozell, the sheriff," he said, sweeping off the worn straw hat to display a bald head and long black sideburns. "I hear you folks are looking for someone."

X. introduced Vianna and himself. "His name is Tom Fulton and we were told in San Francisco that he planned to come up this river and look for gold. Do you remember anyone by that name?"

When he said he didn't, Vianna described Tom. Again, the sheriff's answer was negative. "How come you're trying to find this man?"

Vianna invited him to sit down, and she gave a truncated version of the story. "After all that has happened, I'm determined to find Tom, and Mr. Medrano enlisted to come along as my protector."

Sheriff Rozell's grin flashed brilliantly beneath the drooping black mustache. "You sure couldn't have found a better one. You'll need him, too. Once you leave Flume, you leave the law behind." Studying X. thoughtfully, he said, "I've seen you around San Francisco, haven't I?"

"Probably. I've been there for about a year."

Rozell nodded. "I landed there about six months ago. Came out here from New York. Took the land route through the Isthmus of Panama." He held up his battered straw hat and regarded it affectionately. "That's where I picked this up. Wish I had another just like it. Most comfortable hat I ever wore, and I'm afraid it won't last much longer." He got up. "When you folks fixing to start upriver?"

"Tomorrow," Vianna said quickly.

"I sure hope you find the man you're looking for. You've set yourself quite a task. If he turns up here in Flume, I'll tell him you're trying to find him."

"I'd appreciate that, sheriff."

It was noon before Vianna and X. had made their purchases and were ready to start. Knowing their diet from here on out would consist mostly of flapjacks, bacon, hardtack, and coffee, they ate another big meal of steak, potatoes, and onions before saying good-bye to Flume and the civilization it represented.

The land began to rise almost immediately, although they were able for the most part to follow the more level land along the bank of the river. More often than not, it was narrow and rocky. Sometimes the mountain slopes came right down to the water in rocky slides. The mules, their four legs and different center of gravity giving them an advantage, made out better in spots like this than did Vianna and X. Stiff as her new boots were, Vianna blessed X. for advising her to buy them. She wore the legs of her new canvas pants tucked into them. Her shirt was round-necked and buttoned at the throat. A broad-brimmed hat kept the sun off her face, and folded across her mule's back was a heavy jacket, which at the moment she didn't need.

By the time they made camp, she was eager for a rest, wondering how she could keep going for a full day tomorrow. Nevertheless, she cooked supper, observing closely how X. built the fire. It was her first experience at preparing a meal like this, but it turned out rather well. Coffee had never been so welcome or tasted so good. Not knowing how long they might be in the mountains, they had bought tea, too, because of its lighter weight. They finished their supper with a tin of peaches.

After drinking the last drop of juice from the can, X. sighed contentedly. "You're a fine cook, Vianna." They had been on a first-name basis since the trip by packet boat up the Sacramento. "There's nothing like exercise followed by a good solid meal to make a person feel his best. I never felt this good back in San Francisco."

Vianna gave a rueful laugh. "I won't pretend I feel at my best. I had no idea the going would be so rough."

He leaned back against a fallen tree. He was wearing rough prospector's clothes he must have had made for him before they left San Francisco. A soft gray woolen cap covered his dark hair. He looked strange without his well-tailored suit, but Vianna reminded herself that she must look just as strange to him in her men's clothing. She felt awkward and slightly ridiculous. "Do you want to turn around and go back?" X. asked.

"Absolutely not," she replied without hesitation. "I'm convinced that if I don't find Tom now, I never will." The thought of failure firmed her determination to continue this trip no matter how difficult it proved to be. "I can't promise to be able to keep up with you for the first few days, but I'll get toughened into it."

"I don't intend setting the pace. We'll go at whatever speed is comfortable for you."

Vianna didn't know if the light from the fire failed to pick it out, or whether the sadness that lived in his blue eyes was less than it had been when they left Flume. Certainly it would do more for his ego than his job as brothel bouncer, where he was constantly reminded of how he differed from other men. He helped her scrub the dishes with river sand, then urged her to turn in for the night. She rolled up in her blanket, back against a fallen log, face to the fire, and was asleep before she got firmly settled upon the hard ground. She awoke briefly some time later as she turned over and found X. still sitting up awake and staring into the fire. Feeling as secure as a child with a parent nearby, Vianna closed her eyes and went back to sleep.

It took a week before Vianna's muscles and feet became accustomed to the long hours they spent each day traversing the formidable terrain. Suddenly she got her second wind, and from then on she withstood the rigors of the journey without feeling any more than tolerably tired at night. Until then they had not encountered another human being.

Late one afternoon they came upon a claim that was obviously being worked. A portable rocker stood on the riverbank, some rocks from which the clay was being washed still in it. A bucket filled with water stood beside it. Some yards back from the bank, an old fire smoldered. X. stopped his mule beside the rocker and put out a hand to inspect the rocks when a shot rang out and a bullet went singing past his head.

"Get down," he yelled to Vianna, ducking behind his mule.

From a clump of trees behind the fire came the sounds of someone hastily reloading a gun.

"There's no need to shoot us," X. yelled. "We're not after your gold. We're looking for a friend, Tom Fulton."

"Lemme see your gun!" a man's voice demanded.

A pistol and a rifle were part of the equipment X. had bought before leaving Flume. Upon their arrival in that town, Vianna had noticed that most of the men she saw carried pistols either in holsters or stuck in the top of their trousers. "With no law to protect a man in the goldfields," X. had explained, "he has to protect himself."

Complying with the unseen prospector's demand, X. pulled his pistol slowly from its hip holster and held it in the air.

"Lay it in the rocker," came another command. "Now the rifle." X. pulled it from its boot on the mule's back and laid it beside the pistol. "Now come forward!"

Vianna, X., and the mules moved past the rocker. "Far enough!" Cautiously, a man emerged from the trees, his rifle leveled at them. If it hadn't been for the dirt on his clothes, Vianna thought, he could have been about to take the platform and give a speech. He wore a three-piece suit that she guessed hadn't been off him night or day for weeks. A shirt that had once been white and a black hat completed his outfit. His graying hair and beard were so long she couldn't tell whether the shirt had a collar or not. The eyes regarding them from under bushy brows smoldered with suspicion. Vianna held her mule behind X.'s, glad enough to let the giant take the lead.

"We're not claim jumpers," X. assured him. "We're

not even looking for gold. We're just trying to find a man." He repeated Tom's name.

"Never heard of him."

"Describe him, Vianna." When she was finished, X. asked, "Have you seen anybody that fits that?"

"Nope."

"How long have you been here?"

The prospector weighed that question to make sure he wouldn't give anything away if he answered it. "A week," he said at last.

"Did you come from Flume, or upriver?"

"None o' yore business."

"I'm not poking my nose in your business, mister," X. said patiently. "I'm trying to find out if Tom could be farther up the river."

"I wouldn't know. I ain't been up there yet."

"If it's all right with you, then, we'll be moving on."

"That'd suit me fine."

X. jerked his head over his shoulder in the direction of the rocker. "I'd like to have my guns."

"You go up there and wait by that big rock," the miner said, indicating a boulder upstream from his camp. "The lady can bring the guns to you."

X. hesitated, studying the man.

"I'm not aimin' to shoot you," the prospector declared. "All I want is for you folks to clear outta here and leave me alone."

For the first time since Vianna had known X., she heard unmistakable menace in his voice as he said, "I hope you're telling the truth. If you harm the lady, you won't be able to reload fast enough to keep me from killing you with my bare hands."

The prospector spat a stream of tobacco juice to one side without taking his eyes off X. "I know that. And I'm tellin' you true. I mean you no harm. I only want you to move on."

X. nodded and turned to Vianna. "I believe him. I'll go on ahead, and you wait until he says you can follow." He tugged at his mule and strode across the camp to the boulder, where he turned and watched.

The miner said, "All right, lady. Pick up the guns slowly and be on your way."

"I've never fired a gun in my life," Vianna said, piqued and out of patience by the whole incident, "but I might have to learn how." Haughtily she swept up the guns from the rocker and led her mule up to the boulder.

Before starting off again, X. called back, "If Tom Fulton should show up, tell him Vianna Chadwick is looking for him and to wait for her in Flume."

There was no reply from the man who stood there in his filthy three-piece black suit and black hat, still covering Vianna and X. with his gun. X. slapped his mule's rump, and they headed upstream.

Vianna had an itch between her shoulder blades, imagining that gun trained on her back, until they rounded a bend that put them out of sight and out of range. "Antisocial old coot, wasn't he?"

X. slowed to let her catch up. "What you saw was one symptom of gold fever. That man has made a strike. From now on he'll suspect everyone who comes by of wanting to kill him or steal it from him."

"Whatever it is he's protecting, I don't envy him." Vianna smiled up at her big companion. "I'm glad I let you come along."

He came as near to smiling back as she'd ever seen him. "I thought you would be." He lengthened his stride. "Let's put some distance between him and us before sundown."

Vianna agreed wholeheartedly with that suggestion, and increased her own pace.

18

"This is it," X. said, halting his mule beneath a redwood whose thick, fernlike branches afforded a measure of shelter from the rain.

Vianna pulled up beside him, and with devastating disappointment contemplated the narrow stream of water a few yards in front of them. They had reached the head of the American River without finding a single trace of Tom. It had been a grueling journey. To make matters worse, the rainy season had begun a week ago, and she had enjoyed scarcely a dry moment since. She felt as if her skin beneath the men's pants and shirt was all wrinkly from being wet for so long a time. X. had bought a large square of canvas in Flume before they started out, and that gave them a measure of protection from the rain at night when they stretched it across some poles or branches. With their fire burning in front of it, they managed to keep fairly warm. Building a satisfactory fire was almost impossible, however, when wet wood was all they had to work with, and their clothing did not dry completely, even at night.

"You're sure Tom told the girls it was the American River he was heading for?" she asked glumly, gazing at the tiny stream, dimpled from the raindrops falling into it.

"I'm sure." X. drew her farther under the tree, where there was a little more shelter. "He's probably up one of the tributaries. Or," he added, wiping his big face on the sleeve of his jacket, "he might have changed his mind and gone somewhere else."

Each time they'd come to a stream that was running into the American, Vianna would wonder if Tom had gone up it to look for gold. X. persuaded her to stick with the river and search it to its source, cautioning that if they explored every feeder stream, they'd be a year hunting Tom. "And we don't want to be in the higher elevations when the snows begin."

X.'s suggestion that Tom might have changed his mind and gone someplace else was too depressing to consider at this moment, when she was wretchedly cold and weary. She sighed raggedly. "I really expected to find him."

"He might still be around here," X. said, trying to cheer her. "There's a lot of ground we haven't covered. We can't stay with it any longer, though. We can either winter in Flume or go back to San Francisco. If he hasn't come down out of the mountains by spring, we can start hunting him along the tributaries."

Vianna sank down on the thick layer of needles beneath the tree. It was soggy, but it provided inches of protection between her and the muddy earth. "I'm out of money. I'll need a job, and I doubt that I could find any work in Flume except in the brothels." Her face twisted in a droll grimace. "I think I'll pass on that one." Wrapping her arms tightly around her chest for a little warmth, she said, "That leaves San Francisco. Do you think I can find work there?"

X. hunkered down beside her. "I doubt you could find anything but menial jobs, like doing laundry or waiting tables. Nothing for a lady."

Vianna burst out laughing. "I'm sorry," she gasped, apologetically. "What makes you think washing clothes and waiting tables is unladylike work? The most respectable women in the world do it every day in their own homes."

He looked sheepish. "I wasn't thinking, I guess. It's just that it seemed too undignified for you."

"To be perfectly honest, I haven't had much experience at either one of those jobs. Mother spoiled me. She was always waiting on me, doing things for me. But I'm sure I could learn." She chuckled. "Maybe Mrs. Dayton could use me. If I could work well enough to satisfy her, I wouldn't have to worry about not pleasing any future boss."

X. seemed relieved that her mood had lightened. "You wouldn't have to work at all. I won't have any trouble getting one of my old jobs back, and I'll make enough for the both of us." When he saw the appalled look she turned on him, he amended quickly, "It would only be a loan."

"And how would I ever pay it back?"

He shrugged his immense shoulders. "Maybe by the time you find Tom, he'll have his pockets full of gold dust."

"I hope so, but I won't count on it." She sighed, "I just wish I could find him, with or without the gold."

They sat quietly for a few minutes, listening to the patter of the rain dripping from the trees, falling into the brook. It was heavily wooded here and very nearly silent. There were no bird sounds, not even the whisper of a breeze. The water made soft bubbling sounds as it ran over a small mess of trash that jutted out into it for several inches. The stream at this point was so narrow Vianna could have jumped across it easily.

"Do you want to spend the night here?" X. asked at last. "Or do you want to head back downriver?"

"How many hours of daylight do we have left?" Vianna had lost all track of time. The rain hadn't let up all day. Without the sun she couldn't even guess at the hour. She was trying to remember whether they had had lunch or not.

X. pulled out his big gold watch. Without the waistcoat he used to wear, he had no place to attach the heavy chain, carrying the watch loose in his pants pocket. "It's three-thirty."

"Why don't we stay here? We can't cover much ground before dark, and besides, I'm tired." She glanced up at the branches above her head. "This looks like a good place to spread our canvas, too." What she left unsaid was that the sense of urgency that had been driving her each day was gone. The fatigue she was feeling would have been ignored yesterday. The alacrity with which X. got to his feet revealed that he was not tired in the least. Nonetheless, he declared, "You've made a good choice. We should be drier tonight than we've been all week. I'll bring the canvas, and then I'll see how big a fire I can get going."

Vianna sat and watched him do all the work, too tired and dispirited to move. She had counted so on finding Tom on this trip up the river. It would be months before she could begin to search the streams feeding into the American, more months of loneliness and anxiety, of fear that she would never again know the joy of his presence. Oh, if only she could reach out and feel the warmth of his cheek against her hand, gaze lovingly into his smoky gray eyes, hear his voice softly speaking her name! She closed her own eyes and tried to bring him close by picturing his face, but as happened invariably lately, the image refused to form. She couldn't remember what he looked like! But that was nonsense. She was as familiar with each of his features as she was with her own. Why wouldn't his face come to her? Tears stung her eyelids. Tom, Tom, have I lost you forever?

The trip back down the river was no easier than the one coming up. The almost constant rain kept them wet and cold and made their footing slippery and treacherous. On their left, the river rose each day, swollen by runoff from the rains draining off the mountains. The water had been clear before; it was thick with mud now and roared fiercely. As the days passed, the noise grew deafening. They had to shout at each other to make themselves heard.

It was because of this difficulty in being heard that they were eating their cold noon meal one day without trying to converse. Vianna wished for hot coffee to go with their cold flapjacks and bacon, but starting a fire with rain-soaked wood was such a laborious process that they cooked enough extra at breakfast on the remains of their night fire to last them until they made camp at the end of the day.

They had paused to eat at the foot of a sharp slope where a large oak that still retained its leaves offered them shelter enough to keep them fairly dry as they rested and ate. Grass, brought to life by the rain, provided good grazing for the mules farther up the slope where X. had tethered them. Vianna was chewing a mouthful of cold, tough bacon when she saw X. turn his head upstream and freeze, as if listening intently for something. She turned to look, too, seeing nothing but hearing a sound that reminded her of the roar of the wind as the *Trident* fought to round Cape Horn. All at once X. thrust the remains of his flapjack in his mouth, grabbed her arm, and started scrambling up the slope toward the mules. Although she had no idea what was wrong, she didn't waste time shouting questions at him, lunging upward under her own power and trying to keep up with him. It was when she stumbled and in catching her balance glanced over her right shoulder that she realized what was happening. A gray wall was moving down on them, knocking trees down in its path, loosening huge boulders and sending them rolling like marbles before swallowing them up. Vianna saw that the mass of water stood high enough to sweep them away like straws, and she screamed. X. grabbed her around the waist and dove upward like a man trying to propel himself into flight. He made contact with the rocks again, at the same instant the flash flood struck them. As he clung to a rock with one hand and to Vianna with the other, the force of the water washed over Vianna's legs, exerting such a pull that Vianna feared she was going to be swept away. She had wrapped her arms around a large rock, but the pull of the rushing water tore her loose, and for an eternity X., with his arms still around her waist, fought the force of the water wrapped around her legs. She felt his grasp on her slipping as her body was pulled away from his arm at a sharp angle. I'm being torn in two, she thought. In another minute the lower half of her body, already downstream from her head and shoulders, would join the uprooted trees that rushed past.

Above her she heard X. grunting as he struggled to hold onto her, while slowly she felt his big fingers sliding off her waist. Her left hand was free but pinned beneath her. Somehow she managed to pull it out from under her, and with it she grasped X.'s belt. At that same moment, the roaring gray water ripped her away from his arm. She would have been washed away had not X. immediately grabbed the arm reaching up to his belt. She swung like a leaf in a violent windstorm, held to a branch by its fragile stem. Her arm felt as if it were being pulled from its socket, and she realized something had to give, either her arm or X.'s hold on her. The force of the water was far stronger than the giant who held her. She was going to die! What irony that she should have survived the worst storms the ocean could call up, only to perish in a flash flood that carried no more water than one of the waves that had threatened the *Trident*. Tom, my love, is this how it's going to end? A sob choked her, smothered by the stupendous pull of the current that stretched her body to such a degree that she couldn't fill her lungs.

Then the crest rolled on, leaving a current diminished just enough that X., exerting superhuman strength, jerked her legs out of the water and scrambled up the slope another foot, where they lay gasping and speechless with the knowledge of what they had escaped. Below them the river canyon was wall to wall with tumbling gray water. Their noon campsite was buried under more feet of water than Vianna could calculate. It was then that she realized her trousers had been stripped off her, belt and all, leaving the lower half of her torso naked except for her underpants. Her boots and socks had been peeled off, too. She was shivering uncontrollably from shock and the cold.

"Wrap your legs in this," X. said hoarsely, handing her his jacket.

Silently she obeyed, then lay back again against the rocky hillside, feeling her heart pounding inside her aching chest.

It was a few minutes more before either of them felt like talking. By that time the water level had dropped a foot and was still dropping. The decibel level of its roar had lessened, too, so that although they had to speak loudly, they could hear one another.

"You saved my life," Vianna said. "How can I ever thank you?" She was still too weak to sit up and couldn't see X. as she spoke.

From above her and very close to her head, he replied, "That's what I signed on for. No thanks are required." He put his big hand gently on her head. "Are you all right?"

"I think so. Maybe a few bruises."

"I've lived uncomfortably with the fact that I'm a freak for most of my life. Today has made it all worth it."

Vianna turned so she could see him. His oversized face was white, but his blue eyes were almost free of pain. "An ordinary man couldn't have saved me."

He nodded. "I've been lying here thinking about that. Maybe this was what I was meant to do, the reason for everything that happened to me."

Vianna couldn't believe her life was worth that price, but if X. was comforted by believing that it was, she wasn't going to disagree.

"Lie still. I'll go get some clothes for you."

She watched as he climbed to where the mules still grazed placidly, unfazed by the sound and fury of the flash flood. He removed a pack from her animal's back and unrolled it. From it he took her spare pair of men's trousers, some socks, and her old shoes. When he brought them down to her, she sat up and pulled the trousers up over her clammy legs. The warmth was delicious. It was difficult getting the socks over her damp feet, and they were a bit thick to wear inside her old shoes, but she felt one hundred percent better when she was fully clothed once more.

It had stopped raining. The areas of grass between the rocky outcroppings were damp, but that was a condition to be ignored after having their clothing soaked day after day. Vianna and X. moved over to a small stand of trees that would furnish shelter if it began raining again and settled down to wait for the flood-waters to recede, without an idea as to how long that might be.

"I'm glad I had taken the mules that far up the mountain," X. observed. He was still a little pale. "If they'd been swept away, we'd be in a tight fix. No food, no shelter."

"And no extra clothes," Vianna added. If he was still pale, she must look like a corpse drawn from the waters. She felt tinglingly alive, however. All of her senses were extraordinarily sharp. She was acutely conscious of the rough bark of the tree against her back, the heat spreading through her chilled body. The gray sky appeared strangely porous and soft. Beside her legs the new shoots of grass were vividly green among the dried summer growth. The canyon was filled with the roar of the water, but that was the only sound. Overhead, Vianna watched a mountain jay sit with its feathers fluffed sullenly, absolutely silent as its beady eyes observed every move the two humans made.

X. studied the water, which didn't seem to be going down much anymore. The two feet of mountainside that had been exposed by the falling water had a ravaged look to it. The grass was mashed flat, and there were great muddy holes from which boulders had been yanked like teeth and carried away. There was little debris lying about. The current was not yet leaving anything behind. "It doesn't look as if we'll be able to move on today. We'll make camp here."

They spread the canvas over the branches directly above them and then set out to find wood that would burn. It was much later before they had a fire going and a supply of fuel that would carry them through the night. They filled their enamel coffeepot with muddy water and waited for it to boil so that they could make themselves some tea. They needed the stimulant the hot drink would provide, and if they made the tea strong enough, Vianna reflected, maybe they wouldn't taste the mud.

"Will this flood go all the way down the river?" she asked, savoring the heat of the flames on her face and body.

X. moved the coffeepot farther into the fire. "Remember where the canyon widened into that valley we camped in last night? That will allow the crest to spread out. The flood will lose its steam and be pretty tame by the time it reaches Flume."

They had come upon a few miners and prospectors singly and in groups on their trek upriver. None had known a Tom Fulton, and none had been as unfriendly as the formally dressed miner who had held them at gunpoint. Vianna was thinking about some of them now. "I wonder if the men prospecting between here and that valley will be as lucky as we were?"

"I doubt that there are that many miracles available between here and there."

Vianna recalled what X. had told her back in her hotel room in San Francisco about gold-seekers disappearing in the mountains without anyone ever knowing what happened to them. It seemed likely that there would be wives and mothers somewhere who would never hear from their husbands and sons again. As she reflected on this tragedy, a horrifying possibility occurred to her. "Flash floods like this one could hit the streams running into the American, couldn't they?"

"Sure they could, and it's probably happening." As soon as the words were out of his mouth, he realized why she had asked the question, and he added swiftly, "Not on all of them, of course."

"But what if one hit the stream Tom is on and he wasn't lucky enough to get his miracle?"

X. was obviously seeking for some reassurance to offer her, but he found none. After a few moments he said lamely, "If Tom is on one of those feeder streams, his odds are a lot better than if he had been on the river."

Vianna found no comfort in considering the odds. All she could think about was Tom's being drowned. What a cruel twist of fate that would be! Perhaps at some point during these past few weeks they had been within a few miles of each other. Were they destined never to be reunited? Had she missed him by a few months in Lahaina, only to miss him again here on the American River in California? The thought overwhelmed her with despair. She might spend the rest of her life searching for a man already dead.

Nightmares plagued her through the night, but hope rekindled the next morning when the sun rose in a clear sky. After two weeks of gloomy, wet weather, Vianna's spirits rose, too, as she watched the golden brightness light up the mountain peaks, then spill down the slopes, warming their campsite and finally reaching the still-swollen river. The water had dropped considerably during the night, leaving the canyon choked with uprooted trees and rocks and everything coated with muddy slime. As she went down to fill the coffeepot with water, it became clear that although they could resume their journey today, travel would be slippery and difficult.

Grimacing with distaste, she dipped up some muddy water in the pot and started back up to the fire. She was making her way around a big cavity from which a boulder had been torn when something caught the rays of the sun and shot a sparkle back at her. With the toe of her boot she rubbed some of the slime away. Unable to believe what her eyes were telling her, she knelt and cleaned off more of the mud with her free hand. There in the saturated clay lay a gold nugget as big as the knob atop the coffeepot lid.

"X., come quick!" she cried.

Alarmed by her cry, the giant, who had started after the tethered mules to take them down to the water for a drink, dropped the lead ropes as if they were snakes. He came down the hillside at a run, slipping and sliding on the wet ground. "What's wrong?" he shouted even before he reached her.

She held up the nugget so that he could see it, but he was looking into the sun and didn't realize until he skidded to a stop beside her what it was she had in her hand.

"Good God!" he yelled in his high voice. Taking it from her, he washed it in the coffeepot, then took a better look. "Where did you find this?"

"In this hole. I saw something sparkle and I rubbed the mud off and there it was." Vianna had never thought much about money until she found herself in Lahaina without any with which to buy passage on a ship. She had thought a great deal about it since arriving in San Francisco and beginning her search for Tom. There wasn't a cent left of the loan Doctor Young had made her, and if this nugget were worth very much, her financial problems would be solved, at least for a while.

"Hold this." X. thrust the nugget at her and dropped to his knees to dig in the cavity. Handing her a glob of mud, he said, "Wash this in the pot. I can't get my hand in it."

Vianna did as she was told and felt a piece of grit scratch her fingers as the mud dissolved. Bringing it out, she opened her hand. There lay another nugget, much smaller, about the size of a tiny bead, but pure gold.

Teetering on the toes of his boots as he knelt beside the gaping hole, X. raised his eyes from the tiny nugget to Vianna's face. "I don't know whether you've discovered a small pocket or whether you've found the richest strike since Sutter's Mill. The only way to find out is to stay here and pan for a few days."

Vianna was aware of the idiot grin stretching her face. "What are we waiting for?"

Breakfast was forgotten. Using the skillet as a pan, X. worked at the water's edge, washing the mud that Vianna brought down the mountain in the coffeepot. Within an hour, he had accumulated what he guessed to be an ounce of gold. "That's worth about sixteen dollars and is as much as most miners pan in a day."

Vianna gazed with fascination at the mound of bright dust that lay on one of their tin plates. They had found no more nuggets, but the two they had found winked cheerfully at her from beside the gold dust. "It's pretty encouraging, isn't it?"

"That's putting it mildly." X. rinsed the skillet and the coffeepot, letting fresh water flow into the pot for their coffee. It was still muddy, but clearing. "Let's fix breakfast. I'm gaunt as a hollow log, and we've got a long day's work ahead of us."

They panned almost an ounce an hour that day and the next, employing their makeshift equipment. At the end of that time, X. said, "We'd better mark this claim as ours and hightail it back to Flume to have it recorded. When we come back, we can bring picks and shovels and lumber to make a rocker."

The river had shrunk back to its original size and clarity. The sun had shone for the second day and was setting somewhere behind the mountain, leaving them hugging their fire while a chunk of venison, cut from the deer X. had spied and shot at dawn across the river, roasted on a spit. During their search of the river he had shot several of the creatures, providing them with a welcome change from bacon. Vianna had used the last of the saleratus to mix a batch of biscuits, which were baking at the edge of the coals. The smell of crisply browning meat set Vianna's mouth watering.

During the previous day, she had ripped the skirt out of one of her dresses and made pokes for the gold dust, tying the sausagelike rolls at both ends. There were several behind them in their canvas shelter, plus another filled with nuggets of various sizes.

"We've got enough gold to buy us anything we want, provided someone in Flume's got it." X. was gazing downhill at the cavity they had been working. In two days they had enlarged it considerably. "If this stuff doesn't run out, you and I are going to be rich beyond our wildest dreams."

Even in the waning light, Vianna was able to see the excitement in his large-featured face. His wool cap was pushed to the back of his head, leaving a puff of dark hair waving back from the vast brow. "You think this might be more than just a pocket?" Until this moment she hadn't been able to believe it would be anything big, but seeing X.'s excitement aroused her own.

"I'm no expert," he replied. "All I know about mining is what I've heard from men who've done some, and so I'm only guessing, but I think there's a good chance that the whole side of this mountain might be filled with gold."

Vianna drew in her breath, staring at him.

"If I'm right," he went on, "we'll start the damnedest gold rush since Sutter's." He shook his head, contemplating future events. "You won't have to hunt for work in San Francisco. We'll come back here and spend the winter working our claim. We're low enough that we won't have to worry about snow. We'll get us a good tent, maybe even put a wood floor in it if I can find the tools I need in Flume. By spring you may be one of the richest women in California."

Some of the old pain shadows darkened his eyes. "News of this strike will travel up and down the river. Even beyond. If Tom Fulton is in these mountains, he'll hear about it sooner or later, and you won't have to go hunting for him. He'll find you."

Suddenly all this speculation about becoming rich was totally erased by the possibility that the gold strike might bring Tom and her together again. "Do you really think that could happen?" she asked faintly.

"Yes, I do." He turned the roast on the spit. Some fat hissed as it dripped into the fire. He wasn't looking at her.

Vianna knew what was troubling him and said at once, "If Tom shows up, it will change nothing. I'm not stupid enough to discard as good a friend as you've proven yourself to be. And when I tell Tom all you've done for me, he'll feel the same way." She laughed lightly. "Besides, we're going to be business partners. If this mountain is full of gold, it's going to take the rest of our lives to dig it all out."

"It's really your strike, you know. You're the one who discovered it."

"For heaven's sake, that is just plain silly! How can you save my life on practically that very spot and think it doesn't belong as much to you as it does to me? That makes me downright mad, and I don't ever want to hear any more foolishness like that!" She glared at him, her chest rising and falling rapidly beneath the men's shirt.

He held up both hands in a gesture of surrender. "Don't get so upset! I promise I won't mention it again. Whew! I didn't know you had a temper."

She took a deep breath and let it out slowly. "I can get riled like anybody else."

"Yes, ma'am, you surely can." He began slicing the browned roast. "Maybe we'd better eat and change the subject."

Vianna didn't mention Tom again, but she hugged to her the hope that if their gold strike proved to be a famous one, he would come looking for her. And if they were each looking for the other, surely they would one day meet again. This was the main significance of the discovery to her, because without Tom, what joy could there be in becoming the richest woman in California?

19

━━━━━━━━━━━━━━━━━━━━━━━

They packed up and started for Flume the next morning after carefully marking their claim, stepping it off, and noting points of reference in order to describe it to the recorder. All day they observed signs of the flash flood in the river canyon. When they arrived at the valley, Vianna saw that X. had been right. No longer confined by rocky walls, the water had spread out thinly. They had met two young prospectors working as a team in that spot when they were on their way upriver. They were still there. They told of finding the body of a man who had been drowned and washed downstream by the flood. They had buried him that morning.

"A young man?" Vianna asked apprehensively. Although they hadn't found Tom on the river, he could have worked his way down a tributary to it after they had passed by.

"About our age," the husky blond one said. The flatness of his tone was an attempt to conceal his emotional shock upon being reminded that he was not safe from the sudden grip of death, despite his youth.

Vianna asked in a small voice, "What did he look like?"

"A little taller than me, good pair of shoulders. Beneath the mud his hair looked like it might have been sort of red."

X. caught her arm as she swayed.

The blond man's companion spoke up quietly. "He had a finger missing on his right hand."

X. asked, "Did he lose it in the flood?"

The quiet man shook his head, watching Vianna anxiously as he informed them that the dead man had lost that finger years ago.

X. looked down at Vianna. She felt joy flood her face as she said, "It couldn't have been Tom."

They went on. Although the American was higher than it had been below the valley, they saw no more flood damage. There was no sign of the hostile old miner they had encountered on their trip upstream. The rocker that had stood at the edge of the river was gone, and rain had washed away every trace of his campsite.

Surveying the deserted spot, X. commented, "His vein must have run out. I hope the same thing doesn't happen to us." He indicated a fallen tree resting on a pile of rocks. "Let's rest here a few minutes."

Still holding the lead rein of her mule, Vianna sat down gratefully. The ladies' shoes she'd been wearing ever since the flood tore her boots off were not made for hiking. Her feet were bruised and sore.

"I've been doing some thinking," X. said, giving his mule a sharp tug to bring it up to the log. The animal brayed a protest out of pure contrariness but settled in behind the tree as X. sat down on it. "It would be best if we keep our strike a secret as long as we can after we get to Flume. I've got fifty dollars left. That will buy another mule, and we'll need a third one to carry a full winter's supplies. From then on, we'll have to pay for things with our dust." He pulled the poke holding their nuggets out of his jacket pocket and hefted it in his enormous hand. "These we shouldn't mention. If people get the idea we've made a rich strike, they'll be all over us, trying to find out where it is. Paying with dust and filing a claim will tell them we've found something, but we ought to play it down. We can say we've found some color, but don't know how much of it is there. That won't be a lie. There's no need to pass along to them our suspicion that we've found a mountain full of the stuff."

The midafternoon sun was so warm on Vianna's bare blond head that she had been feeling sleepy, but X.'s warning brought her awake. "Are you afraid someone will steal our claim?"

"It could happen. Stakes can be moved, stumps uprooted, and the ground smoothed out to look like that natural boundary marker was never there. But no one can move the boulders we chose as monuments. They can't grind out the X's I chiseled on them, either." He hefted the poke of nuggets once more and put it back in his pocket. "You never know what somebody might pull, though. And if people got the idea this was a rich strike, there would be a regular stampede for this place. That brings up another thing. We'd better buy everything we're going to need for the winter just as soon as we hit Flume. If filing our claim sets off a case of gold fever, every pick and shovel and pan in town will be bought up before you can say scat, with store owners upping the price with each one they sell."

"You mean we have to buy all those things before I can have a hot bath?" Vianna wailed. "I haven't been able to think of anything else since we started back!" Bathing in the cold river without soap had proved to be one of the worst hardships of the whole journey as far as she was concerned.

Amusement lit X.'s face. "I'm afraid so, but once we've got our business taken care of, you can live in a bathtub if you want to. I'll bring your meals to you."

Vianna made a face at him. "That won't be necessary, because eating real meals at a table with vegetables and coffee is another luxury I'm looking forward to."

When they reached Flume toward evening, X. made one slight change in the schedule he had outlined. They checked into their hotel before they did anything else, unloading their mules and taking their gear to their rooms. It was the same hotel they'd stayed in previously, and the fat hotelkeeper agreed with reluctance to heat enough water for two baths, but he gave them clean sheets without being asked. He was changing their beds when they left to buy their supplies. X. went straight across the street to the livery barn with the mules while Vianna headed for the store that provided one wall of the canvas saloon that was squeezed between the store and the recorder's office. "Paddy O'Neal's General Store" the crudely painted sign said.

The two large glass windows on either side of the door provided the only light, and because the store was deep and narrow, the rear of it was rather dark. "Something I can help you with?" came a man's voice from the shadows. "Let's see, it's Miss Chadwick, isn't it? Sure and you were here a few weeks ago, askin' about a man named Fulton."

"I'm surprised you recognized me in these clothes," Vianna said, heading toward the voice.

"It's your blond hair, lass. No one else in Flume has hair like that." He was smiling when she came up to him, a small man with a thick mane of white hair and a ruddy Irish face. "Did ye find your man?"

"He wasn't on the river, but we didn't search the tributaries. We're going back up, and I'm here to buy provisions."

His clear blue eyes widened in surprise. "You're leaving tomorrow, then? But you just got back to town!"

Not wanting to contradict the conclusion he had jumped to about when they were leaving, she replied evasively, "I'm very eager to find Mr. Fulton."

He nodded sympathetically. "A tragic story, lass."

Vianna stared at him blankly. How had he learned about Tom and her?

"The sheriff told me," the little Irishman explained, noting her perplexity.

"Of course." She had forgotten that she had given an abbreviated account of her tale to Buck Rozell that first night in Flume. At another time she'd have enjoyed talking to this bright-faced, amiable man, but to avoid further discussion of her situation, she got down to business. "Have you any potatoes and onions?"

He let out a roar of laughter. "Has an Irishman got potatoes? Sure now, I wouldn't run a store without 'em, hard to come by as they be. Brought all the way from Frisco, they are."

Vianna had nearly finished buying their edible provisions when X. came in. "Good day to you, sir," Paddy O'Neal said. "You and the lass are going to eat well on your second trip up the river."

X. surveyed the two sacks of vegetables and the other food items that occupied a large stretch of the painted counter. "It will be a while before we'll have to start eating flapjacks again, that's plain to see. Which is fine with me. Before you tote up what we owe you for food, I've got a list of things I want, too."

The tent X. bought elicited no questions from the Irish storekeeper, but when he asked for pans for washing gold, Paddy O'Neal's curiosity sprang up like a jackrabbit's ears. "Planning on doing a little prospecting, are ye?"

"Thought we might as well," X. replied. "If we can't find the man we're looking for, maybe we can find a little gold. You wouldn't have any lumber to sell, would you? Enough for a small rocker?"

"You won't be findin' enough wood for a toothpick in Flume. It has to be brought up the river, you see. No mills around here. Terrible expensive it is, too. That's why Charlie Anderson's got his saloon under canvas. He can't afford the lumber yet for a building."

X. lifted a pick from a stack of half a dozen that leaned against a barrel of flour. "I'll take a couple of these."

By the time they'd bought everything they needed, including new boots and clothes to replace those Vianna lost in the flood, Vianna was wondering if one extra mule would be enough to carry it all.

"That will be one hundred twenty-one dollars and seventy-six cents," Paddy O'Neal announced after adding the figures twice to make sure he hadn't made an error.

X. whistled. "Lumber isn't the only thing that's dear in Flume."

"Every pick and pan and potato has to be brought around the Horn, up the Sacramento, and overland to Flume, sir, and each man whose hand those things pass through has to make his profit. Sure and I'm only takin' a fair profit on the goods meself, sir."

X. took some gold dust, rolled in its square of pink gingham, from his pocket, and laid it on top of Vianna's new trousers. "Weigh it out."

Paddy O'Neal regarded the sausagelike roll with some surprise before swiftly untying one end and pouring some of the dust onto a small scale at one end of the counter. "You've already found some gold, I see," he remarked. Pulling his fascinated gaze away from the tiny mound on the scales, he turned his clear blue eyes on X. and inquired, "Will ye be filin' a claim, now?"

"I might. Then again I might look for something better on this trip."

There was no way the Irish storekeeper could know that that poke of gold dust represented only one day's work. "Took you a long time to pan this?" he asked.

X. nodded. "Mighty tedious work."

That was certainly no lie. Vianna had been glad her job was bringing clay down from the hole. She'd never have had the patience to swirl water again and again over it, letting the mud slip over the edge of the pan while trying to keep the gold dust from following it.

Paddy O'Neal poured out about three-fourths of the gold before the scale balanced. Vianna took the poke back and retied it with the narrow strip of cloth she'd ripped from the trim of the gingham dress she'd brought from Lahaina.

"You'll be leavin' this stuff here till mornin' when you leave?" It was less a question than a declaration of fact. Paddy O'Neal wasn't expecting them to carry their extensive purchases across the street to their hotel.

When he discovered that they did indeed plan to do that very thing, he was flabbergasted. " 'Twill be perfectly safe here overnight," he assured them. "There's no need to be a-carryin' all this stuff to the hotel."

"We might start out before you're open tomorrow," X. said. "Our plans are sort of fluid at this moment." He filled his arms and hands, which still left half the goods lying on the counter.

Under Paddy O'Neal's inquisitive gaze, Vianna loaded up with as many of the remaining goods as she could carry.

"We'll be back for the rest in a few minutes," X. said as the storekeeper followed them to the door.

Vianna was aware of the little Irishman's eyes following them every step of the way as they angled down the street toward their hotel. "I think he's suspicious," she said quietly when they were out of earshot.

"But he doesn't know anything for sure. You go ahead and take your bath while I get the rest of this stuff and scout around for some lumber. There might be a little bit of it somewhere that the owner would sell for the right price."

The tin tub was barely large enough to allow Vianna to sit in it, but the water was hot. It was really too hot, but she won a pleased look from the fat hotelkeeper when she told him it wasn't necessary to bring a bucket of cold water to cool it. As soon as he left, she stripped off her heavy men's clothing and eased herself an inch at a time into the steaming water. Glory, it felt good! Once she was all the way in, she leaned back with a sigh. Because of the short length of the tub she had to bend her knees, but the water came up high under her breasts, giving her the feeling that she was submerged. She soaked until the water cooled enough to wash in, then shampooed her hair first before sudsing her reddened body with the half-used bar of soap she'd been given.

She was dozing in the cooling, soapy water, dreaming of Tom and that special night they'd made love in the cave after the rain had kept them away from the beach for a week, when X. knocked at the door.

"I'll be dressed in a few minutes, then you can have your bath," she called.

"No hurry. I just wanted you to know I'm back."

"Did you find any lumber?"

"Not a board. I'll be in my room."

She felt wonderfully light and feminine when she was clothed once more in her only remaining dress. X. put on one of his suits, the gray one with the ivory brocade waistcoat, and as they left the hotel and made their way to the recorder's office, they attracted the stares of the dozen or so people who were abroad on the main street. Two of the observers were prostitutes, identified by their short, gaudy satin dresses and heavily made-up faces.

"Hi, X., honey," one of them called.

"Hi, Lily." Turning back to Vianna, he explained, "She used to work in Frisco until she got caught going through one of her customer's pockets one night. The madam fired her. Word got around and she couldn't get another job there, so she came out here. She may have mended her ways, but I'm more inclined to think the madams in these gold camps aren't so particular about their girls' behavior."

The recorder's office was next door to the town's other café, and as they had discovered during their previous stay in Flume, the same man ran both businesses. The services of a recorder were not needed often enough to make it a full-time job anymore, so Cal Dodge had opened a café. The office occupied the left-hand third of the building that Dodge built four months ago. When Vianna and X. entered it, they caught the smells of supper being cooked in the café kitchen that occupied the rear of the structure. A door stood open between the two places, and finding the office empty, X. went into the café, returning in a short time with an oily-faced man with short, curly, black hair, a genial air, and the look of one who enjoyed his own food perhaps too well. A stained apron was wrapped around his ample stomach. He greeted Vianna in a courtly manner, adding, "Last time I saw you, you were looking for someone. Did you find him?"

"Unfortunately, no."

"But you found gold instead?"

"Strictly by accident. It hadn't occurred to either of us to look for it."

Cal Dodge shook his head incredulously. "Won't that make some of these prospectors curse their own luck?"

X. fingered the heavy gold watch chain that was once more draped across his wide middle, commenting casually, "It's probably only a small pocket, but we figured we might as well be making a day's wages while we wait for Miss Chadwick's fiancé to turn up."

Cal Dodge grinned. "There speaks a practical man." He sat down at a dusty, messy desk, pulled a ledger from a drawer, and leafed quickly through it until he came to the page he was looking for. It was a fresh one, with nothing written on either side of it. "Now, describe your claim to me. Take your time so I can get it all down."

He proved to be a slow writer and a sloppy one. Vianna began to wince after the third blot he made, but eventually their claim was duly recorded. As X. paid the required fee with some of their remaining gold dust, he said, "There are some awfully good smells coming out of that kitchen of yours. What are you serving for supper?"

Cal Dodge was trying to figure out if the poke had originally held more gold and if it had, how much. He made his reply rather absently. "Liver and onions." He rubbed some of the dust between his fingers. "Harry Simpson butchered a beef today, and I bought the whole liver."

Amused by his efforts to try to determine how good their claim was, Vianna said, "After all those weeks up in the mountains collecting that little bit of gold dust,

I'm vegetable hungry, Mr. Dodge. Are onions all you have?"

Deciding he couldn't glean much information from the square of pink gingham, he took up his role as café host with vigor. "I've got potatoes, of course, and I can butter you some carrots if that's to your liking."

Vianna gave him a delighted smile. "That would be very much to my liking, Mr. Dodge."

"Come back in half an hour," he told them.

The meal couldn't have tasted better to Vianna if she had been a sailor coming off a four-month diet of salt beef and ship biscuit.

Heading back to the hotel after supper, they were hailed by Sheriff Rozell, who was locking up his office for the day. "I heard you folks were back in town."

They finished crossing the street and halted at his door. Flume had no sidewalks, nor was lumber wasted on awnings or overhangs. The buildings were flush with the street. Rozell pocketed his key and lifted his ratty straw hat to Vianna, exposing his bald pate and black sideburns. Beneath his curving black mustache his smile was friendly. "I also hear you've filed a claim."

"Word gets around fast," X. commented. He made the other man appear no taller than a small boy.

Rozell chuckled. "*That* kind of news spreads faster than a brushfire in a high wind. Do you figure it's a good claim?"

"It's too early to tell. We panned enough to pay for another batch of provisions, and we'll head back to winter there and work it. If Miss Chadwick's fiancé doesn't turn up, we'll start looking for him again come spring."

The sheriff ran a hand around the inside of his hat, grinning. "You wouldn't want to tell me where your claim is, I suppose."

"Don't believe so," X. replied amiably. "You can be glad it isn't a rich one. If it was and word got out about it, Flume would be a ghost town in a day, and you'd be out of a job."

"I'd buy me a pick and shovel and join the stampede. That's what I came to California for, to find gold. I'm just marking time sheriffin'. One of these days I'll go back to prospecting. It might not pay as well as this job, but it's more exciting, and you've always got that hope that the next place you sink your pick will make you rich." Buck Rozell's dark eyes went to Vianna and back to X. "Paddy tells me you folks already bought your stuff and have it stashed in the hotel so that you can start off early in the morning. Not wasting much time getting back to your claim, are you?"

"We might change our minds and stay a little while longer," X. admitted.

Vianna decided she could truthfully supply a strong motive for their spending an extra day or two in Flume. "After the supper we had at Mister Dodge's café to-night, I don't think I'm ready to go back to eating flapjacks and bacon quite yet."

"Cal always puts out a good meal. I guess you could tell by looking at him that he likes to eat, and people like that make the best cooks. Guess I'll give him my business tonight. I hope you folks will decide to stay around for a few days. It's been pretty dull here, and it's nice to see some new faces." He stuck the straw hat back on his head, touched the brim as he smiled at Vianna, and headed across to the café.

They remained in Flume only one day, pestered by questions from people who followed them down the street, into cafés and their hotel, and generally made such a nuisance that Vianna agreed at once when X. suggested they leave that second morning. It had begun to rain again, and Vianna cursed the people of Flume whose gold hunger was driving them away from solid shelter and good food. Yet she cheered herself by considering the possibility that within a month word might spread over the whole American River valley that the richest strike of the year had been made by Miss Vianna

Chadwick and X. Medrano and Tom would hear it and come looking for her.

It was a three-day trip from Flume to their claim, and it rained almost every hour of that time, going from drizzle to hard shower to drizzle in an unrelenting cycle. On this trip, however, they had a tent, waterproofed with a coating of tar in the way sailors sealed their rain clothing, so that by piling evergreen boughs beneath them to keep them up off the soaked ground, they slept dry and warm.

It was late afternoon when they rounded a bend that brought them in sight of their claim. "What the hell!" X. stopped dead in his tracks.

Vianna couldn't see around him or the two mules he led. She tugged at her own mule and came quickly up to his side. A quarter of a mile up the river, at what she believed must be the precise location of their claim, two men were squatting at the water's edge, swirling shallow pans in their hands. Another was carrying a bucket down the hill to them, while a fourth was shoveling dirt into a bucket from the hole where the boulder had been gouged out by the flash flood. The cavity was twice the size it had been when Vianna and X. had left it.

X. pulled his rifle from the boot on the back of one of the mules, saying quietly as he loaded it, "You stay here with the animals. I'll go up there and see what the devil is going on. That claim is well marked. They couldn't have failed to see that."

"What if they have guns?" Vianna whispered nervously. "There are four of them."

X. peered up the river at them, saying soberly, "I know."

"Don't get yourself shot," Vianna pleaded, clutching his enormous arm.

"I don't intend to. I just want to make damn sure they know it's our claim and that we've come back to work it." He started forward and had covered nearly half the distance when the man who had emptied his bucket between the two others who were panning glanced around before starting back up the slope. He spied X. at once and must have said something, because all four men dropped what they were doing and ran for the tent standing beneath the tree Vianna and X. had used for shelter. One of them dived into it and started handing out rifles that they had stored there out of the rain.

X. hailed them, his voice bouncing back off the canyon walls so that Vianna heard it clearly. "That's my claim you're working, boys. Maybe you didn't see my monuments."

The four men faced him, rifles held warily in their hands. "There ain't no monuments here except the ones we've marked ourselves." The spokesman was a thickset man with a raspy voice. His trousers were stuck in his boots, and he was in shirtsleeves, despite the rain and chill. He raised his rifle. "Stop right where you are, mister. Don't come any closer."

X. obeyed but said, "If you'll check that tree you've got your tent under and that flat rock at the water's edge, you'll see my mark. A big X."

The four men stood very still. Across the distance that separated them from Vianna, she sensed their tension. "We know where the X's are, mister. There's another one on that tree up there, one on that boulder, and one on that fallen log. We know 'cause we put them there."

"The hell you did! My name is X. Medrano and I've got legal proof that this claim is mine in the recorder's office in Flume."

"I don't know what claim you filed on, but it wasn't this one. We filed it with the recorder a couple of weeks ago, and we got a paper to prove it."

"I don't believe it."

"Show him, Lefty."

A black-bearded man pulled something from the pocket of his coat and moved forward a few steps before stopping. His thickset colleague waved his rifle at X. "If you want to see it, come on."

Vianna wanted to cry out to X. not to get that close to them. When he didn't move, she kept still. "Wrap it around a rock and throw it to me," he demanded.

The black-bearded man stooped down, picked up a stone about the size of a potato, and with his rifle held close to his side by one arm, wrapped the rock in the paper and heaved it. It fell a few yards short of X., who moved cautiously forward a few steps and picked it up. He took a long time reading the paper.

"Well?" the stout spokesman growled finally.

X. looked up, letting his eyes roam the four men who stood there arrayed against him, rifles not exactly pointed at him but held in a manner that would bring them into position in an instant. "This is an exact copy changed the names and, according to this paper, this claim is yours, but I'm going back to Flume and talk to the sheriff. When he and the rest of the town find out they've elected a crook for a recorder, this paper won't be worth anything except to start a fire with." He dropped it at his feet. "I'll be back, boys, and when I come I'll bring the sheriff and a posse with me." He backed away from them until he was out of range of their guns, then turned and strode back to where Vianna waited with the mules. "You heard?"

She nodded as he took the reins of his two mules from her.

"Let's go," he said. His large-featured face and high voice were taut. "I want to put as much distance as I can between us and these hard cases before dark. They aren't going to want to let me get back to Flume and report to the sheriff."

Trying to hurry the mules was futile; they had their own pace and wouldn't be speeded up, no matter how much tugging and rump slapping X. and Vianna did. They were forced to stop at dark after traveling only two hours, because the canyon was too rocky to traverse when they couldn't see where they were putting their feet.

"I don't want to risk a fire, and we won't unload the mules," X. said, choosing a campsite that gave him an unobstructed view for a half mile up the river. "We'll stake the mules up there by those trees, and you find yourself as dry a spot as you can and try to get some sleep. We won't put up the tent, because I want to be able to take off fast if we have to. I'll stay down here where I can see them if they try to ambush us."

Vianna believed she could do without supper easily; her nerves were strung too tight to let her feel hungry. Trying to get comfortable in the cold, wet night was another matter. She wished for the piece of canvas they had had with them on their first trip and which they had traded to the livery barn owner for part payment of their mules' keep while they were in Flume. It would have given her some shelter and been quick to grab up and take along if they had to leave in a hurry. Without it she was reduced to finding a place where the tree branches were thick enough to afford her a half measure of protection from the quiet but steady rain. The spot she found wasn't big enough to keep all of her dry if she lay down, so she settled for being reasonably dry above the waist and pulled some branches over her legs and boots in an effort to keep them from becoming soaked.

It was a miserable night. Discomfort and apprehension kept her awake. When she believed it must be nearly dawn, she went down to where X. sat leaning against a rock as big as a house. "They must not have followed us," she said softly, hunkering down beside the huge dark mass of him.

"I don't think we can count on that. It's only midnight."

"Only midnight!" Vianna repeated, incredulous. "I thought it was nearly morning."

"Go on back to sleep. It's a long time till morning."

Vianna was in no hurry to go back to her wet, cold bed. "Aren't you sleepy?"

"No, but I'm hungry. How about bringing me a couple of potatoes?"

She got three from the sack that was still strapped to one of the mule's backs and washed them in the river. The water was ice cold, numbing her fingers. Giving X. two of the potatoes, she sat down beside him and bit into the other one. The earthy taste of the skin and the slightly salty flavor of the crisp flesh awoke her hunger. She had never realized how good a raw potato could be. They whispered companionably together as they ate, both straining their ears for the scuff of boots or the rattle of a displaced stone. No such sounds came to them, and at last Vianna went back to try to get some sleep.

She came to with a start when she felt a hand on her shoulder. It was X. The darkness was fading, the sky beginning to gray. She could make out the oversized features of his face easily and was calmed by his expression.

"Let's get moving," he said quietly.

"They didn't come?" Vianna asked groggily.

He shook his head, remaining squatted beside her. "Maybe they aren't going to. Or maybe it took them a while to make up their minds to do it. If the latter is the case, we've got to try to stay ahead of them."

Vianna didn't have to go down to the river to splash water on her face. It was still raining. They started off, stiff and cold and hungry.

They halted at noon, built a fire, and had a hot meal. It revived them both. "Make up a bunch of flapjacks so that we won't have to build a fire tonight," X. told Vianna.

"Do you still think they might be after us?"

"It's a possibility. If they don't catch up to us by morning, I think we can relax."

Vianna never knew whether X. stayed awake throughout the whole of that second night or not, but when morning came and the claim jumpers hadn't shown up, he was already gathering wood for a fire. "I can't understand it," he said, whittling away the wet outer wood from a big branch in order to get at the still dry wood at the center. "They could have shot us, dragged our bodies up the mountain, and nobody would have ever known the truth about that claim. Why are they letting us go back and report to the sheriff?"

Vianna found that puzzling, too, but she was so relieved to think the danger was over that she really didn't care too much why it had passed. She relished the feeling of safety and the hot breakfast she was able to cook for them. One more day and they'd be in Flume getting this matter straightened out so that she and X. could go back and begin working the claim that appeared to be the best chance she had of letting Tom know she was in California.

Sheriff Rozell listened skeptically to their contention that the recorder had defrauded them. "Cal Dodge was elected by the miners themselves because he was one of the most honest men in Flume."

There were only two chairs in the sparsely furnished office. Vianna sat on one at the end of the desk, and Rozell sat in the other after having offered it to X., who said he preferred to stand. Beyond the sheriff's shoulder, an open door led into the jail, which, so far as Vianna could see, was simply a room with a cot. A ray of sunlight falling across the floor indicated the presence of a window; there was no sign of any iron bars.

X. was pacing the bare planks of the office, causing the whole floor to vibrate. "Either the miners misjudged Dodge or else he's gotten greedy. The paper those claim jumpers showed me had his signature on it, and the description was word for word the one I'd given him."

"They must have sneaked into Cal's office, copied it, and forged his signature. I can't believe he had a hand in it." Buck Rozell's ratty Panama hat was hanging on a peg behind him. He looked incomplete without it on his head or in his hands. Beneath his bald pate his eyes appeared even darker than usual, as black in fact as his thick sideburns.

"We'll never find out what happened by sitting here speculating," X. declared impatiently. "Let's go over and question him."

The sheriff chewed his drooping mustache. "Cal's a friend of mine. I sure hate to go over there and accuse him of anything like this."

X. expelled his breath in sharp irritation. "We don't have to accuse him of anything. I just want you to see his record book with that claim registered in my name and Vianna's. And then, sheriff, I'll expect you to enforce the law and go up there and throw those guys off our claim."

Rozell slapped his hands on his thighs and pushed back from his desk. "All right, let's go talk to Cal and see what this is all about." He pulled his hat from the peg and followed them out.

They found Cal Dodge in his café, drinking coffee at a table near the kitchen door. There wasn't another soul in the place. At this hour of the afternoon, the wooden tables stood bare and empty, a couple of them still damp from being scrubbed of the remains of the noon meal. Vianna caught the sudden wary look in the recorder's eyes as they walked in, but he greeted them in his normal genial manner.

"Well, I didn't expect to see you folks again so soon." He rose and nodded politely to Vianna. There was no apron covering his rotund belly today; it looked solid as a melon. "I thought you were heading back to your claim."

Buck Rozell put his hands on his hips. "They said when they got there, some other fellas were working it and had a paper proving it was theirs. How could that be?"

Cal Dodge pursed his lips. "There must be some mistake."

"You're damned right there's been a mistake," X. exploded. "I want you to show the sheriff your book with that claim recorded to us so that we can get the law back there and throw them off."

"I sure will," Cal Dodge said at once. "Come on, Buck."

They followed him through the connecting door between the café and the office, which was open. He went right to his desk, pulled out the ledger and flipped through the pages. "Here it is." He scanned it swiftly, then turned the book on the gritty desk top so that the sheriff could examine it.

Rozell leaned over it, read the claim, then checked the signature at the bottom. "It's dated November seventh. Is that right?" He glanced up at X.

"It is. And," X. said, pointing at the page, "you'll see that I put my mark, an X, on a redwood and——" He fell silent, staring at the record. "What the hell! This isn't a description of our claim." He straightened and glared down from his considerable height at Cal Dodge. "So you *are* in it with those other four guys!"

"I don't know what you're talking about. This is the description you gave me."

By this time Vianna had come forward and was examining the book. "Something has been torn out." She ran her finger along the middle of the book. "Two pages are missing. See?" She lifted a couple of tiny ragged fragments of paper that remained in the crease between the pages.

"Two pages," X. said slowly, fixing his eyes once more on the recorder. "Our original description and the copy you gave to those claim jumpers." Without turning, he said to Buck Rozell, "There's your evidence, sheriff."

With a long, sharp fingernail, Cal Dodge loosened the fragments of paper, blowing them out of the crease. "I'm a messy writer. I blotted those two pages so bad I had to tear them out. That's why they're missing."

Vianna spoke up. "Those pages came right before

the one with this phony claim of ours on it, which means you were recopying our original claim. I remember the blots you made when you took down the description we gave you, and they weren't serious enough to have spoiled it."

Cal Dodge leaned back in his chair, hands clasped over his bulging stomach. "I like to keep a neat book. I did it over three times before I got a page that was free of blots."

Vianna flipped through the ledger. "These other pages have blots on them. Why were you so particular about ours?"

"Because I really messed yours up."

"For Christ's sake, that's the flimsiest story I ever heard," X. snorted. "Sheriff, this man and those other four guys have stolen our claim."

"Now, wait a minute. Cal's story sounds all right to me." Rozell pointed a swarthy finger at the ledger. "That looks legal and accurate."

X. was white around his mouth. His voice was under such taut control that it was thin and low as he declared, "Any fool can see this man is lying."

Something flickered in Buck Rozell's black eyes. "I don't think Cal is lying." His voice was flat. "It's your word against his, and I've known him a lot longer than I've known you, mister. If you've got any solider proof than your word, I want to see it."

X. pointed to the fragments of paper Cal Dodge had blown out of the ledger to the floor. "That's my proof."

Sheriff Rozell made a kicking motion with one foot. The air current that resulted sent the tiny flakes of paper fluttering about the floor. "You call that solid evidence?" Coldly, he said, "You're a troublemaker. I'll give you till nine o'clock tomorrow morning to get out of Flume."

X. made no reply, but stood for some moments staring first at the sheriff, then at Cal Dodge. After another long, measuring look at Rozell, he took Vianna's arm and led her out. She was sure he wasn't conscious of the way his fingers bit into her flesh.

"What are we going to do?" she asked when they were out on the street. X. was propelling her toward the lower end of Main Street nearly as fast as she could walk.

"I don't know." His eyes were glassy.

Puzzled, she asked, "Then where are we going?"

This last question seemed to penetrate his fury. He slowed and looked around, his eyes slowly focusing. "I need a drink. You go on to the hotel. I'll be over later."

Vianna stood there watching as he turned aside and entered the canvas saloon they'd just passed. She had never seen X. take a drink since she had known him. She was angry, too, at the trick that had been played on them, but she didn't want a drink. She wanted to talk to somebody. She went into Paddy O'Neal's General Store next door.

"Sure and it's the pretty blond lass, herself," the Irishman exclaimed through the crackers and cheese he was nibbling. He got down off the high wooden stool to stand behind the counter, brushing the crumbs from his mouth. "I thought you and the big fella had gone back to your claim."

"We did," Vianna said disconsolately. "Some claim jumpers had taken it over."

He blinked his clear blue eyes. "You don't say! Claim jumping, is it?"

She told him what had happened. As she spoke, he cut her a narrow wedge of cheese from the big orange wheel he kept covered with a damp cloth. When she came to the part of the story where Sheriff Rozell refused to believe his friend Cal Dodge was capable of any chicanery, Paddy O'Neal rubbed his ruddy face thoughtfully with a small hand, and when she finished on an indignant note with the order they received to clear out of Flume, Paddy said, "Sure and it's got a bad smell to it. It isn't the first time something like this has happened, either. Not that we've had any claim jumping around here for several months, because the veins ran out in this place. Before they did, we had several cases of mistakes and arguments about which claim belonged to who. People around here just started to get suspicious of Cal Dodge when the gold petered out. Most of them moved on to new fields, but the few of us who stayed still wonder if Cal and Buck Rozell didn't have something going between them. I know for a fact that Cal sent some gold back to a bank in San Francisco, and you can't tell me he's makin' out that good with his café. The job of recorder doesn't pay much, either."

Vianna absorbed this information with such intense interest she forgot to eat her cheese. "I don't think you have to wonder any longer about the sheriff and his pal, Dodge. Anybody with an open mind would have rejected Dodge's lame excuse about blotting those two pages." She cast a helpless look at the ruddy Irishman. "Without the law behind us, what can we do?"

"There you have me, lass. I don't know."

They were silent for a time, contemplating the dilemma. Vianna bit absently into her cheese.

"Those claim jumpers," Paddy said, breaking the silence. "What did they look like?"

Vianna described the thickset spokesman. "There was one with a black beard called Lefty, and I didn't pay much attention to the other two. One was blond, I think."

"I know 'em," Paddy said, somewhat excited. "The big man is Bruno Pruett. He and Lefty Harper had a claim north of Flume until it petered out. The blond one is Heck Swartz, and I'll bet the fourth man was Fred Thacker. The four of them live together in a house behind the butcher shop. They don't work or go out prospecting. They say they're still living off the gold dust they took out of their claims, and that might be. They ended up with the best claims in this area after some shenanigans that were a lot like the one that's being pulled on you."

Vianna swallowed a mouthful of the rubbery cheese. "It sounds to me like a neat little band of thieves, Mr. O'Neal."

"That it does, lass." He shook his white head. "What does a town do when it finds out its sheriff is a crook?"

They didn't come up with an answer to that or to Vianna and X.'s problem in the half hour. She didn't stay any longer, because she couldn't wait to inform X. that there was plenty of evidence indicating Sheriff Buck Rozell was the head of a gang of claim jumpers. She started at once for the hotel, hoping he had had his drink and had gone back there.

The lowering sun was in her eyes as she crossed to the hotel. Only three men were abroad in the street, which was still puddled with water even though it hadn't rained all day. One of them was standing in front of the hotel. Vianna glanced at him and nodded pleasantly. She had moved a few steps past him when he spoke. She froze at the sound of his voice. It couldn't be happening! Surely it was a dream!

Slowly she turned.

20

With the sun now at her back, she saw his face clearly. "Tom!" The cry came out no louder than a whisper. She couldn't believe he was real and not a dream. Yet there he stood, handsome as ever, his hair waving up and off his broad brow, glinting like burnished copper in the rays of the setting sun. His belted trousers rested low on his lean hips, and his dark wool jacket emphasized the breadth of his shoulders. The sight of him made her dizzy, and she wanted to hurl herself into his arms, but his face was like flint, and his once smoky gray eyes were cold as ashes.

"You didn't know me." His tone was bitter.

"The sun was blinding me," she explained in a small voice. Her heart was pounding so hard she could scarcely breathe. "I've been trying to find you."

"So I heard. I didn't know whether to believe it or not." He regarded her coolly. "I didn't have anything better to do, so I decided to come to Flume and check it out." He had been holding a broad-brimmed tan hat. He put it on now, pulling it low to shade his eyes, enabling him to get a better look at her. "You've changed. In more ways than one."

Paddy O'Neal had a small mirror for sale in his store. It hung safely behind the counter, out of reach. Vianna had seen herself in it just a short time ago. She was well aware that her face had lost the girlish look it had when Tom fell in love with her in Govans Harbor. The physical and emotional strains of the past year and a half had planed away the plumpness, leaving the bone structure clearly visible. The mouth was firmer, and her eyes no longer looked naively at the world. Tramping through the mountains had slimmed and hardened her body. She looked very much like a boy in her men's clothes.

"I've changed in appearance," she said steadily, "and I'm not the impulsive, foolish child you knew back in Govans Harbor. In other ways I have changed not at all."

"That's hard to believe."

"How much of my story have you heard? Who told you I was looking for you?"

"A prospector I met in the mountains. He said he'd been working a claim on the American when you and a giant of a man came by one day and asked if he knew me."

"Was he dressed in a black suit and black hat?"

"That's the one."

"There's a lot you don't know, then. He ordered us off his claim at gunpoint. He doesn't know why I was looking for you." She moved a step closer to him. "It's a long story and a terrible one. Will you let me tell it to you?"

He lifted one square shoulder. "That's why I'm here."

"Come to my room. We can talk there."

The fat hotelkeeper fixed his protuberant eyes on them as they came in, turning to watch them go down the corridor. Vianna ignored him, dazed by the presence of Tom only inches away from her. There was no chair in her room, and he refused her invitation to sit on the bed. She didn't want to sit down, either. Her emotions were in such a turmoil that she needed to move around. Hat in hand, Tom leaned against the empty wall across from the bed, his face closed and tight as he looked at her, waiting.

Could she overcome his obvious hostility? Harriet's letter in Lahaina had told her how angry Tom was when he arrived back in Govans Harbor to find that she had married Eban and gone off with him on a long whaling voyage. Yet the many times Vianna had imagined their reunion, Tom's anger had evaporated the moment he saw her again. They had fallen into each other's arms and kissed away all the misunderstandings and horror. It hadn't happened that way, and unless she could melt his bitterness, her search for him would end in more heartbreak.

Clasping her hands tightly in front of her, she said quietly, "Eban tricked us both," and began the incredible account of her experiences from the moment she was handed Tom's spurious farewell note.

He broke in almost at once, flushing angrily. "You should have known I wouldn't have left you! How could you believe that note?"

"Because of what you told me about your father and the way you felt about being tied down with a family." She kept her own voice calm.

His flush deepened, and he said no more.

When she came to the description of her wedding night, Tom tensed, pulling himself away from the wall, wadding the wide brim of his hat in his clenched hands. His eyes bored through her as if he were actually seeing the scene.

Vianna moved about the small room, describing those months as dispassionately as she could, trying not to relive them, but when she came to the part where she lost the baby, her voice faltered. "I wanted it so much, Tom. I believed then . . . that it was all I would ever have of you."

Tom's face had lost every bit of its color. "Goddamn his soul to hell!" he exclaimed hoarsely. "He murdered our son!" He dropped his hat, striding toward her. "And he came within an inch of killing you!" He caught her in his arms, murmuring her name over and over, as she broke into wild sobs, his cheek pressed against her hair.

"And I thought I had had a bad time of it this past year," he said huskily when her storm of weeping had waned to quiet tears. "My poor Vianna!" He gazed down at her, his eyes misted. "I've spent all these months being mad at you, being exactly what I was accusing you of being—childish. I should have been searching for you, trying to track you down and explain that I hadn't deserted you."

Vianna's sigh cracked in the middle. "It's over. Let's not look back. We can start over from this moment."

"Thank God you came looking for me, but how did you know I was here? How did you get away from Eban?"

She told him the rest of the story, drawing an incredulous look when she reached the part where she began her visits to San Francisco's brothels. He held her away from him, shaking his head and examining her almost as if she were a stranger he was meeting for the first time. "You went to those places yourself?"

"Who could I have sent? I knew no one. Besides, if they had come back without any news of you, I would never have been satisfied that they had done a thorough job." She traced his left eyebrow lovingly, letting her hand trail down the side of his firm jaw. "I knew I had to find you here or give you up forever, and I couldn't face the prospect of life without you."

Tom buried his face in her hair for a moment, unable to speak, then kissed her. She had kissed him so many times in her dreams and in her daytime fantasies, always with the result that she was left frustrated and unbearably lonely. She might have believed that this was a dream, too, except for the joy that swelled and swelled and was still there within her when he raised his lips from hers.

"It's real!" she exulted. "I really have found you!"

Tom grinned, then sobered. "I'll kill the next man who tries to separate us. Who's this big man the old prospector said was with you?"

"His name is X. Medrano. He's the one who actually found out for me where you were."

"The Eunuch?"

"You know him?"

"I've seen him a few times. You can't be in San Francisco more than a few days before you hear about him or see him. You must have met him at the Gold Dust."

"He quit there and was working at Ruby's. He remembered you and offered to question the girls at the Gold Dust to see if any of them knew where you had gone. When he told me the girls said you were heading for the American River, I knew I had to go there, too, and try to find you."

"How did he end up coming with you?" Tom's tone was brusque.

Vianna told him about X.'s sudden infatuation with her and his apprehension at the thought of her roaming the gold country unescorted. "He has been brother, father, friend, all rolled into one," Vianna declared. "He was absolutely right about my needing someone to protect me, too." She described to Tom their journey up the American, the flash flood as they came down, and how she'd have been swept away except for X.'s colossal strength.

The jealousy betrayed by Tom's tone and expression when he began to question her about X. died a quick death. "It sounds as if we both owe him a debt we can never repay."

Eyes twinkling, Vianna said, "I discovered something that may repay him in part." She explained to him how, on the morning after the flood, she had found the gold nugget. He sent a whistling breath through his teeth, and when she went on to inform him how many ounces of color they had taken out of the pocket in two days, he was flabbergasted.

"Jehoshaphat! I thought I had a good vein up on the Feather River, but it wouldn't compare with this one."

"Someone's trying to cheat us out of it."

His arms loosened about her. "Who?" he demanded, his mouth hardening.

"According to Paddy O'Neal, their names are Bruno Pruett, Lefty Harper, Heck Swartz, and Fred Thacker."

"Those are the same bastards that stole my claim from me! Drove me off with their guns. I rounded up half a dozen other prospectors by promising to let them work my claim for sixty days if they'd help me get my claim back. Took me two months to find that many guys up in that country. We went back to my claim, but Bruno and his gang nearly wiped us out. They are real gunmen. My miners weren't any match for them. I heard about a month ago that the vein had played out." He cursed and added ruefully, "It was big enough to have made me a rich man if I could have got it back."

With her hands resting on his lean hips, Vianna exclaimed helplessly, "We haven't got a chance against them! Paddy O'Neal says people around here suspect that they're part of a gang headed by Sheriff Rozell. The recorder, Cal Dodge, is thought to be in on it, too. There's no doubt in my mind that he is, after the way he lied to us about our claim." She told him about the phony claims Dodge had recorded in the ledger.

Tom was gazing over the top of her head toward the window, a thoughtful, faraway look in his gray eyes. "If we could get enough men together, maybe we could run Bruno and his thugs off. It would take a small army." He brought his gaze back to her. "Where's Medrano?"

"After we left the recorder's office, he said he needed a drink."

"Understandable," Tom commented dryly. "I think I'll go out and find him. I want to talk to him before he gets too drunk to listen."

X. chose that moment to arrive. When Vianna let him in, it was obvious at a glance that he was cold sober. He shook Tom's hand warmly, and with a smile sent in Vianna's direction, he said, "We've made quite a search for you."

"So Vianna has been telling me." Tom looked the

giant squarely in the eye. "I want to thank you for saving her life."

Rather shyly, X. said, "No thanks needed. I just happened to be in the right place at the right time."

"Well, being there was your idea, and I'm thankful you persuaded her to let you come up here with her."

"It wasn't easy."

Tom laughed, glancing at Vianna. "I'm sure it wasn't."

"It was easier than either of you thinks," Vianna protested. "I was scared to death at the thought of starting out alone." She scanned the chairless room. "I wish we could all sit down."

X. said, "We can." He slid down the wall opposite the bed and drew his long legs up, clasping his hands around them. "This is fine for me."

Vianna pulled Tom down beside her on the bed, holding his hand. "I told Tom about our claim. He said those are the same men who stole one from him." She and Tom relayed to X. all the information they had on the gang of claim jumpers and their suspected alliance with Buck Rozell.

X. hunched his enormous shoulders. "I'd have to be an imbecile not to have known he and Dodge were crooked snakes after what they pulled on us." He said to Tom, "You should have heard the bald lies they told Vianna and me about how our claim ended up in the hands of those other guys. Either they thought we were dumb enough to swallow them, or else they figured there was nothing we could do about it." He ran his tongue under his upper lip and made a sucking sound. "They figured wrong. I let it slip in the saloon that Vianna and I made a big strike about sixty miles up the river. After I pretended to be disgusted with myself for being so loose-mouthed, I said, 'What the hell,' and proudly showed them our biggest nugget. Within ten minutes the place was empty. Everyone was off to buy prospecting gear and head upriver. Even the saloon-keeper took the fever. He started out of his place like a cat with its tail on fire. Going to try to sell his stock to the other saloons in Flume. Before he got out the door, I bought his shelves to build a rocker with."

Vianna observed glumly, "The rocker won't be of any use to us if we don't get our claim back."

X.'s eyes took on a peculiar shine. "We'll get it back. I'll hire some of those men to help me drive off those claim jumpers. I didn't want to hire them here in Flume. Rozell might send out more men if he learned my plan." To Tom he said, "I'm glad you turned up. I sure can use your help."

Tom patted the pistol in his belt. "I'm a little better with this thing than I was the last time I tangled with Bruno and Lefty. I've been practicing."

X. nodded his approval. "I doubt that we can expect much in the way of marksmanship from the prospectors we'll be able to hire. If we can hire any. They may be too anxious to find claims of their own to stop and fight our battle for us."

"Why don't you offer them the privilege of working your claim for a month?" Tom suggested. "They know it's a rich one. It might dampen their fever for finding their own."

"Now there's an idea!" X. slapped his knee. "Can you start in the morning?"

"I need a few things." Tom stood up. "Especially more shells for my gun. And I'd better get cracking while there's still stuff to buy in this town." He touched Vianna's hair. "I'll be back in a little while."

It was two hours before he returned. The stores were so busy he had to stand in line to make his purchases. "It's a real stampede," he informed X. and Vianna when he finally got back. "Buck Rozell may wake up tomorrow morning and find himself sheriff of a ghost town."

They went to supper and found the café empty of other customers. "I may have to close up and follow the crowd," the owner declared glumly as he served them.

During the meal a friendship developed swiftly between Tom and X. Vianna observed the evolving relationship with relief. There was none of the rivalry and hostility between them that she feared there might be, even though X.'s love for her was devoid of all sexuality. In lowered tones, to prevent the café operator from overhearing them, the men discussed the means by which they could regain possession of their gold claim. Without a word having been said on the subject, X. and Vianna regarded Tom as their partner. When Tom referred to "your claim," Vianna corrected him. "My half of the claim is as much yours as it is mine."

He turned his eyes on her. "The situation is a little awkward. I'm not your husband."

She met his look straight on, replying steadily, "As far as I'm concerned, you are." The effects of their reunion—first the stiffness, then the tears, followed by the worried consideration of the problem regarding their claim—had checked their physical hunger for one another. It had awakened in Vianna while she waited in her hotel room for Tom to return from his hasty shopping for provisions, and it had grown during supper. She couldn't keep her eyes off him—the hard planes of his face, the sensually curved mouth, the strong brown neck. Whenever his glance met hers, she felt the impact of his own desire. She was aware of her cheeks' growing pinker and pinker during the meal. At this moment they were absolutely aflame, despite her steady voice.

X. spoke up. "For all intents and purposes, I'm considering you her husband, too. The horror she went through with that bastard can't be called a marriage. He cheated you out of a wedding, but that's only a technicality."

"Well, it seems I have a wife whether I want one or not."

Vianna's glance flew to him, her heart plummeting at the flat tone of his voice. When she saw the amused gleam in his eyes, her heart halted its downward rush so abruptly it pushed the breath from her lungs, making her gasp.

Realizing the effect his teasing had on her, Tom said reproachfully, "You still don't trust me, do you?" He was hurt.

Vianna covered one of his hands with both of her own, replying in a small voice, "It isn't that. I can't believe everything is going to be all right. I guess I'm afraid that one way or another I'll lose you again."

The wounded look on Tom's face faded. He put his free hand over hers. "I'm not ever going to leave you again. I promise." His voice was deep and strong.

She gave him a misty, radiant smile.

When they finished eating, X. drained his coffee cup and said tactfully, "If you'll excuse me, I've got some things to see to before morning. What time shall we start out?"

"I'm in favor of starting as soon as it's light," Tom replied.

"Fine. I'll see you both in the morning."

Tom and Vianna looked at each other. It was the first time they'd been alone since X. had come to her room and found them together. There was no reason now not to reveal their desire for one another. It blazed from their faces, burned in their clasped hands.

"Let's go," Tom said hoarsely.

As they hurried through the busy street, they were the object of many curious glances from men who had heard about the gold strike and were rushing through preparations to head up the American to claim a piece of it for themselves.

Vianna and Tom were only vaguely aware of the attention they were attracting. Liquid fire flowed from the hand she held in the crook of Tom's elbow, down her arm and through her body. The bustling crowd was a blur. The lobby of the hotel was empty. They headed for Vianna's room without speaking. When the door closed behind them, she went into his arms with a choked cry, seeking his lips, wanting to feel his hands on her burning body. Because there were no words to express what they were feeling, they made love in silence, letting their hands and lips and bodies declare the wondrous love they shared.

Later, lying blissfully in Tom's arms, her face against his warm, muscular chest, Vianna said, "I'll never take happiness for granted again. I had it all those years I was growing up and didn't know it. The only real unhappiness I experienced during that time was the good-byes I said to my father whenever he sailed away, but it was short-lived. Within four days I would settle back into my usual routine, unchanged and unmarked because my misery was so brief." She tightened her arms around Tom. "This last year and a half has been hell on earth. At the moment I feel as if I had died and gone to heaven."

He moved his cheek caressingly against her hair. "If you did, then I came along with you." His hands kneaded her back, betraying the intensity of his emotion when he said, "Vianna, I want you for my wife. I want it legal and binding, with no way for anyone to ever separate us again. I want you to go back to San Francisco tomorrow and start divorce proceedings against Eban."

She pushed away from him, exclaiming, "I won't leave you. Not so soon. We've just found each other."

His reddish-brown hair was mussed, giving him a boyish look. "As soon as X. and I get this gold claim settled, I'll join you in San Francisco, and if all the legal work is finished, I'll take you back to the claim with me."

"Tom, I'm not going to leave you!" Her refusal was made softly but firmly. "Not yet! I'll go to San Francisco later. For now, I want some time with you. How can you think of sending me off before we've spent even twenty-four hours together? You can't want to be with me as much as I want to be with you, or you couldn't even consider it."

Tom groaned, pulling her close again and running

his hands hungrily over her slender body. "I want to be with you," he said huskily, "but I want it to last forever. I want to erase all of Eban's legal claim to you so that he can never cause us any trouble again."

"He doesn't know where I am." Vianna spoke soothingly. "We don't have to worry about him anymore."

"Did you write and tell your mother you were coming to California?"

"Yes, and to Harriet." Suddenly she understood what he was getting at. "They won't tell him, not after reading what I wrote about what he did to me."

"Eban is insane," Tom reminded her. "If he continues to believe he has been chosen by God to punish you, he'll never give up his search for you."

Vianna shivered. "All the more reason then why I shouldn't go to San Francisco alone. If he found me there——" She couldn't finish. She couldn't even complete the thought. It was too horrible.

Tom remained thoughtfully silent for a while. Finally he said, "You might be right. We'll wait and see how this gold claim fight turns out. You and X. and I might all end up back in San Francisco with a sad tale to tell about how we lost the greatest strike since Sutter's to a gang of claim jumpers."

Relieved that she had won her point and could remain with Tom, Vianna inquired half shyly, half brazenly, "Meantime?"

Tom's seriousness fled. He gave her a roguish grin. "Meanwhile we have some catching up to do, and although this hotel room can't compare with our cave by the sea, I believe I can become properly inspired again . . . and again . . . and again. . . ."

———————————————

21

Vianna was in a state of honeymoon euphoria when they started off at dawn the next morning. Early as the hour was, the exodus from Flume had already begun. They joined the ragged but steady stream of men and mules that moved up the street, past the butcher and blacksmith shops at the far end, past the sparsely scattered houses and outbuildings at the edge of town, and out into open country, hugging the bank of the American River, which provided the only road into the wilderness. A few of them Vianna recognized as businessmen who were abandoning their stores and shops, temporarily if they failed to find a good claim, permanently if their vein proved rich enough. Most of the men were strangers to her, miners and prospectors from the area around Flume whom the rumor of this new strike had reached. She was amazed at their numbers. She wouldn't have believed there were that many people in the vicinity.

It wasn't until the next day, when X. began scouting ahead of them and behind them for men who were good gun handlers, that recognition of the danger lying ahead of them began to penetrate Vianna's exquisite joy at being with Tom again. During the search of the American for Tom, X. had taught her at her request to use both a pistol and a rifle. He had been amazed at how swiftly she had developed her skills with them both. She had been no less amazed, because she had always been clumsy when it came to anything mechanical. In the upcoming fight, she was secretly determined to take part. She had not mentioned that fact, however, knowing it would have drawn roars of protest from X. and Tom. The fear she began to feel was not for her own safety; she was sure the men would not allow her in the front line of attack. Her anxiety was for Tom. Now that they were together again, she began to develop a morbid fear of losing him. Fate could be incredibly cruel. How well she had learned that lesson! Someone was sure to get killed in the gun battle coming up. The thought that it might be X. was horrible, too. She had come to love him like a brother. But Tom was her life. She could never endure the agony of losing him again.

"I've got five men lined up," X. announced that night. He had been ahead of them all day and was waiting on a small shale beach when they arrived there in late afternoon. He took his two mules from Tom and tied them to a nearby tree. He had a fire started and a pile of wood stacked to one side. The sky was clear; they would not need to set up the tent. "They're willing to help us for the privilege of working our claim for thirty days. I've given them written permission."

"How good are they with guns?" Tom asked.

X. shrugged. "Like you and me, they aren't exactly crack shots, but they claim they're pretty good. They're all ahead of us. We're going to meet in the morning at the falls."

Tom nodded. 'I know the place. Have you got a plan?"

Vianna listened closely as she placed some potatoes in the fire to roast.

"Just before you get to our claim," X. explained, "there are the remains of an old rockslide. The flash flood took out the lower rocks, but there are plenty of them left—big enough to give us cover. It's in range of the claim. We can sneak up and open fire on them. The claim is on open, sloping ground. Except for a tree or two above it, there isn't any cover. If we're careful, we can take them by surprise."

Vianna recalled the boulder-strewn area X. was talking about. Some of the edge of her anxiety was taken off as she realized his strategy was a very good one, giving them several advantages over the claim jumpers.

"How far are we from there?" Tom asked, untying his blanket and Vianna's from one of their mules.

X. was smoothing a bed of coals on which to place the skillet, looking like another of the river's huge boulders in his hunkered-down position. "We're a couple of miles from the falls. From there to the claim it's about a two-hour trek. We should have this whole thing settled one way or another by noon tomorrow."

One way or another. Vianna began slicing the bacon, wondering how much they would eat. If the men's stomachs were as knotted up as hers at the prospect of the gunfight tomorrow, she wouldn't need to fry more than a few slices.

The men's appetites were unaffected, however, and when she asked Tom later how he could remain so cool, he said, "I'm not cool. I can hardly wait to tangle with Bruno Pruett and those other bastards."

X. had taken a few logs from the fire and moved upstream far enough to give them some privacy, building his own fire to sleep beside as he had the night before. Vianna and Tom sat with their backs against some debris left by the flood, a blanket under them, another over their legs, their feet to the fire.

Tom hurled a twig into the flames with a hint of savagery. "I've got a score to settle with them. I didn't think I'd ever get the chance." In the flickering light, his face was hard and shiny.

The barely controlled violence his movement betrayed increased Vianna's fear. "But what if——" She faltered, unable to finish.

They were holding hands. He turned toward her, lifting her hand to his lips and gazing at her above it. "Nothing is going to happen to me." His voice rang with certainty.

"How can you be so sure?" she whispered.

"Being with you again has made me feel like nothing can ever harm me again. It's more than a feeling. It's a belief, and with faith like that, no bullet can touch me."

"I wish I could feel like that," Vianna said wistfully. "Being together again has done just the opposite for me. I'm terrified of the possibility that I might lose you a second time."

Tom chuckled. "No chance. You're stuck with me, for better or for worse."

"Is that a promise?" she murmured.

"You bet it is," he said, looking deeply into her eyes before bringing his mouth down on hers.

Swept away by the passion his kiss aroused, Vianna forgot her anxiety. The ecstasy that enveloped them isolated them from the rest of the world. She fell asleep with a rapturous smile on her face.

When they rendezvoused at the falls the next morning with the men X. had hired, Vianna recognized two of them. One was Charlie Anderson, owner of the canvas saloon, who had sold his shelves to X. The other was the blacksmith from Flume, Otto Johansen, whom she had seen often in his open-fronted shop, working at his forge. Anderson was young, rangy, and tousle-headed. In contrast to his boyish appearance, his manner was quietly confident. The blacksmith was older, with a mass of coarse, dark hair and sparse, yellowed teeth. Neither of them had mules. They carried their scanty supplies in knapsacks strapped to their backs, their picks over their shoulders. Vianna was too nervous to catch the other men's names, but by the time X. had explained his plan and they had covered most of the distance to their ambush point, she had sorted them out, at least by their first names. Frank was the one with stooped shoulders and a caved-in chest. The roly-poly fellow was Conrad, and the one with the foxy face was called Red, for obvious reasons. From the shabby look of their miners' outfits, Vianna concluded they had been in the mountains a long time.

All three led mules loaded down with all the paraphernalia required to exist in the wilderness for long periods of time, including rifles. Anderson and Johansen wore pistols stuck in their belts.

X. outlined his plan, then asked if any of them had any questions.

Conrad, the tubby one, piped up. "You sure there are rocks big enough to cover me?"

As the others laughed, X. assured him, "There are some there even big enough to cover me."

Red wrinkled his foxy face. "What are we waiting for? Sounds to me like those guys won't be able to get a good shot at us."

They moved off in good humor. Even Vianna felt more cheerful. But at the end of two hours, when X. called a halt and warned them that the claim was around the bend, her heart began to pound.

"I'll bring up the rear," X. said. "They'd be on their guard the minute they caught sight of me. The rest of you can move up without attracting their attention. Leave your mules back here with Vianna. I'll give you five good minutes, then I'll move up and join you. Pick your cover, but leave a big one for me."

As they loaded their guns and checked their ammunition, Vianna said to X., "Why waste me back here tending the mules? You know I shoot well. Give me your pistol, and I'll move up behind you." She gestured toward the mules, which were being tied to trees by their owners. "They don't need to be looked after."

Taken by surprise, Tom spoke up before X. had a chance to reply. He commanded sternly, "You stay here!"

"But with me you'll be eight against four," she protested. "And I'm a good shot, aren't I?" she asked, turning to X., who was loading his rifle.

"You're a good shot," he conceded, ramming the bullet home. "But you leave this job to us."

"It's my claim, too," she reminded them.

They exchanged a look that made her feel like a

willful child. X. went back to loading his rifle, leaving Tom to deal with her. "Now, Vianna," he began, "I want you to promise me you'll stay back here, out of range."

"There's surely a rock out there that will shield me, too. I would think you'd be glad to have another gun on your side."

The other men were silent but listening as they made their preparations.

"We don't need you," Tom informed her. "We can handle this." He shoved his loaded pistol into his belt. His coat pockets were bulging with extra shells. Regarding her rebellious expression, he moved closer to her and spoke in a low voice. "Now, I don't want any tricks, Vianna. What good is it going to do either of us if I come out of this alive but you're dead? Promise me you'll behave and stay back here where you belong." When she hesitated, he warned, "Either I get your promise, or I'll tie you to a tree with our mules."

"You wouldn't!"

"I would!"

Tartly, she exclaimed, "I'm beginning to have second thoughts about you."

He gave her a saucy grin. "I'll erase them tonight."

"You're very sure of yourself, aren't you?" she huffed.

His smoky eyes possessed her as he teased, "No more so than I am of you."

His glance sent heat coursing through her body; his remark caused her to drop her eyes in embarrassment. She turned away, thwarted and nettled, but when a moment later Tom said quietly, "Let's go," she whirled, wanting to run and throw her arms around him, holding him back from the danger that awaited beyond the bend. He saw her movement and sent her a caressing smile. Then he strode off, leading the others. Vianna pressed a hand to her lips. A moment later, he was out of sight.

Off to her left, X. was silently counting out the five

minutes he was giving them to get into position for the attack. Vianna's throat tightened painfully, and she rushed to his side. Stretching on tiptoe, she pressed a kiss just under his jaw. Flushing, he gave her a look of complete adoration.

"Be careful." Her voice shook.

"All right," he replied, as if he hadn't really considered it before.

Shots rang out. X.'s massive head came up. "What the hell! They couldn't be in position yet!" He took off around the bend at a run.

Vianna followed, dashing with him to what remained of a large grove of trees. The flood had stripped the land bare of everything about a hundred yards back from the normal bank of the river. From the edge of the trees they had a good view of the quarter of a mile or so that lay between them and their claim. Between them and the rocky area they had chosen to launch their attack from lay a stretch of sandy ground that still bore marks of the flood—stumps of bushes, bits and pieces of wood, the tops of once-buried rocks. Tom and the others were lying facedown in that open area, dead or pinned down by gunfire coming from the very boulders they had been heading for.

As Vianna bit off a scream, X. cried, "Hell, there are five—no, six—guys out there behind those rocks. Rozell must have suspected we were planning something and sent two guys on ahead of us to warn Pruett and the others." He shouldered his rifle and began firing toward the attackers.

Vianna's eyes were riveted on Tom's fallen form. Unaware of what she was doing, she was whispering, "No, no, no," in an unending litany. As X.'s rifle fire began to sing over the heads of his fallen comrades, she watched in exquisite relief as Tom raised up slightly and shot toward the rocks with his pistol. Three of the other men did the same.

"They're sitting ducks out there!" X.'s tone was agonized.

It was true. There were only the ragged remains of some bushes for cover, and at the moment Tom and the others couldn't make a move toward them.

"Take this pistol." X. shoved it at her. "If we can keep those bastards busy enough, maybe Tom and the rest can take cover."

Vianna grabbed the pistol eagerly. Choosing a boulder from which shots were being fired at Tom, she sent dust and rock chips flying into the air and into the face, she hoped, of the thug who was trying to kill Tom. Until she emptied her gun, she had the satisfaction of knowing that her target couldn't get off a single shot. She ducked over to X. for more shells.

"Good work," he said approvingly.

Her second barrage gave Tom time enough to slither quickly over to a scrawny, denuded bush that wouldn't have given adequate protection to a rabbit. Red and Charlie Anderson managed to take scanty cover under the hail of X.'s rifle shots.

X. was cursing. "There isn't enough cover out there, and it would be suicide for them to make a run for it and try to get back here. If only we could get behind them!"

Vianna was too busy to look for a way for that to be done, but after another brisk salvo from her pistol, X. called her over to him. Never taking his eyes from the battleground in front of him, and firing intermittently as he talked, he said, "Take the pistol and some shells and circle through these trees. When you get to the mountain, pick up as many men with guns as you can and the bunch of you start firing at these bastards from behind. It doesn't matter if the men with you can't hit a barn from forty feet. All we need is a diversion. With you shooting at their backs, they'll have to turn, and that's when we'll rush them." He squeezed off another shot that whined as it struck rock. "Even if they see you come out of the trees, you'll be out of range of their guns. Do you think you can do it?"

"Of course I can, but you need my gun right here.

You can't keep that gang busy enough to protect Tom and the others."

"Yes, I can, Vianna. They have no chance this way. You and I can use up all our ammunition and end up right where we started, with Tom and the rest lying out there in the open to be picked off like squirrels on a branch. If you want to save Tom's life, do as I say."

Put like that, it was unarguable. Vianna filled a pocket with shells and took off, running as fast as she could run through the trees and away from the river. A stitch knifed through her side, but she didn't slow down. On she sped, clearing the trees after a few minutes and streaking across open ground to where the mountain began to rise. Its gradual slopes swarmed with prospectors swinging their picks, examining rocks, or moving slowly with their eyes fastened to the ground. Sounds of the battle had drawn the attention of some of the gold-seekers. Others, if they had taken notice initially, had already resumed their search for the precious metal that other men, at that very moment, were trying to kill each other for. Scrambling up the slope to the nearest prospector, she gasped, "Do you have a gun?"

The particular prospector that Vianna gasped out her question to was one who happened to be more interested in the gunfight than in gold; however, the thought of being a participant rather than an observer started him shaking his head.

"That's our claim down there," Vianna said swiftly. "You can work it for a few days if you'll help us now."

That changed the aspect of the situation for him. "I'll help," he said at once.

Vianna picked up two more men the same way within minutes. They took cover behind the tree under which X. and Vianna had camped. Down the slope and downstream, easily within range, were Bruno, Lefty, and the other four men, crouched behind the scattered boulders. Vianna and her companions let loose a hail of bullets. She gave a triumphant shout as her bullet found Bruno Pruett. He spun, his right arm hanging useless, shifting his gun awkwardly to his left hand and trying to aim it up at them. Caught in a cross fire now, Lefty Harper and the other four men scrambled among the rocks, trying to find cover. Lefty went down almost at once from bullets fired by Tom's group. One of the newcomers fell, too.

That was enough for the blond thug Paddy O'Neal had identified as Heck Swartz. He stuck a bandanna at the end of his rifle, waving it in the air and yelling, "We give up! Stop shooting!"

His friends must have approved his actions, because those who still could threw their hands in the air, holding their guns high above their heads. As X. emerged at a run from the trees, Vianna saw Tom leap to his feet and race for the rocks. Relief and joy brought a small cry from her. Right behind Tom came Red, Charlie, and Otto Johansen. Conrad was lying in X.'s path. X. swept up the rotund man under one arm and carried him forward. By the time he arrived, Tom and the others were collecting the guns of Bruno's gang.

Vianna ran down the slope, past the excavation that was her claim, and threw herself against Tom's side. "Are you hurt?"

His hands were full of rifles and pistols, and he could only grin down at her. "Not a scratch."

"Thank God!"

"I guess we needed you after all," he conceded.

She replied archly, "I come in handy in all sorts of ways."

"So I'm learning."

She went over to X., who had laid Conrad on the hillside close to their claim. Blood was staining the roly-poly man's right trouser leg. Putting her hand inside X.'s big paw, she said, "Are you all right?"

"I'm fine." His face flooded with affection and approval. "You saved the lot of them."

"It was your idea," she reminded him. To Conrad, she said, "Are you hurt bad?"

"I don't know." He was green with pain and shock.

She and X. knelt beside him, ripping his pant leg and baring a thick, hairy leg. The bullet had gone into the flesh above and to the outside of the knee. X. examined it closely. "If it hit a bone, it couldn't have more than nicked it, and the bullet went clean through. It will hurt like hell, but you'll be all right in a couple of weeks."

The gang of claim jumpers hadn't gotten off so lightly. Lefty Harper and one of the newcomers lay dead. Bruno Pruett was still on his feet but leaning against a boulder, clutching his right arm. Fred Thacker was slumped on the ground, blood pouring down his face. Heck Swartz and the other gunfighter were untouched, standing surly and silent, hands on top of their heads, looking into Red's gun and foxy face.

It was Bruno Pruett whom X. and Tom confronted.

"Hello, Pruett." Vianna had never seen an expression on Tom's face like the one he was wearing now, tough and menacing. "It's a different story this time, isn't it?"

The barrel-chested claim jumper glowered at him.

Tom said, "You don't recognize me, do you?"

"I recognize you," came the growled reply.

"Good. Then you know that my finger is itching to put a bullet through that thieving heart of yours right now."

Fear flickered in the bellicose face. His eyes darted between Tom and X. like a trapped animal. "You've got your claim back. Isn't that enough?"

X. held his rifle loosely at his side, but he loomed threateningly over the wounded man. "It's too bad Vianna's shot didn't puncture that bulging chest instead of catching the shoulder. But as long as he's still alive," X. said to Tom, "let's use him as a messenger. He's the best of the whole mangy bunch to take a warning back to Buck Rozell."

"Maybe you're right."

X. turned back to Bruno Pruett. "You tell Rozell

that if he or any of the rest of you bastards ever turns up here again, we'll shoot you on sight. Think you can remember that?" His high-pitched voice dripped sarcasm.

Pruett glared at him but didn't answer.

The tip of Tom's pistol waved slightly as he said in a lethal voice, "You didn't answer my friend."

"I can remember it," Pruett declared swiftly in a loud voice.

X. said, "All right. Clear out of here. I want to be looking at your backs in two minutes."

"What about them?" Pruett asked, nodding toward the two dead men without taking his eyes from Tom and X.

"We'll bury them. Now get going!"

Still clutching his shoulder, Pruett started off without a word to his companions. But they had heard it all and followed with alacrity, even Fred Thacker, who staggered a bit as he moved off, pressing a dirty red handkerchief to his head wound.

Vianna moved up beside Tom, and the three of them watched the thugs head back down the river. Heck Swartz paid no attention to his wounded colleagues, passing them up without a word. Within a couple of minutes they all disappeared into the trees. "Do you think they'll come back?" Vianna asked uneasily.

Tom and X. exchanged a look. "If they do," Tom told her, "they'll get exactly what we promised them."

22

Vianna glanced up from the letter she was writing as the door to her office opened and a short man with tangled gray eyebrows and a springy step came in.

"Mornin', Vianna! Break out your book. I've brought you some work!"

"Stumpy, you mean it? You've found color?"

The little man grinned from ear to ear. "I finally did. Ike Covell just gave me the assay report. I don't know how big the vein is, but it's a rich one."

Vianna cheerfully pulled the ledger off a shelf behind her desk. When the mountain on which she and X. had found their gold had proved, as X. forecast it might, to be full of gold, she, X., Tom, and the other miners who had found claims on it decided to organize a town. Vianna suggested that because they had found a pot of gold, they name the town Rainbow. Everyone concurred, and at their first election, she had been elected recorder. X. had accepted the job as sheriff reluctantly, because he hated violence, and argued that he had a mine to run. But the miners of Rainbow insisted that his size would discourage most trouble before it got to the point where he'd have to use his muscle or his gun. As for the claim, they said, he could still help Tom run it, because they were all going to be so busy digging for gold, they wouldn't cause enough trouble to make sheriffin' a full-time job. For the time being he lived and slept in her office.

The X-Vi-Z mine, as Tom proposed they call it, proved to be incredibly rich, and to Vianna's great pride, Tom turned out to be a clever businessman. Within a month after they started to work, he had picked up five claims that surrounded their own from men who preferred gold in their pockets to digging it out of the earth. By the time another month had passed, the excavation had eaten back so far into the mountain that they had to cut timbers to shore it up. Six men were hired to help with the work, and two more claims had been bought up to add to the X-Vi-Z. When Vianna wasn't busy fulfilling her duties as recorder, she took care of the mine's growing payroll and records.

People were still pouring into Rainbow. One of the first to come was Paddy O'Neal, who set up his store, the nucleus of a business district that was stretching out along what had become Main Street. Others from Flume followed, including the madams with their prostitutes.

"Sure and Flume's a ghost town, they tell me," Paddy O'Neal informed Vianna one day as she bought some flour from him.

"I wonder what's happened to Buck Rozell and his gang."

"Someone said they moved down to the Calaveras River. They're probably up to their old tricks down there."

The stage that ran to Flume now came on to Rainbow. The traffic was so heavy between the new gold camp and San Francisco that the line ran three coaches a week. Someone had set up a sawmill five miles from town, and Rainbow was no longer just a tent town. Most of the businesses on Main Street were wood-frame buildings, though still unpainted. Tom had hired a carpenter to build a house for Vianna and himself on the hill behind the grove of trees from which they had launched their very nearly abortive attack on Bruno Pruett and his gang. It too was unpainted, but with furniture, carpets, and wallpaper brought from San Francisco, it was cozy and comfortable and more. With their new wealth Vianna was able to buy the best of anything that was available, and as a result, their home would have been considered luxurious by anyone's standards. Paint for the exterior had been ordered and was due to arrive any day by the freight line that now operated from the mouth of the American River to Rainbow.

Despite the easy access to San Francisco now, Vianna had not gone there to consult a lawyer about divorcing Eban. She was afraid she could not obtain a divorce without his finding out where she was. The terror this possibility called up was stronger even than her desire to be legally married to Tom. For the time being they were living together as if they were lawfully man and wife.

"All right, Stumpy, locate this claim of yours for me," Vianna said, pen poised above the thick ledger.

Sitting down across the desk from her, the leathery little man threw one muddy booted leg across his other knee and began with gleeful relish to describe the reference points to her. It was across the river, which was still swollen by winter rains and dangerous to cross. The miners who had claims over there came to Rainbow in their canoes and boats no more often than they had to, buying several weeks' provisions at a time. There were periods when the American was so wild that it would have meant almost certain death to have tried to cross it.

"There are so many of you over there now," Vianna observed, "that someone ought to rig up a ferry. The type with ropes so that the raft wouldn't get swept away."

"I wish they would. I had a time getting over here this morning, and it looks to me like the water's rising." He waggled his muddy boot. "Maybe one of these days somebody will get disgusted with prospectin' and decide to go into the ferry business."

Vianna read back what she had taken down to make sure she hadn't made any errors. "That's it, then.

Maybe your vein will run straight through to the other side of the mountain."

He sprang up off the chair and danced an exuberant little jig. "It might be another X-Vi-Z mine!"

Vianna laughed. "I hope it is."

She told Tom about the new strike at noon, when he came home for dinner. He listened with interest, but he obviously had something else on his mind. Halfway through the meal he said, "I'm ready to leave for San Francisco on the next stage and see about getting you a divorce."

She lay down her fork, the old feeling of dread creeping over her. "What if I can't divorce Eban without revealing where I am?"

"If that's the only way it can be done, we'll do it and then deal with him if he wants to come here and cause trouble." He looked straight into her eyes in a forceful way. "I don't like our situation. I want you safely married to me."

"I want it, too," she said miserably, "but not at the risk of more trouble with Eban. Just the thought of his coming here terrifies me."

Tom stretched his arm across the table toward her, his hand open and inviting hers. She put one of her icy hands in it. "I won't let Eban hurt you ever again," he promised. "Trust me."

She felt the living warmth and the solid strength of his hand enclosing hers and read the gritty resolve in his face. "Yes, I trust you," she said simply.

He nodded, pleased. "We'll leave Thursday morning."

The next day, Wednesday, she sat at her office desk, writing to her mother. It was raining hard and the afternoon was dark. The letter would leave on the same stage she and Tom would take the next morning. As she was dipping her pen in the tin inkwell, the stage arrived, pulling up in a splatter of mud at the stage office directly across the street. Vianna watched the driver jump down from his seat, landing ankle deep in mud. He stretched hugely, then went to the door of the coach, which someone inside had already flung open. She watched, her curiosity aroused. Except on extremely rare occasions when there were women aboard, the drivers usually left the passengers to debark unaided. She never found out who the woman or women were, or even if they existed. The first passenger off the coach was Eban.

She thought afterward she gave a cry; she recalled clearly that she froze, the pen falling from her lifeless fingers to roll off the desk to the bare wooden floor with a clatter. Even through the rain-streaked window there was no doubt that the man in the short, heavy sailor coat was Eban. He was hatless and clean-shaven. His long, harshly lined face stood out palely above his dark clothing. He was staring straight at the recorder's office. For one horrified moment Vianna believed he had been able to see her inside; then she realized he hadn't when he sent his glance up and down the street before striding around the coach to claim his baggage. No longer paralyzed, but trembling, Vianna watched him reappear a few minutes later and plod off toward the hotel and out of sight. She stumbled up off her chair, gripped by panic. Her only thought was to get to the mine and tell Tom. Throwing her tarred canvas cape around her shoulders and a shawl over her head, she crept out the door. There was no sign of Eban. She started running through the mud to the X-Vi-Z.

They were no longer placer mining. The pocket of loose gold had run out, but there had been a vein behind it. They were bringing rock out of the belly of the mountain now, rich ore that had to be loosened with picks wielded by hired crews. Vianna was gasping painfully for breath when she reached the black mouth of the mine, shored up by timbers and surrounded by mounds of loose rock. Tom and X. were examining a wheelbarrow full of ore that a big-jawed young man had just brought out. Tom saw her coming and hurried down to meet her. "What's happened?" he asked before they came together.

"Eban!" Vianna croaked. "He's here. He just got off the stage!" She gave him a wide-eyed, stricken stare.

"The bastard found you." Tom cursed, and an ugly expression passed across his face. "Don't worry." He put out an arm, and she slumped against his chest. His voice sounded hollow in the ear she had pressed to his shirt as he said, "Let's go tell X. He's the law. He can order Eban out of Rainbow or throw the son of a bitch in jail until he agrees to leave."

With his arm still around Vianna's waist, he yelled up at X. and motioned for him to come down the slope. The big man arrived in a rattle of loose stones, rain streaming off his broad-brimmed hat.

"Eban just arrived on the stage," Tom informed him without preamble. "Vianna saw him."

X.'s face went hard. "Where is he now?"

"He went to the hotel." Vianna's voice was reedy.

X. stared off toward the sprawling cluster of buildings that was Rainbow. "I'll go have a talk with him."

"I'll go with you." Tom turned to Vianna. "We'll drop you off at your office. You stay there until we're through."

She shuddered. "I don't want to be alone. I'll be less afraid if I go with you."

Tom hesitated. When he saw X. nod, he said, "All right, I guess you might as well be in on this, too. You might even enjoy it." This last remark was made with the bitter relish of a man about to settle a huge score.

They slogged through the rain and mud back to town and down the street, past the new hotel that was being built, to the only one doing business at present. The chipper, bespectacled owner glanced up from the paper he was reading behind the raw wooden counter that served as a desk.

X. asked immediately, "Have you got someone named Eban Stanbro staying here?"

The hotelkeeper said with a note of curiosity in his

voice, "As a matter of fact, I do. He just came in on the stage."

"What's his room number?"

"Six."

X. led the way down the uncarpeted hall to the door marked with a crudely painted "6," and knocked.

A moment later Vianna found herself looking into the face she had hoped she would never see again. The thin mouth had grown even more cruel; the deep-set eyes burned with a maniacal gleam. He showed no surprise at seeing her. "Did you really think you could escape me?" he demanded with undisguised triumph, scarcely bothering to notice the presence at her side of Tom and X.

X. pushed past him into the narrow cubicle that held a single bed and nothing else. His head almost touched the low ceiling. There hardly seemed room left for Tom and Vianna, who stood just inside the door, close but not actually touching. Vianna could feel Tom's barely controlled fury throbbing in the air between them.

Continuing to ignore X. as well as Tom, Eban said, "You weren't very clever, Vianna. It was your use of the name Mrs. Nathaniel Sawtell that gave you away. The agent with whom you booked your passage became curious when no one in the community knew an attractive young woman by that name. My company's agent heard about the small mystery and informed me of it when I came back to Lahaina. When I heard his description of you and the name you tried to disguise yourself with, I knew at once it was you and followed you here."

The furrows running from each side of his nose to the corners of his mouth deepened, and his face turned gray. "You've become a notorious woman! Everyone in San Francisco has heard of you and your partners in this X-Vi-Z mine." For the first time he acknowledged the presence of X. and Tom, favoring them with the same type of stare he would have fixed upon sailors who needed to be reminded that they were in the presence of the captain and master. As his eyes came back to Vianna, he hissed, "Your vileness seems to be limitless."

Tom grunted, hurling himself forward and crashing a fist against Eban's gaunt jaw. Eban was the taller and heavier of the two, but his rigid, graceless body fell back against the foot of the bed, and he would have fallen to the floor if he hadn't managed to grasp the metal bed frame and hold himself up. Tom was on top of him, ready to strike again, when X. caught him with both arms around his chest and pulled him away.

"Let me at the bastard! I'll kill him!"

"I know you will." X. gave Tom a sharp shake. "I'm not going to let that happen, for your sake and Vianna's. You've both got enough ugly memories of this guy without adding that one." Still holding Tom, he addressed Eban. "In case you haven't noticed my star, I'm sheriff here, and I'm telling you to clear out of Rainbow on the morning stage."

Eban pulled himself erect. Blood trickled from the side of his mouth, and there were red marks, left by Tom's knuckles, on his jaw. "I intend leaving in the morning. With my wife."

Vianna came forward, moving around X.'s huge frame to confront Eban with clenched hands held stiffly at her sides. "I'm not going anywhere with you ever again. As a matter of fact, I was preparing to leave for San Francisco tomorrow to file for divorce." Making this blunt declaration filled her with sweet satisfaction.

He stared at her in blank shock. Apparently the idea of divorce had never occurred to him. "You can't get free of me! God has given you to me to punish!"

Tom made another lunge for him but was stopped by X.'s restraining arms.

"If you so much as lay a finger on her again," X. warned, "I'll put you in jail and throw away the key."

"She's my wife! I can do what I like with her!"

"Not here in Rainbow you can't."

"I'm not leaving without her! You can't prevent a husband from taking his runaway wife back home!"

"I can and I will. The law is flexible in these gold camps, and Vianna is regarded with affection by everyone in town. If you make any attempt to harm her or to carry her off, the miners here will give me any powers I need to deal with you."

"If I don't get to you first," Tom put in. "Let me go, X. I won't kill the son of a bitch with Vianna standing here watching." X. hesitated a moment, then released Tom, who grabbed Vianna's arm, saying, "Let's go."

As they went out, they heard X. issue a final warning. "I'll be at the stage in the morning. You'd better be on it."

The hotelkeeper must have heard Eban's shrill shouts and his body crashing against the iron bed, because he eyed them curiously as they came up the hall and went out the glass-paneled door.

"Do you think he'll leave?" Vianna asked anxiously when they were once again on the street. The rain had let up momentarily, but the fat, dark clouds overhead were preparing to release more.

"I don't know," X. replied. "But don't worry. If he doesn't, I'll make sure he's put someplace where he can never bother you again."

Tom spoke up. "Meantime, I don't want to leave Vianna alone for a second. I've got to get back to the mine, but I can get by without you for the rest of the day," he told X. "Why don't you stay in your office and keep Vianna with you until I close the mine tonight?"

"That's a good idea." X. shot Tom a sober look over Vianna's head. "Watch yourself. That guy's so crazy there's no telling what he might do."

"Don't go!" Vianna begged, suddenly fearful and clutching Tom's arm. "Stay with us."

"I can't. I've got to see that they shore up the tunnel ceiling before it caves in on them." He gave her a tough grin. "I can take care of myself. He won't catch me unaware again."

"Can't you close down early?" she asked.

"I'll try."

Vianna spent the rest of the afternoon in X.'s office, her eye on the hotel entrance. X. made coffee on top of the heating stove, and they sipped it as he caught up on some paperwork. It began to rain again, heavily and steadily. Eban did not leave the hotel, yet Vianna's uneasiness was unrelieved until Tom arrived about six o'clock to take her home.

Neither of them slept well that night. Finally Vianna whispered, "You aren't asleep, are you?"

"No."

She snuggled close, and he put his arms around her. "X. is right, you know," she said. "Eban is so crazy there's no telling what he might do. I don't think my divorcing him and marrying you is going to stop him from believing I still belong to him. I'm afraid he'll just go on causing us trouble."

"You may be right, but let's take one thing at a time. We want to make sure he's on that stage when it leaves. If he isn't, X. will lock him up until we can figure what to do with him."

"It was stupid of me to have called myself Mrs. Nathaniel Sawtell."

"No matter what name you'd have used, the agent would soon have realized no one knew you. And Eban would have recognized you from the description the agent gave to him."

"I suppose so." She pressed herself tightly against Tom's warm, hard body, exclaiming, "Oh, God, I wish he'd leave and get on his ship and sail away and I'd never have to hear his name again as long as I live!"

"Maybe he will." He kissed her softly. "Go to sleep now." He yawned. "I think I can."

She did manage to sleep some, awakening to a day as dark and wet as the previous one had been. At first she thought the roar she heard was caused by wind,

and since wind was a rare phenomenon in this part of
the country, she went to peer curiously through the
window. The trees between the house and the river
were scarcely moving. Suddenly the noise struck a chord
of recognition. Whirling away from the rain-splashed
window in dismay, she said to Tom, "The river is up!
We may be in for another flood!"

He had been rubbing his bristly face and yawning,
but at her alarmed exclamation, he came instantly
awake. "If the water gets as high as it did last time, it
could wash the whole mine clean and collapse the
tunnel for sure." He began pulling on his clothes. "I'm
going down to have a look at it. Get dressed and come
with me. We'll have breakfast downtown."

Vianna dressed quickly in pants, shirt, and miners'
boots and wound her blond hair up, securing it with
the carved wooden combs given to her by Wakea in
the jungle above Lahaina, reflecting tiredly as she did
so that Eban's sudden appearance yesterday was catas-
trophe enough without having a flood on top of it.

One look at the river eliminated this new worry. The
water was high and wild, white water making it look
like a miniature raging sea, but it was a long way from
being a flood.

"We won't be seeing the miners on the other side till
this goes down," Tom said loudly above the roar.

Some of them were at work, early as it was, moving
doggedly through the rain in their zealous search for
gold. Vianna studied the raging water, remarking pensively, "I was telling Stumpy Pratt the other day that
someone should set up a ferry that could be pulled
across on ropes. Even at the best times it's chancy getting across here in a boat or canoe. You'd be taking
your life in your hands to get out there today even on
a ferry. What we need is a bridge."

Tom grinned indulgently. She had become Rainbow's
biggest booster, feeling very possessive about it. After
all, she had seen it grow from a flood-gouged cavity
in the mountainside to the sprawling, busy place it was

today. True, it was ugly. Even her fond eye admitted that. Shacks and tents and even cruder shelters were still scattered randomly about the gulch and slopes, but she loved it. Going back to Govans Harbor with its reminders of whaling and ships and the horrors these had caused her would have been unthinkable, even if she hadn't found Tom here. Now that she had, Rainbow's emotional hold on her was complete. She took great satisfaction in seeing it develop and prosper. The need for a bridge to link the mines on the far side of the river with those on this side had come to her suddenly as she regarded the swift, swollen river. "All in good time," Tom told her. "Let's go eat breakfast."

There were now three cafés in Rainbow. They chose the one from whose windows they could see the stage office. Halfway through their meal, the stage came down the street from its barn and parked outside the office. The wheels sank deeply in the mud. The rain-swept street was empty. Tom pulled out his watch. "It's due to leave in fifteen minutes."

The driver jumped down and went into the office. Vianna pushed her plate away, no longer able to eat. She peered up the street, but the hotel was beyond her range of vision. A few minutes later she saw X. emerge from the sheriff's office with a huge square of tarred canvas in which he had cut holes for his head and arms thrown over him. A wide-brimmed hat kept the rain off his face. As he gazed around, Vianna waved through the window. Her movement against the kerosene lamps inside the café caught his attention, and he sloshed across the street.

" 'Morning," he said, coming over to their table.

"He hasn't shown up yet?" Vianna asked at once.

He shook his head. "I've been watching."

Tom pulled up a chair from the empty table next to theirs. "Might as well sit down and have a cup of coffee while we wait."

X. sat without removing his dripping slicker. He

looked like a big tent with a head thrust through the top.

"The river's up," Vianna said absently, drumming her fingers on the bare tabletop.

"So I heard." X. caught the eye of the proprietor and indicated he wanted coffee. "I didn't go down. I wanted to keep an eye out here."

"There's no danger of flooding," Tom informed him. "At least not yet."

"Good. As soon as we get this bastard on the stage and out of here, I'll go with you to the mine. We ought to figure out a way to keep the water from getting in it in case of another flood."

"Right."

They sipped coffee, talking desultorily and scarcely taking their eyes off the portion of the street that held the coach and the stage office. Two passengers arrived, both men, neither of them Eban. Finally X. drained his cup and stood up. "I'm going to the hotel and roust him out."

Vianna spoke up. "Maybe he's in one of the other cafés."

"I'll check. You two stay here and keep an eye on the stage. I'm going to ask Russ to wait until we get this guy on it."

They watched as he crossed the street, spoke to the driver, and headed out of sight in the direction of the hotel. In ten minutes he was back, wearing a formidable frown. "He's not in the hotel or the cafés. Herb says he hasn't seen him this morning. We checked his room. All his stuff is still there. It hasn't been packed. Looks like he has no intention of leaving."

A chill ran up Vianna's back beneath her shirt. Tom kicked back his chair as he stood up. "That son of a bitch is going to be on that stage when it leaves if I have to break both his legs to get him in it." To Vianna he said, "You'll be safe here. Wait for us."

She was so tense she couldn't even nod, yet she wasn't surprised. She had never really believed that

Eban would depart meekly on the stage this morning. Getting him out of her life was not going to be that easy.

"More coffee?" Wes Powell, who ran the café, was at her elbow, showing his broken front teeth in a smile.

"Yes, thanks. It looks as if I might be here for a while."

Fifteen minutes later a strapping young man stuck his head in the door. He worked at the X-Vi-Z mine, and when he saw Vianna, he called out, " 'Mornin'. I didn't know you were here. Tom sent all of us guys out to look for this big sailor that X. has ordered out of town. Guess he isn't in here." He ducked out again.

Forty-five long minutes later another miner came in and, at the sight of her, headed for her table. It was Elmer Cook, a middle-aged man with a square, solemn face who worked a claim near the X-Vi-Z. He removed his soaked hat, saying, "I'm to tell you the sheriff wants you at the mine. I'm to take you there."

Immediately suspicious, Vianna asked, "Did X. tell you this himself?"

"No, miss. Some feller called out to me from the mouth of the X-Vi-Z. Pretty excited he was. He said Tom had been shot and the sheriff wanted you brought right away."

"My God!" Her suspicion was extinguished instantly by panic. Eban had done it! She was sure of it! She sprang to her feet, yanking her cape from the back of her chair. "How bad is he?" she cried as she flung it around her.

"I don't know. I was just told to get you there as fast as I could."

She pulled her shawl over her head as she ran for the door. Once outside, running was impossible. Floundering through the mud, struggling to keep her balance in the sticky mire, she was nearly wild with fear. If X. wanted her to come to the mine, it could mean only one thing. Tom was hurt very badly. Badly enough to die. Her breath came in short, moaning gasps. She was barely aware of Elmer Cook as he followed along in silence, earnestly fulfilling his role as guard to get her safely to the mine.

Enough discarded rock had spilled down in front of the mine entrance to make climbing the slope easy. There wasn't a soul to be seen. The broad mouth of the mine with its timber supports gaped blackly. A half-filled ore car sat just inside, deserted by the men who had been recruited to help in the search for Eban. Vianna hurried past it into the mine, calling, "Tom! X.!"

A blood-chilling giggle echoed past her down the tunnel, and Eban's voice, sounding hollow, declared, "You've seen the last of him, Vianna."

She whirled, almost colliding with Elmer Cook, who was still following her. Eban was emerging from behind the ore car where he'd been hiding. There were red patches over his cheekbones. His eyes were sunken and gleamed with a feverish light. He wasn't wearing any rain clothing, and his woolen jacket and trousers were soaked through.

A hatred, almost murderous in intensity, welled up within Vianna at the sight of him. Through clenched teeth she demanded, "What have you done with Tom?"

"Unfortunately, nothing. He isn't here. But I knew my little tale would bring you."

Elmer Cook turned an agonized face to Vianna, realizing he'd led her into a trap. "I thought he was one of the new miners!" He cast a desperate look around, and spying a pickax leaning against the wall of the tunnel, he dived for it.

Eban sprang forward. With hands clasped and using his arms as a club, he struck Cook across the back of the neck, felling him. Vianna tried to dart through the narrow space between Eban's thick body and the ore car, but he caught her. Her scream was choked off by one of his strong-fingered hands. "You are mine, and I'm taking you away from here." The words came out of his thin blue lips as prissily precise as if he were taking tea in her mother's parlor. "Those disgusting animals you've surrounded yourself with can't prevent it. I'm your husband, and it is my duty to cleanse your soul of the corruption you've heaped on it." All the while he spoke, he was dragging her toward the entrance. Reaching it, he peered out.

Vianna cast a frantic glance around, too, hoping someone was near enough to see them. The mountainside was deserted. Eban started down the rock-strewn slope, pulling her along, one hand still clamped so tightly over her mouth she began to taste blood. When she saw the dinghy drawn up on the riverbank and realized it was to this he was taking her, she screamed against his crushing hand. No boat of any kind could enter those angry, rushing waters without being overturned, its occupants dashed to death against the black rocks or sucked under by the current and drowned. She struggled desperately to get free, pulling them both down in a tumbling slide. The instant his hold was broken she screamed so loudly she thought her throat would burst. Surely someone would save her before she was thrown into that boat and swept to her death.

Eban regained his balance and caught her, striking her across one side of her face so hard that for a few moments she was too dazed to do more than fight feebly as he pushed her into the dinghy. He shoved it the foot or two necessary to get it into the river, then jumped in himself.

"You'll kill us both!" she cried, trying to sit up.

"Get down and keep still." He was seated on a thwart, and grabbing the oars, he started rowing into the current. "Have you forgotten that I've handled boats in water thrashed to foam by harpooned whales? You'll live, Vianna! You'll live to be purged of your depraved appetites!"

The current took them and sent them spurting forward as if the small vessel had been shot out of a giant hose. She began to scream, partly from fear, mostly from a desperate hope that someone would hear and come to her rescue. What anyone could do for her at this moment, she hadn't an idea. The boat was out of control. Eban had lifted the oars out of the water, holding them ready, but to thrust them back down into the wild, powerful current now would be to flip the craft and spill them out.

Ahead of them lay the stretch of open ground that separated Rainbow from the American River. It was filling with men, streaming down from the primitive wooden village. They had been alerted somehow, perhaps by her screams, to her peril.

Eban was laughing maniacally. "Now you know what it's like to be taken on a Nantucket sleighride!" He continued to laugh, the ghastly sound ringing out over the roar of the water. "I've been on one ever since the day I married you," she shrieked, gripping the sides of the boat, rigid with terror.

There was no mistaking the immense figure of X., who was in the forefront of the crowd pouring toward the river. They were still too far away for Vianna to make out any more individuals, but she was certain the smaller figure at X.'s side was Tom. The sight of them sent a shaft of hope streaking through her, but its life was brief. What could they possibly do? There were rapids at that point and beyond, a maelstrom of white water and black rocks. X. and Tom must have realized this at that very instant, because they swerved and started downstream. Some of the men followed. Others continued to run toward the bank.

"Eban, for God's sake! The rapids!"

Her warning drew his eyes from the river to her. They were opaque, wild. His thin lips twisted in a mirthless smile showing his gums. "It's right that you should be afraid, Vianna! If you died now, your un-cleansed soul would burn in everlasting Hell!"

His glance jerked forward again as the boat brushed a rock. The bow swung toward the bank, and for one glorious instant Vianna thought the craft was going to shoot toward the point where the miners had gathered. She could see them easily now. They lined the river's edge; some were even forming a human chain and moving into the water, which, though quieter near the bank, was still almost too swift to allow a man to keep his feet. But the raging current would not let go. It whirled the boat back into midstream, and seconds later they entered the rapids. Eban dropped one of the oars into the water and worked it furiously, fighting to prevent the craft from being pushed crosswise of the current and capsizing. Through the blinding spray, Vianna watched the point of land with its potential rescuers swiftly draw closer. The boat would never make it, though. Black rocks thrust up through the raging, foaming water. They would be dashed to pieces against one of them any instant! Skillful as Eban was with a boat, he was no match for the raw power of the rain-swollen river in its mad rush down the mountains to the Sacramento and thence to the Pacific.

The vessel whirled first this way, then that way, light as a wood chip in the angry water, with Eban using one oar, then the other, then both to keep the small craft from upsetting. Since they had entered the rapids, he hadn't made a sound.

The human chain had paid out as far as it safely could. Vianna could see the men's faces, strained and wet, as they stretched their arms to the utmost. She made a rapid survey of the situation. There was no chance that they could snare the boat, but if she jumped, could she make it to that closest grasping hand? She wouldn't know until the last moment. Clutching the sides of the boat, she pulled herself to her knees and crouched, ready to spring if it looked as if she had a chance. The craft was bobbing sharply, tossed like a ball in a whirling roulette wheel. The jarring shocks made Vianna feel as if her bones were crumbling to powder.

The outermost reaching hand was only a hundred feet downstream now. Vianna kept her eyes riveted on it. At this point it appeared as if the boat would pass within thirty or forty feet of it. A long jump would still land her in the frothing water too far away for the hand to reach her. Yet it might be possible to lunge a bit closer or to grab one of the smaller rocks jutting up from the riverbed and hang on, hoping an eddy would sweep her toward the bank. It was a slim chance, but the only one she had. Sooner or later, the boat would capsize. At this point, at least, there was a chance of rescue.

With every nerve and muscle taut, she readied herself. The hand held out to her belonged to Red, the miner who had helped drive Bruno Pruett and his gang off the claim. She saw his foxy face clearly as she leaned forward.

"Jump!" he shouted. "We'll get you somehow!"

At that moment, the whirling rapids spun the boat, turning it completely around, its bow pointing upstream, its square stern plowing through the boiling water. Finding herself suddenly on the far side of the boat from Red and the rest of the human chain, Vianna collapsed into the bottom of the boat, heart in her throat. No small craft could remain upright going stern first down these rapids. Over the curved side of the vessel, she caught sight of a bunch of miners on the opposite bank, watching with set, helpless expressions as the boat rushed past. They had no way of knowing what was happening. She made out the small form of Stumpy Pratt. When he recognized her, he let out a howl of alarm and started running downstream.

Another abrupt spin brought the boat around, its bow slicing the water once more. Behind them, Vianna saw the human chain pulling in toward the bank, its rescue effort a failure. Some of those who had stood watching were already running down toward the next point, where Vianna could see a knot of men gathering on the spit of land that jutted out into the river. Standing head and shoulders above them all was X. The river narrowed at this point and became quite deep. She couldn't begin to calculate how deep it must be with the water as high as it was today. In any event, it was far too deep to allow for another human chain to form. The only hope for rescue here was if the current would hurl the boat up onto the spit. Vianna saw that this was a possibility, given the narrowness of the river, but she knew Eban would never permit it if he could keep the dinghy in midstream. Swift and deep though the water was at that point, it did not froth madly as it was doing here in the rapids. Its relative safety had Vianna praying that they might reach it even if they swept helplessly by X. and the others.

She could see Tom now. X. was holding him around the chest from behind as he had held him in the hotel room when Tom had tried to hurl himself upon Eban after knocking him down. "No, Tom, no!" she screamed as she realized he was trying to throw himself into the river in an attempt to reach her.

A grunt from Eban drew her attention back to her own predicament. Looming directly ahead at the end of the rapids was an enormous black boulder, and the boat was aiming straight for it like an arrow. Eban plied the oars in a desperate attempt to change the dinghy's direction. The craft swung this way and that, shooting all the while inexorably at the rock. When Vianna realized nothing in the world was going to prevent their smashing against it, she closed her eyes and murmured Tom's name. At the same instant that she heard the bow splinter against the rock, she was thrown into the air.

Her landing in the deep water was soft, but she was sucked down at once by the current. *I'm drowning,* she thought, with a sort of wonder that her life was about to end. The next moment, however, she was tumbled to the surface by the same capricious current.

It swept her along, but at least her head was above water. Ahead she could see the spit. X., Tom, and the other men were a blur. If she could only swim and choose her direction! But her boots weighed her down like anchors. Risking being drawn under again by the current, she doubled up, sending herself underwater but managing to tear off one boot. A few moments later, she pulled off the other.

Lighter by pounds, she began swimming, trying to free herself from the onrushing water, which would sweep her past the spit. Suddenly she was sucked down again. Her lungs were almost empty, and she felt the frantic need for air almost at once. This time the current did not thrust her back to the surface. Her lungs involuntarily sought to fill themselves with air, and she felt the cold water pour into her nose and down her throat.

She could never recall what happened after that. The next thing she knew, she was rising to consciousness with Tom's voice speaking her name in anguished tones. She tried to say something, but no words would form. Her eyes fluttered open and there he was, kneeling over her, his handsome face drained of color, his rusty hair darkened by the rain. A cough tore its way up from her chest, so painfully that she knew she must have been coughing and retching for some time. Tom pulled her over on one side, but the cough brought up no more water.

"How did I get ashore?" she managed to croak.

"The current almost threw you up here," Tom replied in shaken tones. "It was sheer luck. We couldn't have got to you."

"But you would have tried. I saw X. holding you back." The big man was crouched on her other side, as pale as Tom was. Vianna gathered her strength and gave them both a weak smile. "I'm all right now. Stop looking as if I had died." Behind X.'s head, she saw the rest of the crowd staying respectfully back. "Eban?" she whispered.

"Stumpy and the others have his body on the other side. His neck must have broken when the boat hit the rock." Tom spoke in a flat, unemotional tone.

"He's dead?" Vianna asked, unable to believe it.

Tom nodded.

"I'm free, then," she said slowly.

X. spoke up. "And so is he. May God have mercy on his soul."

They were silent for a moment, each of them thinking his own thoughts about the man who, with his twisted mind, had wrought havoc upon so many lives, including his own.

"We won't have to go to San Francisco now," Vianna said at last.

Tom disagreed. "We'll be going just as soon as you feel well enough to travel. We're going to get married there."

"But I don't want to be married there!" Vianna protested weakly. "I want the wedding to be here in Rainbow, and," she said, as the idea grew, "I want it to be the biggest, most elegant wedding folks around here will ever see, the kind they'll still be talking about years from now, when Rainbow is old and settled and full of churches and schools."

Color was returning to Tom's face, and he grinned. "I won't quarrel with that. We'll have a minister come out from San Francisco to perform the ceremony here." He cocked an eyebrow at her. "You do want to go to San Francisco to have your wedding dress made, don't you?"

"Of course. How elegant could I be in miners' boots and pants?" She gazed up at X. "Will you give me away?"

Affection glowed in his large-featured face. "I'd be proud to."

Vianna struggled to sit up and made it with Tom's help. She peered across the river at the far side, where men were still gathered around the body of Eban. She shivered slightly. Tom pressed her hand. "Take me home," she said quietly.

He helped her to her feet, and the three of them turned their backs to the river and started back toward Rainbow.